CONVERGENT COINCIDENCES

CONVERGENT COINCIDENCES

BOOK II
THE LEAP YEAR SERIES

RICHARD BLAND MILES

aventine press

Copyright © July 2021 by Richard Bland Miles
First Edition

All rights reserved. No part of this book shall be reproduced or transmitted in any form or by any means, electronic or mechanical including photocopy, recording, or by any information and storage retrieved system without the written permission of the author.

This book is a work of fiction. Names and characters are products of the author's imagination. Any resemblance to actual persons, living or dead, is purely coincidental. Some events and incidents actually occurred but were enhanced or supplemented as needed. Names of some institutions and businesses were changed, others remained fixed.

Historical events and data are accurately depicted. All merchandise and products are true to their time. Television shows are correctly sequenced. Recognizable persons, authors and their books, singers and their recordings are properly described.

Published by Aventine Press
55 East Emerson St.
Chula Vista CA 91911
www.aventinepress.com

ISBN: 978-1-59330-999-2

Printed in the United States of America
ALL RIGHTS RESERVED

*For the still beautiful Georgiann
who was at the core of some convergent coincidences
a long, long time ago.*

Acknowledgements

My reviewer and critic, John Gatschet, who provided insightful suggestions, ideas and changes.

To Kelli Blohm, my other wonderful reviewer who can catch any error while offering solid advice for change.

To Cathy Macek and Tim Macek who provided automotive expertise.

My wife, for her always helpful suggestions.

Memoriam

In memory of Aunt Georgia or "Georgie," without whom, a lot of wonderful things in life would not have been possible.

In memory of my Grandmother Miles who would read to me frequently — when she became tired, she would tell me that was enough for now. Without fail, I would beg her to continue. She always would.

In memory of the Jesuits — Robert R. Lakas, S.J., William C. Doyle, S.J. and John Kavanaugh, S.J., all of whom provided positive guidance and unwavering support.

Author's Notes

"Thinking is hard work, which is why you don't see many people doing it."

Sue Grafton

"Things are not always what they seem; the first appearance deceives many; the intelligence of a few perceives what has been carefully hidden."

Phaedrus

"We can believe what we choose. We are answerable for what we choose to believe."

John Cardinal Newman

A dollar in 1964 = $8.00 in 2020

PREFACE

Convergent Coincidences, caused by nothing more than Chance, are a striking and remarkable set of circumstances which materialize, then intersect to connect a few individuals who forge unwavering bonds, as together, they pursue common goals or desires, sometimes continuing throughout their entire lives.

Even at the beginning of the mid-60s, the youth of the time were still simply typical teenagers. They hung out and "goofed off", flirted, dated, went steady, broke up, then started through that cycle again — ad infinitum. They even studied during the school year, worked summer jobs, trying to grow up enjoying those "so carefree years". At least, that's what their parents tried to persuade them to believe that's what they should be doing. However, it seemed like it took a lot of stumbling and bumbling to get through them. The parents were right — it was best to be lighthearted and untroubled. They could have added — unknowing.

Viet Nam was not even deemed a "Conflict" yet, but more than 150 soldiers had already died with 9000 deployed there when the Marlowe family moved to Wyandotte in 1963. Overnight, the idealism and dreams that created a magical aura faded into the mist, as Jackie so correctly predicted, "there would never be another Camelot". The American public was kept in the dark as the Government's foolish involvement in the South Vietnamese quagmire steadily increased, culminating with Americans being horribly deceived by Johnson and McNamara, resulting in The Gulf of Tonkin Resolution, giving the President broad war-making powers. The underpinnings of this Conflict began breeding problems for society like a fast growing, undetectable cancer. The counterculture movement, bolstered by the SDS and the hippies [or hipsters who had taken over from the beatniks], began to exponentially accelerate its rise. Marijuana and drugs, previously the purview of lowlifes, were quickly becoming mainstream. The Gates of Hell had cracked open.

All of this, of course, happened a long time ago as Richelieu Marlowe was beginning his junior year in a new school in a new city. He, along with his sister and others, experienced how Chance could trigger a series of Coincidences which meshed together so thoroughly and intensely.

Richard Bland Miles
July, 2021

AUGUST

As my mother pulled out of the parking lot of Melton's, the family restaurant in Auburn, I happily answered, "Thanks Mother, for letting me drive almost to the Kansas line. It was good practice for my test next week."

"Well, I would let you drive all the way, but I don't know if a Nebraska learner's permit is good in Kansas. Best not to take a chance. We should be in Topeka soon, then it's a straight shot into Wyandotte."

My sister DeeDee, now sitting in the front seat, announced, "I can't wait to turn sixteen."

I bet you can't ... you already look sixteen ... even older.

"Only eleven more months, Mother, then I can drive too. I'll take you shopping."

"Yeah," I teased, "for groceries."

"No, you big idiot ... shopping for clothes and shoes and accessories, go to lunch, the movies, other girl stuff ... *fun* girl stuff."

DeForrest Danièle and I could not have been physically more dissimilar except for height. DeeDee is about five foot nine with auburn hair and vivid green eyes, their color our grandfather Richelieu calls "Paris green". She bears a moderate resemblance to our mother who passed on her high cheek bones, straight-edged nose, porcelain skin and the beautiful eye color. I just got thick black hair from her. My very dark, almost black eyes come from my father. I'm five foot eleven now, but I'm going to get to six feet and beyond, like him.

I had the back seat all to myself — never been here before. My mother had bought the '63 black, two-door Ford Galaxie 500 "Custom Fastback" about three weeks ago, trading in the old '58 Country Squire wagon. Certainly unbelievable my mother would buy such a cool car. I figured she would buy a lime green four-door Dodge Hideous or a Plymouth Embarrassment in breathtaking

Yellow Cab yellow. Sometimes my mother can be surprisingly hip and really with it. I stretched out lengthwise and began thinking about this move.

So we're doing this to be closer to family. But the only one left in Wyandotte is Aunt Danièle. Grand-père and Grand-mère Richelieu moved ... uh hmm ... seven months ago. Really liking Florida.

Offutt must remind Mother too much of Dad. Bet we're moving from the Air Base to get away from all those memories. Oh God, she really broke down at his grave after those Memorial Day services. She was a mess ... a complete mess. My miserable, heartbroken mother, Geneviève Georgette Richelieu Marlowe, widowed at 37.

Thanh Da area in Saigon, Vietnam, morning of May 12, 1962 ... evening of May 11 in Omaha. Forrest Macey Marlowe ... killed by a sniper's bullet. **Dead at 38! Just 15 months ago**. *God, I miss you Dad. Oh God, so much ... so DAMN much. Maybe this move will get rid of these damn nightmares.*

Probably miss some of the guys, like Luke and Hermie. DeeDee will miss them more than me. That girl is boy-crazy. Yet fun ... even if she is my sister.

And you, Linda ... I'll write ... maybe even call you. No wonder I went steady with you this summer. You're incredibly cute with an incredibly cute pair. Oh wow ... in your blue and white two piece at Peony Park or The Officer's Club Pool. How you stayed in that low-cut top, I'll never know. Oh, but you didn't stay in your top two nights ago in your parents' dorky '61 Parkwood. 'My amazing twins ... fantabulous going away presents for you to always remember me by.' That's right Linda, won't be able to forget your two beautiful baseballs

Aaaah baseball. Maybe I'll start at first base for St. Ignatius. Wish I could have played more at Loyola ... still not bad for a sophomore. And a damn, damn good season in the A League. Hit .345 ... five home runs. Guess I'll miss some of the Cardinals too.

"Richie, are you still with us?"

Why does she still call me 'Richie'? Well, Dee Dee, too ... so does Aunt Danièle.

"Don't worry Mother, he's just thinking about Linda. How much he misses her. Richie, aren't you going to miss Linda?"

I smiled whimsically, "Yeah, some ... I guess." ... ... *Certainly her pair of baseballs. Whole new meaning to the saying, 'play ball'.*

"Oh, you bet he will, Mother. He'll miss making out with her."

"Bet you'll miss Hermie and Luke more than I will," I weakly retorted.

"Even though we never went out, I *know* they both liked me. A whole lot."

"Angel, I told you repeatedly you were too young to date Hermie." My mother continued her chiding, "He's two and a half years older than you. *And* I know Luke wanted to date you too ... he was much too old as well."

"I am a sophomore now. I should be able to date whoever I want."

"Only farm boys can drive at fifteen in Kansas, but I think just tractors." I snickered. "Anyhow, don't think there're many farmers in Wyandotte."

"Who says I have to date only fifteen-year-olds?"

"Why don't we talk about school? Oh Angel, I know you will like Notre Dame de Sagesse."

"But there's no boys there!"

"*Really?*"

****

"Well, children, here we are. Our new house on Washington Boulevard. Oh, there's Aunt Danièle already. Even the movers beat us here."

My aunt, Danièle Madeleine, is my mother's younger sister by exactly a year, both born on the eighth of October. She's a few inches shorter than my mother at five foot four, having a more slender frame. Even though they share only a slight facial resemblance, it's easy to tell they are sisters since both have the same black hair and lovely green eyes.

The marital separation of two and a half years has really been tough on her with the divorce granted this month ending her four-year marriage, finally dumping the whoring drunken bum, Harry Brooks, along with his name. The completion of its dissolution had been even rougher on her, so my aunt — Danae* as everybody

---

*__Danae__ is pronounced DUH-neigh ... the 'da' in soda plus the sound a horse makes

calls her — had taken an extended vacation for four weeks and stayed with my grandparents in Naples, flying back home from Florida last night. Due to these marital problems over the last two years she lost a lot of weight, yet still is attractive. According to Grandfather Richelieu, she and my mother are still "Flowers of the Aquitaine". Aunt Danae is a topnotch legal secretary for the Ellis and Mullins Law Firm, who are probably the best in the city of Wyandotte. My mother always said she should have gone to law school. However, after college, she went to Florence then Paris and fell in love with both cities, living about three years in each place. She came back to the States and went to work for the firm about nine or ten years ago. Conveniently, she lives not far away in an apartment off of State Avenue by Kensington Park.

"Aunt Danièle! Oh, Aunt Danae! Oh my best Aunt!" my sister exclaimed and hugged her tightly as they kissed.

"DeeDee honey, you just keep getting prettier every time I see you. Would you look at **that** shape, those—! With that hair, those eyes, and flawless complexion. Oh, the guys will be flocking to meet and date you! And I'm still your only Aunt."

"Hey, still my only Aunt, I think you've shrunk some more," I teased. "Oh Richie, you just keep getting taller and more handsome," she exclaimed as now she had to look up at me slightly more. "Your hair is **a lot** longer and those soft, dark eyes have become ... yeah, sultry. The girls are really going to fall in love with you!" She pushed back a curl that had fallen over my forehead. We kissed each other on the lips, hugged tightly, and I gave her a kiss on her forehead to complete our ongoing personal ritual.

As the two sisters hugged and kissed fondly, my aunt declared, "Oh, I can certainly tell they are related to me. How was your trip?"

My mother said, "Oh, fine, Richie drove almost halfway." Then in a more subdued tone, "How are *you* doing, Maddy? I've missed you so much."

"Flight last night was nice ... on time. I'm okay. I really missed you too. But thank God you're here, Georgie. At last. For good."

Aunt Danae changed her tone and the subject completely, "Your house is fabulous. Just terrific!"

Something's up. Their childhood code of using middle names. Signals a needed private conversation.

Following that cue, we all went inside to tour our "fabulous" house. When we were eating lunch my mother had given us the particulars on the house. It was designed with a center hall plan, built in 1928 and is about 3300 square feet. I walked through the front door and into the entry hall, seeing the dining room to the left and a study to the right — Mother would use for her stock market investments. The stairs to the second floor are on the entry hall's left side just beyond the dining room. I walked straight ahead into the living room then off of it through a large kitchen, noticing a wide doorway to the dining room. From the kitchen, there was a short hall with the laundry room on one side and a generously spacious guest half-bath on the other. At the hall's end was the door to the garage. We went upstairs to check out the three bedrooms with their good-sized bathroom. Lastly, the large master bedroom and its bathroom. I would have the bedroom with a view of the backyard and the bathroom to myself. DeForrest would be in the bedroom looking out onto the street, adjoining the master via the Master bath which she would share with our mother. The fourth bedroom, on the other side of my bathroom, would be used for storage and a sewing room.

My mother's description was quite precise. This house was certainly much nicer than the one in Omaha. I guessed she used some of my father's insurance money for its down payment.

As the movers brought the furniture and moving boxes into the house, my mother directed where everything was to be placed and positioned. Both DeeDee and I took our marked boxes to set up in our rooms. After the movers finished, we decided to go eat dinner. Aunt Danae suggested The Indian Head, a new restaurant on Minnesota Avenue.

As we entered, my aunt waved a big hello to two men in a booth who were giving their orders to an older waitress. After we had been seated, the shorter of the two came over to the table.

Ted Laird, one of the partners of the firm, smiled widely to welcome Aunt Danae back, saying everyone had missed her and would be quite glad to see her back on Monday. He, especially, saying he had a brief he wanted her to review as he warmly patted her shoulder. Laird and my mother exchange pleasantries and DeeDee and I were introduced. There was more friendly small talk then he returned to his table.

My mother had previously mentioned he was Danae's attorney for the divorce and "one of the best." He was about their age, my mother's height, wasn't cool-looking and was starting to go bald.

DeeDee asked straight up, "Is he married?"

Aunt Danae responded, "No, divorced with two kids. He would welcome some encouragement from me, like responding to that shoulder rub. He won't be getting any, divorced or not."

My mother then suggested, "Just go see Monsignor O'Reilly and talk to him. He can work miracles."

"Gi Gi*, you know I would need one for dealing with *Mr. Harry Brooks*," giving my mother a look which meant "change the subject".

"Let's see what's on the menu. Children, remember it's Friday." A plain-looking Candace — according to the slightly chubby, young waitress's protruding badge from her large bust — eagerly came over to take our drink orders.

✸✸✸✸✸✸✸✸✸✸✸✸✸✸✸✸✸✸✸✸✸✸✸✸

On Saturday, Aunt Danae came over to help complete the move in. Around noon, my aunt suggested, "Richie, why don't you drive my car when we go get lunch. It'll give you some varied practice for your test ... different car and a stick. Your Nebraska permit is certainly valid."

"Wow, outta sight! Sure."

Aunt Danae's car was a cool '57 Chevy Bel Air Sport Coupe with a 283 V8 engine with a four-speed manual transmission on the floor which Macek's Mobil and Garage custom installed when she purchased the car in May that year. Still a beautiful,

---

***Gi Gi** is pronounced Zhee Zhee ... as in first syllable's French pronunciation of the designer Givenchy

2-door, two-tone in black and ivory. Its only negative was it happened to be one of the things that attracted Harry the Prick to her. According to Mother, she drives too fast, loving to shift gears "at her discretion". My grandfather told me once he knew of at least four speeding tickets she had gotten since she had purchased the car, mysteriously three of them became only warning tickets. Aunt Danae admitted to DeeDee and me she acquired her passion for stick shifting and fast cars during a week in Monte Carlo at the Grand Prix when she met some of the drivers — "particularly one Italian" — and winked. Accordingly, two Christmases ago, DeeDee and I bought her a large silver-plated California Custom T handle for the gear shifter. We had "Grand Prix 1950" engraved on it. She loves it.

We drove to a hamburger place on State called Zesto's to get lunch for the four of us. Aunt Danae had no idea why everyone called the drive-in "Zesto's" since its neon sign on the street clearly proclaimed, "Peter's". She thought maybe it was the previous owner's nickname or some strange, whimsical reason. No one seems to know. This was where all the high school kids ate, hung out or just drove through on weekends. The drive-in was the largest I had ever seen and was shaped like an elongated Greek letter Ψ [psi] without the bottom of the stem. A car would pull in one side and exit out the other. There was parking all along the sides except at the back where there was only room to drive behind the building which housed the kitchen and the waiting carhops. The middle piece of the letter was a narrow island, extending from the front of the building to the street with parking on both sides, but much less desirable since backing in wasn't allowed.

My mother had given me money for the lunch but my aunt wanted to pay. My instructions were "absolutely not, under no circumstances" should I let her pay. While pencil-shaped, ordinary-looking Anita took our order, my aunt had become completely distracted by a brand new, black Stingray "Split-Window" Coupé driving through and even more by the guy at the wheel. As she drooled over both, I slipped the carhop $7 and mouthed for her to keep the change. The order was quickly delivered and my aunt tried to pay for it. Anita merely replied, smiling happily, "Paid for." My aunt laughed, said how sneaky I was.

After we returned home, lunch was quickly re-heated. As we began eating, Mother said, "I called St. Pat's and Monsignor O'Reilly is saying the 9 o'clock High Mass, so I thought we could all go to church there. I left my name with the housekeeper to talk with him afterwards. I haven't seen him in at least five years." My aunt readily agreed, happy for the chance to see him again.

Better go to confession for 'my going away presents'. Won't look too good to my mother and aunt if I don't go to communion. Give DeeDee ideas. The Church of St. Joachim and St. Anne is only a mile and a half or so ... I'll just walk over. Hope I don't get yelled at too much for my 'festivities' at the drive-in. Sure looked fabulous AND certainly felt fabulous. Oooooh sooo damn fab-tab-u-lous.

My confession netted me a hefty penance and the stern admonishment to "*never* come back to confession with that sin again." If I found another Linda and happened to engage in the same "cultural activity" — as one of the Loyola Jesuits put it — I'll just go to a Jesuit. *Certainly* not back there.

The Church of St. Joachim and St. Anne was a conspicuously well-maintained, built in the same Neo-Gothic style like St. Patrick's Cathedral, but it couldn't compare. The Cathedral was at least three times as large and built out of white Carthage stone with three tall spires and the main one is at least 150 feet and marks the chapel. The interior is truly beautiful with towering vaulted ceilings, painted in various religious themes. The entire altar area was built in white Italian marble and consisted of the elevated main altar extending up two stories to almost touch the dome ceiling with twenty-foot stained glass windows behind it, providing a great accent. Additionally, there were two side altars, an ornate communion rail and a spiral staircase pulpit which wound at least twelve to fifteen feet above the congregation, from which Sunday sermons were delivered. Even the Stations of the Cross which ringed the nave area were framed in the marble.

Always, always totally impressive. Maybe I will just go to Mass there. I know DeeDee will go with me. Maybe Mother and Aunt Danae. Everybody ... just like old times.
Except Dad!

SHIT! JUST SHIT!

****

Right after Mass, we met the Carsons — Mrs. Carson, Ronald, Edward and Claudia — outside the side entrance. My mother and Mrs. Carson exchanged pleasantries and started working out a tentative carpool schedule for DeeDee and myself. I would drive Mondays and Thursdays and Ron, the senior, would drive the other three days. He and Eddy, a sophomore, both had bright red hair and were about five foot eight or nine. Claudia, a junior, was short, plain-looking, also red-haired, freckled with a friendly nature. She would drive on Wednesdays. One of the two seniors would drive on Mondays and Tuesdays and the other on Thursdays and Fridays. One of the three girls would pick up DeForrest and Karen Reynolds who lives only three or four blocks away. My mother said she would call Mrs. Carson tomorrow and they could figure out the share of the cost for DeForrest and myself. Mr. Carson who sung in the choir, sauntered up to the group and jovially introduced himself to the four of us. Ron said the best pick-up time for each other would be at 6:45. Claudia felt closer to 7 o'clock for them was adequate. We said our good-byes, nice that the two families were able to meet and get acquainted.

We walked over to the Chapel as suggested by the housekeeper to wait for Monsignor O'Reilly. In about five minutes, the priest and a guy who probably went to high school, maybe college, came walking over to us. After my mother and Aunt Danae both hugged and kissed the priest on his cheek, he shook hands with DeForrest and me, telling us how grown up we were. He introduced the guy as Roland Bush, one of his best singers in the choir, a good student, and quite a nice young man. He was slightly taller and a little bigger than me. As I shook hands with him, I noticed he and DeForrest were seriously checking each other out.

I was caught between two conversations.

"I was deeply saddened when I heard about Forrest. He was one of the best, a man of solid integrity. I'm so sorry. I will remember him during the 10:30 Mass."

"Thank you, Monsignor. Your kind words do provide solace. I still miss him ... so very much. He always loved the Cathedral."

"Well then, you should join St. Pat's. I won't tell," Monsignor said, then laughed.

"I'll be a sophomore at Notre Dame de Sagesse. Do you go to Bishop McKenna? St. John Vianney?"

"Yeah, a senior at McKenna. *Sure* you're only a sophomore?" the guy teased.

"You should come to dinner next Sunday, Monsignor."

"What kind of classes are you going to be taking at Sagesse?"

"That would be very nice."

"We can talk about the good old days when you were a Curate and we were in pigtails here at St. Pat's," my aunt laughed.

My widely smiling sister readily responded, "The usual sophomore stuff ... Latin, French, English and ugh, geometry."

"Check your schedule and I will call you this week with a time."

"Know what you mean ... more Latin, English, Accounting, Spanish ... just more stuff."

"I'm going to plan on it. Sorry, I've got to run — back to the rectory, then get everything ready for the 10:30 Mass. Just wonderful to see you again. Oh, good. Here she comes." The Monsignor chuckled, "I'll leave you with your old school chum. Come on Roland."

"Nice to meet you, Roland. Maybe I'll see you sometime soon."

"Count on it, DeForrest. Wonderful to meet you. What a striking name!"

"Thanks. Byeeee."

"Bye for now."

A nun, about the same height as my aunt, was approaching quickly.

"Becky? Becky Goodman? Oh, my heavens! It's been sooo long. Too, too long."

As they warmly hugged and kissed, the former Rebecca Goodman gushed, "Oh, Gi Gi, it's so terrific to see you. You look wonderful. And yes, it's been years. Danae, not as long, but still it's been some time." They also hugged and kissed.

Sister Cecilia was deeply sorry to hear about my father and often remembered him in her prayers. Mother gratefully thanked her. "Of course, these are our children." My mother re-introduced us to the nun who seemed very happy to see us again. At least she didn't say, "Oh my, how you two have grown" and all that crap. As she and I exchanged polite greetings, she did a double take, saying she thought she was seeing a young Forrest. She commented DeeDee was a quite attractive young lady, taking after our mother and aunt. They decided they hadn't seen each other in about ten years.

Aunt Danae broke in, "Congratulations! Lee Talbot at the firm told me you've been promoted to the Principal at McKenna from being Principal here."

"Yes, it's true." She looked very amused, "Who would have thought after the mischief we got into *here*," Sister Cecilia's slight grin broaden widely, "then a little more at McKenna" and she nudged my mother, "that I would end up being *the Principal* at both schools."

My aunt and mother joined her laughing. I could easily see my Aunt Danae in some "mischief." Actually, a lot. But my strait-laced, always by the book, Mother?

"I'm truly sorry girls, but I need to go back into church for the 10:30 Mass."

"You must come with Monsignor for dinner next Sunday."

"Oh, I'd love to. Really. But the convent has our monthly devotion to The Blessed Virgin. I'd certainly take a rain check. Honestly Gi Gi and Danae, I really would. I do want to catch up on the past ten years." She grinned, "Maybe relive some of those great, older memories."

"Great, Becky ... er, sorry ... Sister Cecilia, we'll set a date."

"Wonderful! Oh please, save 'Sister Cecilia' for public, otherwise I'm still Becky."

"Then sometime next month, Becky. At the latest."

"Deal! I've got to run. I'll be sure to include Forrest in my prayers tonight when I am praying for Kenneth and Kenneth

Junior." She hugged my mother and aunt and smiled warmly at DeeDee and me.

****

As we were going home, DeeDee turned to my mother in the back seat, "Mother, that Roland is dreamy. I hope he asks me out on a date."

"He looks too old for you."

"No, no, I'm sure he said he'll be a Junior." I knew he had said Senior. DeeDee shot me a lightning strike, pleading look not to say it, so I continued with my self-imposed silence. She quickly changed the subject, "Mother, who were Sister Cecilia's Kenneth and Kenneth Junior?"

"That, Angel, is a long story. Such a terribly sad one. Over a year and half after Becky and I graduated from McKenna, she married Kenneth Patterson when he was on leave the Saturday before Valentine's Day in 1944. Tragically, he was killed on D-Day during the invasion of Normandy at Pointe du Hoc, a few miles from Omaha Beach. Their baby's development was badly flawed and most people erroneously thought it was due to the great shock of his death. After her painful delivery, the poor little thing only lived a few hours and was baptized Kenneth Junior. Becky became extremely distraught and came to St. Patrick's to pray daily for almost a month. She was praying before the statue of the Infant Jesus of Prague and suddenly had a vision or revelation. She saw an angel standing over a seated Kenneth holding their baby on his lap. The angel told her she would make an exemplary nun. When she made her commitment, both Kenneth and the baby smiled. What is truly strange about this happening is there was an old nun, Sister Aloysius, tidying up near the vestibule. She swore she saw a bright light for some moments by the eighth station of the cross, very close to the statue. However, I should point out Sister Aloysius always had problem eyesight, even when both Danae and I had her for third grade."

"Wow, that's still real spooky," said DeeDee in amazement.

"Well, in fairness, adding to the ethereal aspect ... after the word got around, skeptics said it was only bright sunlight passing thru the light-colored pieces of one of the stained-glass windows. So, they went at the same time about a couple weeks later, but no light. Then it was decided, it must only occur on the exact day like at Stonehenge. Children, remember ... like when the four of us were there ... summer solstice of '61. So, they waited until the next year. It rained. The following year, it was cloudy. Finally, the third year, it was sunny. But no bright sunlight on or around the statue, either an hour before or after the designated time ... or the day before or after. Poor old Sister Aloysius had died in the interim, but the story of the light and Becky's vision lives on. Within days after it happened, she entered the convent and adamantly will not talk about her experience."

Aunt Danae shifted course, "Rebecca always was very smart, highly organized. She'll be the first nun to be McKenna's Principal and still young. Very close to forty though." In the rearview mirror, I saw her lean over and teasingly push my mother. For about the hundredth time, I wondered what those two were like as teenage girls. Sometimes they happily act like they still are.

The three girls continued happily chatting non-stop during the rest of the drive home. As we got out of the car, Mother asked, "Richie, what do you want for breakfast? You haven't said a word to us since Mass ended. Actually, before it started."

I faked a sullen look, "Can't get a word in edgewise with you three females."

"O my poor baby nephew."

"O my poor, poor big brother."

"We all are soooo sorry." They all laughed which did make me smile.

****

After dinner, my aunt left and DeForrest went to her room to read and play records, so I asked my mother, "Aunt Danae is terrific to have around. Why doesn't she just move in with us? Into the sewing room. She could save a lot of money. You said she didn't have much."

"Richelieu, she has her own life." However, her words unconvincing; her expression distracted; her thoughts were on something else — something worrisome.

※※※※※※※※※※※※※※※※※※※※※※※※※※※※

On Wednesday, I easily passed my driver's test. After my birthday dinner, I celebrated by asking DeeDee to go to Zesto's for a malt and some cruising. You never could tell what cool chicks might be on the prowl on a warm summer night. On Monday morning, she had called up Karen Reynolds, also a sophomore, so they could meet and get to know each other. In those two days, they quickly became fast friends, thus she wanted to take her with us. I said sure, why not?

On the four-block drive to her house, she asked, "Don't you think Roland Bush is handsome?"

"Yeah ... guess so. I'll trust your judgement *for that*, but what about your judgement in lying to Mother *for his year* in school?"

"You can't tell her. If she thinks he is only a year older, she would let me go out with him. But two years or more ... never. Swear, Richelieu. Book of Secrets, please?"

The Book of Secrets dates back to when DeForrest and I were probably about eight and nine. Anything we didn't want our parents to know was to be kept between us in our mythical 'Book of Secrets'. Once placed in there, it stayed.

"You don't know anything about him. He might be a dud date."

"Oh no! I can tell. He's so handsome. The Monsignor likes him, he's smart and sings in Cathedral's choir. Swear Richie, swear."

"Okay DeeDee, I swear. It's in the Book." When we pulled into the driveway, I exclaimed, "Wow, this is huge. A real mansion."

"Yeah, six bedrooms, four and a half bathrooms, four-car garage and maybe twice the size of ours. Her father is Dr. Reynolds, the best surgeon in both cities. Oh, there she is."

Karen was probably five foot three, maybe four, blonde hair, a little on the pudgy side yet still a fairly decent shape. DeeDee got out of the car and Karen slid in next to me. Nice facial features. Wonderful, beautiful blue eyes. And my sister was setting me up.

"Rich, my best friend, Karen Reynolds. Karen, this is my brother, Rich."

"Hi, nice to meet you, Rich."

"Great to meet you, Karen. Your house looks really terrific."

... ... Like your light blue eyes ... God, they are alluring.

"Thank you. When we get back, come in and I'll give you the nickel tour."

"Sure, okay. That'll be great."

As we pulled into Zesto's, Karen mentioned Wednesday nights at the drive-in are never real busy, even the summer. There were a few parking spots on the highly desired exit side, so I backed into the first one. It wasn't the easiest job with Karen right next to me. I think DeeDee had a little room between her and the door and was crowding Karen into me. A carhop came out to take our order. I thoroughly looked her over. Medium height, slender, not much of a bust, quite pretty, vivacious, a great smile. When she was walking back, I got a good eyeful of a pair of shapely calves and a great butt whose curves fortunately weren't completely shrouded by her carhop Bermuda shorts.

After some minutes, Karen saw someone she knew driving through and asked to honk the horn, so I did for her. She waved to some guys in an Oldsmobile 88, but they didn't wave back. The guy sitting shotgun took a hard look at Karen, then me.

"Oh, they are from McKenna," Karen explained willingly.

I noticed when the Olds pulled out of the exit, it hastily sped down the short distance on the wrong side of the street to re-enter the drive-in. They eased past us, then backed into a space a couple of places down. Mr. Shotgun came over to DeeDee's side, said his name was Stan Something then started talking to Karen who was trying to ignore him. Number Two and Number Three were now out and began chatting up DeeDee forcing Stan Whatever to come over to my side.

"You always date two girls at a time, buddy?" he demanded loudly.

Aah, just great! Must be Karen's old asshole boyfriend. My kind of a real fun celebration. ... ... "My dating mores are not your concern. And I'm not your 'buddy' either."

"OH YEAH!" he countered defiantly, spouting smoke with no fire at all.

His feeble retort confirmed he took my pompous answer as an insult, *exactly* as it was meant to be. I began to size him up. He was five foot six maybe seven, slightly chubby and looked like all fluff which he undoubtedly was. Still looks could be a little deceiving. I discounted his two buddies since DeeDee was easily handling them. They were only interested in her, not their little friend's girl problems.

He pleaded, "Karen, will you please talk to me. What if I call you later?"

"Okay. But only if you go away **now** and leave **us** alone."

The carhop had come with our order about the time Little Stanley moved over to my side of the car and she was waiting patiently with our shakes and the malt. He turned, then deliberately knocked one off the carhop's tray. He then stomped over to the Olds.

"What a damn child! A senior, too!" Karen said disgustedly.

As the shocked carhop hastily placed the tray on the window, I reassuringly said to her, "Don't worry about it. I'll pay for it." I smiled at her very warmly, "Would you please get me another one? Thank you," When she bent down to scoop up as much of the ruined shake as she could into the fallen cup, my eyes became riveted on her butt. They followed her derrière's own delicious shake as she hurried back to the ordering area.

Yep! A great tush! No hiding her shapely cheeks in those unattractive uniform shorts.

My sister broke up my mental drool, exclaiming, "What if he wanted to fight you? There were three of them!"

"You had two of them nailed down. They were only interested in coming onto you. Little Stanley didn't want to fight. He's just jealous. Good job, Karen. Think you succeeded very well."

"You see, we had been going steady for a couple of weeks. Like I told DeeDee on Monday, things were fine, until I found out he snuck out with some Slovak slut, Valerie Something-bitch-vich. So I broke up with him. Now he wants me back. That's, sure as hell, not gonna happen. Don't ya think so?"

I think most Catholic girls swear more than Protestant girls.

"Oh, most definitely, Karen. Stan sure didn't **act or look** like he was worth keeping around. Don't you agree, Rich?"

"Yeah ... sure ... not worth it. Great song though," I said as *Pipeline* by The Chantays began playing over the Drive-in's loud speakers.

My sister and Karen continued jabbering about Little Stanley cheating with this Sallie or Valerie. How terrible that was, how terribly 'dirty and grubby the skank was', how terrible something else was, and how terrible on and on.

My replacement raspberry shake was brought out quickly by the pleasant carhop. "Thank you and please keep the change for *your* trouble." I teased with a 'come on' smile, trying to impress her a little with the nice tip and a lot with the inviting grin.

At least one worked well as she responded with a highly flirtatious smile, "Oh, no trouble at all. Thank you very much. Come back soon and ask for *me*." She pointed to her blouse label, "I'm Cathy."

I expanded my smile, "I certainly will, *Cathy*. And I'm Rich."

"Oh, I bet you are. Judging by this new, absolute cherry Galaxie and outta sight Madras shirt. Plus your cool manner to put down that mouthy, rude little jerk. Rich, if you need anything else, *you* just honk, and *I'll* be right back in a flash."

"Oh, I will." She smiled, took the tray and left.

So when she was about fifteen feet away, I honked. She quickly returned grinning and bowed, "Yes sir? Anything else, sir?" Joining her laughter, I could only shake my head side to side. As she hurried back inside for more orders, I wanted to follow her — to continue flirting with her. Sadly, only my eyes were able to make a repeated derrière focused trip.

I could tell neither of my companions were pleased with my fooling around as they had ended their conversation about the branded 'Slovak Slut' before Cathy and I had finished exchanging smiles and flirts with each other. Regardless of what they thought, when I pulled out to leave, I honked again and waved to Cathy. She enthusiastically waved back. In facial attractiveness, she was certainly above average. Had a great-looking butt and legs, yet a small bust — still she definitely had an above average body. Personality in spades, enhanced by that great appeal from her sparkling brown eyes. Certainly would look much nicer in anything other than her drab uniform blouse, Bermuda shorts and flight cap. I liked her and was positive the feeling was certainly mutual. A great birthday present, so score one for the new guy in town. I'll be back!

※※※※※※※※※※※※※※※※※※※※※※※※※※※※

Karen proudly gave me a tour of the interior of her house which was impressive. I also was able to meet Dr. and Mrs. Reynolds and two of her four siblings. As we got ready to leave, Karen thanked me for the malt. I told her she was welcome and thanks for coming with us, then wished her a goodnight.

On the short ride home, DeeDee asked, "Well, Richie, what did you think?"

"About?"

"Karen! Don't play *dumb* with me."

"She seems like a nice girl."

"And? ... *And*? You know she has a huge crush on you already. Would you take her out on a date again?"

"Again?"

"As in tonight. I told you to quit playing dumb with me. It was so cool the way you put that guy down."

"Karen wanted to get even. Who would blame her? Little Stanley Whoever seems like an idiot twit. And clearly out of her league. Why'd she go with him? 'Cause he's a senior?"

"Well yeah, that's true. Looks cool to be dating a senior."

"Sure does look cool," I smirked, "especially if the senior's a tubby, incredibly rude runt who cheats on you with some grubby slut. And, my little sister, that wasn't a date ... not with you along."

"Okay, bag the shit about chubby, cheating senior runts. **Would** you date her?"

"Yeah, maybe."

"Oh, I get it ... Linda is still on your mind."

"Dunno, maybe."

"Oh, I met the other two girls in the carpool. The seniors."

*Aaaah ... senior girls like Linda, the **always** good-time girl. ... ...* "What are they like?"

"Richie, they are very nice girls and have good personalities." Dating code for "not your type". Good to have a sister screen dating possibilities.

※※※※※※※※※※※※※※※※※※※※※※※※※※※※

The rain had already started when I woke up Thursday, continuing unrelentingly into the night. Confined by the weather, I spent the day reading Raymond Chandler's *The Big Sleep*. What a great mystery! Friday morning found me bored, so I went for a walk around the whole curve of Washington Boulevard to St. Joachim and St. Anne's. The architecture in the area was really interesting. There appeared to be some Chinese influence in their designs. All the houses had some similarities yet very different overall. This architect Curtiss had designed a lot of really cool houses.

I was a couple blocks from returning to the house when I came upon a guy just sitting on his front steps, also looking bored. As I walked past, he got up. He looked to be about five foot ten with a medium build, light brown hair and about my age. He said hi and I said hi back. He asked if I lived in the neighborhood and I said yes, we had just moved in a week ago, pointing further down the curve.

He came towards me to introduce himself, "My name is Mick Hayden. Are you going to start school at Prescott?"

I extended my hand, saying, "I'm Rich Marlowe. No, I'll be going to St. Ignatius over in Kansas City."

Mick was also a junior and pitched for Prescott's baseball team. When I told him I was hoping to play first base, we laughed as it meant we would be playing against each other in the Border League. His parents were both CPAs and had their own firm which specialized in corporate tax. They were at work and he was just killing time. I asked him if he wanted to go meet my family and he said sure. Walking down the street, we shot the bull more about baseball and our favorite major leaguers we followed.

My mother was patiently waiting on the phone with some brokerage house in New York, trying to get a hold of their Ford Motors analyst. I introduced Mick to her then we went into the kitchen where the Sagesse Sisters — as I had dubbed the two — were hanging out. Mick, of course, knew Karen since she only lived a few blocks from him. As I introduced DeForrest, she checked him over like she did every good-looking guy while Karen gave me a flirtatious smile and said hi.

DeeDee then suggested, "My mother's too busy to help me make lunch. Why don't we all go somewhere?"

Mick added, "How about Blender's. Right Karen?" Karen readily agreed. He explained, "Pretty much caters to high school and junior college students but totally different from Zesto's. A regular restaurant." Having never been there, DeeDee and I both said sure.

Blenders was almost empty so after we ate, we decided to just hang out there for a while, talking and playing records on the jukebox.

"Karen, did you make up with Little Stanley Whatever?"

"That damn cheat, that piece of senior shit."

"I'll take that as a resounding 'No'." We all laughed.

"I am completely available," she said looking straight at me with those inviting glacier blue eyes. So thoroughly mesmerizing. I thought about asking her out, but she seemed somewhat immature. I wonder if she thought her swearing made her seem older? Were smoking and drinking next on her rungs to "maturity"?

As we talked more, I got to know Mick — my instinct was right — he was a good guy. I think DeeDee liked him too. Karen flirted with me. I flirted back. Since it was Friday night, we all wondered what we would do. DeeDee suggested the four us go to the movies. There was one, *The Great Escape*, which she and I had not seen. Mick said he had already seen it, but he would like to see it again and would drive. I was pretty sure Karen had seen it too, but she didn't say. So we all agreed and left. We dropped off Karen and Mick and on the quick drive home, I asked her what she thought of Mick. She thought it was way too early to tell. I said he was a good guy.

DeeDee slightly changed the subject as we got out of the car, "You had acquaintances in Omaha, but never any real close friends."

"Oh yeah. What about Luke and Hermie?"

"Hermie," DeeDee explained, "did come around a lot. But it was to see **me**. He wanted to date me. Badly ... reeeel bad-leee! And Luke ... well, Luke was just your teammate on the Cardinals ball team. I'm **the one** he was soooo interested in. He seriously wanted to date me, too." As we walked in the back door, DeeDee immediately went to pick up the phone to call Karen.

Well, that was damn good to know — I only had "good buddies" because both had the hots for my sister.

****

Mick and I decided Steve McQueen was great, especially with the baseball and glove scenes. The girls liked James Garner. We drove through Zesto's but couldn't find a decent spot. I looked hard for Cathy. No luck. Nobody really felt like Blender's again, so we called it a night.

At Mick's, we split up. He walked DeForrest home while I walked Karen to her house. We held hands and talked during the two long blocks. On her front porch, we talked a little more between two short kisses, then I said goodnight. On my way home, I decided I liked Karen, but there was nothing saying, "Go back for more!"

Since I didn't pass Mick on my way from Karen's, he — or more probable, DeeDee — must have already said goodnight. She was waiting for me when I walked in. I immediately asked her what she thought about Mick.

"A nice guy and fun." ... ... *That English poet, Alexander Pope, said, 'To damn with faint praise.'*

"But how about Karen?"

"Nice girl. Fun too. She's not a Linda." ... ... *Damning with faint praise, Part 2.*

****

Saturday, around noon, I heard the mail slot clang. After I finished reading the last couple of pages of a chapter of another Chandler book — *Farewell, My Lovely* — I went to check if my course schedule from St. Ignatius had come. On the way down the stairs, I heard it clang a second time and guessed the postman had forgotten something. On top of the stack were three smaller, white envelopes and I quickly looked through the rest of the stack. Unfortunately, my letter from St. Ignatius wasn't there.

As I neatly placed the mail on my mother's desk in her study, I suddenly realized two of the smaller envelopes were written in my father's hand, *addressed to himself* at a P.O. Box here in Wyandotte with no stamp, no return address. The third wasn't marked at all. Why send letters to yourself eight thousand miles away? Who delivered these? Not through the Post Office. I found her letter opener and gently sliced open the three envelopes. I took them to my room and shut the door.

The first contained a single folded sheet and simply said,
  #33   The Painted Dog ——3K
       6/5/62
       Duc Phan

The second one was very similar,
  #35   The Flying Goose —— 2K
       9/5/62
       Minh Trang

The third one, similar, but with a cryptic comment and not addressed,
  #36   The Painted Dog —— 2K
       10/5/62
       Duc Phan
     ≈≈≈ DEAL !!! ≈≈≈
     $$$ & 2 Am Pass

All dated within the week he was killed. I decided not to show them to my mother. It would just be upsetting to her and I didn't have a clue what they meant. Where was #34? Why was it missing? I put them in the back of my desk drawer. Over the course of the following weeks, I would take them out, look at them, yet couldn't decipher their meaning even a little bit.

✳✳✳✳✳✳✳✳✳✳✳✳✳✳✳✳✳✳✳✳✳

On Tuesday, both DeForrest's and my letters were in the mail. She was over at Karen's, so I put hers on her favorite place — a large chaise lounge where she sprawls out to read, write and do homework on her portable desktop. I wondered if she still pictured herself as Empress Josephine Bonaparte, languidly resting on her pillows, daydreaming about boys.

I spread out on my bed and opened mine to check out my schedule:

8:10 — 9:00	Religion	Fr. Morrison
9:10 — 10:00	French III	Fr. La Croix
10:10 — 11:00	Ancient Civilizations	Mr. Bannister
11:10 — 12:00	English	Fr. Fitzgerald
2:00 — 1:00	Lunch	
1:00 — 1:50	Adv. Algebra / Trig	Fr. Hoyle
2:00 — 2:50	Latin III	Fr. Lo Bianco
2:50 — 2:55	Dismissal	

These were the courses my mother and the principal, Father Carroll, had discussed, so I wasn't surprised. I was pretty sure having Religion first thing in the morning would put me back to sleep. I called Ron Carson to get the scoop about the teachers. He responded with a complete rundown. Morrison is formally Vice Principal and informally the "Enforcer," nicknamed "The Moose" and incredibly boring, except when it came to discipline and punishment. La Croix is a good teacher and a nice guy. Bannister is new and will be the head basketball and baseball coach. Fitzgerald is an ex-cop, very tough with an even tougher demeanor. Fr. Hoyle, an eccentric older priest, nice guy and extremely good teacher. Lo Bianco is incredibly hard. I would really have to study my ass off with the writings of Cicero. We talked a little more, ending with he would pick me up next Tuesday, bright and early at 6:45.

Mick called and said he and Pamela — his girl from last spring and early summer — had gotten back together again thanks to their date last night. It all began two weeks ago when she had come to watch him pitch in the All-Star game and he threw two innings of perfect ball. She and another girl were in the upper part of the grandstand so no one could easily see and recognize her. The other girl, Caroline, persuaded her to go talk to him after the game. Everyone was celebrating, then a big busted blonde went over to give him a hug and a warm kiss. So she dejectedly thought she was his date. Mick laughed and said it was his engaged cousin from St. Louis. Seeing him with another girl, just confirmed she had made a mistake. She thought she would wait until she saw him again.

Next time she saw Mick, he was with a different girl — a good-looking, dark reddish brown-haired one. They were doubling with another couple Friday night, driving through Zesto's. She couldn't take anymore and called him on Saturday morning, asking him to take her out. They went to The Indian Head restaurant to talk over dinner. She said she had greatly missed him and was terribly sorry she had given his ring back before she left for Chicago. She really had been down in the dumps for most of those six miserable weeks without him and badly wanted to go back to being steadies again.

Mick said, "Your sister is a lot of fun and terrific looking," then added, "but DeForrest is not Pam. What about Karen and you?"

I chuckled, "Oh, there's **no** Karen and me."

"Good, I want to fix you up with a date for Friday night. We'll double. Her name is Caroline Cunningham. She's really cute ... fairly smart."

"But?" Wanting to find out **now** — not when I picked her up — about her less flattering characteristics. Maybe she could do Ipana ads like Bucky Beaver.

"Butt?" He snickered, "Oh yeaaah ... *a fabulously nice* butt." Continuing seriously, "She's short, about five two, brown hair, brown eyes. Great set of knockers for her size with that marvelous butt ... a ter-ri-fic bod. *That's* why you would like her. And she's Catholic," he kidded. "*That's* why your mother would like her." I thanked God he didn't say, "nice girl with a wonderful personality" like DeeDee's seniors.

"Where would we go?"

"The movies, then Zesto's or Blender's. Or maybe even Allen's Drive-in, but the crowd there is a little rougher. Have you been there?"

"Nope."

"It's all right, like Zesto's. On State ... the other side of 13th street. Kinda of completes a longer loop for cruising."

"Okay, I'm game."

※※※※※※※※※※※※※※※※※※※※※※※※※※

DeeDee wasn't too pleased when I told Mick had fixed me up with a blind date. However, when I said I was going to double with Mick since he was back with his old girlfriend, she was totally indifferent.

On Wednesday, Mick showed me a couple yearbook photos of Caroline, but they were fairly grainy, large group shots. She still looked like she would be attractive. Mick gave me her number and I called her on Thursday, just to introduce myself and to get acquainted a bit. We began by talking about her classes at Prescott. She was taking a General Education path and thought she might go to secretarial school or just get some kind of a job after graduation. I told her generally about mine, then mentioned after the movies, we might go to one of the hangouts. She said great and we hung up. Mick was right, she seemed nice.

The next night, Mick picked me up and as I left the house, DeeDee yelled, "Have fun with Jane Doe*."

I got into the car and he introduced me to Pamela. Her big, gorgeous brown eyes were a trifle close set and her mouth was slightly overly generous, but still quite good-looking with long, brown hair. Seemed to be medium height with a nice set of knockers. The rest of her was hard to judge, sitting in the car. We picked up Caroline and decided to go see *'Beach Party'* with Frankie Avalon and Annette Funicello at the Avenue Theatre then to Blender's.

Everything Mick said about Caroline was true. She was really cute and above average smarts. *And what a body*! Truly, she had "*a fabulous butt*". On my scale, it was the best I'd seen in a really long time with breasts larger than any guy would expect on a short, slender, lightly sun-tanned body. Her personality was refreshing as she could be funny or serious, genuine too. Spoke her mind with some conviction like the Irish Catholic she is.

But he forgot one thing. She smoked! A lot! As my mother always put it, it would be like kissing an ashtray. Close, because when I kissed her goodnight those few times, it was like kissing smoked barbecued breath mints. DeeDee and Mother wanted to

---

*In '60s teenage slang, **Jane Doe** or John Doe was a blind date

know if *I had been* smoking. My clothes must have reeked from it because my mother told me to give them to her, then she hung them in the garage.

Lying in bed, I recalled when my father caught me smoking, telling me it was okay to smoke, after all, I was a teenager now. So while we talked about baseball and girls, particularly Bonnie Jo, he told me to keep smoking, inhaling each cigarette drag. He even lit up one with me, but I noticed he wasn't sucking much of the smoke in. After about my fourth fag, I decided those were enough for this time. Within a few moments, my stomach started to feel queasy and I was getting lightheaded. Moments later I threw up. As I was puking, my father told me while I might think it looked cool, my body was telling me something entirely different. His lesson cured me on smoking.

※※※※※※※※※※※※※※※※※※※※※※※※※※※※

Mick called me the next morning and asked me what I thought. I told him he was more than right about everything but forgot to tell me about her smoking. "Yeah, well most guys don't care. Is it a showstopper?"

"No, no ... not yet.

"Would you take her out again?"

"Of course."

"How about tonight?"

"Uhhh Mick ... don't think she'd go with me on such short notice."

"Oh, short notice or not, she'll go out with you tonight. Got my ears full, taking Pam home. Why do you think girls go to the toilet together?"

"See who can piss the longest? Maybe, the farthest ... like guys?" We laughed at my crudities.

Mick, still snickering, said, "There is a party at the Lake tonight, mostly Prescott and McKenna, I'm sure Wellington too. There will be a band and it will cost a buck a head to get in."

"Sounds great. I'll call right now. Still got her number etched in my brain. Drexel 1 - 6180. I assume this Lake has water?"

"Yep. And a lot. Pretty good-size one. The road around it is real curvy."

"Like the girls." We laughed again.

Caroline immediately said yes, saying it would be nice to see me again so soon. I told her I felt the same and would happily pick her up about 6:45.

****

We arrived about 7:30. There were probably 100 to 125 guys and girls who appeared equally split by gender. Maybe half had dates, leaving quite a few singles in male and female clusters, both thoroughly checking out the opposite sex; some subtly, some overtly, all intently. The six packs of beer were readily flowing. I noticed there were quite a few bottles of the hard stuff opened also. The Wild Ones were a fairly decent band as their loudness covered some of their shortcomings but, unfortunately, they only knew one slow song. Any other slow dances were on records played thru their hi-fi system speakers during the band's break.

As Mick predicted, all three schools were there. As we approached the Lake entrance, he commented the rivalry existed on the gridiron, the court, the track and the diamond, but not at parties and the hangouts. It wasn't uncommon for a couple to go to different schools.

During the band's third break, I didn't see Mick and Pamela around so I mentioned it to Caroline. She laughed, saying, "Yeah, they went outside to get some Lake air. We could get some too. If you would *like to*."

Sure, I understand. Watch the submarine races. Look for the Wyandotte Lake Monster. ... ... I snickered, "Yeah, it is a little stuffy in here."

As we began to walk out of the shelter house down to the lake, two guys came running through the front doors yelling, "RANGERS! Park Rangers!" This I didn't understand.

About twenty guys and ten girls in various stages of inebriation stumbled past us and out the double French doors on the side. "In need of lake air too?" I asked jokingly.

Caroline smiled, "Not exactly, this happens at almost every band party. We parked in the lot near the road and walked down to the shelter house here. Anybody can tell it's the Park Rangers when they drive their red and green marked car into that upper lot. So the warning is given and all the underage drinkers leave quickly. Those caught could be arrested but only rarely does somebody get tagged because it takes the Rangers too long to get here. When it does happen though, it's because they're too drunk to get out fast. The age for beer is only eighteen so somebody legal acts like the beer is theirs. However, the hard liquor bunch really leave in a hurry, not forgetting their bottles which, of course, would be confiscated. The age is twenty-one for booze. Regardless of how old you are, it's still easy to get anything you want."

We continued walking down to the lake and I took her hand in mine. I broke the silence in a teasing tone yet I was serious, "Did you forget your smokes tonight?"

"As the nuns always told me, I have other bad habits. Might even show you a few. You know, I just seem to be talking all the time. Both last night and especially tonight. You never really say very much."

"It's fine. I like to hear you talk."

She abruptly stopped. "No guy has ever told me that," she said astonishingly. "Sometimes they will tell me to just shut up."

"If they're smart, it would be for this." Leaning down, I pulled her to me and kissed her for a few moments.

After I ended the kiss, she said happily, "Please interrupt me anytime for—"

"For this?" I kissed her hard and she responded with greater intensity.

There were five or six benches, all with couples on them in various joined positions. Even in the dim light of the area lanterns, slightly enhanced by the almost full moon, we could see one couple being particularly passionate. She was halfway braced up against the arm of the bench. He had his hand under her peasant blouse which was billowing like a small sail in a strong breeze. Her hand was between his shadowed upper thighs. She said something in his ear and they both got up and quickly headed down a wide, paved path that cut through the woods. During Caroline's watchful gaze, she began to snicker as we sat down on the still warm bench.

We started to talk less and less, making out more and more, progressing with intensity. After we broke apart from an open mouth kiss which quickly developed into some Frenching, the devil in my mind wondered what other activities Caroline and I could participate in. The angel was taking a nap.

I teasingly asked, "Didn't the nuns tell you that type of kissing is 'just so unchaste' for a good Catholic girl?"

"Oh yes, just so terribly impure and sinful ... which is why it's so much fantastic fun," and she laughed. "I figured we might be engaging in this little activity and the breath mints I've been using don't really work that hot, so I gave up smoking for tonight. Frenching has always been at the top of my bad habits list. You have a very talented tongue."

"Truthfully, I have been complimented for a few things, but never my tongue. You are extremely proficient yourself. Thought of the Olympics?"

She wondered what proficient meant and I told her 'skilled' but in her case 'gifted'. She responded, "Ooh, thank you my devil," kissing me on my cheek as I kissed her neck. She asked, "Would your so mar-vel-ous mouth give me a nice hidden hickey, but not on my neck? My mother would just kill me. She's declared 'any appalling love bite would mark her daughter as a very fast girl with loose morals'. It's her old-fashioned Catholic way of simply saying 'slut'. Please, below my neck, definitely where a collar would cover."

"Happy to plant a strawberry on you."

She unfastened the top two or three buttons of her blouse and pulled it sideways so I could easily find a place which would be completely shielded by any collar. During the simultaneous movement of casually shifting her blouse and twisting her torso, her bra strap fell off her shoulder and her cup slightly fell down. This quick sequence resulted in displaying most of the beautiful slope of her breast. While the top portion was nicely tanned, the bottom part was a wonderful snow white. After I visually devoured my momentary *au naturel* gift, Linda's two white baseballs came fleetingly into my mind. Imagining what the rest of Caroline's would look like, I envisioned a fabulous sphere with her now barely hidden nipple and areola, all prominently exposed.

While she turned to discreetly adjust herself, here came Mick and Pamela down the main lane. When Caroline shifted around, she too saw the couple approaching, and exclaimed, "Damn, is it that time already?" Her tone implied she realized her promised hickey wasn't going to happen then, so she subtly fastened up her buttons.

Mick replied, "Yep, it's 11 o'clock."

"Crap! My damn midnight curfew. Rich, I'm sorry. Hate to be the party pooper, but I need to leave."

"It's okay." ... ... *Just when things were getting **really** interesting.*

"Yeah, it's fine. We were coming to find you guys anyway. But we didn't think we would find you way down here," grinned Pamela, "*so close* to the Path's *charming* entry."

Caroline began giggling and Pamela joined her. I was sure the actions of the previous couple of this bench could somehow account for their snickering.

Mick explained to me the following week about the Path's allure. A well-crafted, silver charm — called Path's Entry which depicted the beginning of the Path — was sold in the Lake's gift section of its Gear and Outfit Store. One would be given to a girl after the couple engaged in sexual intercourse in a sufficiently secluded spot off the 3.4 mile trail. For obvious reasons, the charm was almost always kept hidden by the girl. Guys enjoyed its double entendre name. Only years later did the Park officials finally realize the charm's significance. They immediately quit selling them, however, a secondary market already existed at pawn shops or open air street markets.

****

Mick was right about the road. It wasn't easy at all, even with a few final streaks of sun as we drove to Shelter House #2. Our exit from the park was in pitch black, with the trees blotting out any moonlight. Thus, I kept the brights on as I drove slowly until we reached the Ranger hut at the entrance. There was a drive-in theatre about 1½ miles from the lake and aptly named

The Lakeside Drive-In. *Irma LaDouce* was playing and Shirley MacLaine was on the screen.

I offered to take Caroline home first but she said she would rather stay with me. So we dropped Pamela and Mick at her house where his car was.

As we drove to her house, she pouted, "I didn't get my heavenly hickey that my delightful devil promised me."

"I'll remedy that *immediately* upon arrival." Caroline smiled and nodded.

After I parked, I noticed she already had undone her top buttons again. shifted her collar and blouse which now displayed a small but sufficient patch of bare shoulder. During the next half minute, Caroline received my very best effort.

"Thank you, Rich," then begun kissing me intently. However, she quickly pulled back, "Oh, damn it. Just damn it! I want to stay here with you, but I *have to go* in. My mother will turn on the porch light at five minutes after midnight." She patted her lower neck and shoulder, smiling, "But I've got my strawberry to remind me of you all week."

As I walked to her door, holding her close, I stopped and gave her a short French kiss. She gushed, "I had a terrific time with you and your talented tongue and luscious lips."

"You have some really good alliterations," I laughed.

She looked a little quizzical, so I quickly continued, "Your tongue has a flair of its own. I had a great time Caroline. Next weekend? Would you like to go out?"

"Oh yes, I would like that so much. Call me, Rich. Soon? Please?"

"Great! I'll call before Wednesday night ... sooner. Promise."

She took a single step up on the porch stoop, which almost equalized our heights. We tightly embraced and began to French intensely. I could enticingly feel her breasts as she firmly squeezed against me, much more than when we were slow dancing. She had to thoroughly feel me too. I was solidly erect. My hand found where her blouse had become untucked, slid to her navel where my thumb began to gently circle its rim, interspersed with light pressuring touches to its shallow center. We continued to kiss, still Frenching. After about seven or eight revolutions, she pulled away, breathlessly murmuring something to God. Then distinctly, "Night Rich. Thanks," and kissed my cheek.

As she turned to go inside, I responded softly, "Goodnight, Cara."

Walking to the car, I thanked my two instructors — wherever they were — Scarlett Charlotte for the Frenching lessons and Red-Hot Rusty for the navel techniques. Yet frustrated though. I had imminent designs to continue gliding up her bare midriff to that overfilled cup. Then emptying it.

I started the car up, hearing Elvis belt out *Devil in Disguise*, followed by the yearning and eagerness of the Four Seasons for their *Candy Girl*. During the drive home, the music continued but I wasn't listening. I could only think about Caroline. I really liked her. Sexually, of course, I wanted to feel up and see those tempting tits. Sooo badly. And what a butt! But there was more. Was it her wit? Her cute looks? Her personality? Her audacious attitude? I couldn't put my finger on it. But there was this exuberant chemistry between us. I liked her so damn much. I did. I *really* did.

SEPTEMBER

I had christened Mother, Aunt Danae and DeForrest as Greek goddesses — "The Three Graces". One represented grace and elegance, another personified charm and joyfulness, and the third exemplified beauty and youth. Their main role was to bestow the gifts of giving happiness and the feeling of well-being to the people around them. My Graces fit the descriptions excellently.

The Three Graces and I went to the 9 o'clock Mass which DeForrest had suggested. My mind started to wander about fifteen seconds into the sermon which one of the Assistant Pastors was giving. Even though he was rebuking the parishioners regarding the sinfulness of lust, it was bore-ring. I would lay odds **if** he ever dated, none of the girls were a bit cool — just homely and nun-like virginal.

*Father ... Lust is a must! My lust last night certainly was. Ahh, that beckoning shot of her breast slightly spilling out of its cup. Didn't Shakespeare say ... 'Methinks her cup doth runneth over?' Yeah, next time ... I'll relieve those overburden cups of their soft, rounded wonders And stroke **them** instead of her navel! Yeeeeah!*

Oh sly, Dee, sly. And why would DeeDee want to go to a High Mass? High Masses are longer and have a lot of singing. But singing means a choir ... choirs have guys. The only choir guy DeForrest wants to see is Roland Bush.

The choir always took Communion last after they finished its hymn and would file down from the choir loft. There he was and here was DeeDee watching him intently, even as he knelt down to receive the Eucharist. When he was walking back to the loft, he looked piercingly at our pew, specifically for her. He smiled and since she was looking back, I'm sure she smiled. Hell, I would have done the same thing, maybe even waved at a good-looking choir chick I wanted to get to know much better.

Knowing some form of exchange took place between them prodded me to seriously scrutinize the six, nice Catholic choir girls. I spent the remainder of Mass answering the subsequent self-test question —

Given the following characteristics of
- (1) Plain looking
- (2) Flat chested and/or ironing board butt
- (3) Chubby or larger
- (4) Slovenly in appearance — e. g. hair
- (5) Atrociously dressed — e. g. clothes

Choose which answer best describes each girl,
- (A) two of the above
- (B) three of the above
- (C) four of the above
- (D) all of the above
- (E) none of the above

There were certainly no E's and only two A's, three B's and one C. But they all could sing extremely well. Why wasn't there an E? Just *one* terrific E?

After Mass, we went to see the Monsignor at the Chapel to confirm dinner. DeeDee had her radar on high alert as she swept the parking lot for Bush. He predictively appeared again with the priest. They went straight to each other and they had their own private conversation. Mother and Aunt Danae exchanged pleasantries with the Monsignor. I was bored. Dinner was to be at 1 o'clock and would be a prime rib roast. He was looking forward to it and went into the rectory. I retrieved the car, driving it back to the Chapel to pick those two up. Instead of waving to get DeForrest's attention for a third time, I simply laid on the horn. This irritated both my mother and aunt and embarrassed DeeDee, but it worked.

"You didn't have to do that!" she said huffily as she climbed into the back seat.

"*Really?*"

"**Really!**"

"Children, neither of you are ten, so both of you quit acting like you are."

Dinner was very good. How could it not be? With two French cooks and one in training? During dinner, the two "older girls" reminisced with the Monsignor about the "good old days". I could tell DeeDee was getting more and more antsy to change the subject to Roland Bush. She would be playing with fire if she brought up his name. All the Monsignor had to say was the word "senior" and her dream would go up in smoke. But DeForrest always did play with fire, so she lit the match.

Monsignor O'Reilly thought very highly of him. He had sung in the choir for four years, was very devout regarding the Church, but unfortunately had no vocation to be a priest. He would continue to be an honor student in his **senior year** and was definitely going to college next year. The priest continued to rave about him and his family. He was the only child and his parents were highly thought of and were quite active in the parish. He then surprised everybody, me included, by saying he would be an excellent Catholic boy for a nice, pretty Catholic girl, like DeForrest, to date. **THE** seal of approval! DeForrest was ecstatic.

When those three started cruising down Memory Lane again, DeeDee and I asked to be excused.

As we walked up to our rooms, she gushed happily, "Now all I have to do is figure out how to get him to ask me out."

"Attracting guys never has been a problem for you, DeeDee."

"I really like him already. He's soooo good-looking. He's funny. Has a great personality and—"

"Just be careful."

"Like you and Linda?"

"Now what the hell does that mean?" I challenged her as I followed her into her room where she reclined on her chaise lounge with a satisfied, smug look.

"I know the two of you went to the drive-ins, **not** the regular theaters, like you told Mother. And her mother too! Even though you always picked a movie that was showing at both. But, you big idiot, I'm sure Mother knew anyway."

"Who told you that?"

"Hermie. Oh, it wasn't hard. I could get him to tell me anything about you for a kiss. Luke, too."

"What? How?"

"Easy. Mother would go to the Base Exchange or a noon daily Mass. Maybe to the brokerage house or other errands. You'd be messing around the Officer's Club pool, ogling the girls in their two-pieces. I'm eleven months younger than you, not eleven years. I'm not sexually naive or stupid."

"Never thought you were. What else did my '*buddies*' sell me out on?"

"Not much, really," she giggled, "but it was sooo easy. The making out was really great. With both of them!"

"Luke is ten or twelve months older than *me*! Hermie is almost two and a half years older than *you*! Mother would *kill you*!"

"Look, all they ever wanted to do was wow and kiss me. Hermie telling me how pretty I was and Luke saying I was 'just gorgeous.' Guys, even older ones, can be maneuvered with decent flirting and teasing, followed by solid making out. I got Steve at your Loyola to do my algebra homework for a quick make out at the Base library. We'd go between the stacks."

"Yeah, some real friends of mine! Wasn't Steve your boyfriend? Then that conceited Rory just replaced him."

"Well, yeah, Steve sorta was, but then school ended and he went to Winnipeg for the summer. Guess Rory kinda was too ... both more like fillers until something better came along ... which never did. Oh but Rory sure thought *he was* ... you know, with our partying at the pool with his buddies and the girls."

"Back to the Choir Boy. Bet he's seventeen already. Just watch yourself."

"Eighteen in January. Hey, changing the subject, did you know McKenna is having a class reunion? For Aunt Danae's year ... '43. Those two are going to check it out. Maybe find some old flames and fan those ancient embers."

We both laughed.

DeeDee became serious, "It would do Mother some good, you know, to get out, have some fun, meet some nice guys ... after all, she still looks really good at thirty-eight. Aunt Danae has been thru hell with that slut chasing alkie. Even so, she still looks really cute. Could use more than a few pounds though. Way too thin! Maybe they both can find some nice guys."

✽✽✽✽✽✽✽✽✽✽✽✽✽✽✽✽✽✽✽✽✽✽✽✽✽✽✽✽✽

Labor Day blew by and Tuesday morning came early — very early. Ron Carson's few remarks about my instructors were dead on. Fr. "The Moose" Morrison was going to be a challenge all right — to stay awake.

In French, Fr. LaCroix was only allowing us to speak in French, "*après tout, c'est le français III*" [after all, it is French III].

Ancient Civilizations was going to be cool with Coach Bannister and the Romans, the Greeks, Etruscans, Phoenicians, Babylonians, and of course, the Egyptians.

Fr. Fitzgerald, the ex-cop, had a hard demeanor which I knew scared some of the guys. Being around military all my life, he didn't faze me. In fact, I liked him. Especially when tonight's assignment was to read the first page of *To Kill a Mockingbird*. Nobody dared ask why only one page. I immediately knew why. After reading the first page, you wouldn't be able to put the book down. I ate lunch by myself in the little park area, reading more than the first page.

Fr. Hoyle was a little old Jesuit, always smiling. It was extremely obvious he knew and could teach anything mathematical.

Latin was probably going to kill me ... oh that was quite clear. We were going to do a lot of Cicero and "when you boys get a little tired and sleepy, we will do some of Martialis and Catullus' poetry. Specifically their love poems on Fridays to sharpen you up for your dates."

So I summarized:

Religion	Really boring, hard to stay awake
Français	Good, a little work
Ancient Civilizations	Great, would be fun
English	Great, but a lot of work
Adv Algebra & Trig	Great, with an even greater teacher
Latin III	God help me

DeForrest's classes were fairly similar, except she had Geometry which she said she would hate. Languages, whether dead, foreign or just plain old English, were always easy for her. History wouldn't be bad and religion would be "neat". I asked her how that could be. "The priest is young and really handsome. All the girls have crushes on him."

Within a day, she was already in with one of the two cool girl cliques, thanks to Karen introducing and bragging on her. She was christened with the nickname of "Frenchy" from her two middle names of Danièle and Richelieu. Karen is called "Sailor", yet I didn't see the connection until DeeDee said it was because she could swear like one. Made perfect sense. Experiencing her crudeness in mixed company, I could only imagine her vocabulary with just girls.

She asked how many friends I had made, then backed off and revised it to acquaintances. I said none.

"Richie, try to make some friends this year. There was no one at Loyola."

"There's Mick down the street. He's certainly becoming more than just an acquaintance."

"He goes to Prescott, you big idiot. Guys at St. Nate's. Try, please?"

"Okay, I will. Are you going to miss your goofy buddies, Helen and Beth?"

"Nah. Well, maybe some. They were sorta squirrelly and giggly, especially around the guys at the pool. The ones I still miss are Olivia and Clara Jane. Remember, I talked about the three of us tried smoking and drinking at our sleep-overs. We would talk about girl stuff a lot. You know, like comparing cool guys, the best ways to make out, what gets you all hot and bothered **and more**. Only C J liked smoking. Liv and I really hated it ... made me nauseous. But **all of us** loved comparing the girl stuff. Liv is still at Darby near Livorno and C J is at Elmendorf. Said the winter there was colder than a witch's teat."

※※※※※※※※※※※※※※※※※※※※※※

That night, I called Caroline and asked her to go out cruising then to Blenders on Friday night. I didn't want to drive back to St. Ignatius to watch the team beat the crap out of some public school and I sure didn't care about watching Prescott. She happily agreed. Caroline confirmed her classes were nothing spectacular, except she was excited about a new class — Shorthand. The remaining were pretty much what she expected from her schedule of Business Math, a Social Studies class called Marriage & Family, English, a Home Ec cooking class and Study Hall. She asked me about mine and I sort of downplayed them, saying similar to hers — Math, English, Social Studies too — lumping Religion and Ancient Civilizations in there — and Languages. But no Cooking or Shorthand which made her giggle.

She paused, then snickered more, "I have a disease of the tongue and mouth. Only you can heal me. I'll stick out my tongue. Ahhhhh. See?"

"Oh quite so! Yes, the Doctor knows what malady you are suffering from and he will make a house call Friday night with a guaranteed old French remedy. However, you must leave your cigarettes at home for the cure to be truly effective."

She seriously whispered, "I really want to see you. Rich, I can hardly wait. I will leave my fags here. Definitely."

****

The best news of the week came Thursday morning during Father Carroll's infrequent morning announcements to say there would be informal baseball tryouts beginning a week from Monday. Mr. Bannister wanted everyone, football players included, to fill out information cards near the bulletin board in the main hall.

At lunch, I glanced at the card's required information. There were the basic particulars but also asked position, experience and some baseball vitals. When I started to fill mine out, I recognize John Nelson from my class who was completing his too.

"You're Marlowe, right?"

"Yeah, I know your name is Nelson."

"Yep, but everybody calls me Jack. You transferred in this year, right? Sit in back. Never say much."

"Came from Loyola in Omaha. Name's Richelieu, but I go by Rich."

"Didja play for them last year?"

"Yeah, both years as second-string first baseman, but I got to play about a third of the time last year. How about you? What position do you play?"

"Third base, just part-time last year like you, but towards the end of the season, I did start. Hoping to continue starting. There are two other Richs who played last year and a Rick who will make the team. You should go by Lou, you know, since you play first base, like Lou Gehrig. He was the best."

"Now that's a coincidence. The bat I use is a Lou Gehrig Louisville Slugger. It's a 35/35. A little heavy sometimes but when I get a good stroke ..."

"Hmmm. Yeah, fairly large, same inch and ounce. Sounds like a good, solid bat. That's fate telling you to put Lou on your card for good luck. Where do you live? I live south of the Country Club Plaza, off Ward Parkway."

Yeah, I'll be like Lou Gehrig. ... ... "Oh, I live in Wyandotte. I'm going to use Lou. Thanks."

"You eaten lunch? Or ya eat with a bunch of guys?"

"No, I haven't. I really don't know anybody."

"I'm going to eat outside. Wanna join me?"

"Sure."

We finished filling out our cards, went into the cafeteria then took our food outside. Jack said that he didn't hang around much with the guys from St. Ignatius. There were the jocks, both football and basketball. The book baggers — real smart guys who study all the time and whose entire female interaction is limited to their sisters and mothers. Another crowd were weekend junior beatniks who thought they were cool because they could act beat and smoke in the lunchroom. Plus a few other insignificant groups. His father had told him no group should define who he was. He took it to heart.

Jack seemed popular enough as guys would walk by and say hi. They had no idea who the hell I was. He had a girlfriend who went to St. Catherine's. A short, blond, blue-eyed senior. A real beauty. Her parents didn't like him at all. He didn't give a shit. As long as she did. They were going to the movies tomorrow night and out cruising around tonight. I told him I might go steady with a girl who was also short, very cute with a great body. I would know after this weekend for sure. As the preliminary bell rang for Math class, we decided we would play some catch during Monday's lunch. I had met several guys this week, but he was the only one I liked. Maybe it was his attitude, his natural cockiness — I'm Jack Nelson — take me as I am or get the hell out of my way. Either case, I don't give a shit.

****

On the drive home Friday afternoon, I told the Carson brothers I was sure glad to see the weekend, but had a ton of homework to look forward to. But what I was really looking forward to was French kissing Caroline while I completely fondled her beautiful set of tits — not just glimpsing some tan-lined spillage. I had just spent the last four days with only males. **I was Horn-ee**. And the more I relived our Saturday night "activities" on her front steps, the more my H-level increased. Yet I found myself also wanting to be with her, just to be together.

Caroline answered the door, wearing a white fitted blouse trimmed in green. Her tight green slacks and medium heels purposely emphasized her fantastic butt which I drooled over as I watched her walk into the dining room to get her purse. She looked really good with bright red lipstick, minimal rouge and light green eyeshadow. I wanted to jump her right there in the living room. I doubted if either her chain-smoking mother or cigar puffing father would notice since they were glued to the TV, watching Don Ameche's *International Showtime.*

She slid in the driver's side to sit close to me, I complimented her, "Hey, you look really, reeel-eeee nice tonight."

She snickered, "Well, thank you, flattery *might* get you *somewhere.*"

With that come-on, the degree of my horniness soared. Fortunately, it was fairly dark since it was a little past dusk with some rain clouds in the west. I informed her, "The Doctor needs to examine you … **now**," and leaned over and kissed her neck and earlobe as she smiled delightfully. As she opened her mouth to say something, mine covered hers with my tongue diving in. I frantically swirled my tongue inside her mouth and all over her tongue, finished by momentarily sucking on it. Having caught her off guard, an almost breathless Caroline happily sputtered when I stopped, "Whew ... weeee. The Doctor ... certainly is **in**! ... **in** my throat!"

The Doctor would rather be IN your bra! And he will be ... IN just a little while.

After she quickly regained her normal breathing, she suggested, "They should coop you up more. After Blender's, there's a place I **really** need to take you. My big strawberry was perfect. Almost the size of a half dollar. A nice deep red. I think it even glowed in the dark," and she snickered. "But it is now just a very hazy hickey and I want one of its longer lasting relatives, so bright it radiates heat."

"The Doctor knows exactly how to heal the patient, but a more intense treatment will be required." We both laughed. As we drove away, she moved close to me, placing her left hand loosely on my neck or right shoulder. I planted my hand almost midway up her left thigh, moving it only to make the occasional turn or lane change, which did cause me to brush against her breast a few times. That sensation, followed by some thigh-squeezing, caused a few predictable erections. We cruised up and down State and Minnesota — talking, teasing, laughing. I was having a great time with her. Since I had never been through Allen's, we decided to check the place out. As we went through, Caroline honked and waved to a big busted, chubby, peroxide blonde who was leaning on a guy as he straddled his motorcycle.

"There's Candace ... Candy. She graduated last year. Waitressing somewhere."

"Yeah, at that new place. The Indian Head. When my family went out for dinner, she was our waitress. Pretty good one, too."

We barely beat the football crowd at Blender's who came piling in. The Prescott guys and girls were ecstatic since their team had drubbed Wellington badly by a 27 - 6 score. We grabbed a booth and ordered a couple of shakes. I was still hungry so I added a hamburger — of course, no onions — and some fries too. Caroline waved at some guys and girls she knew, especially Shirley and

Lorraine, two of her new girlfriends who were in her Shorthand, Marriage & Family and Cooking classes. They eagerly came over after claiming a table with their stuff.

Lorraine Holliday's family had just moved to Wyandotte from Little Rock since her father had taken a job with the Phillips 66 refinery. She was plain and broad-faced, medium height with a large frame, probably considered herself "pleasingly plump" as evidenced by her tightly packed, slightly bulging jeans. Her overly large breasts were *truly* pleasingly plump, as she advertised them in a screamingly tight, plunging blue sweater with cleavage rivaling two small honeydew melons. Her whole sensual effect, completed by wearing white lipstick and too much blue eye shadow and heavy eyeliner, unfortunately, gave her look a definite slutty edge.

Shirley Spencer, "Sherry" as she called herself, transferred from one of the rural schools — Townsend High School. She seemed to be fairly good-looking, had a thin face, about the same height as Lorraine. She was equally tarted up, also wearing white lipstick with thick eyeliner and ample red eye shadow. Her dishwater blonde hair was piled high on her head in a disheveled beehive. A noticeably tight, red surplice sweater with a fitted waist, firmly wrapped her much smaller yet still fairly sizable packages. Sherry's jutting posture indicated her pair were proud to be on display. Her eyes scouted the diner, eager for any male attention who wanted to scrutinize them in closer detail. Or who wanted to check out her shapely legs and butt in her tight, matching red skirt, hemmed inches above the knee. Unfortunately, Sherry's appearance, even though much thinner and much more attractive, still duplicated Lorraine's decidedly air of sluttiness.

I didn't recognize anyone. But I told myself, I had only lived here three weeks plus I went to a school across the river. Still did get a fair share of longer than normal glances from a few girls.

I devoured my burger while we both finished our chocolate shakes and my fries. Caroline then nervously pulled a pack of Larks from her purse, unwrapped the cellophane and laid the cigarettes on the table.

I emphatically pointed at them, "Thought you weren't going to bring *those*?"

"Oh," she responded in a feigned casual tone, "I bought a new kind of breath mints yesterday, Clorets. Don't worry, they work wonders. Think this new Lark brand of cigs will make me look so very cool when I smoke them?" She nervously snickered, " 'Cause it'll be a Lark." And she pulled a cigarette from the pack.

Now I was irritated at her. Caroline had promised no cigarettes tonight. "I don't think any cigarette makes a girl look 'so very cool'. A girl should have her own natural cool. Breath mints or not, kissing just isn't as good with smoking. Besides, it's really bad for your health. You should just quit. Tonight!"

Caroline's temper flared up as she snapped at me, "We aren't going steady! You can't tell me what to do! That crap about your health is **Shit**! Put out by a bunch of dumb ass doctors who wouldn't know enough not to piss into the wind. Just pure **Bull Shit**!"

Which pissed me off royally. The conversation now was accelerating down a one-way road named Nowhere Good. I demanded forcefully, "Okay, how about doing it just for me then? If we were going steady, then you would quit? **Right now**!" I flipped the pack away from her, almost to the window.

This angered her all the more. She snatched up the pack, snarling, "Oh hell no! Not even if I had your God damn fraternity lavaliere*. You still couldn't tell me what shit to do. Or what shit **not to do**!"

She immediately flipped open her lighter, lit up, took an extended drag, then blew the smoke out of the side of her mouth towards the window. Moments later, she inhaled another lengthy mouthful and exhaled the smoke through her nose. I continued waiting.

So different from last Saturday night. And tonight ... in front of her house ... then cruising. I don't get this.

Caroline took a third, long drag and the smoke escaped in between her hot, staccato bursts, "Carl Farris is a senior. ... ... Team's tri-captain. Right tackle. ... ... Asked me out. Tomorrow night. *Doesn't give a shit* if I smoke, 'cause he does too."

---

*Giving a **lavaliere** necklace or pin symbolizes a long-term commitment between a couple and generally viewed as the stage between going steady and being engaged

*Now I get it ... But I'm the one who **doesn't give a shit**! ... ...* Completely losing my temper, I growled, "You two idiots are made for each other! **We're leaving ... Now**!"

Instantly, dynamite exploded. Caroline screeched, "**Kiss my sweet ass**, you arrogant Uptown White Collar Boy. **I'll go home with whoever I want**." She steadily spat out her next barrage, "**You ... can ... go ... straight ... to Hell. Rot there ... you conceited ... GIANT PRICK!**"

She smashed her cigarette savagely into the ashtray, grabbed her purse, snatched up her cigarettes and lighter, hastily slid out of the booth to quickly join her two girlfriends.

I watched as Sherry lit up, following Lorraine who was already exhaling a small-size cumulus cloud of smoke, slightly dangling her cigarette between her fore and middle fingers. Her thumb was neatly tucked under her gaudily adorned ring finger with the entire hand near her face. Still failing a movie scene attempt to look "so very cool". Yet both were succeeding quite well in their "come-on looks". Caroline was eagerly welcomed as two guys made room for her in the booth. A few more were standing close by, talking and flirting while they glimpsed down Lorraine's sweater. Then she leaned over and her overflow became more pronounced. Invitingly so. Two guys became completely fixated on Lorraine's risqué, teasing waterfall. I wondered which one would succeed in picking her up — and succeed in what else with her.

The plastic ashtray kept smoldering — like I was. I violently shoved it, causing the plastic ashtray to ricochet off the window at the end of the table. When it finally came to rest, it was upended with the dying cigarette butt and ashes scattered everywhere. I stayed in the booth for a couple minutes. Still tightly wound and firmly pissed.

I could always go over to that table. Ask her to come back to ours. Ask her not to go out with the football player. Ask her to go steady. Yeah, right ... NONE of that 'ASK' BULL SHIT ... IS ... EVER ... gonna happen.

I yanked three dollars out of my billfold — more than double the bill — flipped them on the table and got up out of the booth. Out of the corner of my eye, there was a flicker of the back side of a slender, extremely tall girl with long golden-brown hair. Her great butt and long shapely legs, wonderfully arrayed in a tight green pencil skirt, easily glided into the girls' toilet. I could wait for her to come out. But why? I had never seen any tall, slim girl with a great-looking butt and legs whose face and bust could match them. Always a pancake-flat chest with a quite plain or even homely look. I went straight out the side door, not looking back at the newly formed trio and their admirers. Probably couldn't see Caroline anyway through all their damn smoke.

****

I came through the kitchen from the garage. My mother was just finishing sweeping up some broken glass off the floor. "Richelieu, watch your step! I dropped a glass. ... Well, that was a very quick date."

DeForrest appeared out of nowhere, "Did you have a fight and break up?"

"You can't break up if you were never together. We only had two dates. Plus tonight. Whatever that disaster was."

"Karen would sure take you back."

"You need work on your dating definitions. 'Take you back' implies we had gone together at some point in the past. Karen's nice. But she's not for me."

"Anybody can tell you are back in school. We are getting anything from definitions to detailed analyses. Oh well, tomorrow night, Karen and I are going to a McKenna party. You should come with us. Or too ashamed to be seen with two attractive sophomore girls?" she teased.

"Thanks, but I've a ton of homework. We argued about her smoking, then I really made her mad when I told her cigarettes don't create cool. That a girl creates her own cool ... a natural cool."

"Richie, do you think I have 'a natural cool'?"

"Yeah, a lot. Sometimes too much."

"Now that's the nicest thing you've said to me in a long time." She rewarded me by kissing my cheek then continued on her way up the stairs and to her room.

"What happened, Rich? But only if you want to talk about it."

Certainly leaving out the enticing sexual memories, I filled her in with only highly edited details, concluding with, "I really do like her, but I wish she didn't smoke. I wish she was a little more ambitious. Doesn't care about college. Just basic, run-of-the-mill dreams. I'm sure this date with the other guy was her bargaining chip. She would give up this tackle and go steady with me, but continue to smoke. Mother, I was beginning to really like her. She's an incredible amount of fun to be with. Very, very cute. A terrific, great personality. Funny. Genuine and honest, not pretentious."

I turned to go to my room, laughingly saying, "Who in their right mind would choose a tackle who smokes over a first baseman who doesn't. Ya gotta wonder. But she's Catholic, so you would have liked her immensely!"

I went to my room and laid on the bed. I had quit grinning. It wasn't funny anymore. I did like her. A lot. Certainly sexually, but there was something more. I still didn't know what the allure was. That unmistakable chemistry between us. Regardless of her A-bomb detonation, she didn't blow up that strong attraction. It still was there. In spades.

She's great to be with ... makes me laugh. Makes me feel good to be with her. Genuine, honest ... like I told Mother. Not fake like other girls can be.

She can make out and French. Not to mention her bewitching butt and beckoning breasts. There, my contribution to sexual alliterations. Really odd though ... when she gets aroused, she unconsciously creates them.

Awww, Shit! SHIT! Damn it! Why didn't I just take her to the drive-in? That Lakeside one? We'd French, give each other hickeys. I'd easily be caressing those soft, rounded mounds before the first show ended. Boy, did I screw up. BUT GOOD!

But that smoking ... just couldn't take it. If she just would give it up. Who am I kidding? Even so, we would have gone nowhere. No thoughts about college, no dreams or ambitions after high school. Dad wouldn't have liked her lacking that desire ... maybe not even Caroline herself. Could tell Mother SURE doesn't.

Shit ... so what if she lacks the desire to be educated more or ambitious. Damn it, I still really like her ... she has that natural, fresh charm. So cute ... a great body for a short girl. With a short temper ... and a BAD one. God in Heaven, never saw any chick explode like that! Oh well, Caroline's history.

But WHY do I still like her so damn much?

I decided to call Linda, hoping she was home. Surprisingly, she was. We talked for about fifteen minutes, first about school, then lying to each other by saying how much we missed each other, then very quietly reminiscing about our last drive-in date. I did miss making out with her and especially her "baseballs". I realized as I went to sleep — not much else. Not like I did with Caroline. Damn.

****

DeeDee still wanted me to go to the party with them and said thanks but no then asked how they were getting there. The party was just a couple blocks from Karen's, so they would walk. My mother and aunt, after dropping off DeeDee at Karen's, were going to a party at one of the law partners' homes to celebrate something. Now I had the whole house to myself — to do homework. After watching *Route 66* and *The Twilight Zone*, I decided to work on my assignment for Ancient Civ's. If you are going to do homework on a Saturday night, might as well do the subject you like.

DeForrest called about midnight from Karen's to ask if I would come get her. Even in our neighborhood, our mother strictly forbade her to walk alone at night. I, of course, could walk by myself as DeeDee teased "nobody would want me." I told her I would come to Karen's and we would walk home. I needed some air.

On the way, DeeDee mentioned Roland Bush had come late to the party, but she was still able to dance with him for a few records.

"He is soooo nice ... a good dancer, too. Really smart. He asked me out for next Saturday night and, of course, I said yes."

"Don't you think you should ask Mother first?"

"Oh, she'll agree. After all, the Monsignor 'recommended' him as a nice Catholic boy for me to date. I really like him. One of his friends asked Karen, so we are doubling. You really missed your chance with her," she teasingly said.

"Yeah, my kind of girl. One who swears like a sailor."

"Richie, no girl is perfect."

"Only you, DeForrest Danièle."

"Why Richelieu, such a 'perfect' compliment!" This was immediately followed by her scoffing, "A **perfect line** of bull shit! You're so full of crap! Whatca doin'? Staying in practice for the next girl?" Then with seriousness, "Look at the past month. You said you didn't like it when Linda was sometimes loud and boisterous. You didn't like that Caroline smoking. And Karen because she swears a lot."

"I did like Linda a lot and she liked me a lot. And she liked vodka a lot. When she drank, she was more fun and definitely wilder. Always wanted to party, be at the pool, go to the drive-in or cruise on Dodge making the loop from Todd's to Tiner's. A great summer chick. Really great! But she didn't care much at all about after high school, especially going to college. Dad told me, over and over, 'Only date smart college girls. Then marry a highly intelligent, great beauty, one like your Mother'."

"Wow! You never told me she drank." Then she began to giggle happily, "Daddy always told me the same about guys, only marry a good-looking one ... **like him**." I smiled, but her recollection quickly twisted into an unintended gut punch.

Moments later, I continued, "Caroline was definitely fun. Great to make out with. Very honest but stubborn. Nobody could tell her what to do or what not to do. Which led us to the problem of her smoking. I told her it was bad for her health. She should quit. It smells and it's no fun kissing a breath minted ash tray. All of which really pissed her off but good. She has an exceedingly short fuse on her temper. **IT IS** surprisingly intense. She called me an arrogant Uptown White Collar Boy, told me the health statement was bullshit, I could kiss her sweet ass, then go straight to Hell and rot there, and ended by calling me a conceited giant prick. She's right about one thing, she does have a great-looking, sweet ass. And, maybe I am a little arrogant and conceited." I moaned slightly, "I liked her. A lot. Really a lot."

"Ha, she must have been totally pissed at *your* arrogant, conceited ass," shifting my comment away from the amazing look of Caroline's.

"Karen is nice. Really nice. I like her as a friend. The swearing is just my excuse. There just wasn't anything for me past her beautiful blues. I'm sure she's really worse when it's just you girls."

"Yeah, she's pretty bad. Not all that bad with guys, just some to shock them."

"No guy wants a girl who swears like that. Makes her seem cheap, slutty. She'll attract the wrong kind of guy. Hmmm, maybe that's what she wants. Like some leather jacket from Allen's Drive-in."

DeeDee laughed, "She keeps talking about bringing some biker guy home just to piss off her parents." I thought of the chubby, big busted Candace with her biker.

"That would certainly do it." I unlocked the door and we went inside.

****

Lunch on Monday found Jack and me eating alone. Last Friday two baseball lettermen, Rich Trent and Rich Harris, had joined us and were moaning about their bad luck with girls. But that night was going to be different. They were doubling and their dates were girls from St Maggie's. We guessed not much changed since they weren't here, yakking and bragging about the girls in glorious detail.

"So how'd it go with 'Little Caroline'?"

"Well, you know I told you 'Little Caroline' smokes. She won't quit to keep dating me. She already had a Saturday date set up with a smoker lineman, no less. I'm sure the deal would have been she wouldn't go out with him if I gave in on the smoking."

"Did you?"

"Hell no! And this first baseman had second base made. No doubts."

"You gave up a 'two bagger' because of a little smoke? What a dumb ass! God, I shouldn't even be seen with you."

"Yeah, I regretted it when I got home, I regretted at Mass and I regret it now, but the smoking would have just continued. If I was only interested in playing with her tits until something better came along ... sure, I could overlook the smoke. But I was beginning to seriously like her. No ... I already do ... or did ... a ton. Whatever. Shit, I don't know. She was terrific."

"Lou ... Lou ... Lou, when will you ever learn? Any girl willing to let you play with her tits is fun to be with. By definition! Read that somewhere in the Bible."

We laughed, but I said seriously, "Come on Jack, you know what I mean."

"Yeah, I do. So I am going to introduce you that rarified air of St. Catherine's honeys. They are the best."

"Best at what?"

"At what? At what, you ask? Everything! Camille told me if your girl didn't work out, she wants to fix you up with Brenda who's a senior too, medium height, kinda flat-chested but a great butt. Has a cute face with brown hair and really, really smart. What do you say for Friday night? We'll meet at The Nu-Way. Maybe get a little to eat, listen to the juke box some, talk a lot. You can take her home. You'll like her. All right?"

"Sure, okay."

****

On Tuesday, I dropped the Carson brothers off, then I pulled up to the garage door. When I got out to open it, I heard a noise. There was Harry Brooks — Aunt Danae's Bozo Ex — standing off to one side of the driveway.

"Hi, Rich. How have you been?"

"Fine, Harry. What d'ya want?" I opened the garage door behind me.

"Oh no, it's what **you** want."

"What the hell, Harry? Been drinking? As usual?"

"Now be nice to me. I have something you might want. And no, I'm stone sober. Two days. Going to prove to my Elle I can do it. Don't need that God damn Alkie Anon place she and everybody else kept telling me to go to."

"Good for you." ... ... *Sure don't give a shit. Why did my Aunt ever let him call her just 'L'? Danièle or Danae is so much nicer sounding.*

"You the one that picked up those envelopes?"

"Yeah, I have 'em. Nobody else knows about 'em either."

"That's good. Look, I'm sorry for that little mail stunt. I was drunk and I wanted to get even with Elle and your family. Our divorce was just finalized. Rich, I miss her. God, I miss my Elle terribly. Maybe by staying sober, she'll come back. Got a good job. Start tomorrow at Simpson's Body Shop. An estimator and finish painter."

Only if Aunt Danae is crazy! ... You treated her like SHIT on the sole of your shoe.

"About that mail ... Forrest began sending me these envelopes. He didn't trust anyone in that office he worked out of. Told me never to open them. Never under any circumstances. So he would send me different kinds of envelopes for proof and safe keeping, mostly like the ones I left. He said he had to trust someone, so it had to be someone in the States. You were too young and he certainly wasn't going to upset your mother with it. We were always 'Brothers in Arms', you know, since I was in Daegu, Korea while the *Real Big Shit* hit the fan there in June of '50. And he knew I needed money for my investment ideas. He would send a $10 money order with each batch of envelopes, like that last group. Some of the small ones were addressed so he could mail them separately. Which he would do. He told me to hold everything in a safety deposit box. Well, when he was killed, I destroyed everything, but missed those last ones."

"Proof of what exactly?"

"I don't know exactly, but it had something to do with intelligence work."

"Well, no shit Harry! He **was** a Major in SAC's intelligence division."

"No, I mean it was an investigation into wrong-doing in the military. Our military, Viet Nam's military with Vietnamese and American criminals. He needed me to hold the proof. I figured it was big. He and I met at Windsor's. He told me again I had to keep my mouth shut if I wanted any more money to be sent.

This was when he came home on leave when everyone was here in Wyandotte for that Christmas in '61. Unfortunately, Elle and I had just separated."

Because you began picking up and screwing those bar sluts from your favorite dives. ... ... "Windsor's. Your favorite bar. Come on, all this cloak and dagger shit."

"You don't believe me, do you, you little Asshole. Well, I still have some proof. It'll cost you."

"Thought you gave up drinking?"

"I need to eat and pay rent. Fifty dollars and I will tell you everything. Tell you what, give me $25 before I talk and then $25 afterwards if it all sounds good. I'm willing to do it this way because I know it's all good stuff."

"All right, when?"

"Next Monday night. At—"

"No Harry, no bars. Aah ... the Public Library at 7 o'clock ... in the Periodicals Room."

"Make sure you bring the money. Say, have you got any on ya now?"

"Yeah, here's $5. That's all I have on me. You'll get the rest of the money. But your stuff better be worth it."

He simply turned his back and left. I probably had just pissed away five bucks, but I needed to know what those envelopes meant. **I had to know**. Now to figure out how to find the remaining $45.

As I walked into the house, my mother said, "Was that Mick I heard you talking to?"

"Maybe yes or maybe no. Maybe it was a beautiful non-Catholic girl and I didn't want you to meet her just yet."

My mother smiled sweetly and went into her study. I went upstairs and pulled out the three envelopes for the umpteenth time. They made no more sense now than they did when I picked them up off the floor with the mail.

During the night, I had the God Damn Nightmare again. There was my father in his dress uniform, standing in front of a white picket fenced house which I think was where we lived when I was about four or five. He looks at me like he is expecting me to respond to his question or statement. There is a shot and he drops to his knees, then falls flat on his face with a large bleeding hole in his back. My mother comes running out of the house, screaming.

I woke up sweating and terrified — like every time before — still deciding never to say anything to my mother. During that *first and only time,* when I was telling her about the nightmare, it quickly started to overwhelm her, reminding me of when the officers told her of his death. So I described to her only part of the damn thing. When she hastily regained her composure, she said she wanted to take me to a Shrink if they continued. **No way!**

****

School these past couple of weeks has been damn rough. Religion was a sleeper as Moose droned on and on about concupiscences. He could even make lechery and "young men's carnal desires" sound boring. French wasn't too hard, I just had to pay more attention to grammar. "Old Civs", as it began to be called, was great. We were going to learn about Egyptian mathematics, astronomy, and medicine in their times, how they practiced scientific surgery and their mummification process. We were beginning to discuss how the Babylonians used algebra and cuneiform writing. This was going to be terrific. English was great also, but hard — a lot of books to read and essays to write. Math was actually enjoyable with old Fr. Hoyle. Latin was incredibly damn hard.

Now I completely understand the old refrain:
>Latin is a language
>Dead as it can be
>Latin killed the Romans
>And now it's killing me

However, I decided Friday the 13th was not going to be bad luck for me when I easily found The Nu-Way, just off the Plaza. Jack stood up and waved me to the booth. He first introduced me to Camille — she was **fabulously good-looking** — beautiful, natural baby blond hair and deep blue eyes. Then quickly announced, "This is Brenda Cox." Jack was fairly right in his description of her. She was probably medium height, did have a very cute face, brown hair cut in the short, curly Italian style which made her look a little boyish. I like a classy feminine look. Her bust was *assuredly* pancaked with only slight curves. Definitely flat-chested.

We all had shakes and talked. Jack and Camille left around 9 o'clock — Jack saying they had some place to be and winked at me when they said goodbye. Brenda then ask if we could leave shortly because she and her Mother had to run quite a few errands, so they were starting early in the morning.

She was certainly smart, taking Classical Honor courses in Languages and History and thought she would be an attorney. Brenda talked quite a bit, mostly about herself. Yet she seemed worth a second shot as her talkativeness could be only nervousness. As I was taking her home, I said I knew it was short notice but would she like to go out tomorrow night. She confidently agreed, "Sure, that would be nice." We decided to go to the Broadmoor — sort of a nightclub for teenagers on the other side of the Plaza — for some dancing. We had a better than average length, yet still chaste kiss good night. I decided walking back to the car that had to be lengthen and more. A greater wish was that her tits would quadruple in size overnight. But Jack was certainly right about her butt — two wonderfully curvaceous cheeks packed nicely in tight slacks.

During my drive home, the comparative thought of "sure has a terrific ass, just not as great as Caroline's". The memory of her strutting into the dining room in those tight, green slacks kept popping into my head. Thinking Caroline was "history" was obviously flawed as I seriously wondered where she was and what was she doing. Since it was still relatively early, I drove through Blender's, then Zesto's looking for her. Also Cathy, promising myself I would ask Mick about my carhop queen and get her phone number. A last circuit up and down State. Neither one to be seen. Shit, Caroline was undoubtably with that damn lineman. And he's probably doing exactly what my religion class daydreams were — intensely Frenching and feeling her up. On every damn date.

****

On Saturday, I went to Safeway to buy a few things that my mother needed for dinner that night. I was wearing some old, beat up shorts with an equally old powder blue cashmere V-neck sweater. I had cut the sleeves off when one elbow had worn out. And due to my growth, it was now shorter length. They were out of Eskimo pies, so I asked one of the stock boys if he knew of a store that I might find them. He told me Ball's at 18th and Central would definitely have them. I vaguely knew where it was. Somewhere on the other side of St. Patrick's. However, I found it easily, pulled in the parking lot, and went into the grocery store to look for the frozen food section.

Oh my God! ... Look at that Amazon! She's beautiful! Gorgeously long, long legs. Look at that wonderfully curved butt! Long beautiful hair!

Wowzer! Wowzer!

The girl was extremely tall, maybe even six foot, with golden brown hair. She was dressed in a white blouse with red polka dots and red shorts. Her long legs made the pair appear shorter. As she bent over one of the frozen food cases, the fabric seemed to shrink farther, exhibiting even more of those magnificent thighs and distinctly accenting the curve of her butt. I stared intently, gawking at this girl's fabulous derrière and thighs, hoping for a wondrous glimpse of a sliver of butt cheek. My intense wish was she only would stretch just a little further. My mental craving caused a completely unwanted erection which totally destroyed my plan to go over to meet her.

How to hide this huge bulge? She could easily see it in these crappy shorts. No length left on the sweater to pull over and hide it.

Oh God, what an embarrassment!

I turned and moved close to the frozen food cases, then shuffled down the aisle, hoping the cold might shrink my predicament. It didn't. When I found the Eskimo pies, I grabbed a couple boxes, held them in front of my bulge. I glanced back at her. I **had** to see her again. She was looking right at me but only for a moment or two, then she pushed her cart into the next aisle. She joined an older woman, probably her mother, yet the two didn't facially resemble each other at all and the girl was a good half-foot taller and the mother was fairly chubby. I watched them go through the check-out line then walk out the door.

Damn this giant hard-on, really screwed it up. Oh that's it, go away ONLY after she's long gone. Shit, I really wanted to meet her. What an absolute goddess!

As I pulled into the garage, I realized she was the girl in Blender's last weekend. The one walking into the girl's toilet. Well, there goes my theory how a tall girl's appearance of her front can't match or exceed her backside's bonanza. The goddess A-bombed that to Hell.

My infatuation with her had exploded. I had to meet her.

****

After DeeDee left on her first date with Roland Bush, my mother came into my room and said, "Well, he seems very thoughtful and well-mannered. I believe that in time, I might be able to like him."

"C'mon Mother, he wants to date your daughter more than just tonight, so he'll be very respectful and nice to you. And Monsignor thinks a lot of him."

Since we were on the subject of dating, I asked, "When are **you** going to start dating again? You'll never meet anybody cool at the grocery stores, the banks or your favorite, the brokerage house."

My mother remained her usual stoic self, "Oh, Rich, it's not as easy as you think when you're my age. Men are still primarily interested in *that* one thing, not necessarily a fully developed loving relationship."

"Ooh." I wanted to change the subject desperately. I knew my mother was quite savvy about the "games" men could play, but didn't want to know **how** she knew. Fortunately, my thoughts turned to this afternoon. **I** did meet someone at the grocery. Well, I sorely wish I could have. I didn't want to be late for my date with Brenda or 'Bree' as she went by, so I told Mother quickly, "There was this girl at Ball's. **Great-looking**! Not merely good-looking. She had it all. She was completely, totally fab."

Driving out of the garage, it dawned on me Mother really had no thoughts about marrying again. I believed she was still completely in love with my father.

****

Even though it was crowded, we got a table quickly since I handed the hostess a couple of dollars. More of my father's expertise, "Tipping and tipping well will almost always gain you swift and excellent service." Bree talked even more, tonight's topic seemed to be all about the injustices in the world, ending with the U.S. beginning a quiet military action in Viet Nam to stop Communistic expansion. I started to say I knew all about it, but I just let it go. She was just okay as a dance partner, although she acted like she was better than she was. Slow dancing with her reminded me of my lessons as an eight-grader with "Pancake Pamelas" as we guys called those noticeably flat-chested girls. A few times I looked for the tall, golden brown-haired goddess, wishing she would be here. Though it was early, I figured it was time to leave and go make out.

While I was taking Bree home, she asked if Lou was short for Louis or something similar. I told her Richelieu. However, I don't think she believed me. Did I mean "like the Cardinal in seventeenth century France"? I started to explain but she began to delve into the history of France at that time. I knew a lot more than she did, even could have corrected her twice, as I always listened intently when my grandparents talked about the history behind our names. When we parked in front of her house, I wanted to make out to see if she could be quiet, and more importantly, if she was a good make out. Our first kiss was a brief one. The second one, much longer with some mutual passion. As I tried a third kiss, I hoped for even longer and more intensity. But she pushed me away, telling me she barely knew me.

That pissed me off, so I challenged her, "During last night and tonight, you talked about school, plans after it, even world events and lotsa other things. I think I know you well enough."

She said she hardly knew anything about me. Obviously, that was because she needed to shut up and listen to me when I tried to talk which was infrequent. She said she wanted to go in and I certainly accommodated her. I didn't try to kiss her good night, but, at least, she did finally shut up. No attraction with her whatsooo-ever.

Since it was 11:30 when I drove back into Wyandotte, I decided to cruise up and down State, looking for what or who — I didn't know. No Cathy in Zesto's. I *had* to ask Mick about her and get her number. As I drove into Blender's, I thought about going in to single out a babe from a bunch of unattached girls, but arrogantly surmised any chicks there without a date, probably wouldn't be to my tastes. Resembling somehow, in some way, the huge mistake I had just left. And if I saw Caroline, it could lead to a fight with her Bozo lineman.

I stopped at the light at 30th, thinking, "Aww shit, go home." As I glanced across the traffic lanes, there **SHE** was — in a '58 Chevy Biscayne, heading in the opposite direction. She was talking to her date, but looked over, seeing me. Our eyes locked solidly for several moments, but the light changed and the car pulled away. I was left almost catatonic. The guy behind me blared his horn. I looked in the side mirror to see the shrinking twin set of double round tail lights. The end to a "wonderful" evening.

※※※※※※※※※※※※※※※※※※※※※※※※※※※※※

Driving to Mass, all we heard was the continuation of my conversation with DeeDee about Roland this and Roland that. I was ready to puke. She **really** liked him.

Unfortunately, Karen had a terrible time with her date, Ronnie Kovac. Earlier, DeeDee had stopped her gushing about Roland long enough to tell me that during the two girls' bathroom break, Karen called him "a horny sonuvabitch pig prick". Some of his "compliments" were cloaked in suggestive terms, capped off by "accidentally" copping a feel of her butt during The Cascades' *Rhythm of the Rain*. He apologized but she knew he enjoyed his hand rubbing over her ass. She continued with a litany of swearing, interspersed with barfing gestures. When they came out of the bathroom, Karen said she wasn't feeling well and needed to go home right away. I asked what should Karen expect. She was crude herself with guys. DeeDee said she never made even one provocative comment to that horny shit from the start of the date.

When we pulled into St. Pat's parking lot, I finally got the chance to describe my goddess, DeeDee exclaimed, "She was at the party last night! Had to be her. Can't be that many fabulously good-looking, extremely tall girls with light brown hair. This girl was a little taller than me. She had a date, naturally, but the guys were still hanging around her, trying to get a dance with her. The guy she was with, was really handsome. Seemed real happy together. Maybe she's Catholic and goes to McKenna." Everyone laughed.

All throughout Mass I kept thinking about her and how to be introduced to her, then make a date with her. She had to have a flaw somewhere. Maybe she wasn't too bright. No, according to DeeDee, she acted smart enough. Maybe she talked strangely, like a little girl, or high pitched or like a duck. I was going to drive myself nuts with this. A girl like that would be going solidly steady.

Later that afternoon, I walked Aunt Danae to her car, bringing her 'care package,' from dinner with me. We kissed good-bye, hugged then I kissed her on her forehead. As she drove away, Roland pulled up. He said he was in the neighborhood and thought he would just stop by and say hi. I said I would go get DeeDee. Going into the house, a lightning bolt struck me.

Inside, I yelled to DeeDee, "Rollie baby is here."

I knew it would take at least five minutes before she made her appearance, having had to check everything over at least twice. So I went back to Roland and asked, "There was a real tall, great-looking girl with golden-brown hair at last night's party. Ya know her name?"

He hesitated for a few moments, then said, "I know who you are talking about. Don't know her name. I'm pretty sure she goes to Wellington. Certainly doesn't go to McKenna. Her date probably goes to Wellington too."

I found out some time later he knew her name **and** she went to Prescott. He had met her at the end of the summer and had a wild desire to date her. So he wouldn't tell me as the on-going word was Wyandotte girls thought St. Ignatius guys are highly intelligent, cool, looks ranging from good to handsome and all with reputations of "being very fast". Of course, that's certainly not all correct. All the guys are intelligent. And only some are cool and good-looking. Add also highly confident or just plain arrogant **and** yes, fast — to varying degrees — caused by spending the entire school week with only smart, heavily disciplined and certainly horny guys. Regardless of what is fact or fiction, fortunately for Wyandotte guys, St. Ignatius's guys stick mostly to Missouri girls from the co-ed public schools and St. Maggie's or girls only like Sagesse and St. Cat's. Oddly, even the ones who live in Wyandotte or Johnson County go for the Missouri girls. Go figure that one, but my last date was with a St. Cat.

Later that afternoon, I called up Mick to see if he knows anybody for Wellington girls. His cousin Mel goes there, so he gave me his number. Then I thought I would cover all the bases, so I asked him about Prescott. I described the goddess as terrific looking, having golden-brown hair, great legs, great butt, slender. He was getting over an early season cold, and just as I say "tall in height," Mick starts to sneeze and he hears "small". He says I am perfectly describing a girl at Prescott. She's real good-looking, has a great personality, a cheerleader and a senior, but is going steady with the captain of the basketball team. Couldn't have been her as she would have been out of town all day and Saturday night for some Girl's State convention. If she breaks up with the guy, Mick will tell me immediately. She sounds like my type. I didn't know I had a type. I found out months later this had made perfect sense to him when he told me he heard the "small" in height description and the only two girls he had seen me with were "small" or short girls — Karen and Caroline.

I called cousin Mel immediately, told him Mick sent me and described my goddess to him. He is positive the girl is a senior who just made Homecoming Queen, has long, brown hair and eyes, great personality, slender, tall, nice body, most guys think she is very attractive. Confirms what Roland thought. Would not be his choice for a girlfriend, since she is a little taller than he is. Made perfect sense when Mick told me some time later his cousin is only 5 foot 7. However, she is going very steady with a Wellington guy. I thank him and hung up. Suddenly, the antenna of the Biscayne flashed into my mind which had green and white ribbons tied on it — Wellington colors.

Shit, Shit, SHIT. Dammmn it! — That's her. I was so damn depressed. Guess I thought all I had to do was be like some knight, put on my shining armor, go on a quest for her, searching everywhere, questioning everybody, following all the signs to finally happen upon her. She would be there, just waiting for her knight.

****

Jack heard all about my date on Sunday, so Monday at lunch, he told me I was "too fast". Towards the end of the second date, I made her nervous, especially when I came onto her. Sometimes, it seemed like I was pre-occupied. I was very hard to get to know. I told Jack that was only because she talked about herself, her school, her family, the world and everything else in God's universe. Brenda couldn't keep her mouth shut and listen for shit. Her nickname shouldn't be Bree — it should be Breezy! We laughed and wrote her off. Camille told him Antoinette Faber had become available. Jack said she was filthy rich, good-looking with nice, **average** size knockers. And a decent shaped butt. Was I interested? I said of course.

****

Baseball practice started with Coach Bannister outlining his goals for the week. He knew he was missing four guys who were playing football now. Still there were sixteen guys who showed up for the tryout. No one would be cut. It was just very early 'spring' training. He watched intently as we all warmed up. The coach made some notations on his clip board, then named "two squads" of eight players. Jack and I were on the Blue squad who took the field while the White squad took batting practice. I was assigned to first and Jack to third. Then the squads reversed and it became my turn to bat. The coach was still pitching, each batter getting five swings. I had brought 'Lou II' with me and partially hid it under my Loyola warm up jacket, both of which my mother had purchased for me last winter. It was the unwritten code, placing the bat like that says it is for my use only. I had three good hits, one was really exceptional. Probably the furthest I had ever hit a ball, bouncing once then rolling into the parking lot. All in all, I had an excellent tryout while Jack had an even better one. Both of us were satisfied with our practices.

✻✻✻✻✻✻✻✻✻✻✻✻✻✻✻✻✻✻✻✻✻✻✻✻✻✻

That night I met Harry Brooks exactly at seven, having told my mother I needed to do some research for a paper at the Library. DeForrest said I was probably meeting that girl who came into the backyard last week. I said it certainly was the same person.

"Ya got my money?"

"Hi to you too, Harry. Yeah, here's a twenty." I flipped the bill at him.

He grabbed the money, stuffing it in his pocket while furtively looking around.

"There's no one here except a couple of old men and a young librarian."

"All right, here is what your father told me. This is God's Truth, I swear. Major Forrest Marlowe was posted as a security military advisor to the Saigon Chief of Police to advise on various potential problems, like methods to handle crowd control or insurgency type problems. That kind of stuff. But he had another job ... undercover type ... to investigate a drug smuggling operation utilizing Vietnamese and American, both military and civilian. A month before he was killed, he wrote me saying he had enough proof to show an American military connection which acts as a conduit to bring drugs into the country on returning military transports from Tan Son Nhut airport to military airports in southern California. Someone with Las Vegas underworld ties, picks up the drugs, distributes them. Then launders money through a 'legitimate' export-import company, Bradford Universal in LA. He said all he needed was a little more proof and his case would be complete. He never could use the office in Saigon as there were two American soldiers and some Vietnamese cops involved. He never named names."

I had started making notes like Fr. Fitz had told us to do when researching for a paper. Then Harry passed me a 8 x 10 black and white picture of a beautifully featured woman of Asian/Caucasian mix. **Completely naked**! The nipples on her jutting out medium-size breasts were aroused. She was smiling as she lay against some propped up pillows, one leg spread widely with the knee bent, resting on the bed. The other was partially hanging off the side of it. The fingers of one hand spreading her vulva, and the surrounding pubic area completely hairless. The other hand is beckoning a man to come back, obviously for more sex. And that man in the other part of the picture is **MY FATHER** in civilian clothes. He appears to be heading towards the door, looking back, saying something, maybe good-bye.

I was completely shocked, "This is SHIT! **My father** would **never**, **never** touch a whore like this. He loved my mother too much." I lost my temper and raised my voice, "**This is pure SHIT**! How did you get this **God damn picture**?"

Now loud enough to be heard over the noisy oscillating fans, the young librarian stood up with a highly distressed face to emphatically warn me, "Any more of **that** language, you will leave immediately! Keep your voice down and be quiet!"

I quickly went over to apologize to the librarian. She was a small busted, attractive blonde whose nameplate identified her as 'Miss Rosalind Black'. "I'm very sorry, Miss Black. Some news was very upsetting. My apologies to you. It won't happen again. Sorry again."

She strongly yet sympathetically said, "I understand, young man, but **you will** keep your voice down. Watch that tongue of yours! **No more swearing**!"

"Yes, ma'am. Thank you. Sorry." I walked back to Harry.

"Just cool down, kid. Your father sent it to me. He claimed it was a fake but a damn good one. Said he had been in her house where it was taken. Met her a few times there while looking for this slanty-eyed shit — one of the smugglers at the beginning of the chain — who wanted her for himself. But she's *a very high-priced* call girl — clearly way outta his league. This expensive whore would even proposition your father every time he saw her. He did pay her once to set up a meeting with this little gook, waited with her for quite a while, but he never showed. The gang got wind of the extent of his investigation. So it was a blackmail scheme to silence him. He either lost his proof and cooperated or Geneviève would be sent the picture with this letter from the whore saying she was pregnant with his kid. He mailed them to me in case they possibly sent copies to her. I guess to show he knew about it in advance but I don't know how he was going to convince Geneviève it was a fake. I tell you kid, it sure looks very real and very, very damning."

His arousal was increasing — the picture was starting to turn him on, "A big Air Force Officer stud, like your dad, could have his pick of the top of the line expensive Saigon call girls, like this luscious, intoxicating piece of Eurasian strange. During France's dumb-assed pre-WWII escapades in that shit-hole place, her gook mother got knocked up by some Frog. That's why this hooker whore's got lighter skin, larger eyes and a higher nose. But best of all, those *full* primo tits! Yeah, look at that inviting, tantalizing pussy! Says give IT to me rough and reg-u-lar-ly! That hot piece of ass belongs in *Playboy*. Better yet, in my bed. Ooh yeah!"

The picture does look real. Damn it ... ... very real. Couldn't be ... can't be ... IT JUST CAN'T BE! NOT MY DAD! NOT HIM! NEVER! Please God. Please!

The writing in the short letter was poorly scrawled in bad English but the gist was there. Pregnant and his.

"There must be something to prove these are terrible lies. Can't the Saigon police do something? Make her confess it was all a lie. What about the Air Force?"

"Not really, kid, and why? Your father is dead. Your mother doesn't know any of this damn shit. The Air Force wouldn't want to tarnish your father or more importantly, themselves, by bringing it up. You remember how the communists' story went ... that drugged up Viet Cong radicals in Saigon decided to kill the first American officer they could find that morning ... or some shit like that. The shooting was in retaliation for Robert McNamara's visit days before when he bull shitted and said he was 'very encouraged' and he had seen 'nothing but progress.'

Thus, your Dad's death, according to what the Air Force obtained from interrogations and the numerous propaganda leaflets, the commies made **their** point to the people in Saigon ... and in other areas of South Viet Nam ... that horse's ass McNamara shouldn't be 'very encouraged' as shooting a Major was hardly evidence of 'nothing but progress'. So the Saigon police arrested and executed the four Viet Cong involved in the plot. Anyway, the case is closed and nobody there cares now. Welcome to the real world, not yours of sheltered privilege."

I took the picture and the letter and handed him his $25 in an envelope. As I got up to leave, he said, "Oh, I had a copy of the letter and picture made. You know, you **might** want to **donate** some more money to me in the future," then smirked as if he was about to pull off a big deal.

I spat my words at him very forcefully but quietly, "I don't have any more money. This drained me, you Bastard. So you are going to blackmail me? Shit, I don't think so, Asshole. Go ahead, **show** the picture. I'm not stupid! Then you will never get back with Danièle. Never! I will make sure ... God damn sure ... you won't!"

He laughed, "Oh well, you're young, so I thought I try and sucker you. All right, then here is the real deal. You help me get back with my Elle and the copies of the picture and letter disappear."

"How many copies do you have?"

"Only the one." He laughed viciously, "With *that kind* of photo, it was all *your* money could buy. Not the sort your local Rexall Drug reprints. A deal then?"

"What am I supposed to do?" I agreed very reluctantly.

"I'll let you know, next Monday, same time, same place."

The next day, I was a total wipe-out. I slept terribly and while I didn't have the nightmare, its presence recurred in my sleepless thoughts. I almost fell asleep in Moose's class which would have been suicide. Thank God, I got through everything including Latin, even though Lo Bianco called on me and I was totally unprepared. Certainly would have been dead meat, but the bell rang before he could select a passage. He always remembered and would try me sometime later this week. At least baseball practice mostly kept my mind off of it.

That night, I prayed to the Holy Ghost for help. I hoped He still remembered me. During the next half hour, the beginning of a plan began to take shape. I would ask Fr. Fitz after English class if he would hear my confession, then ask his advice. The seal of confession would, of course, guarantee his complete silence and just as importantly, he would know how to handle it. The word was he had been not just a cop but a detective before he joined the Jesuits.

After English the next day, I told Fr. Fitz I needed some advice desperately and would he hear my confession. He said to meet him in the chapel in ten minutes. I told of my messing around with Caroline and some other minor stuff. Then I told him the problem, reading from and elaborating on my notes from the meeting with Harry, then showing him the picture with its accompanying letter. He said he would have to think about it seriously to come up with a way to proceed. This will take some time, but on the good side my mother doesn't know anything about it. I told him Harry the Prick wants to genuinely get back with my Aunt Danièle, so he would never show the picture or letter or say anything to my mother. But the jerk still tried to use the threat of exposure into giving him more money, thinking I was naive enough. I was afraid if this crazy scheme didn't work, he might even try to blackmail my aunt in coming back to him. My aunt might do it since she loved and cherished my mother deeply, thus would do anything to protect Mother's memories and strong feelings of love from being crushed. In the past couple years, Harry had become a right nasty Bastard!

For penance, he gave me three Our Father's, Hail Mary's and Glory Be's and said I should do something nice for my mother. I gave him the three numbered envelopes. I had previously noticed the picture was marked #25 and the letter was #26. Neither was #34. As I handed him both items, I asked him if he thought we could prove my father's innocence. He said he wouldn't give me any false hope, although he said Harry knew much, much more. He had some thoughts, would evaluate them and let me know, maybe in a few weeks. I thanked him profusely. He just smiled, "I'm Father Brown." I didn't know what he meant until days later.

※※※※※※※※※※※※※※※※※※※※※※

Baseball practice the rest of the week went great. On Friday, we had a five inning intra-squad game and Jack hit a single and a home run. I had a triple and a long fly that the left fielder, Rich Harris, made a spectacular catch of. In the field is where Jack really showed how really good he was. He backhanded a shot, tried to plant himself in foul territory but slipped as he threw. The ball skidded into the dirt and took a strange hop caused by the english Jack had put on it, but I still snagged it up for the out. We laughed about it later. I told him neither Jones or Kline could be close to beating us out. He agreed I wasn't too shabby, but I still could learn from the master.

He and Camille were going that night to the movies. I had a date too — my Latin book. I had just squeaked by with Lo Bianco yesterday. Jack told me God had made Saturday nights for horny guys to go out, meet good-looking, frisky girls and both engage in "real fun stuff." He had read that too in the Bible somewhere. I really laughed hard. He also said Camille would finalize everything to fix me up with Antoinette and he would let me know Tuesday. Jack was becoming my first real close friend. That and baseball were the only things going well.

※※※※※※※※※※※※※※※※※※※※※※

The first autumn cold front had pushed through on Sunday and far much cooler than the previous Monday. While I waited in the periodicals room, I began to drool over a spectacular looking Librarian who was on evening duty — terrifically well-built as evidenced by her snuggly fitting evergreen sweater. I eagerly went over and asked her about books on Babylonian cuneiform. She had nice warm, smiling eyes which, like mine, were very dark brown, essentially matching her black hair. 'Mrs. Dianne B. Scott,' according to her desk nameplate, was the only good-looking unrelated female I had talked to in days. She stood up to guide me to a corner area in an adjacent room where that topic's books and card files were kept, walking a few feet in front of me.

Really, really beautiful ... about five-and-a-half foot tall. Wow! What shapely legs. And a great derrière in her matching evergreen pencil skirt ... What movement in her walk. Terrific breasts ... nice hair. An absolute Goddess!

Shit, she's already married ... like that matters ... she's probably ten years older.

God, I'm so incredibly horny.

I gratefully thanked her as she showed me the section, sorrowfully forgetting my impossible dating scheme. I could only watch her body stride so wonderfully, so effortlessly out of the room. She was, without a doubt, The Goddess of the Tomes — straight from the Elysian Fields.

After I finished my futile daydreaming, I found some books for my term paper and was checking them out at the main desk when Harry finally showed up. I could smell him ten feet away. He was drunk. Completely. I told him I would drive him home. Yes, in his car. His immaculate, beautiful 1958 Sierra Gold Impala convertible. I did, but I could only do it with the window rolled down.

He babbled, talked and swore some guy or guys are following him. I asked, "Were they pink and each one had a trunk?" while I helped him up the stairs of his walk-up. Inside, he nosedived onto his bed, falling asleep quickly.

Seeing the copies of the letter and the picture sticking out of a book, I took them. After all, I'd paid for them. I left him a note, saying I had taken the items, but I had agreed to help him with Danièle, so I would. I almost choked writing that, but my father told me "When you give your word ... you **must keep** it!"

Seeing a bunch of empty pint bottles of Jim Beam in his trash can, I finished the note with, "Absolutely quit drinking! Go to Alcoholics Anonymous!" When I left the apartment of the converted house, I noticed there was a guy acting like he was polishing his car. Who does that at night? It wasn't even a cool car, maybe a four-door black Buick or DeSoto. Harry's paranoia had rubbed off on me. I walked the six blocks back to the Library to get the Galaxie and my library books.

****

I had just started watching TV on Friday night, when the phone rang. A frantic Aunt Danae was screaming Harry was at the door to her apartment — dangerously drunk and belligerent. If she doesn't let him in, he is going to break down the door. I told her to call the Police, then lock herself in the bathroom. We would be there immediately. I yelled for my mother to grab her coat and I filled her in as I drove like hell to Aunt Danae's apartment. By the time we reached the apartment building, the Police had already handcuffed Harry and were pulling him through the smashed-up door. I took one look at the apartment — chair knocked over, table overturned, a broken Jim Beam bottle, the place smelling like bourbon. My poor aunt was sobbing terribly, clutching her chest with one hand and holding the side of her face with the other. The Son of a Bitch had beaten her soundly.

I turned and ran towards the police car. Before they could put Harry inside, I pushed the smaller cop out of the way and slugged the Bastard in the jaw as hard as I could, knocking him into the trunk of the cop car. Then I grabbed him by his hair to smash his face into the trunk lid of the cruiser. Fortunately for Harry — and me — the bigger cop quickly pulled me off him, warning me, "That's enough. I understand your wanting to bash his head in, but no more. Otherwise, I'll arrest you too."

Heatedly stalking back to the apartment, I noticed a guy in a black Buick driving away. I was sure it was the same guy who was in front of Harry's Monday night.

Standing outside of her apartment, there was an older couple, Warren and Sarah Luverne Walton, with whom I had made friendly small talk on previous occasions. Mr. Walton explained, "This scoundrel was yelling and screaming all sorts of crazy stuff. He still loved her. He wanted her back. He would do anything to get her back. That he could prove the Air Force, the Las Vegas mob, and some Bradley or Hadley Industries, and only God knew who else, were all in cahoots to smuggle millions of dollars of horses or something into the United States. He loved her. Let him in, he just wanted to talk, he adored her, they were meant to be together forever. They killed Horace or Boris to shut him up. The same incoherent rant over and over and over."

Sarah Luverne chimed in, "After she wouldn't let him in ... my oh my, he called poor Miss Danièle some terribly vile ... ooh ... just obscene names. Then he kicked the door in. Thank the Lord, two minutes later the Police showed up."

I thanked them for their concern and telling me of Harry's ravings, then went back inside.

My mother was holding my aunt, trying to comfort her, talking to her. She was holding a bag of frozen peas on the right side of my aunt's face. Her voice was colder than the plastic sack and I only caught the last of her words, "...with us tonight. Tomorrow, you are moving in with us. Maddy! Do not argue with me."

"Okay, Georgie. You know best. Always look out for me. Why does he keep hurting me? Keeps on. More. Oooww! And more. Why Georgie? Ooww!"

"Oh, Maddy please don't cry. Please! Please Baby! I was deathly afraid of this shit continuing and that God damn bully hurting you more! Oh, Maddy baby, I won't see this keep escalating, getting worse and worse. And I know **it will!** I'll see his conniving, scheming chicken shit ass in jail! My God, hitting and knocking you around. The woman he loves so much and can't live without!"

What? Never heard Mother swearing and losing her temper like this! What did Danae mean 'KEEPS hurting her'? He's beaten her before? When?

"**Forrest**, stay with your aunt, keep the bag on her eye and cheek. I am going to pack some clothes for her."

My mother rarely, rarely called me Forrest and when she did, I was in incredibly deep shit or something was very, very serious.

My aunt clung tightly to me, crying as I put my arms around her and held her firmly, still making sure the sack was properly positioned on her face. "Hold me Forrest! Keep me safe Forrest! Like you did in Florence!"

Aunt Danièle has never called me Forrest. In Florence? That area in North Omaha?

I told my aunt everything was okay now, she was with us, over and over. My mother finished packing the suitcase. Danae continued to cling tightly to me, whimpering with her arms around me. When she shakily got up, her slacks, widely ripped down one side of her leg, fell to the floor. I pulled them back up to cover her and decided I would just pick her up and carry her to the car to lay her down in the back seat. As I drove away, my mother who was now holding her, told me to take her as fast as I could to Providence Hospital to be checked over.

Close to the hospital's emergency doors, I lifted my aunt out of the car and carried her again. As we neared the door, my mother came back out with an orderly and a wheelchair and began barking information and instructions to him and to the nurse who appeared at the door. To me, "Go get DeForrest at Karen's! Now!" On the drive, I cursed myself soundly and repeatedly for being taken in by that son-of-bitch's scheme to help him get back with Danae. So he could beat her more? **What else?**

My Aunt was checked over, and the ER doctor told her she would have some very ugly bruising both on her face and her left breast. She was given pills now and for later. A nurse found some safety pins for her slacks. The four of us came home around eleven and my mother and DeeDee put her to bed in my mother's room. Mother insisted upon sitting up with her for the night. I found out the next morning that about five o'clock, DeeDee got up to relieve herself then requested, finally adamantly pleading with our mother to go get some decent sleep in her bed. She would stay with our aunt. About 9:00 a.m., my mother went in to check on both of them, and Aunt Danae said she felt like coming down to breakfast. The four of us began talking while DeeDee began to cook.

I went over to my aunt and said, "Aunt Danae, it's terrific you are moving in with us. Because **you** are the best Aunt ever. My Three Graces, all together in one house. But you have to share a bathroom with your sister again." DeForrest would be sharing *my* bathroom since she was moving into the sewing room. She was far less happy about that than I was. Oh well, a small price.

As predicted, Aunt Danièle's cheek and eye were starting to turn an ugly black and blue. Last night my mother told DeeDee and me the bastard had slugged her at least twice in the face after he grabbed and viciously twisted her left breast followed by a hard punch, both causing the area to bruise badly. She looked terrible, horrible. I could only hope his face looked worse.

She weakly smiled, tousled my hair and kissed me, "Thank you, my Richie."

DeeDee then announced, "Yeah, Sir Richelieu of the Hoel Shire even punched the jerk out last night."

Both my mother and aunt looked astonishingly at me with my mother saying, "What? When?"

"Oh, it was when they were taking him to the cop car. I only got in the one good pop. A cop pulled me off before I could do anything else. You are safe here, Aunt Danièle, I swear." My mother and my aunt exchanged some sort of knowing look.

Aunt Danae smiled warmly, "I know you always protect me Forrest, ... er Richelieu, my brave, handsome Prince Richelieu," and started to hug me tightly but it hurt her too much.

"You need to put some weight on. It was easy to carry you, My Little Auntie." It wasn't easy at all, but no one needed to know. I kissed her forehead.

She whispered by my ear, right side clinging onto me, "Such a bull shitter!"

I became very serious, "I'm *unbelievably* happy you're here for good. I've always missed you when you weren't here!"

That caused her to burst into tears, but now she did hug me tightly, wailing "Oh, my Little Forrest." She clung to me for a few moments, kissed me on the lips then on my cheek. She smiled at me, then went to Mother who wiped away her tears, whispering something inaudible. DeeDee's happiness was obvious as they hugged and kissed. My aunt gushed, "I'm so incredibly happy to be here with my family for good." DeeDee had finished cooking and served us. The four of us ate the first of our many breakfasts together.

Mother called Ted Laird and told him what had happened. He called back about twenty minutes later saying Harry Edward Brooks had been charged with assault and battery, public drunkenness, disturbing the peace and destruction of private property. After he spent the night in the drunk tank, he was arraigned this morning. He was released by Judge Milton Wade, based on his "personal recognizance since it was his first offense". Laird said first thing Monday morning he would obtain a formal restraining order against Brooks to make sure she doesn't have to see or deal with him in the future. My mother thanked him.

DeeDee stayed with our Aunt when Mother and I drove to her apartment to bring her car, clothes and some of her stuff back to the house. I asked her about his bullying — how long had it been going on? Did he ever hit her before? Couldn't Aunt Danae do something?

Mother A-bombed me. "Forrest, you're old enough to hear and know about these types of marital problems. That jackass started his damn bullying after they had been married a year or so, but it was all verbal. Never touched her. Blamed her for anything that went wrong, including when his so called 'investments' went bad, losing jobs, gambling losses. Then the drinking started. He beat her for the first time that night after he came home, bragging about his wretched infidelities with…"

My mother didn't finish. Didn't have to as the damn whore of Saigon appeared, laughing at me. Taunted me by pointing to her exposed genitalia.

"Danae left him and moved in with our parents Septmber '61. Never saw or talked to him. He had an expensive teenage call girl named Noëlle Kringle or something Christmasy for a short time. Followed by a dark-haired floozy, named Elaine Debussy … supposedly fairly resembled Danae … moved in for quite a while with him until he badly beat her. Followed by any promiscuous thing in her twenties to drink and have sex with."

"Then in March … a few months after your grandparents moved to Naples … Harry called to come over to her apartment. To talk and apologize. He brought her roses and after filling her with complements, he started trying to kiss her. She didn't want him to, told him it was too soon and he needed to leave. The Bastard grabbed her, shook then slapped her, pushed her down onto the couch, yanked her skirt over her waist, then wrenched **everything** underneath it … garter belt, hose, panties **and** a bloody pad hooked into a Kotex belt … down **and off**. She had given up struggling to keep them on for only a few moments as he was badly hurting her! When he saw she was menstruating, he smacked her again because **she** was having her period **then**.

Didn't stop him though as he brutally penetrated her*. She just let him finish it. She didn't want to be hurt any further."

My mother took a deep breath, "After he ejaculated and moved off her, he grabbed her panties, cleaned himself off with them. To emphatically show her he could do anything to her he wanted, he forcibly shoved the soiled panties inside her bruised and bleeding genitalia, hurting her even more. After he yanked his trophy out, he crammed them into her mouth, pull them out then took the panties with him. Thank God, the Bastard didn't get her pregnant, but she did get a **gonorrhea infection from him**. She finally **gave** that odious, wicked son-of-a-bitch his well-deserved, long overdue divorce papers."

Must have meant 'COULDN'T get her pregnant' ... happened during her period**

My mother had become highly animated, extremely pissed off. I had never seen her like this. "Of course, she became very afraid of him but never said anything, except to me. That's when I decided we would move to Wyandotte as soon as possible. I was seriously considering it anyway."

"His violent behavior became increasingly worse. In mid-July, Danae was leaving for work and he was hiding outside her door, maybe drunk. When she turned to lock it, he grabbed her from behind by her breasts, crushing and pulling her by them as he yanked her to the stairs of the lower walkout apartments and threw her down them, calling her obscene names as she fell. When that nice Sarah Luverne heard the noise and came out, he took off. Danae called me, told me the fall bruised her body some but her breasts were hideously bruised and swollen ... she had almost passed out. We decided she should leave for Florida that night. Last August, I should have further insisted she move in with us but she felt he wouldn't try any-thing since he was warned

---

***Spousal Rape Laws** did not exist in 1963; what was done was morally and heinously wrong but perfectly legal; changes to the law started slowly in the '70s, progressing until their completion in the '90s

A sexual myth of '50s and '60s prevalent among teenagers was a girl **couldn't get pregnant during her period; Conception is, of course, certainly possible yet rarely does occur

'very persuasively' by her two cop buddies to stay away from her, plus she thought the three of us living here would keep him away too. And importantly, she was starting to date again ... actually, one of those cops and ... well ... if the occasion arose ... to be sure of needed, uninterrupted privacy."

Mother was still incensed as she related his last night's rant. "He broke in before she could get to the bathroom. He demanded 'how many different cops are you screwing every weekend'. When she told him no one, he twisted then hit her left breast as hard as he could, knocking her to the carpet, yelling '**You're a cop whore!** Let's see how many of your cop boyfriends will drool over your face and pathetically dinky tits, all bruised and swollen like your... "uh ... his obscenity for female genitalia ..." is gonna be.' That depraved man then said he would continuously shove a 7-Up bottle up her for a while after he 'climaxed' in her. He ended menacingly, 'Your tits and ... ... blank are all **mine! ALL of you is mine! To do with what I want.**' He jumped on her, violently struck her breast again, then pinned her arms to beat her cheek and eye. Got up and ripped her slacks as he was again going to—. Well, the police quickly came in, pulled him off and arrested him."

Even before my mother finished, I was already making plans to use Little Lou for beating the shit out of the Bastard. We'd ensure his face, nuts and dick would be beaten soundly until **they** bled and **they** were bruised and swollen. She had already read my mind — as she could — making me swear an oath to my father I would NOT go have a "talk" with him. She admitted the restraining order would be a worthless piece of crap, so if he showed up to see Danae — at any time, at any place — I could have a "talk" with him "in any language" I so desired. In my mind, he was nothing but a drunken, whore chasing bully and coward. After this last beating, Mother painfully revealed she knew if he ever got Danièle alone again, he would go berserk and **try to kill her**. She **knew** he would. She was **positive** he would. That really and truly scared me shitless.

※※※※※※※※※※※※※※※※※※※※※※※※※※※

"How are things going with Roland?" I asked DeeDee that night as we both went upstairs to get ready for our dates. "This must be your fourth date with him."

"Sixth! Counting Sunday afternoon. Oh Rich, he is really terrific and wonderful to me. Last Sunday, he gave me perfume ... a bottle of Christian Dior's Diorissimo. Oh, I really, really like him. So ultra-sweet and cool," she gushed. Then lowering her voice secretly, "He treats me like I'm older, like I'm already a senior. Sophomore boys are so lame, so boring! Even most junior boys ... no, no, not like you. He always knows where to take me and what to do on a date. He is smart, knows a lot about music, not just rock 'n roll. Has talent for languages like me. He's witty. Of course, he is really so handsome. His parents are wonderfully nice to me."

"You sound pretty gone over him. But doesn't he ever ask you what you would like to do?"

"Well ... not so much ... no, guess not. He just always knows great places to go and what to do. You see how sweet he is to Mother and also Aunt Danae. He really is the most! Oh yeah, I really, really like him. A lot. Just so much."

"Well, that's great," I said enviously, remembering "Breezy," the self-centered bitch of a couple weeks ago. Hopefully, tonight would be totally, totally different. Jack and Camille had made good on their promise for a second shot with a St. Catherine's girl. I was to meet Antoinette Faber with them at The Nu-Way.

****

I finally found a parking place and hustled to the entrance's double doors. Jack and Camille were just leaving the Diner as I walked in. He explained his parents were going to an important fundraising ball at St. Luke's Hospital. Dr. Nelson's car was running sporadically, AAA was having to tow it, so they needed his mother's car. They were very sorry, but they had to go. I told them it was fine, saying to Camille, "Antoinette looks like a dream". She was attractive, confirmed by warm hazel eyes, a winning smile, nicely built with upswept blond hair which undoubtably had been professionally coiffured. And style. Oh God, *plenty of style*. She was impeccably dressed in an expensive ruby-red dyed-to-match sweater and stretch pants with stirrups and pointy-toe black, leather ankle boots which perfectly matched her designer Coach handbag. She was definitely a girl who had an open allowance.

We talked for over two hours about a lot of different topics like school, fashion, college plans and more on clothes. As we started to leave, she apologized for monopolizing the conversation with her fashion talk. I told her she was just easy to listen to. Her ideas on clothes, design and tastes were interesting. I always liked being with great-looking girls who are wonderfully dressed. Ones, like my sister, who knew the newest styles and could talk knowledgeably about them. I told her she certainly was three for three, so that made her definitely not a dumb blonde. That made her laugh and she warmly thanked me for those compliments by wrapping my arm with both of hers, tightly holding onto me as we slowly walked to my car.

We parked in front of her house and we immediately began to kiss, then heavily. After a long open mouth kiss, she called me Teddy unconsciously. She apologized quickly.

"I'm so sorry about calling you Teddy. Wasn't very nice. I guess I'm not over him, even though that damn jerk cheated on me. With some Northwest **whore**."

"He's a very lucky guy for you to still feel and think that way about him. He's an idiot to have cheated on you. My God, **a real damn idiot! I sure wouldn't**! You are like a Roman goddess with your beauty and grace. You have more style and class than is legal!"

She looked at me, dazed for an instant, then eagerly kissed me, excitedly. After a few intense moments, we broke apart, then she repeated more passionately, much longer which I eagerly returned. When we parted again, she was breathing a lot quicker, barely able to gasp out, "Ooo-hhhh." Wildly excited, she stammered out, "Lou, for you only. Never have let Frenching happen on any first date of mine."

Immediately, Antoinette began very deeply, intensely Frenching me. After an incredible, wonderfully long a minute or so of wrapping tongues, her mouth grabbed my tongue to strongly suck for a couple moments, then abruptly let go and ended the kiss totally.

The reason for that immediate termination — my hand was under her sweater and deftly moving up.

She quickly caught my fingers, stopping their quick rise up her bare midriff after a pause at her navel for a few intense caresses. Before that they once lightly grazed across one breast on the outside of her sweater. During my exploration, they slowly glided over and back her quite pointed nipple, regardless of its being covered by her bra and sweater.

Hastily she panted out, "Lou ... need ... to go in ... **now** ... before you ... get into my ... and fond— Want to ... so much. ... ... Be another ... first date first ... can't let you. ... ... So mixed up ... with Teddy ... shit ... just SHIT!"

I stammered out, "Damn ... I understand." But my penis absolutely *did not*. And the rest of me didn't want to either. However, I jokingly added after I regained *my* breath and some semblance of normalcy, "Thannnk you for the best French kiss of my life. My neglected tongue and tonsils' cranky dispositions are long gone."

She laughed, energetically kissed me on my cheek and made a short scoot to the passenger side. I went around to open the door, sure that it was Shakespeare who said, "A great make-out by any other name would still be as sweet".

She apologized again as I helped her out of the car, "I'm really, really sorry. You're a great guy. So funny. Such a stud with those dreamy eyes. I **really** could go for you big time ... just so damn much. But the timing for us is just so out of sync. I have— **No, I need** to get over Teddy completely. Wouldn't be fair to you. Obviously ... I called you by his name. When I do, I promise to focus on **only you and me**." She giggled then she teased, "Are all the guys at St. Ignatius such great make outs? And with *such damn tantalizing fingers*?" She playfully slapped one of my hands and laughed flirtatiously.

Before I could answer her, a car pulled up, tires screeching. Shit, this had to be the "real idiot" Teddy. A guy got out of the car quickly but just stood by the door, waiting. For me? For her? Then he started walking towards us.

Well shit ... after enjoying a great make out session ... excluding being called by the wrong name ... encouraged by an A+ French kiss, intensifying with a breast brush with nipple skim then some navel rubbing, on my way up to those fairly medium-sized ruby-red grapefruits under that ruby-red sweater ... I ALWAYS end it with by having a fight.

About my size ... ... No ... he's a little bigger ... ... Shit, this IS not good.

Antoinette yelled nervously, "Teddy, don't ... don't make any trouble!"

Teddy stopped and quickly confessed, "I won't! Don't want any either." Then to me, "Just want to talk with Antoinette. All right?"

"Only if she wants to talk to you." I almost added "You dumb asshole" but that would have only started God knows what. She obviously agreed because she began to walk towards him, meeting him in the middle of the street.

"Thanks. I'm Ted Burrows."

I didn't follow her over and offer to shake hands. The instructor of my "boxing class" told us this is how the unsuspecting fool gets sucker punched. While you extend your hand, your face takes a nice, solid shot.

"I'm Marlowe. Goodnight Antoinette."

She turned and smiled warmly, "Goodnight Lou. Thank you for a great night."

"It was my pleasure." I got into the car for a very frustrating drive home.

Well, that was shit ... just Shit.

I really could go for her. God, she's good-looking ... loaded with style and flair ... decent chest and butt. Yep, our damn timing is just out of sync. My total 'timing' was intensely making out for fifteen minutes after spending two and a half very enjoyable hours getting to know her. And timing IS everything.

My sexual frustration made me think of Caroline and I persuaded myself I could find her. So I drove up and down State Avenue looking for her, going through Zesto's, Blender's, finally Allen's. I did see Sherry flirting with some bikers then happily getting goosed by one of them. I didn't stop and interrupt her fun to ask where Caroline might be, now convinced she had a date. I took my disappointment home and we went to bed.

❊❊❊❊❊❊❊❊❊❊❊❊❊❊❊❊❊❊❊❊❊❊❊❊❊❊❊❊

Aunt Danae and I went to early Mass at St. Joachim and Anne's. She wore her big, Ray-Ban sunglasses — so-called Aubrey Hepburn shades — heavy makeup with a large scarf. We sat in the choir loft. Fortunately, there was no one else there and we waited until everyone in the nave area had left. When we got back to the house, DeForrest and my mother had already gone to the 9 o'clock at St. Patrick's. To see whom, I wondered. We ate breakfast when they came home then the three of us went over to Aunt Danae's apartment while she laid down to rest. We cleaned it up and packed up her remaining clothes along with her crystal and other keepsakes. The movers would come for her furniture as the rest of the pieces had come furnished with the apartment. The insurance companies could sort out the damage.

Yesterday, when we cleaned out the sewing room, Mother decided that the room assignments had changed. DeeDee and I would switch bedrooms and Aunt Danae would have the sewing room as her bedroom. My mother simply said she was use to sharing a bathroom with a male. I think DeeDee asked for the switch, knowing she could be occasionally embarrassed with me seeing her lingerie, hose, a set or two from her ever growing collection of baby doll pajamas, and especially those "feminine personal products and accessories" as they called them in Kotex magazine ads. The switch was fine with me, as long as I had a bed and place to study. Until the new bed came, my aunt and mother would sleep together in the master. They laughed about it, saying how it was just like when they were little girls. It was good to see them laughing again.

❊❊❊❊❊❊❊❊❊❊❊❊❊❊❊❊❊❊❊❊❊❊❊❊❊❊❊❊

On our way to lunch Monday, Jack said, "Camille thinks you are a wonderful human being, somehow bringing those two lovebirds back together. When Teddy found out Antoinette had a date, with a St. Ignatius guy no less, he realized he didn't want his Northwest sleaze, Patty Beth Landis, all that much." He snickered,

"Those initials of hers gave her the nickname of Peanut Butter Legs. He wanted Antoinette back very badly. She really liked you, but ..."

But not before I was rewarded with Antoinette's exclusive first date French kiss, regardless abruptly ended due to a good start at first date petting. Sweater grazing that glorious grapefruit and its excited peak ... ... Ooooh.

"...hear what I said? God, you're so damn dull. Dip Shit, it's because **they spread so easy**! Anyway, Camille feels very badly for you. She likes you. Why? God only knows. So she wants to fix you up again. Three's a charm."

"When Camille hears Antoinette has broken up with Teddy for good, let me know. I could really, really go for her. She sure had Antoinette pegged right. Yeah, let's try it again. Camille may have good taste in girls, just not with guys."

Jack made a funny face and we both laughed.

OCTOBER

On Tuesday, I related the past weekend events to Fr. Fitz in the confessional. I was becoming a regular for this sacrament. He became disgusted when I told him the Prick slapped my aunt then forcibly took her while she was menstruating. She had quit struggling, so he would not hurt her more. Just passively laid there while he finished his thrusting into her, ending by brutally creating his trophy. Some months later he mauled and crushed her breasts so hard she thought she was going to pass out, followed by pushing her down a flight of exterior apartment stairs. Finally, last Friday, terribly beating her face and breast, began to tear her clothes off to rape her. Fortunately, the Police came as he just started ripping her slacks. He had planned after his rape to continually ram a pop bottle into her genitalia.

Father pointed out he was a very sick man. This type of situation was not new to him. He had seen it too many times. I asked him if my mother was right — would he really go nuts and try to kill her? He tersely yet emphatically responded, "**YES! Most assuredly! Be very watchful.**" He said to keep him apprised of anything new. He pointed out it was not a coincidence about the man in the black car. For penance, he gave me one Hail Mary and to study harder. Lastly, he adamantly said, "Remain vigilant with your aunt. Extra vigilant!"

When I walked into the room for the start of classes on Wednesday, Jack was smiling. So I went over to him and he said, "It's all set up for Gloria."

Immediately, Moose walked in to begin the class with a prayer, and I hurried back to my desk. Jack said loudly, "Remember Gloria."

Moose immediately jumped on Jack, "Nelson, what did you just say?"

"Just '*Ad majorem Dei gloriam*'*, Father. You know, to start the day right."

"Nelson, keep the day going right by leading us in the prayer. In Latin!"

So he did. And easily. Jack always could pull a rose out of a bucket of shit.

As we walked to lunch, I said, "OK, Gloria or Gloriam, why is she worth trying to get on Moose's bad side this morning? Risking demerits or a jug?"

"Oh, just staying in practice. Gloria Crockett is the girl for you. She's a senior, about five-five, brown hair, brown eyes, decent looking with an *absolute killer chest*. You'll love her."

"If she's this hot, why is she instantly available? Or another 'Teddy' just waiting?"

"Well, someone did dump her or she dumped him. A couple weeks ago. C'mon, whaddya say? We'll meet at the Broadmoor. Change of scenery for good luck."

"Sure, why not. I'll give her a shot. Three's a charm."

"Friday night, it is."

❈❈❈❈❈❈❈❈❈❈❈❈❈❈❈❈❈❈❈❈❈❈❈❈❈❈❈❈

I was early when I walked into the Broadmoor, so I wasn't surprised not to see Jack, Camille, and my date, Gloria. As I gave my name and paid the cover charge for our foursome, I slipped the attractive, older hostess — Ingrid as detailed on her fancy badge — two dollars and was immediately seated at a good table. When the trio came in, I stood up to get their attention.

Gloria was close to everything Jack had said to expect. I thought she would be better looking as she had a rather long, thin nose and her chin fairly receded. However, easily gliding over to the table, she certainly substantiated Jack's description of "an absolute killer chest," which was well displayed in a tight lime sweater, accented by her coordinating navy slacks and heels.

---

* '**Ad majorem Dei gloriam**', a Jesuit motto or saying which translates '**For the greater glory of God**'

Camille introduced us and she smiled brightly in a very pleasant manner. This still had promise. We all talked, ordering our cokes and shakes. After we danced to a few fast songs, a slow number began, Bobby Vinton's *Blue Velvet*, followed by Lesley Gore's *You Don't Own Me*. We were close enough to where her major-league chest would intermittently brush against me. Didn't seem to bother her as our "contact" kept repeating. **Certainly** didn't bother me. Well, it did start to cause some bother in my pants. We continued to talk about our schools and she asked me if I knew any girls from St. Catherine.

"Yeah, I know Brenda Cox and Antoinette Faber."

"Oh, Cox, the narcissistic, know-it-all. Some girls claim she's a Sappho. I'm sure they're right, just from the way she always intently **gawks at me**." Her emphasis undoubtedly implied her large knockers. "Oh, she does date guys … at most twice … then done. Guys must figure it out. Seems like she's always with her little boy girlies. Now, Faber is a poor little, *very* rich girl who thinks she's the next Coco Chanel. But she can't flaunt a school uniform any more than the rest of us." Bitterly added, "But **does she** ever when we don't have to wear our crappy uniforms."

"Do you know any guys, other than Jack, from St Ignatius?"

"Sure, I dated Tom Strickland, Mike Thomas and Terrance White, pretty good football players. Chris Ewell … oh, that very nice-looking basketball player. Eddie Williams, runs the 100-yard dash. St. Nate's jocks, all like you. Or it's a St. John V's guy. My parents would both have heart attacks if a public school Non-Catholic showed up at the door for me."

Hmm, wonder if she knows there are a few 'Non-Catholics' at St. Ignatius?

After we finished dancing to a few more fast songs, Camille asked Gloria to go to the powder room. Watching them, confirmed my partial glimpses — her butt was almost flat — a sharp contrast to Camille's nicely shaped one.

"Well, what do you think?" as Jack paid me for the cover charge.

"Well, she puts the 'Cat' in St. Catherine's. She doesn't like either Breezy or Antoinette. She truly believes and even says some of the St. Cat girls claim that Breezy's butch. Says the Lesbo's always staring at her. Undoubtably her knockers. She doesn't like it ... or her."

"Yeah, not surprised. Probably just jealous ... especially of Antoinette. Camille has heard that about Bree. Says it's not true. Just envy because of her real high grades. Hangs out with some girls who are nothing to look at ... never date. She does though, fairly regularly. But never steady."

"Jack, I'm not so sure. Oddly, both she and I were intently eyeing the same really stacked, good-looking chick that Saturday night. Awww, I dunno ... she was probably just envious as hell of the girl's great-looking tits since I bet Breezy can't even fill an A cup. Flat ... sixth-grade flat."

****

Brenda Jewel — 'Jules' — Cox always deeply missed Phyllis Prince, her first and very intense love;
They met through a common female cousin in the spring of her junior year;
Her 'Prince Philly' was from Prescott, always called her 'my Jewel', hence Jules;
Before school started in the Fall, Phyllis dumped her hard, declaring she craved and loved sex with males much more — like the two guys during the past six weeks;

Brenda was heart-broken, devastated;
Brenda re-named herself Jules after she finished high school, graduated from Fontbonne College, a Catholic and all women school where she had two girlfriends, each with a good-size bust;

Jules decided to go to Hastings Law School in San Francisco;
During her second year, she met well-endowed Constance Hargrove on the UC Berkley campus who was finishing her doctorate, they moved in together; Constance became a professor of Medieval History Jules became an attorney in the field of women's rights;

After five years together, Jules was finally caught in her intermittent, yet persistent infidelities with her hair stylist;
A vicious argument ensued and Constance revealed

> she was having an affair with a male professor in her History Department; They split up, Jules went to live with Alice, her buxom stylist — only for a time;
>
> Partner free in 1982, she enthusiastically participated in an 'old-time 60s Love-in'; A three-day lovefest of opioid drugs involving needle and syringe sharing combined with her sexual experimentation with various bi-sexual partners, both female & male;
> AIDS was just being realized as an epidemic, and tragically she contracted the disease during this orgy-type Memorial Day weekend spree — as did six other participants; Brenda Jewel Cox died in 1984, at age 38

****

"Speaking of big tits, would you look at those very *attractive*, huge knockers on that *unattractive* redhead? Can she dance! Reeel nice. Bouncy, bouncy! Bet she gets a lot of dates regardless of her looks! Oh yeeeah!"

Lorraine's honeydews instantly came to mind. "Because she's smart, has a great personality and a lot of fun. I can see her list of favorites to do ... likes to watch old movies, take long walks, **loves to be motor boated.**"

When Jack finally quit laughing, he said, "Oh, I bet she's a lot of **fun for that ... and more**! She reminds me why the old saying, 'Anything more than a mouthful is a waste' is so damn dumb and totally wrong." Then he gestured towards the door, "Hey, we're going to split when they get back from the toilet, after they finish discussing you, fixing their faces, and 'tinkling'. Where in the hell did 'tinkling' ever come from? Or 'make a puddle'. So how's a girl gonna make a puddle when she's pissing into a toilet bowl *full of already pooled water*?"

"Tinkling is just a girly euphemism. Their supposed 'quiet, gentle ringing sound they make urinating in the bowl' as my father once described to me. My Three Graces use it all the time. I mean, doesn't it sound a lot more socially graceful for a girl to say, 'I'm going to tinkle,' rather than whining to her boyfriend, brother or father, 'I have to go peeeeee' like some little third-grader or your paradox about 'puddle making'." We both laughed and he agreed.

The girls came back, wondering why we had been laughing so hard. Jack responded with, "Dancing and motor boats." And I added, "euphemisms." Neither girl believed us.

After Camille and Jack said good-bye, Gloria suggested, "Let me pour some of my coke into yours. I've something special just for us in my purse." She guardedly opened her rather large purse and I saw the top of an already opened pint of Gordon's Gin.

Had a good sip or two in the stall while she was 'tinkling'?

"Here, give me your coke, then mine." Under the table, she poured some of the alcohol into each one. "Have to be careful or they'll throw our asses out if we get caught. To a wuunderful evening." We clicked glasses and took a drink. I had tasted booze quite a few times. Her mix was strong.

We danced some more, talked some more and Gloria drank more. I declined as I knew I had a good drive after taking her home.

After about an hour, she came very close to me and whispered in my ear, "Would you like to go somewhere nice and quiet."

I nodded, "Course, I would." ... ... *Let the make-out begin ... ... and meet the willing inhabitants of your bra.*

She sheepishly grinned, "Gotta gooo make a quick puddle. Meet ya in front."

Good ... She's already a little blitzed.

While Gloria "made a quick puddle," I took my very long, not so quiet, not so gentle, relieving whizz into a urinal.

When I drove out of the parking lot, she moved over to sit very close to me and began playing with my ear and hair. I asked, "Where to, O tour guide?"

"My house. Not far. We can certainly 'talk' there." She giggled. "I'll direct you." After she unscrewed the top of the Gordon's, she took a sip straight from the bottle and held it to my lips. I joined her with a good sip.

She began chattering non-stop, "St. Cat's is like a convent. No guys! My mother's idea! Spent years in a convent. A real one! Almost became a nun. Treats me crappy sometimes. Wants me to be one. Some of the nuns think so too. 'Dresses toooo short! Toooo much lipstick! Tooo much makeup!' Shit like that! Tonight's was 'your sweater's tooo tight! Don't dress like **that**'. She'd like it if I wore my shitty school uniform skirt on dates. **But** only if I didn't roll the dammn waistband up*. Wanna look cool. How can ya be cool? Can't dress like frump-pee shit! Like ya wanna be some wallllflower. Or dresssss like you were in grade school. *I wanna be noticed, specially by gggguys.*" She hiccuped. "Oh, sorry." Then sort of giggled after taking another gulp.

"I would notice you *anywhere, anytime.*" ... ... *With* **those TITS**! *O Hell yes!*

"You know, you're niceee ... so are thooose eyes." She now snickered loudly. "Okay, we'll play a game when we get to my house," as she took another swig.

"Great. What kind?" She only continued to giggle then poured another short gulp down me.

Before I was able to pull over to the curb, she had wrapped her arms around me, kissing my neck and cheek. After about only five minutes of kissing and trivial babble, we advanced to open mouth. She was coming on strong. So within a moment or two, I touched my tongue to hers to start some Frenching. After a couple of minutes of wrapping tongues, she stopped, pulled away to purr devilishly, "Bet I know something you want badly. Heh heh ... to play with my *big, sensational, firm...*" Her eyes slid down to stare at her tits. "Oh, I'm right, St. Nate stud. *I know* you want 'em. You keep drooling at 'em. But you gotta win my game first."

"Hell yes! These tantalizing large grapefruits in your tight sweater have captivated my attention all night," and I pointed — my finger only an inch away from them.

"Well, thaaaaank you. Game time! Should be easy for you, living with three females. What is the cup sizzze of my brazzziere?"

"Okay, I'll play with you. Then *literally* play with you too," I laughed. Then I became serious, "But why does living with three females make it easy?"

"Silly, I know you guys look into lingerie drawers or feminine laundry to check out bra sizzzes."

---

*In Catholic co-ed high schools ('60s and probably later), girls would roll up the waistband on their uniform's skirt to be an inch or two shorter & more appealing

"What? That's crazy! I don't know and don't care what size bra any of my three females are! The only time I ever **noticed** anything at all was when my sister started to develop, growing out of her training bra."

"Don't get so damn pissy pissy with me. If it's a racy brazzziere, guys'll rub all over the fabric. Caught one of my brothers with my only real sexy one. Bought it on a dare. Said guys imagine it's their girlfriend's. I'm sure these *kinds* are used for their repeated, sinful self-abuse. But guess what? I'm wearing that sexy one now ... you can see it and as you call 'em 'these tantalizing large grapefruits' if you win."

Of course I don't fondle the mountain of bras at home. We'll see if I remember anything from Linda's 'demonstration' of her 32Bs. Gloria's way, WAY bigger than she.

I quickly concluded by answering, "You're definitely a C cup."

"Correct, give that man a kiss." She did on my ear after gently tugging on the lobe with her teeth.

"Now what is the band size?"

"Band size?"

"Yes, Silly. The distance 'round my ribcage. Under my brazzzziere."

Chest circumference ... she's a bigger build, so bigger around. Why are they always even numbers? Whatever ...... add 2. ... ... "Oh okay, hmmm ... that's called 'band size'. I'll go with a 34. You're a 34C."

"Right again and you get another kiss."

She dragged her tongue slowly across my lips. I was starting to feel high from the gin. Didn't care. I liked where this was going.

"Now how big are they?" And distinctly pointed at her tits.

I was feeling good and somewhat silly. And so, so horn-eee.

Shit, I don't know. ... How big is 'an absolute killer chest'? Linda happily proclaimed 'my twins just increased to 34" ... gonna get a lot bigger'. Ha! Probably still praying for softballs ... which she'll never have no matter how many guys 'rub 'em and rub 'em'.

She continued to smirked, "C'mon! *How big,* Lou-ee?"

So add 2" for 36". Mr. Gordon Gin says 'they look so prime in that sweater of lime'. Add another inch ... make it a prime number of 37. ...

... "You are a very invitingly prime looking **37 inches.**"

Gloria's mouth dropped open, erasing her smile, "You ... you ... won." No enthusiasm or thrill in her voice, but only bafflement by her defeat.

The Buzz hit wonderfully as my thoughts envisioned what "kinds of time" waited for me. ... ... *Time to claim my reward of those ample 37 inch double prizes.* **Time** *to release them from that confirmed 34C sexy bra.* **Time** *to feel some* **BIG, soft tits**.

The immediate placement of my hand under her sweater with its deepening grasp on her breast, was met with shock. Gloria suddenly pulled away, screaming, "**NO! NO!** Stop pawing me! I'm a good girl! **I'M PURE! CHASTE!**"

Astonished, I said, "What the Shit! You said I won!"

"You did ... ... but you're **never** going to touch my ... my ... me again. Mother says it's thoroughly indecent. Terribly sinful! Kissing is fine, but only **bad** girls let themselves be felt up and groped! Pawed like **that**! No other guy ever got all three right, so it was easy to stay sinless and pure. I **am not going to be** a Jezebel to satisfy your licentious, carnal desires."

You Deceitful Bitch! Pseudo Slut!

I was hotly pissed, intensified by the gin buzz and now denied a promised remedy for my horniness. "No, **what you are** is a prick-teasing pussy who plays a sensual game promising your big tits for the prize. You lost, so now you hide those proudly paraded tits behind a bunch of fake morality bullshit!"

Quickly she recovered from this vulgar insult and screamed, "**I'm a what**?" As she spat out the response at me, I caught movement in my peripheral vision and reacted instantaneously. Her slap still caught me on my ear which probably hurt as much as the aimed for cheek would have.

I quickly got out of the car, yelling at her, "Get out of my car, you crazy, screwed-up bitch."

"I am not crazy, I am not screwed-up, and I am certainly not a harlot, regardless of your plan to turn me into yours," she yelled back.

"Okay, you're not crazy. You're just drunk. You lost control during making out. Went further than you wanted. Get your damn, nothing to-look-at, pancake flat ass and your narcissistic thirty-seven inch tits outta my car. Out! **Now bitch**!"

"I am not drunk either. I am always in control of myself when I drink or do some kissing. *Whatever* I do. Always in control. Always! As it says in the First Epistle of Paul to the Thessalonians in chapter 4, verses 3 and 5, 'abstain from immorality ... not in the passion of lust like the Gentiles who do not know God'. I'm going inside now. Don't even think about coming close to defile me again, you devil sent from Lucifer!"

She crawled out the open driver's side, grabbed her large purse and wobbled hurriedly away from me, mumbling, "Always in control! Always in ..." She fell down in her yard, stood up with great difficulty and staggered the rest of the way to the front door. "In control" of what? Hopefully her bladder? Certainly not her equilibrium and possibly not her mind.

****

Gloria de Virgine Crockett — [or Latin translation, 'The Glory of a Virgin' Crockett] immediately joined the Sisters of Charity upon spring graduation; Her mother and father were euphoric, Both older brothers thought she was making a very grave mistake;

After five years Sister Felicity began her first teaching assignment of Chemistry at McKenna High School; There was chemistry of a more intense personal type — she and Vice Principal Father Thomas Mayer fell in love;

Principal Sister Cecilia, surmising their relationship, waited until the school term ended, then told her she would be leaving in two days for the Convent in Topeka; Gloria did leave, not for Topeka but to Baltimore where the priest happily joined her and his family; She was released from her vows and the priest was finally laicized;

Her parents disowned her completely, her brothers were overjoyed for her; They married in the Church, Mayer was an outstanding public high school principal; When their five children were older, Gloria went back to teaching Chemistry at the all-girls Catholic High School of Baltimore; Their marriage was a very happy, loving and devout one

****

DeeDee came into the living room as we were waiting for Mother and Aunt Danae to go to church. Mother was probably doing some of her makeup magic on Danae's bruised area. "Roland asked me to go steady with him last night. He says I am, without a doubt, the only one for him. He tied the ring to a red rose stem. How romantic! I was going to tell Mother, but she's still worried how that terrible beating is affecting her little sister. Aunt Danae's not quite her old self yet, but I'll figure out how to tell Mother. And soon. But I had to tell someone! I'm so happy! So, so happy!" After she finished her two and a half twirls, she begged, "Book of Secrets?"

"Sure, it's your love life." ... ... *For those who have some. And I worry about MY little sister too.*

❊❊❊❊❊❊❊❊❊❊❊❊❊❊❊❊❊❊❊❊❊❊❊❊❊❊❊❊❊

On Monday, I wasn't able to talk to Jack until lunch when he quizzed me, "I understand you didn't like Gloria at all. Odd, 'cause I thought you two were really hitting it off. Said you wouldn't even walk her to the door."

"That **bitch** is a lunatic! She's nuts! She's totally crazy! **I'm not kidding**!" I related the whole evening from when the drinking started to me driving away from her house, asking The Holy Ghost to descend upon me and let me know what took place.

Jack exclaimed, "Jesus, Mary and Joseph! All the Saints in Heaven! I had no idea. I know Camille doesn't either."

"Sounds like she has serious problems with her mother, too. Winning her tits' game kept her 'pure'. Hard to tell how a guy got an offer to play. She wasn't a rookie at drinking at all. Maybe to dull her feelings or inhibitions so she could make out and get in the mood to play her game. Maybe to blot out her controlling mother. Or both. Who knows? Who cares? Maybe it's that inhibition shit Moose keeps harping on."

"Yeah, maybe. She's the weirdest prick-tease I have ever known or heard about. She's just incredibly bizarre with all the 'chaste and pure' bull shit after she repaints the inside of your mouth using her tongue as a brush. Then Game Time! But where she's thoroughly twisted is thinking you actually play with the family bras. That's sick! **Real sick**. I'm clueless about my sister and my mother's **and** I'm keeping it that way. I have never heard of a girl quoting the Bible on a date. Verses about Moose's favorite subject ... Lust! Serious Shit! I guess this means no more dates with St. Catherine Honeys?"

"Jesus Christ, what do you think? Girls from St. Cat's aren't soft little kittens. No, that's not right, there's one named Camille. The first Cat is narcissistic and rude. The second is terrific, but uses me to force her boyfriend to shit or get off the pot regarding her. Accidentally calls me by his name because she's not over him. The third Cat becomes drunk to kill her feelings or inhibitions so she can play a game focusing on her tight sweater tits, but goes stark raving mad when she loses and has to pay up, spouting quotes on lust from the Bible. I'm going back to dating only Protestant girls. They are well-mannered, don't get drunk, don't smoke, don't swear, know what guy they want, certainly are not crazy or quote the Bible."

As soon as I finished saying those perceived Protestant girls' positive attributes, a drunken, bra whirling Linda materialized, laughing at me; joined by Scarlett Charlotte, the older, proficient Frenching teacher, saying something highly suggestive with her cigarette dangling; Olga was there, telling me to touch her hurriedly, to put my hand down her partially unbuttoned dress like the other times; Bonnie Jo reminded me she was the first girl I felt up — but only on the outside of her sweater; Red-hot Rusty pulled down the side of her high waisted bikini bottom, displaying her beautiful butterfly tattoo, asking if I wanted to kiss it.

Jack was conclusively going on and on that was a bunch of crap or something similar. "...you don't really believe that bull shit you're spewing."

"Okay, all right. That, obviously, is not true. Reformation chicks do the same shit too. Hell, I don't know, maybe Catholic girls can get some sort of a Papal Dispensation for their crazy antics."

Jack laughed, then became serious again, "Still Gloria is bad, bad shit. I'll only tell Camille about the boozing. Leave the game show shit alone. But tell me honestly, how **did** you get all three?"

"I'm a first baseman, idiot. I have to know the exact size of any spherical type object I need to catch, field or *feel* for the out," I said with my usual first baseman arrogance. We both laughed but then I confessed, "Just very good mathematical logic, of which Father Hoyle would be proud. Well, no ... no he wouldn't. It was simply, incredibly shitty, bad luck."

****

Tuesday was the Richelieu girls' birthday and DeeDee and I decided to take them out to an early dinner — since it was "a school night" — at a new, elegant French restaurant which had just opened, called Lafayette's. The bruising on Aunt Danae's eye and cheek was finally gone or at least completely concealed by my mother's expertise with a makeup brush. Also finally gone were her anxieties and nervousness. My sister and I had pooled our money as we always did. I had gone to Macy's to buy some perfume for Aunt Danae. When the saleslady gave me a whiff of Chanel N°5, I was convinced. It had a fantastic scent. I vowed on the way home, if I ever found a solid, wonderful girl to go steady with, I would definitely buy this perfume for her. The size I bought was expensive, but my aunt had been through Hell lately. It was time for her to start a new life and I figured the perfume could only help. DeeDee found a lavish, emerald green blouse at DuVall's on the Plaza for Mother. Because the Prick Bastard had drained me, I was short and DeForrest covered me with a loan. They loved their presents and the dinner. DeeDee and I were happy to see them both laughing and enjoying themselves like old times.

****

Saturday night was the big twenty-year reunion for Aunt Danae and Mother. DeeDee and I went to Zesto's for a quick dinner. When Anita — the plain, pencil shaped carhop — took our orders, I asked, "Where's Cathy? I never see her."

She quickly informed me, "Cathy Winters is not only Prescott's head cheerleader and the best one, but the steady girlfriend of the football team's fullback and one of the best players." I was somewhat shocked, only hearing Malcom or Mel something. "They started going together the day school started. Cathy doesn't work during the school year."

I said to DeeDee, "Can you hear this extra loud flushing noise for all my wishful plans with Cathy." She gave me a look of sympathy.

My older graces had spent the afternoon at Salon Silvestri, getting their hair done in some sort of current hair style. DeeDee said both were "very elaborate up-dos." Whatever both were, they looked very chic. DeeDee decided she would be the commentator at the Richelieu fashion show using her hairbrush as a microphone.

As Aunt Danae came down the stairs, "And here is Danièle in a dress of black wool with pleats at the hips and a slimming black satin cummerbund at the waist accented with a large bow in back. A nice wide neckline with elbow length sleeves. Her hair is in a bouffant style with flicked up curly ends. Some very stylish eyeliner with green eyeshadow to accent her green eyes. Very nice indeed."

"Our next model is Geneviève who is wearing a heavy sculpted red silk cocktail dress with slightly dropped waistband trimmed with a bow and rhinestones at the left hip. A round neckline with back zipper. Tonight she has opted for the beehive hair style which is backcombed and lacquered nicely with Aqua Net ... our sponsor. She has more than a hint of grey eyeshadow to enhance that dress matching red lipstick. Stunning."

"Amazingly done, girls!"

While DeeDee said they were both concerned about turning forty in a couple of years, tonight they looked beautiful, stylish and so ultra-cool. They were going to make a lot of wives envious as hell.

"Wow, folks. The Richelieu sisters are back in business and on the town tonight. And they look fabulous," I said in a teasing tone.

I congratulated Danae, "Aunt Danièle, you look fabulously great, just terrific."

"Thank you, Richie honey," and we kissed and she hugged me, then I gave her my forehead kiss.

I had not seen my mother really dressed like this since the '61 New Year's Eve party with my father. "Mother, you look really beautiful."

She smiled affectionately, brushed my cheek with the back of her fingers, then kissed me gently. "Thank you, my little Forrest."

The lipstick from those two kisses would be my final lip allotment for quite some time.

DeeDee had expressed the same impressive sentiments to each one, receiving her lightly touched kisses and hugs. "Good night girls! Go break a few hearts!" DeeDee laughed with them as they left, but turned to me and seriously said, "They're sure going to turn a lot of heads. Male *and female*."

Roland came over about an hour later "to watch TV" in the living room and left exactly at DeeDee's midnight curfew. I had to promise her if I went to the kitchen, it would be via the dining room, announcing with loud steps coming down the stairs. I went to bed about 12:30 but couldn't sleep well.

Not sure why I did, but earlier I had called Linda and was informed "our devout Lutheran daughter has *another* date with her very nice fellow from *our* church". Her mother's attitude was like "so you, Catholic boy, don't need to call here again." I had forgotten to ask "Ole Strait-Laced Grace," as Linda always called her, if they were going to the drive-in to ignore the movie, drink vodka, heavily make out, and play some baseball.

I put my Wyandotte memories together with nice but immature Karen, ballistic Caroline, frigid Brenda, hot Antoinette, and the fruitcake Gloria. Hadn't been in town for two months and already dated five totally different girls — no, not completely different, they **were** all Catholic. That was the problem, only now I was serious about it, not like when I kiddingly told Jack that. Only Reformation chicks from here on. Ones that don't drink like Linda or act with Charlotte's roughness and crudity, Bonnie Jo's immaturity and possessiveness or Rusty's cheating. The abrupt break up between Olga and me was due to her father's sudden transfer, but she seemed hardly upset when we said good-bye. Time to hit up Mick to fix me up. I had not seen much of him. He was always with Pamela and I was always with a St. Catherine's mistake. I definitely would call him tomorrow.

The troops landed at 2:05 and woke me up when they came thru the front door laughing and talking and hustling into the living room then the kitchen and back again.

I knocked on DeeDee's door, opened it slightly and stuck my head in enough to loudly whisper, "Ohhhh Dee."

No response.

Then louder, "Dee! Get up!"

"Damn you to Hell, Richelieu! What in God's name *do you want*?" She snarled, "It's two o'clock, you big idiot. The damn house better be on fire."

"Better. The girls picked up some guys. I'm going to eavesdrop. Meet you at the landing."

DeeDee hurriedly had put on one of her heavy, matronly pink robes over her "color of the night" baby doll pajamas to join me. They were having a great time. They would laugh loudly, followed by loud shhhhing. For about twenty minutes, we listened on the landing like two kids on Christmas Eve trying to overhear hints about our presents. We did hear a few specifics, such as Aunt Danae, laughing loudly, "Carl! You didn't!". Later Mother saying, "No Rex, it was a …" Undoubtedly, they were having a great time.

Both DeeDee and I were happy for them and decided to hit them up in the morning. She teased, "It's because I wore my emerald green BDs tonight … the symbol of hope, rebirth and renewal."

"Or for envy and greed," which earned me a playful push.

"And always a pink robe … represents playfulness, femininity, and tenderness. It's the color of universal love of oneself and of others."

We snickered, then quietly said good night for a second time and went to our rooms.

****

DeeDee and I were up much earlier than the partying sisters and we waited in the kitchen to pounce on them. Finally around ten o'clock, they made their entrances which were extremely different than last night's. No makeup, their hair was still nice but a little off, even with both 'dos' wrapped in toilet paper. They looked really tired and, without a doubt, so far from fabulous in their drab housecoats.

Aunt Danae begged, "Oh God, DeeDee, honey, please tell me you have coffee … strong, sooo strong!" Mother's desperate expression duplicated her sister's desire.

DeeDee said she had, then acted very serious, like a parent, "All right, young ladies, you just sit down!" She served each one, inquiring, "I want to know all about these two boys ... Rex and Carl."

They both sipped their coffee, finally beginning to somewhat wake up. As DeeDee refilled their cups, they began to smile, then started to snicker like teenage girls. Mother replied, "How do you know about Rex and Carl?"

"Well, we both heard you and your 'pick-ups' when you came in," I fibbed.

"Oh, we're sorry, but we were having a great time." Mother explained, "Carl Gibson was the quarterback in Danae's year. Rex Finnegan was a star forward, extremely smart ... the class salutatorian. He went to Prescott, a year ahead of Carl. Carl and Rex were next door neighbors when they grew up. They were always best buddies. Since Carl didn't want to come by himself, Rex came with him. Like I did with Danae."

Now completely awake, Danae said to Mother, "Don't forget to tell the children you dated Rex. Took you to both Prescott and McKenna proms."

She painfully smiled, "Gee ... thanks, *Danièle*."

"What happened, Mother?" DeeDee inquired, really wanting to know.

"Oh, Angel, it was a long time ago. We started dating in March and right before my Prom, we started going steady which lasted throughout that whole summer. We had some really good times."

"Yeah, but ... but," Danae interjected, "he was seeing Mary Jo Phelps from Prescott then *that* Marie Simmons. Both on the sly. Mary Jo was a nice girl but Marie was McKenna's most blatant whor—"

Mother cut her off, "Marie Simmons was a girl we went to McKenna with. Yes, she had a bad reputation. And yes, he was cheating with both—"

Danae interrupted her, "She was called 'Fast and Free Marie,' or 'Fondle Me Marie.' Oh, Momma sooo despised him. Let's see ... she called him '*Un tel païen indigne de confiance*. [Such an untrustworthy heathen] She was right about—"

Mother cut her off again while both DeeDee and I chuckled. "Thank you, *Little Sister* for the risqué nickname memories. Yes, Momma somehow knew he would cheat on me. 'Not only not Catholic, not even baptized. *Un païen!*' [A heathen] Oh, she intensely disliked him! But Rex left to go to college at Duke University and I went to KU in the fall. I met your father and Rex didn't exist anymore."

"Did he ever get married? Is he still married?"

"Yes, a girl from back East he met when she was doing graduate work at Duke. No, he divorced her after about ten years."

"Time to quit grilling poor Mother. So Aunt Danae ... a quarterback. You dated him in high school?"

"Well, yes, but we broke up because of Ruth Byers. I liked him so much. In fact, *way too much*! He was my first love then he broke my heart until that beautiful Roger Sparks from St. John V's came along a month later. Carl married her and before you ask ... yes, they divorced after three kids and twelve years of marriage. 'Little Ruthie' is still really frumpish and fat! You saw her Gi Gi. Same slovenly look as the last time I saw her at the grocery!"

"Meee ooow, hiss, hiss!" imitated DeeDee, as she quickly popped a couple strawberries in her mouth.

"Let me get this straight, you two girls brought divorced men into this house after two o'clock this morning. DeForrest, what kind of an example is this for us two very impressionable teenagers?"

My mother laughed at us, "Oh children, you are so funny. We were having an awful lot of fun. Reliving old times, good times, happy times. We had no idea of the current time or cared."

DeeDee wondered, "Are you going to see them again?"

"Maybe if Carl grows a lot of hair back and loses thirty pounds." She kidded, but then seriously added, "Plus we are both divorced."

"So what?" I interjected.

Mother grimaced, "Oh, Richelieu, *please* don't start on divorce and the church."

"Don't forget priests marrying, and there's birth control and also women priests like there were back in the seventh century in Ireland—"

DeeDee interrupted, "Are you going to see Rex again?"

She hesitated, "Yes, I have a date with him Saturday night." She rapidly changed the subject, "We need to get ready for noon Mass."

"Oh no! My communion fast ... those strawberries. Greeeat!"

I knew that fruit scarf was intentional. Communion would be about 12:50 and a good half hour or more before her *now* three-hour fasting time would elapse. Wonder what she and Rollie were doing on the sofa here last night? No surprise I had to announce myself, then detour through the dining room to the kitchen so I wouldn't see them. I hoped she knew what she was doing. I was beginning not to like him. Not at all.

****

Earlier our mother told DeeDee and me that she and Rex were going to dinner to a place on the Plaza, aptly named the Plaza III. After dinner, they would be going to a nightclub for dancing and drinking. I asked her if she could finish these activities in a suitable amount of time as she had a midnight curfew. She just laughed, said don't wait up for her. Danae would probably be home around eleven or twelve from a girls' night out.

Rex Finnegan rang the bell precisely at 6:30. As I invited him in, he said, "You must be Rich. I'm Rex."

"I am. Nice to meet you," as we shook hands. He was about my height with brown hair and medium build, square jaw, brown eyes. Actually a pretty good-looking guy. His clothes were immaculately tailored, looked straight out of Gentlemen's Quarterly. He had on a starched light blue shirt, a blue and red striped tie, matching red handkerchief in a muted blue striped three piece suit.

DeeDee came into the hall and I said, "This is my sister DeForrest. DeeDee, this is Mr. Finnegan."

"Hi, Mr. Finnegan, nice to meet you."

"Oh, both of you, please call me Rex. Well, *your* beauty and style certainly rival your mother's, DeForrest."

"Thank you, Mr. Finnegan."

"Rex, please."

Our mother came down the stairs, looking very elegant in a black crepe cocktail dress. Yessir, my father sure knew how to pick them.

Rex said my mother looked every bit as stylish as last weekend and they should be going.

As they walked down the sidewalk, I shouted, "Remember your midnight curfew." My mother simply put her right hand in the air, turned it backwards, waving good bye.

"Well, what do you think?"

"I am NOT ... going to like that ... that Prick," DeeDee said slowly.

"Huh? What? Why? He seemed okay to me."

"This is for the Book of Secrets."

"Sure. Fine."

"I don't like the way he looked me up and down and up again. I know guys look me over, sometimes a bunch. Sometimes exactly like that. **This** guy is an ancient forty. That *comment*! Waaay strong. He could have simply said I was pretty like Mother." Then she mocked in a low voice, " '*Your* beauty and style *certainly rival* your mother's!' Then ogling me like some real horny high schooler! The date's with Mother, not me. What a Lech! Yuck! Double Yuck! Oh damn, Rollie will be here in ten minutes to take me to a McKenna party. I've got to check my makeup. And my outfit."

"Don't forget to tinkle," I teased.

She gave me a pained look like I was being infantile then hustled upstairs into her bathroom.

Eight minutes later Rollie rang the doorbell, just as I distantly heard the toilet flush.

That night I had the nightmare again. It was getting worse — more graphic. My father seems to be more desperate for an answer. There was more blood. My mother was shrieking louder. I'll talk to Father Fitz about it soon. There will be no damn Shrinks.

※※※※※※※※※※※※※※※※※※※※※※※※※

First thing, as we got into the car to go to 9 o'clock Mass at the Cathedral, was to begin to interrogate my mother. I noticed even Aunt Danae's ears were perked up. But my mother simply deflected us by saying, "After Mass, we'll go to the Indian Head and I will tell all."

After the Consecration, I noticed DeForrest became very hesitant and nervous, however she went to communion. A few minutes later, her "perfect" boyfriend and the rest of the choir were at the communion rail.

They have been dating for six weeks or so. At least once, mostly twice a weekend, plus some Sunday afternoons. Now going steady ... now engaging in— ? Other guys still try to get a date ... the most she does is flirt ... but only a little. She's really crazy about this guy, really nuts over him. He seems a tad too 'Eddie Haskell' with Mother and Aunt Danae. I'm just the Beaver to him ... but if he hurts her, he'll think a lot differently, like I'm 'Paladin'.

Mick's lining up a nice Protestant girl ... a good-looking one ... maybe likes to make out ... a lot ... an awful lot ... and other stuff too.

After Mass was over, DeeDee was frowning and still looked worried. She quickly begged, "Richelieu, please pick me up at the Chapel back door, pleeease?"

"Sure, Dee." If it's Richelieu, it must be serious. She quickly headed in the opposite direction.

As usual, my mother and aunt saw some people they knew and stopped to chat. I saw no one. After about ten minutes, I went to my relegated task of chauffeur and waited for the two older Graces. When we picked up DeForrest, she was happier and in a much better mood. Whatever it was, looks like they made up or fixed the problem.

At the restaurant, after we had ordered, DeeDee begged, "Come on, spill it."

My mother very calmly said, "We had a very nice time. Dinner was extremely good and very well done. After we finished, we went to The Inferno, a very elegant nightclub. We danced, had a few drinks and talked about old times again. Rex introduced me to the club's owner, Fred Reed. Later Rex told me this Reed is an extremely good client of his."

"I also met the club's new dancer and singer, Christy Taylor who joined us during one of her breaks. A friendly, beautiful girl who has very black hair and green eyes ... like us, Danièle. That great, rare combination! Ha, who knows, maybe we're distantly related since she grew up in Wyandotte but graduated last spring from high school in Hays. Rex had met this girl at the Starlight's production of *Gypsy* this summer where she was one of the dancers. She had a slightly expanded minor part as one of the chorus girls with a few comedic lines. Loved working with and learning from Gisele MacKenzie. Then she was in *The Wizard of Oz* as part of the dancing and singing Ensemble. Christy then laughed, saying she was Rex's protégée and he was 'simply the most wonderful man' as he obtained this limited engagement at The Inferno. He's helping her on her next rung to becoming a star on Broadway."

Mother took a long drink of her coffee, "She dances extremely well, but just fair as a solo singer. Her skimpy outfit with its deep décolletage certainly helped garner the males' approval and loud applause. Well, in fairness, women liked her performance too. Probably wishing they could look like she does ... that scanty costume thoroughly displayed her quite good-size bust, pancake flat stomach and great Bridgette Bardot legs. Honestly, I have to admit she has an abundance of genuine sexual allure, her slinky attire notwithstanding. *And* only eighteen, but looks *and* acts much older."

DeeDee impatiently said, "Okay. Enough about a possible tenth cousin. And then? And afterwards?"

"And afterwards what? A lady only discusses her date in generalities."

"Or only with her sister, like in high school," Aunt Danae chimed in. "I don't remember any Taylors. Have to be on her mother's side." My aunt became serious, "Are you going to see him again?"

"Next Saturday night. Haven't decided what we are going to do?"

I decided I would start asking the obvious questions. "What does Rex exactly do for a living?"

"He is an investment advisor at First National Bank and Trust, a Senior Executive Vice-President."

"You mean he is a stock broker? I thought you said you were much better than the vast majority of stock brokers."

"Well, he does have to be licensed as a broker, but he's much more. His responsibilities include reviewing and possibly revising a person's investment portfolio. He manages the client's personal portfolios to help them maximize their rate of return according to their investment objectives. A personal asset adviser."

DeeDee interjected, "Are you going to let him manage your money?"

"Well, we're having lunch on Wednesday to discuss potential stock and bond opportunities."

I added, "I bet you could teach him a thing or two."

Aunt Danae piped in, "Even about investments."

My mother made a sour face but then joined in our laughter.

****

When I came home from school on Tuesday, there was a police car and an unmarked one in front of the house. I ran like the wind to the door, mind racing.

Did that Asshole try to attack Aunt Danièle again? WHAT did he do to her this time? I'M GONNA KILL THE BASTARD! ... COPS OR NO DAMN COPS!

Just as I pulled the front door open, I almost collided with two police officers who were leaving. The policewoman told me a drunken Harry Edward Brooks had run his car into Wyandotte Lake and had drowned. They were sorry for my loss. He evidently lost control of his car, launching it off the big fishing dock and into about twenty to thirty feet of water. Aunt Danièle was still named as his emergency contact with the law firm's address and number on the card that was in his billfold. They had gone to Ellis and Mullins to tell her and bring her home. A detective had just arrived a few minutes ago. I thanked them as they walked out the door.

Aunt Danièle was with my mother on the sofa in the living room. Mother was holding her hand and had her other arm around her. They both wordlessly acknowledged me. I couldn't tell if my poor Aunt was upset by his death. She just shifted her gaze back from me to continue staring at the fireplace.

The newly arrived detective was standing by the sofa. "I know this is very hard, Mrs. Brooks ... er ... Miss Richelieu, but could you please come with me to identify the body? Your sister could certainly come with you."

That's Bull Shit! She's not going anywhere close to the morgue. ... ... "No Detective," I interjected, "I'll go instead. Do you want to leave now?"

My mother started to object, then said nothing.

"Again, I'm sorry, Miss Richelieu. Son, I'm ready when you are."

"Aunt Danièle, are you going to be all right? Do you need anything? Is there anything else I can do when I'm out? Of course, I'll get your car."

She quietly said, "I'll be fine. Thank you for going, Forrest. And my car."

Detective Morris and I introduced ourselves and as we left, he began to explain some of the details. The accident happened before noon today. The ambulance driver and medic guessed Harry's alcohol content was "incredibly high". The Lab and Automotive crews were going to pull his beloved '58 Impala from the lake this afternoon then do their routine checks on it. An old man and his grandson were fishing near the dock. The grandfather said they heard tires screeching and the car was veering out of control but it never slowed, just straight onto the dock, smashed through a dock post and wildly veered off right into the lake.

As Morris lit up an Old Gold, he said he talked to Park Ranger Williams, who was on duty at the entrance hut. He said Brooks stopped about 8:30 and asked if Shelter #2 was open yet. He was told yes. There was another man who stopped about 9 o'clock and said he was thinking about renting a shelter for a party and which ones could he look at. The ranger said only #2 was open. The man was not easy to identify as he had his hat pulled down and the ranger didn't really think it would be important. Morris said that's why the guy was a Park Ranger, not a cop. No attention to detail.

"What kind of a car was he driving?"

"Good question, Richelieu. All he could remember was a black four-door. Maybe a Buick. Wannabe a cop?"

"No, maybe an architect."

"Yeah, well they havta be attentive to detail too."

The room was particularly cold. Detective Morris guided me over to one of the three shrouded gurneys, checked the tag on the big toe, and asked me if I was ready. I nodded and he pulled the cover back.

There was Harry.

Stunned, I sucked in a quick breath. His face grotesquely contorted, a ghastly, horrid white. A long, irregular gash on his left temple, exposing a thin crack in his skull. There were contusions on his forehead. His mouth torn crookedly, missing teeth, nose smashed. I had to turn away.

"That's him."

My stomach started to churn. I hurriedly left the room, followed by Detective Morris, who pointed me to the toilets down the hall. I ran through the nearer door, beseeching God for a toilet close, only to see two shocked young file clerks — one at the mirror, the other coming out of the first stall with her skirt and slip hiked up to her waist, fumbling with a twisted garter belt strap, hotly saying something like, "… after this, panties over belt…". I managed to dodge past her and barely made it to the still gurgling stool to begin throwing up. A second wave followed rapidly, and after some retching, then the final heave. The girls must have left because Morris came in to check on me. Said no big deal about the vomiting, that with violent deaths, a lot of people throw up. Morris drove me to the law offices to get Aunt Danae's car. Driving home, I couldn't quit focusing on that's how death looks before the embalming and funeral home niceties. Although I still felt like shit, I took solace knowing my aunt didn't have to see his mangled face and head.

My aunt was laying down, having taken some tranquilizers. My mother was beginning dinner when DeeDee came into my room. We began talking about the whole sordid mess. I told her a little about the morgue and throwing up in front of the two girls in the women's toilet. She said Aunt Danae had seemed stunned by his death. Was it sweeping relief he could never harm her again? Neither of us could figure out how she still could have any feelings whatsoever for him because of all the heartache and misery he created for her — his bullying, his uncontrolled drinking, his week with a teenage hooker, his live-in slut of many months, his bar whoring, and lastly, breaking in to rape and beat the shit out of her.

Finally I relented, telling her when they were separated, how he violently and degradingly took her sexually by force. Having her period. His trophy. The clap. Months later, how he badly mauled and severely bruise her breasts. Shoving her down her apartment building's stairs. Lastly, Father Fitzgerald's dire warning.

Already a pissed DeeDee finally exploded, "That is so God damn humiliating and vile! Any so-called 'man' is a repulsive, nauseating Shit Hole Prick Bastard! I don't give a damn what they **don't** call it because they weren't divorced, that's **RAPE**! Taking his trophy ... her menstrual stained panties with his putrid gunk and her saliva on them ... what a **sick** pervert! Gave her the clap, too! **What**, next time savagely rape and torture her? Batter and beat the shit out of her until she was dead? If he couldn't have her, then no one else could. **My God**!"

I agreed, "The Great King of Assholes. I will never understand all that crap he dumped on her, like his shitty life was her fault. Throwing their money away, all those whores. Forcing himself on her. Repeatedly attacking her. She has to be greatly relieved he can't hurt her anymore."

"Yeah, a great relief. Daddy would never be unfaithful like that bastard prick, even if he got propositioned by some beautiful call girl whore when he was on foreign assignment. He deeply loved Mother so much. I know ... know he ... he did." Mentioning our father was the final straw in all this sordid talk. A tear started to fall down DeeDee's cheek and she hurriedly left to cry privately.

The beautiful Eurasian whore's face appeared again with a scheming and secretive smile. God damn that slut bitch!

****

I went to confession the next day with Fr. Fitz, telling him everything that happened including the third incidence with the man in the black four-door Buick. His comments were, "Poor tormented man. I will pray for his soul. This becomes more and more tangled."

I confessed all about crazy Gloria. I was so focused and worried about Aunt Danae, I had forgotten to mentioned Antoinette in my last confession. I decided against discussing my nightmare. Maybe I didn't like my mother dating Rex. Maybe I didn't like her dating. Period.

"For your penance, one Our Father and you are to be extra mindful and caring with your aunt." Quickly his tone changed and was very stern, "A rosary for your activities and desires with the tempting, amoral rich girl **and** say another rosary for playing that lewd game and your related actions with that very bizarre, miserable girl. **And** say a third rosary for her to find help to overcome her wretched unhappiness."

Then he became vehement, sharply forceful. Far worse than in class. "Marlowe, quit screwing around, looking for outwardly nice girls yet still slutty! Damn it, find some **morally decent**, intelligent ones. With real personalities! **Genuine, substantive young ladies**!" He pointed his finger about an inch from my nose, staring fiercely at me, "**DO IT!**"

"Yeeess Father, I ... I will," I replied shakily.

****

Both my mother and aunt felt there was no need for a wake for Brooks, but they did ask Monsignor O'Reilly to say the Requiem Mass. He delivered a touching eulogy, dwelling on Harry's war record and life prior to his crazy, violent years. While God would forgive him, I couldn't. Not for all his unbearable misery he heaped on my poor aunt. Then horrifically traumatizing her these past eight months — maybe even longer. I grudgingly prayed for his soul to be in Heaven. I still couldn't forgive the prick.

Detective Morris was in the church's vestibule, saying he was sorry for the intrusion. When would a better time be? Mother told him to come to the house after the burial, muttering something about the sooner, the better.

About three o'clock, the detective rang the bell. I invited him to the living room where we were. My mother offered coffee or tea, maybe a sandwich. He declined. Morris said he had a few points to mention. The car is completely totaled. Danièle sort of snorted a laugh. She said he loved that car more than he ever loved her. The detective also mentioned the post-mortem proved he was very drunk. The fifth of Wild Turkey he had in the front seat had completely shattered. He had quite a bit of money in his billfold — three $1 bills and two $100 bills. His death was thus ruled by the coroner as drowning exacerbated by cranial injuries caused by a vehicular accident while driving under the influence of alcohol. He thanked my family for their hospitality. I quickly offered to see him out. We walked outside and I shut the door behind me.

"Detective, you know there are some points that don't add up."

"Such as?"

"He wouldn't buy a fifth of Wild Turkey. He drank only pints of Jim Beam."

"Maybe he got it as a gift." The detective lit up one of his Old Golds.

"Yeah, sure ... along with the two $100 bills. And how did he get **from the shelter** around that winding lake road with brake problems. I've done a round trip to Shelter #2. It's not that easy. Was there any fresh fluid in the parking lot?"

"Kid, are you *sure* you don't want to be a detective? I had the same two loose ends. Didn't know Beam was his booze of choice, so now three. Here's the problem ... the booze and money can be explained away pretty easily. However, there was only one fresh fluid drop in the parking lot, and only a couple spots leading onto the road. Could have been his or someone else's car. There has been too much traffic and previous leaks on the road itself. Nothing that is not easy to explain away. Only a minuscule residual of brake fluid in the reservoir, otherwise just lake water. I don't think the impact of the crash into the post caused it all to leak out ... there was nothing there to leak. But the coroner has already ruled. Oh yeah, the car was still in third gear, so in his drunken and terror-stricken state he probably didn't think about downshifting."

"Here is what I think happened ... A meeting between Harry Brooks and the man in the black Buick at the Shelter #2 is arranged. He goes down to the Path Entry and meets him on one of the benches. It's the only one open year round."

Where Caroline and I made out ... glimpsed her 'spillage' ... a hundred years ago.

"He takes the Wild Turkey with him, knowing Brooks is an alcoholic. They drink and talk and Harry drinks more ... much more. I did find the Federal tax seal strip for that fifth, complete with its wild turkey picture, an empty blank envelope along with some other meaningless trash in the park's bin. Of course, only Harry's fingerprints were found. The man gives him the $100 bills in the envelope as first payment to keep quiet about something. But alcoholics will lose control like the night he attacked your aunt."

He took a long drag on his cigarette. "But the die has already been cast, since the man had cut, probably about two-thirds of the way, through the reinforced fabric on the brake hose which will cause the hose to rupture completely the first time he steps on the brakes real hard. Probably happened at The Corpse's Curve ... as you kids call it ... after he gained sufficient speed. Our mystery man figures with the booze and quickly no brake fluid, Brooks will run off the road and crash. Open and shut ... Brooks is drunk and doesn't negotiate a curve. Nothing is checked because there would be nothing to *check*. The car would be a complete wreck."

"But Brooks knows his car and somehow is able to keep it on the road until the dock area. From the grandfather's statement, sounds like the car was purposely launched off the dock. It was either that or continue around the Lake, finally crashing into some trees or side boulders ... as planned. So we have the car and I know the brake line was tampered with because I believe the hose had a deep cut. The hose was ruptured and given the condition of the car ... could have been caused by a lot of different things."

The Detective took a couple quick drags then went on, "I'm positive Brooks' room had been searched very professionally. If he was hiding something, I'm afraid he wasn't very creative in his choice of a hiding place. A floorboard under the rug in his apartment ... ... of all places. Empty, of course. But that too can be explained away by saying that was Brooks' 'bank' and he made a 'withdrawal' of the two $100 bills. Maybe he was thinking about buying something expensive from the guy in black. There's another very small but important fact which supports my theory. The cop sent over to check his room out found his 'hidey-hole' and called the lab boys. They found some threads to a black jacket or overcoat caught on a rug tack near the hole. Brooks didn't have any coat in black fabric. I can't prove a damn thing. But I know Brooks was murdered."

"So what do you do now?"

"Nothing, they ... whoever *they* are ... covered themselves extremely well. They are going to get away with it." I thanked the detective for his insights and professional manner with my aunt. We shook hands. Before he smashed out his cigarette in the street, he lit up another one with it. Then got in his car and drove away.

※※※※※※※※※※※※※※※※※※※※※※※※※

The following Monday, I met my confessor in the chapel and told him everything the detective had told me. Both the facts and his theory of murder. Father Fitz was sure both deaths are linked somehow. He said since he believes nothing further will happen here, he is going to write up the whole affair and with my concurrence, will send it to a fellow Jesuit in Saigon who maybe has a "proper" connection. Father Fitz also said Brooks knew vastly more than he told me and he had kept every piece of hard evidence my father had sent to the Post Office Box, as demonstrated by the need for "safe keeping" in the now empty floorboard space. I told him he was supposed to rent a safety deposit box, but I bet the money went for booze, a bar pick-up or one of his so-called investments.

"That was *only one* of his fatal mistakes. His biggest one was trying to extort money from these people. While he thoroughly underestimated the safety of his hiding place, he unbelievably miscalculated their sheer ruthlessness for violence."

"He got a couple medals and some kind of meritorious ribbon ... I think for bravery. Even made sergeant while he was in Korea. Must have thought he could get one over on these thugs. And he was a good insurance adjuster for Allstate, really knew cars, but after the first couple of years ... those dating and the first year of marriage to my Aunt ... he got weird. Said he was going to make a fortune, always had the next 'hula hoop' idea. Every failure was her fault, so he continued verbal bullying her and drinking. On the night he first beat her, he started his bar bimbo screwing with two slut cousins. The breaking point for my aunt. That SOB put her through Hell."

"Yes, I'm sure he certainly did, but she still may have cared about him. His degrading, coerced act was the last straw ... she knew she had to divorce him, be rid of him. Only abusive, sadistic bullies act in that manner. And yes, Richelieu, he would have killed her ... if not the next time, then the one following. If he couldn't have her, nobody could. I believe sometime, in one of Brooks' non-inebriated states, he proves to himself he has figured out a foolproof plan of how to make his extortion scheme work flawlessly. Probably starts off by contacting Bradford Industries. Then plans further to get a little money from your family via you and, to complete his fantasy, concocts some crazy plan how to eventually reunite with your aunt."

He took a deep breath, "Regarding Harry and your father ... I'm most assuredly convinced your father **never** showed him any of the evidence, let alone wrote to him regarding the photograph or letter, the drug smuggling operation and the laundering of the money. They never met that Christmas. If they did, your father would have wanted a key to the safety deposit box. He had to have sent Brooks a letter long before all the drinking and adultery started, offering him the deal of money in exchange for taking the *unopened* evidence envelopes to be placed in a lock box *and* his complete silence for *his own safety*. Your father knew what he was dealing with."

"After his death, Harry opens all the documents, complete with your father's comments and notes, finds the photo with the letter, the contact at Bradford, then recreates your father's case sufficiently to realize the potential for extortion. He just needed to figure out how to make it 'flawless'. Sometime Brooks told or showed enough proof to the man in the black Buick to confirm his blackmail evidence. 'They' needed a clean sweep and quickly. To find all of your father's proof and to stop Harry before he began his alcoholic bar bragging, maybe with some of the envelopes or documents as proof, especially to impress a new tavern tramp. This is going to take some time, but I believe we will get at the truth. For penance, say one Our Father and a rosary for the repose of Harry's soul."

****

Almost home from school, Mick waved me down. He got in the car and told me, "I was going to call you, but here ya are. Good news. Pam has fixed you up with Sheila Rhodes for Friday night. Doubling, of course, and it's my turn to drive. There is a band party at Fifth Street Hall. Mostly McKenna, I'm guessing. She's really good lookin', a senior, brown hair and eyes, great set of knockers ... got a ... uh ... well ... decent enough bod. Good actress. President of the Drama Club. Makes the honor roll every time in one of the college prep tracks. She is C of E and she goes to St. Paul's Episcopal where Pam goes."

"This Sheila sounds pretty good. Maybe I'll call her to introduce myself."

"Sure, why not." He kidded, "Just don't mess it up on the phone. Talk at you later in the week. Don't know her number, but she lives on 14th Street ... pretty sure. Good luck. See ya."

Aunt Danae and her two friends who worked at the Law Firm decided to take the early train this morning to Nashville for a girls' getaway. I asked my mother if she had a hand in this outing and she reluctantly said she did, but DeeDee and I were not to say anything. She felt a trip like this would help get her mind off Harry's death. Tonight they would go to the Grand Ole Opry for some Country and Western music. I gagged easily on that. But when DeeDee and I found out on Halloween, they would be seeing *The* Jerry Lee Lewis at the Hermitage Hotel, we quickly changed our minds. Friday, they would go to St. Louis, spend the day and night and take the early train back, arriving late Saturday morning.

I called Sheila to introduce myself. She seemed nice enough as we talked about school and the classes we were taking. Coincidentally, we were both taking Latin and studying Cicero, even using the same textbook. I told her it was killing me, but she said she didn't think it was too bad. I figured she probably was like DeeDee and was just good in languages. Then I found out they hadn't covered even two-thirds of the material we had finished. No poetry at all. As we talked, she seemed to be trying to impress me with her classes and studies. I hoped not another 'Breezy'.

NOVEMBER

On All Saints' Day, the three of us went to Mass at St. Joachim and St. Anne's, then afterwards to breakfast at the Indian Head. DeeDee said Roland had planned a very special surprise for their date tomorrow night, so she should wear her full red skirt and matching sweater which were his favorites. I, of course, had my blind date with Sheila tonight. DeeDee was teasing me about repeatedly going out with "older women" which had become my "modus operandi". I simply told them, if one is cool enough, there is absolutely no pressure.

Mick and Pamela picked me up to go get Sheila who didn't live far from St. Patrick's. When Sheila opened the door to greet me, I could see she was certainly good-looking, about 5 foot 5 with brown hair and attractive brown eyes. My eyes stealthily slid down to glimpse a terrific pair of knockers. Unfortunately when she went to pick up her purse and coat, I couldn't miss her extra large butt and stocky thighs. Undoubtably reined in by a tight, constricting, long-length girdle trying its best to control her sizable butt. Definitely didn't fit Mick's "decent bod" description. Should have been more like "great bod" — great tits and **great** big ass and thighs.

She introduced me to her parents, emphasizing I went to St. Ignatius, "*The* Jesuit school". I helped her on with her coat, said, "Goodnight" and "nice to meet you" to her parents.

During the drive to the dance, the three of them talked in sport generalities. Prescott's so-so football season and the high expectations for the basketball team, maybe even winning state. The football team was playing in Lawrence tonight so not many students would make the trip. The Homecoming Dance was just okay according to Sheila as the decorations could have been done better and so could the music. My private thought was having a nice guy for a special dance could have negated that, but I guess not as she went on to say her date was a dud. She was shocked a *junior* — a Trudy Kingly or something like that — was elected

Homecoming Queen. I was already starting to get a little turned off. When we got to the hall, I paid our $2 admission per couple. After about twenty minutes, Mick and Pamela split and left Sheila and me by ourselves.

"Is there any differentiation in your year?"

"Yeah, there are four classes. And—"

"Well, at Prescott there are three classes of College track paths."

And they are ... The Moe, The Curley and The Larry

"One emphasis is on the Arts and Languages which is *my path*. Another is more geared to Math and Science. The third is Arts & Science. A good blend of the first two. *Everyone else* just takes General Education studies." Her voice was sharply cutting in the last comment, making that group sound like they were pond scum. "Are you taking any other languages, besides Latin?"

"Yeah, French and English." I threw in the English to get a taste of her sense of humor.

She started to say English wasn't consider a "language" but retreated by saying, "Oh just French," like I was a little slow. "I'm taking second year German with my Latin III. I finished two years of Spanish last year. Prescott has the highest number of National Honor Society members in the state and I will become a member this year. How about St. Ignatius?"

And Prescott is probably the biggest school in the state ... so what's their percentage? Shit, this confirms it ...... another Breezy. Time for some fun.

"I never paid any attention to the Honor Society, it's only for seniors," I said in fake humility but rebounded with, "Too bad Prescott is so limited."

"*Limited*? What do you mean?"

"Well, well, well! If it isn't Rich Marlowe, one of St. Ignatius's finest at an activity we both know very well." I turned around to recognize a short, extremely cute girl in a bust clinging, pink V-neck sweater. Wearing an excellent matching color of pink eyeshadow — but too much — and too damn much black eyeliner and pinkish-white lipstick. Overall, precariously bordering on a slutty look.

"Well, hello Caroline," as I instantly had checked her out further without being overtly obvious. ... ... *Caroline Cunningham ... tad slutty looking or not ... your body is still fantastic.*

Ignoring Sheila completely, she begged, "Please ask me to dance later and we can catch up, if you're not still mad at me. I'm **so** sorry. Please?" Caroline displayed a very hopeful look.

"Sure, course I will," I said smiling.

"Excuse me. We were having a productive conversation here until yo—"

"See you later **Rich**," Caroline interrupted. Behind Sheila's back, she stuck out her tongue to curl it invitingly, grinned and strutted away in her tight jeans and high heel pumps.

Oh God, look at that ass wiggle! Wowzer!

She joined Lorraine who waved at me as she was exhaling smoke through her nose, sufficient to fill a boxcar. I returned Honeydew Melons' wave.

"See you later **Rich**," Sheila mimicked almost perfectly and I remembered Mick saying she was a good actress, especially with voice imitations. "Then, you must know that ... **that girl**," her voice inflecting "that girl" to mean "Slut".

"Yeah, had a few dates with her. Lives over in St. James' Parish."

"So she's Catholic then. I've seen her around Prescott with others of *her ilk*." I was going to say something to defend Caroline. I didn't though.

The band finally started to play so we began to dance the twist. I can hold my own when dancing only because my mother insisted on me taking ballroom dancing for two years as an eight-grader and a freshman. I never was great at dancing, however, I learn some steps and found or gained a sense of rhythm.

Sheila had not.

The dance classes were a compromise so I could take boxing lessons. My father "enrolled" me in these "boxing lessons" as they were purported to my mother. These lessons were taught by a drill instructor but were really street fighting techniques which did include boxing but a whole lot more. It quickly stopped the bullying and threats I was then a target of. However, with confidence and some know-how, I found a few reasons and causes to get into fights. Several didn't end well for me. Like the one with a senior over my fiery red-head, Rusty. Cheated on me with the jerk. Afterwards, my "summer love" — now a junior — decidedly dumped me, the lowly sophomore.

After the dance, I asked, "Would you like a Coke?"

"Pepsi, if they have it, sure."

As I was going over to the soda pop stand, I noticed Roland Bush and his two buddies, Ron Kovac and Billy Brewster, and thought about stopping to say hi and be friendly for DeeDee's sake. Then a disturbing thought bubbled up in my mind about him. *Especially* with her. All three were excitingly talking loudly and laughing. They were partially hidden by a large square post, so I lean up against it to eavesdrop on their conversation. I heard rumors these three would go to Missouri to see what they could pick up. Sure enough, Billy was bragging.

"Mine had gigantic jugs, biggest knockers I've ever seen or played with. Headlights and hubcaps* even bigger than your slut's whole teeny tiny pimple tits."

"Yeah, but my scrawny slut wasn't ugly and fat like yours."

"So what! With any of 'em, ya just close your eyes or put a sack over its head." It was Billy laughing. "Lisa's nothing but a chubby, homely, high school whore. But, at the Northland library, we went behind that pigeon-bombed Carnegie statue where there's that hidden area. Boy, did I play with those whopper tits. **Then**, like a good slut, she unzipped my pants, pulled out my cannon, made it fire quickly. Great date! All for a burger, fries and a coke. Bringing chocolates for her tomorrow night, like she needs 'em. Gonna bang roly-poly Lisa. Good and Plenty!" He laughed, "Like the candy. And keep her phone number handy for future nasties."

Bush was laughing too, "Look around. Maybe there's something here for you two. If not, we'll go across the river to find some good stuff." Then Kovac started a detailed version of his "conquest" of his "scrawny slut".

---

*In '60s teenage slang, the term **"headlights and hubcaps"** was a vulgar expression for **girls' nipples and areolae**

Shit, that crap confirms it.

I detoured around them, bought the soft drinks, finally returning to my exciting date.

"Well, here he is now. Mary Lou and Neva, this is *my St. Ignatius* date, Rich Marlowe. Rich, this is Mary Lou Babson and Neva Smith. Senior girls too."

"Hey Mary Lou. Hey Neva."

"Hi Rich. Gee, we never meet any guys from St. Ignatius," said Neva. "Where do they all go?" She giggled, "Can't be hiding." Mary Lou just continued to stare at me.

I just shrugged my shoulders in response, "Most of the guys live in Missouri." That killed that conversation. Weeks later, I found out that those two and a third senior, Maureen Modica, nicknamed "MoMo," were called "Rhodey's Toadies".

"We're going to get a coke too. See you later, Sheila. Bye, Rich."

"Yeah, bye. Here is your Pepsi. Happy times," and I clicked her bottle.

"When you said Prescott was limited, what did you mean exactly?"

"The course selection and duration."

"And?" she said becoming somewhat irritated, which was my intent.

"You have no Greek."

"You have Greek?" she said disbelieving.

"Your courses are only for two years, not four like ours."

"My Latin is third year!"

"Yeah, but you are only two-thirds through what we have translated in the textbook. You haven't done work on any poetry ... *id est, exempli gratis* ... that is, for example ... Catullus' love letters."

Now she was becoming pissed off, insulted at translating the obvious for her. She defensively said, "I **most assuredly know** what i. e. and e. g. mean. At Prescott, we **have** to have a **much** broader selection because of the types of students enrolled."

"You mean Prescott has to cater to all those students in General Education who are limiting the College Path potential possibilities by needing all those trivial courses for their ordinary diplomas."

"Exactly."
Sheila had missed my subtle sarcasm.

Who was worse? Sheila or Breezy? Shit, this one. She's mean ... really nasty.

What did the General Curriculum have to do with her class being way behind us? That's called blame deflection. What a stupid, insensitive bitch!

AND my damn date.

Some McKenna guys whom she knew came over and talked. While a couple of them danced with her, I danced with her plain-looking buddies — the continuously chattering Neva and the quiet and shapeless Mary Lou who would noticeably gawk at me. A guy named Eugene danced with Sheila a few times — seemed to like her. She was enjoying his and the other males' attention.

Maybe I could pay Eugene to take her for the rest of the night. What's the going rate for spiteful bitches?

As the band finished their set, the singer announced it was a ladies' choice and a goldie oldie slow dance. *I Love How You Love Me* by the Paris Sisters began to play.

Out of nowhere was Caroline.

"Would you dance with me Rich, please?"

I said, "Sure," and looked at Sheila. She was pissed.

Caroline snuggled up to me as tightly as she could, which made me think she must be wearing that same flimsy, thin bra again because I could firmly feel her breasts flatten warmly against my chest. So there was that good news which caused some of the bad news. I was getting a first class erection and she had to feel it, just like on her porch step. Far, far worse, she powerfully reeked of residual cigarette smoke. Shelia, in retaliation, was dancing with none other than Bush and had locked herself very tightly into him. He had a very satisfying smile. As he made a dance turn, she was smiling happily. Maybe he was making a similar impression on her.

What would DeeDee think ... seeing him like this and hearing him earlier? And the omniscient Monsignor.

Boy, Sheila ... regardless whatever type of girdle you're wearing ... a long tight one, a panty or some other kind ... that is one hefty ass you have with matching thighs. ... ... "How is your shorthand class?"

"It's wonderful and easy. I got a grade of a 1 in it and also a 1 in General Math. Rich, I made the Honor Roll for the first time since I've been at Prescott."

"I always said you were no dummy. You proved me right."

"Oh God, **thank you** for saying that."

"What did your parents say?"

"Not a **God damn thing**! They don't give a **shit**!" She looked extremely hurt. "Never did. 'Just as long as you pass' ... that's from my father. 'Be a good Catholic girl' ... my mother ... meaning don't become her long definition of *slut*."

"I'm sorry Caroline. That's really too bad. You have the smarts. And a lot. I know you do. You should go to junior college after graduation."

"Oh Rich. You're such a great guy, giving me compliments after I was such a nasty bitch to you." She began contritely, "I thought you would still be mad at me. After all, I **was** so hateful to you ... told you to go rot in Hell ... called you a giant prick. Look, I have a bad temper and when I lose it, I can get horribly spiteful, especially right before my— ... ah, uh. I just got so God damn pissed off at you. And I'm still so ashamed. I didn't mean it. Forgive me? Please? I'm so sorry. I miss you!"

"Easily forgiven and done a long time ago. Although I do recall you did say something about 'kissing your sweet ass.' " Somehow this quickly embarrassed Caroline as she redden up and looked away. I gently turned her face back, "And as I intentionally verified a while ago, **your ass** has lost neither its very sweet look nor appealing jiggle in those tight jeans and heels. Still looks extremely kissable to me."

She recovered, "Well, damn, thank *you* for noticing *my* ass. Rich, only you could convert my insult to you back into a complement for me. Oh damn it, Rich, damn it! I missed you so much. I must have called you at least ten times, but your mother always said you were studying, twice you were on a date. She was very intimidating, like a General. I didn't leave a message. I was too rattled, still worried you didn't want anything more to do with me."

"So that was *you*! But you never even left your name either."

"No, I just couldn't. But I had to somehow get to talk to you, to see you. So I went to Mass at St. Pat's to look for you afterwards. After a few tries, I finally saw you with your family. You were all talking with some people, so I started to come over to you. I was so nervous, I stopped and lit up, took some quick drags, like I did before I came over the first time to see you tonight. The taller, black-haired lady ... your mother I guess ... had been watching me. The General gave me such a domineering look ... such a completely daunting one ... I lost my nerve. I turned around and left."

"You know, a couple times, I cruised around **looking hard** for you. Obviously never found you. Found Sherry in Allen's, but she was with some bikers, enjoying playing grab-ass with one of 'em. Didn't want to bother her."

"Shit, I wish to God you would have found me, talked to me, anything. And yeah, Sherry loves getting goosed ... by guys she really likes a ton."

"What about Carl the tackle?"

"I would break up with him right now to go out with you. Going to break up with that big ape anyway. And I wouldn't sneak around anymore with Terry Massey either."

"Caroline, we both know why it didn't work before."

"I would definitely quit for our dates. I promise!"

"No, I mean quit for *good*. No smoking ever again."

"I have tried **and** tried. But I can't. I just **can't**. I've been smoking since I was in the sixth grade at St. James's. I loved it even then. I would get caught time and again. Third time I was caught in the girls' toilet, I got expelled around Christmas freshman year at McKenna. Then had to make new friends at Whittier. That's where I met Pamela and Sally. Oh, I guess I could lie to you ... say I had quit ... ... no, I guess I couldn't lie to you."

"True, we would never lie to each other. We both would just get mad at the other once again. Oh yeah! I was pissed off at you." Still serious, "You were always so considerate and thoughtful with me. You treated me like I was always more than some dumb, little broad with a good bod."

"You're not a dumb broad! Don't *let anyone* tell you that. You're not!" I smiled, "But you don't have a good body." She immediately frowned. "You've got a **great** one! However, you're **still little**." I patted her on the top of her head affectionately.

She laughed as the song was ending, "Thanks for saying that Rich and this dance. I miss your tongue *and more*."

I'll ditch the mean bitch. Run off with Caroline for another 'great make out'.

I moved my thumb over her sweater a few times where her navel would be and grinned, "Oh, I certainly miss much more than your tongue." Then I began to slowly move my hand upwards. ... ... *Certainly your tantalizing tits. And play my version of grab-ass — tightly gripping both cheeks.*

She caught both my veiled remark and my thumb, "Rich, I'm *sure* we could figure out something. And this ... **this** thumb really and truly messed with me. Oooh, never had any guy feel up and fondle my belly-button. Started to get me all hot and bothered."

"Oh, I certainly intended this thumb to mess with you. Wanted to get you all hot and bothered, Cara."

"You called me Cara again!"

"All the time if it helps you to quit smoking."

She put her head against my shoulder, wrapping her arms firmly around my right arm. "Oh, damn it, Rich, if I could ... if I only could."

As we walked back to where she had asked me to dance, she confessed, "You know big, fat-ass Sheila doesn't really like me since she thinks I stole Larry the Linebacker from her last summer. Which I didn't have to! Even Pamela or Sally Adams don't hang around with me like they used to. But, I guess, they have their steadies and I date the football jocks, plus we have different classes, even clubs."

"Why is that a problem for you? So they have boyfriends? So what? There're lots of others who like you, I'm sure ... like Lorraine and Sherry. *And I like you!*"

"Damn, that's what I always loved about you, Rich, you don't talk much because your attitude does it for you. You don't give a shit what anybody thinks. You're so damn cool."

"I'll find you shortly for another dance, a slow one ... or maybe **something else ... something real, real nice**. I promise Cara," and I winked.

"Bye and thanks," she stuck out her tongue temptingly again and strutted sweetly away. I watched intently, knowing it was for me. Especially when she tossed her butt off-stride, simultaneously waving her finger as she unmistakably pointed it at the parking lot.

Sheila waited a short interval for the air around to become purified again, then returned saying, "I can't believe you would dance with her. She is just so ... so common ... so cheap."

"So *that's* what it is. We have a lot in common and she's a very nice girl." I ignored the "so cheap" comment.

"What! How can you say that? You obviously don't know her. Beginning this summer, she started becoming intimate to steal other girls' boyfriends. She has earned herself a bad reputation."

"But certainly not deserved."

"Well, of course it is! Just look at her! She's a deceitful, trashy little slu—"

I interrupted, "I'm going to get a coke." This was going nowhere good, and it wasn't even 9 o'clock. "Do you want something?"

With her air of superiority, "No, I'm fine." She headed towards the girls' toilet.

Bet she doesn't merely 'tinkle' ... probably 'chimes' loudly. Letting all the girls know it's Sheila, the important bitch, taking her important piss. Wonder how long it takes her to yank down her white nylon monster, chime loudly, then jerk it back up to conquer those mammoth cheeks and thighs.

I'll find Caroline or Lorraine ... tell them I want to leave with them NOW. Then I'll find Mick and tell him I'm history ... so take the 'important' bitch home.

As I was walking over again towards the refreshment stand to find Caroline, I saw Roland Bush again talking with his two buddies. So I went over and leaned up against the post again, still staying out of sight. This time Bush was talking. Maybe it was about one of **his** Friday night conquests. DeeDee wouldn't want to hear this. It would hurt. Badly. Very badly.

Instead I unbelievably heard, "... of your irritating shit. All right, all right! I'll finally tell you two annoying shits. It was gradual ... just like I **did** with Monica Matthews ... started off with making out, then heavily. After a few weeks of increasing love talk bullshit, I asked her to go steady ... setting it all up ... first feeling her up on the outside, then immediately inside for some soft, bare tit. Happened first at her house one night. Oh, hers are fine, **so very fine**, just perfect in size. The next week, I 'begged' to see them. Now I always kiss those flawless virgin nipples and halos. Hot pink in color. Sure different from all the shades of brown I've thumbed and fingered before. They really turn me on!"

"Wow! Never seen pink. Lisa's are just plain old brown, but brown and huge."

"Well, my next step was easy ... maneuver her into dry humping. Now I just pull her down and mount her, and she's trained to tightly lock those shapely calves around mine. I pound her until I shoot my wad, just dry docking the shit out of her. The great thing is she's so naive and innocent. So I always tell her how much I love her, calling her my 'forever sweet one' ... like I called double M. My little auburn-haired virgin needs to hear that shit. Oh, she deeply believes it. After about fifteen minutes of that kind of flowery bullshit, I resume rubbing up those soft tits and lusciously colored nipples and pounding that pussy until I get my rocks off again. She's always willing, always hot. Getting hotter. Has to be so lubed up by the way she pumps and grinds me so hard. Probably smeared all over her panties. Her name even matches her bra cup size ... **DD**."

Jesus Christ! That's DeForrest!

"Tomorrow night ... the grand finale. Another Monica 'bang-bang'. And my second pair of souvenir 'virgin club' panties. **That** first-timer's light blue ones are monogramed with a nice cursive M. Keep in my special place. Never any sleazy whores' undies that have been yanked down more times than you get yo-yoed on a wild roller coaster ride.

He lowered his voice, "My parents are out of town for the weekend, and I'll have DeeDee all to myself in that empty house. After I get her smoking red-hot, I'll work my magic fingers up under that full red skirt which I **told her** to wear ... so no slacks or any type girdle ... start stroking her thighs but going higher, popping those garter straps on my way into a pair of red lace panties. Then I'll slip my two fiery fingers inside her virgin cunt, arousing her so intensely, so thoroughly, all the while telling her 'this is the only way to swear our love for each other' and 'there will always be only you' or some bull shit like that. I'll have her begging for my big loaded dick. Oh yeah, **I'm going to have her**, willingly. OR I'll—"

Aaaarrrrrrraaaggg!!!!

I hit him as hard as I could in the jaw. The punch was a solid hit, knocking him to the floor. Brewster quickly retaliated with a body punch, so I nailed him with a hard cross to the face. The Prick swiftly recovered, hitting me with a strong hook to my left eye. I connected a second punch to his buddy's eye again. While he started to go down for the count, a building collapsed on me as I heard a yell from behind, "You Motherfu—."

※※※※※※※※※※※※※※※※※※※※※※※※※※※

With all the pain and grogginess, I could only wobble badly, even with two guys helping me to a car to lie in the back seat. When I finally became fairly aware, I realized I was in the back of Mick's moving car. Both girls were in the front. I started to get up but my head promptly vetoed the idea. One side hurt, excruciatingly so. There was a towel or some cloth on it and when I touched it, I could feel a sticky liquid, had to be blood — mine. And there was this damn elephant sitting on my chest.

From the front seat I heard, "Why did he slug Roland Bush and start that fight?"

Oh shit .... my head.   Damn .... my chest.

The wooziness had mostly cleared off but at the expense of increased pain. So I tried to keep my mind off of the throbbing by intently focusing on the conversation from the front seat. It helped very little.

"Bet it probably had something to do with Rich's sister. As they were splitting, this Billy Brewster was heard, kinda stuttering, saying that he and Kovac, were only trying to break it up. Which was bull shit because I saw Bush and this Kovac finish by stomping Rich's ribs a bunch of times ... hard. This was all after this Kovac evidently hit him on the back of the head with the pop bottle.

Good thing it didn't break or he would be a lot worse off than he is." It was Mick.

Oh God help me ... ... this hurts! Oooooh!

"So it was Bush, Kovac, and Brewster. Rich must have solidly hit this Brewster because his eye was really bleeding and he was real unsteady while the other two were kicking Rich. Three McKenna guys against only him. Sure was quick ... only fifteen, maybe twenty seconds but the two certainly beat him up badly ... especially using a bottle. In baseball, I learned with a head injury that a doctor should examine it, so we're going to take him to the emergency room."

"Well, I'm not going to *any* hospital," objected Sheila. "I thought guys from St. Ignatius were gentlemen, not common brawlers."

O Jesus! I hurt.

"Too late, we are already here. Now to find the emergency entrance."

O Jesus! This hurts. Oooooh! Shit, my head.

I saw flashing lights — or at least I thought they were flashing — on the main building of Bethany Hospital. And the pain was getting worse. Much worse.

Mick, hurry ... ..., God damn this pain!

Fights ... sure ... anytime. Blind dates ... never again. Bitch! Pretentious Bitch! O God! Hurts like hell. Only wanted to brag ... ... dated a guy from St. Nate's. Poor Caroline ... labelled her a whore. You nasty pompous cunt!

"I'm not going *in there*," came from the nasty, pompous Cunt. Pamela said she would stay with her in the car.

O God! This hurts like shit! Ohhhhh Shit ... ... Shit!

O Jesus Christ help me! Oooow God please help me ... ... this is killing me!

"Oowwww Mick. Oh God, Mick. Really hurts." He had gotten me out of the car somehow and had my arm around his shoulder and he was half supporting me, half dragging me towards the emergency room doors. Mick was apologizing for not helping in the fight, but only saw the end as my chest was stomped, then two of the assholes helped the other shit to hurriedly leave. I thought my head was going to explode and when I tried to breathe my chest felt on fire. Just then an orderly came out with a wheel chair. Before I could sit down, I started vomiting, causing the pain in my chest to skyrocket. I almost passed out before I could finish spewing. The orderly grabbed me, positioning me in a wheel chair. I groaned to Mick to call my mother as soon as he could, then take the girls home.

The next interval entailed several treatments and procedures interspersed with long periods of boredom. After I answered some dumb ass questions to see if I knew who I was, then quickly a pain shot — some waiting — then taking a bunch of X-rays — then more waiting. A nurse checked my vision and reflexes. Finally another nurse came in, gently rubbed some cream on my chest, then tightly wrapped my rib cage. I got tired of more waiting, so I laid down. I felt a couple of needle pricks in the back of my head, meaning someone was doing something back there. A nurse who claimed she was a doctor began stitching up my eye. She said she had finished sewing up my head some time ago, saying it was a good thing my skull was hard. My mother came over to rub my shoulder — one of the few places that didn't hurt.

Where did my mother come from? Oh God, there's My Little Dee. If Bush tries to touch her, I'll beat him senseless with Little Lou. And his asshole buddies too.

The doctor, now promoted from nurse, said I should stay a while to make sure there were no further problems. She wasn't happy about me nodding off while she sewed up my head, so I was going to stay in this ER examining room for a while. She said it was probably just a side effect of the general pain shot, maybe combined with the locals. Since it seemed to be wearing off, she gave me another injection, and she would be back in an hour to check on me and shut the door.

"Richelieu, are you in a lot of pain?"

"Like a truck hit me. Better, especially my ribs. Since they got rid of the elephant. My head doesn't hurt as much. How long have I been here?"

"Well, at least two and a half hours ... probably a lot longer. They could only minimally treat you for a while because of a bad car accident. One person even died. The doctor said you may have as many as four bruised ribs, so they wrapped you up for the weekend. You'll have to sponge bathe. Three stitches for the cut above your left eye. Seven stitches in your head. I have pain pills she gave me for tomorrow morning. And a prescription for after that."

"Is that **all**? So then I won?"

My mother ignored my arrogant, self-proclamation of victory. "Richelieu, what happened?"

"Nothing, just a disagreement with a big jerk and his jerk buddies."

DeForrest insisted, "About what?"

"Guy stuff. Nothing really."

"Mick called us and waited until we got here and made sure you were going to be okay, then took your dates home. He said something about you and Roland got into a very bad argument. **I want to know**!"

"So do I," reiterated my mother.

"No, neither one of you want to know." I was adamant.

"Forrest, I am your mother. **You will tell me**!"

Awww Shit ... Forrest. ... ... "Okay, but not with DeeDee here," I wearily said.

"Richelieu, if it's about me, I have a right to know."

"DeForrest, you won't believe me. You like that Shit Head too much."

"*Don't you call him that!*"

I was trying to stall, but the shot was kicking in. I had no will to hold out. "Well, it has to do with DeForrest. And deeply intimate. Still want to know?"

"Now, Forrest!"

"I'm going to tell you the whole truth. Neither of you will like it. Obviously, I sure as hell didn't. Bush tells you he goes out sometimes with the boys on some Friday nights. He and his two buddies go to Missouri to pick up sluts. Tonight at the dance, I overheard the three of them talking and laughing about what a great scheme they have going. One began to relive and describe in some detail his current on-going conquest. Their fast and easy pick-ups' physical attributes are like prizes. Then they brag about their activities with them. The rest is vile. Hideously vile."

"**Forrest,** I want to hear it," my mother said solemnly.

Now the pain is better. Doesn't hurt like before.

"**Now Forrest! Now!**" my mother yelled at me.

That shook me out of my relaxed state. "Oh, God help me! About an hour later, I overhear this bastard Bush start bragging in very graphic detail about his weekly petting activities with a girl he calls his 'innocent, so naive, so gullible, auburn-haired virgin who has beautiful, perfect size tits' with unusual colored nipples ... uh ... pink. Firm calves and thighs for tightening him into her while he dry humps her a couple of times on each date."

DeForrest suddenly sucked in a breath making a low, sharp moaning noise.

"Then, what he's going to do with her tomorrow night at his house when nobody's home for the weekend. After he fondles her and gets her really excited as he said he always can and does ... Oh Christ, forgive me ... he is going to put his hands under her red skirt ... which he told her to wear ... so nothing in the way to her red panties. He'll move up her thighs, stroking them. Next, he'll slip his hand into those panties, then his fingers inside her. While he gets her really wet and aroused, he'll emphatically lie to her about how much he loves her as he enters her for her first intercourse. Same thing he did with some other girl. I decked the Prick, and the three of 'em teamed up to put me here."

DeForrest came out of her delayed momentary shock, shrieking, "**No, no, no**! Our love is special and unique! There's only been me! Only me! He even calls me his 'forever sweet one'. He would never talk about me like I was some street whore, some common slut just for the taking! **That's not me**! He **loves** me! You're just jealous of us because none of those St. Cat bitches or any God damn girl can meet your absurd "big stud" expectations. You're wrong about Roland. Dead wrong! **YOU SHIT**! I hate you, Richelieu! You vicious, nasty Prick! Mean, terrible **BASTARD! HAAATE YOOOU**!" And she began to cry violently and ran out of the holding room.

Even through my increasing drugged state, I could tell Mother was incensed as she hissed, "How do you know he was talking about DeForrest?"

"Dee has auburn hair.

"**Forrest, and?**"

My mother now was glaring at me, "**FORREST! What else?**"

"Said he was going to take her red panties as a trophy. For his virgin collection. Said even her name matched her bra size ... DD."

My mother snapped, "That imbecile is not even close, she just filled out into a C ... last spring." She was as cold as an iceberg, like last month when that other Bastard beat up poor Aunt Danae. While it was probably the shots, she was starting to scare me. "Enough of his terrible smut! I'm going to find your doctor. We are going home and we're going to completely sort all this damn filth. **NOW**!" She stormed out the door, slamming it. I was now really woozy so I laid back onto the examining table.

Where are the cute Candy Stripers? Must be the first C my smart sister ever got in her life. Heh, Heh.

I waited for the Candy Stripers, but only the doctor came in to check me over again. She said I seemed okay to leave. The nodding off and uninhibited talking were due to the drugs. If there were any problems to bring me back at once, then she released me. An orderly wheeled me to the front door where my acutely incensed mother was waiting with the car and my sobbing sister in the backseat. No one said a word on the way home. I staggered a little as I followed them through the kitchen. Our mother fumed, "DeForrest, please go to your room. **WE are going to talk later**!" DeeDee was still crying. "Forrest, in the study! Please!"

Still with 'Forrest' ...... Shit.

She closed the door, still maintaining her glacier demeanor. "You gave a fairly clinical account regarding Bush and DeForrest at the hospital. Now you will tell me, verbatim, exactly what he said. The exact words. His exact description."

"Mother, please no. It's worse than rough locker room talk."

"I don't give a damn! I need to know to help your sister! And DeForrest needs help. Desperately! As a senior, I thought that

Shit would be too old for her, however, Monsignor O'Reilly highly recommended him. It was obvious she was completely smitten with him after Mass on that first Sunday. He's always been very courteous and mannerly with me ... *seemingly* very respectful of her. I hoped then believed he would be an excellent boyfriend for her. A handsome, devout young man, in the Cathedral choir, an honor student, from a very good family, an athlete. I was so damn wrong and so was the Monsignor. Oh, what a God damn mess! I was fooled, like my poor Angel ... my little Danièle. So terribly, terribly duped! I had no idea of the appalling direction and intensity of her dating activities with this horrible creature. Manipulating her by creating, then feeding off her vulnerability and naiveté. How vile! **God damn him**! All within two months!"

So I told my mother, word for word, what the Son of a Bitch said. I started out by pretending I was back in the locker room at Loyola. Then I realized my mother had gone to college and probably seen and heard a lot of this type of shit from Dad or her girlfriends, so this was nothing new. But this was still shocking. This was about **DeForrest**!

As I finished, I was starting to feel like hell again. My mother began to pace back and forth for a few moments, stopped and concluded, "Thank you Forrest, I can still fix this for DeForrest." I had no idea what she meant, other than things would be fine, once again.

I forced myself to get up to walk over to kiss her goodnight. My mother said with tears in her eyes, "I certainly never approved of your father having you take those so called 'boxing lessons'. It was one of the very few subjects we argued about. **Because** it didn't end with resolving the bullying you endured. You simply continued to get into fights on the Base. But tonight I am very proud of you for what you did. Forrest, I can see your Father in you tonight. He never played just when the odds were in his favor or played only when he wanted to. He always did the right thing, no matter what the cost. He always went up against the side that was wrong, no matter what his chances were. I really loved that about him. And **I hated it. HATED IT!**"

Twin torrents flooded down her cheeks and she turned away from me, walking to the double windows. Despite her try at concealment, I went to her, turned her back around and tried my best to hug her which hurt like hell, but I didn't give a damn. Remembering I still had my handkerchief, I quickly opened it and gave it to her. She wiped her eyes and face. While she swiftly regained her composure, I gave her my nightly kiss, then an extra one. I gently rubbed her shoulder, saying, "Mother, tonight it was only three of them against me. I may have lost the fight *but I won the war.*"

She sniffed slightly, patted my cheek softly then kissed it, "I know, Forrest, I know you did. But you paid a terrible price. Paid dearly!"

"My pain will all be gone in a week. If his scheme to seduce then betray DeForrest had worked ... like with that other girl ... God only knows when her pain would have left her. For that, I would have beaten the God damn Bastard senseless ... and more." I didn't wait for her to scold me about my swearing, but turned and hobbled up the stairs to my room, vowing to God and my Father I was going to fix that Son of a Bitch for BOTH their pain and suffering.

****

When I woke up on Saturday, I wasn't sure if I ever wanted to get out of bed again. I remembered Mother had come in a couple times during the night to wake me to make sure I didn't have any problems with the concussion. The last time, when she was standing over me, thinking I had gone back to sleep, she whispered, "Thank you, my darling little Forrest," and kissed me on my forehead. As she left, I could hear her praying, "**Forrest, my Heart**. Please, please help me to…"

I still had a solid ache in the back of my head, my chest hurt like hell and my eyebrow felt sore and swollen. Those pain pills the ER doctor had given me, were only to be taken with food. I was starving, then I remembered why. I had thrown up everything from yesterday outside the emergency room. I went to the toilet and urinated. As expected, that extremely vital department was in good shape, no pain. I gingerly put on my robe, grabbed the pills, and hobbled down to the breakfast room. Mother probably wasn't up yet due to her checking on me and I figured even if DeForrest was, it wouldn't matter. She wouldn't be speaking to me now or for days. Worse — things would never be the same between us.

Then I figured out how she was going to communion yet doing those increasing stages of petting. Moose had talked about some Canon Law during the first couple of weeks of school. There needs to be a "grave reason" and if she started not going to communion, Mother, being Mother, would figure it all out quickly. That would be extremely grave enough for DeForrest. She was utterly infatuated and totally under his control — convinced she and that Prick were so completely in love with each other. Our mother would put an abrupt and final end to it. That would make it "critically" grave. Given the "no opportunity to confess," she would need to "make an act of perfect contrition then go to confession as soon as possible" — like Monday at school. Evidently, every Monday for weeks. Oh God. My poor Little Dee.

As I walked into the kitchen, I waited for her chill. Unbelievably, DeForrest hurried over to me. She had been crying — considerably. Eyes red and swollen, face puffy, nose red. Appeared totally ghastly. She tried to speak but could only choke out, "Rich ... sorry ... last night." She sniffed deeply, "What I ... what I called you ... didn't mean any ..." A few tears fell down her cheeks as she continued stammering, "Richeeee ... you have to forgive me ... you **have to**." She began to wail loudly and her tears increased their flow rapidly. She flung herself down at the breakfast table and buried her head in her arms, moaning "Oh God ... **please** ... **for** ... **give** ..."

I really felt like shit, even without the pain of the beating. I grabbed a dish towel, painfully pulled a chair next to her and lifted her head up gently. I began to wipe her tears away to ease *her* pain, "Of course, I forgive you." I kissed both her cheeks.

My poor Little Dee ... my baby sister. ... ... "Please don't cry. You will always be My Little Dee. I **will always** love you. No matter **what you do,** no matter **what you say,** no matter **what happens. Nothing** will ever come between us. **I won't let it**!"

She reacted to this with even more intense bawling, but now burying her face in my shoulder. After a long time of crying and sniffling, she settled down somewhat to say, "I'm sorry ... so very sorry ... you were badly beaten up ... my damn naiveté. My childish fantasies ... about love. That I knew how ... to clearly handle guys ... even older ones. That I knew I was in love. That I knew what I was doing, trusting that ... that ... as we *repeatedly* did all those intima..." This caused her loud crying to recur and tears flooded her cheeks again. I affectionately wiped her face again and wrapped my arm around her to hold her against my left shoulder. After some time, she kissed my sore eye and cheek a couple of times then hugged me which hurt. I didn't care.

"Richey Rue ... you always have protected me ... now even against myself. **Thank you. I love you so much,** Richey Rue."

"And I will always, **always** love you, My Little Dee."

We kissed each other on the lips for a long, heartfelt moment to firmly confirm our reconciliation and even with my pain, we embraced again for a time. Her tears were now of happiness as was my broad, beaming smile. We both felt elated to be best friends again. She finally regained her normal composure, then said as she pointed at my chest, my eyebrow, then made a circling gesture for the back of my head, "Do you hurt a lot? I know I caused all of this pain for you. I'm deeply sorry." She began sniffing again, "Richie, I can't tell you how much."

"Yeah, I do hurt, but what's important is that **you** are okay. I'll be fine. I heal quickly, ya know. Remember that time last year in Omaha? Well, okay, twice. Ha! Don't worry. Everything has worked out. Really! Did you sleep at all last night?"

This brighten her demeanor considerably as she wiped away the residue of her tears, "Richey Rue, you are the absolute best brother. Yeah, some ... maybe a few hours ... It's ok. Are you hungry? Mother got up a while ago and just left to pick up Aunt Danae at the Union Station. I could fix us breakfast, maybe bacon and eggs? Toast?"

"Oh yeah, Aunt Danae, I completely forgot. Yeah, I'm starving, that would be great, My Little Dee. Please."

We hugged once more and I tried to get more comfortable at the table, then DeeDee gave me some orange juice for my pills and made our breakfast. We talked while we ate, even laughing at times. After we finished, I started to tire. She offered to help me up the stairs, but I didn't need any. My Little Dee stayed with me after I crawled back into bed.

❈❈❈❈❈❈❈❈❈❈❈❈❈❈❈❈❈❈❈❈

Richelieu never once doubted the beating he took wasn't worth it, He and DeForrest became much closer;

He never asked and only some months later he was told just a small part of what was said in the very explicit mother and daughter talk;

DeForrest's extremely deep-seated feelings of a love — though misconstrued —emboldened her to engage in those intimate activities; Then she was forced to realize she was being despicably used and cruelly betrayed; This incident and its brutal lecture taught DeForrest about males in a vile, odious way; In future, she became much shrewder, more astute and highly selective if she decided to go out with a guy or continue with future dates;

However, Richelieu could still sense she had recurring thoughts from this treachery which disturbed and upset her — she continued to suffer

❈❈❈❈❈❈❈❈❈❈❈❈❈❈❈❈❈❈❈❈

I could only imagine the kind of night Mother must have had. I knew she couldn't have slept well, if at all. Had to be a disturbing and agonizing long night, especially getting up to check on me those times after having a lengthy and excruciatingly painful talk with DeeDee. When she and Aunt Danae came home, both Graces came to look in on me. Mother appeared completely exhausted. My little Grace was still baby-sitting me but happily joined our mother to go into the master bedroom.

My aunt gave me two big kisses, checked me over again, worrying exactly like my mother had about my injuries. I lied, telling her I was too tough to hurt. She didn't believe me, telling me I was always such a bullshitter. Then she leaned over me, tenderly caressing my cheek, saying, "Your father would be proud. Very proud! It's exactly what he would have done." She pulled back to look at me then kissed me again. "Oh my Forrest! My Little Forrest!" She started to cry, so I quickly asked about her trip. Wiping away a tear or two, she told me she and her girlfriends did have a terrific time. The Grand Ole Opry was fabulous but Jerry Lee Lewis was a little too wild, yet still performed a great show. We talked for a little while, then Aunt Danae said I should rest. She needed to unpack and maybe rest a little herself. I could tell she knew about DeeDee. And it bothered her greatly. So did my condition. I now realized she thought of us as more than niece and nephew. A lot more. We thought of her as more than our Aunt. Much more.

****

Early that afternoon, I really needed to get some more pain pills. Mother said she would go to the pharmacy for me, but I just laughed at her, said I was fine. But I wasn't. I hurt, really and truly hurt. She was completely exhausted and certainly didn't need to run my errand.

While the prescription was being filled, I felt strong enough to walk up the street to Ball's for a box or two of Eskimo Pies. Slowly moving down an aisle, I suddenly saw **HER** from the back — the tall, slender, golden brown-haired goddess in a pair of tight jeans.

God ... Oh God! There SHE is! THE best looking girl ever. Golden brown hair. Incredibly, wonderfully tall. Oh God those legs ... must go on for miles. Look at that butt! Oooh fantastic!

Can't just introduce myself looking like I had just escaped from Dante's Inferno. Damn it, may never see her again for weeks, even months. How to approach her? Oh, please turn aro — SHIT!

My wish was granted. The instant she turned around, I ran into an eight-foot display of Tide, knocking down some of the detergent boxes. I started to replace the boxes but it was excruciating when I bent over. The Goddess immediately came over and offered, "Could you use some help?"

"I think I can manage," I groaned painfully. "Thank you for off—" as I dropped the box.

"Here, I'll help you," she said and replaced that one and the other three boxes.

"Thank you. I was looking for Eskimo Pies."

The Goddess happily pointed, "They are over in the next aisle. In the same place they were the last time I saw you here."

I started to laugh but it hurt like hell, "Right. Forgot which aisle. Thank you for replacing the Tide. I'm Rich Marlowe."

"You're welcome, Rich. I'm Autumn Knight."

"That's a pretty name. Unique too." ... ... *God, please help me. I sound like an idiot.*

"Thank you. Were you in an accident?"

"Ran into a door." ... ... *Actually, a helluva beating.*

"Was it a revolving door?" She started to snickered but stopped quickly. "Oh, sorry, your injuries aren't funny. They must really hurt."

"Oh, it's okay. Only hurts when I laugh," I said trying to make light of it. ... ... *Or talk, eat, breathe ...certainly to bend down.*

"I'm a Junior at Prescott, but I haven't seen you in the halls there."

"No, we moved to Wyandotte three months ago from Omaha. I'm a Junior too. St. Ignatius, the Jesuit High School."

As I took a needed breath, she smiled teasingly, "Oh, **I know** all about St. Ignatius."

"Really, I didn't think many guys and girls here in Wyandotte, especially Prescott, knew much about it."

"Very true. But my older sister is engaged to be engaged to a guy who graduated from St. Nate's las year. Not sure what that really means."

"It does sound serious."

"Oh, **that** it is. Look, I would love to talk with you more, but I need to get home and get ready."

For a hot date. Lucky guy. I'm already jealous. ... ... "Could I call you sometime, maybe meet for a coke some Saturday afternoon? I promise I will look much better and be less clumsy. I would like to talk with you more ... but maybe ... you're going stea dy."

She smiled a beautiful, wonderful smile and her light brown eyes sparkled as she declared, "I won't go steady. My number is Finley 3-1416. Call me, maybe next Saturday afternoon we can meet."

"Terrific, I will call you this week."
"Don't you want to write my number down?"
"No need."
"Really? Well, don't forget your Eskimo Pies." She laughed merrily and began to push her cart to the checkout counter.
"Thanks again for your help," I called after her.
She turned, smiling beautifully in her departure.
Thank You, O God. Thank You for sending me the Goddess again. This is what Helen of Troy must have look liked.

I gingerly went into the next aisle and picked up the Eskimo Pies. When I finally made it to the checkout counter, a long line had quickly formed. For a moment, there was Autumn striding past the front windows. I could only gawk.

That bend for the Tide box really cost me. I put my Eskimo Pies in with the frozen peas, deciding to come back since I was having some serious pain. I sat in a booth in Ryan's Pharmacy, quickly took the pain pills then ate a couple Three Musketeers bars and drank a coke. I rested there, sipping another coke, fantasizing about my golden brown-haired Goddess until I felt strong enough to leave and go back to Ball's. All the way home, I continued my daydreams.

✣✣✣✣✣✣✣✣✣✣✣✣✣✣✣✣✣✣✣✣✣✣✣✣✣✣

Those wonderful visions abruptly ended because when I walked through the front door, I telephoned the Chicken Shit Cocksucker. He was shocked.

"Shut up and listen to me, Asshole! If I hear anything about your 'activities' with my sister, whether they are actual or just your warped wishful thinking, **you will be damn sorry**."

Immediately Bush was condescending, "What are you going to do, beat me up like last night? Guess you need to be reminded **you're** the one who ended up going to the hospital, not me, Shit Head. Oh, and how is **your head**, **Shit**?" He laughed nastily.

"Head's fine, but you're not listening, Prick. I'll go to Monsignor O'Reilly, tell him the full story, including your Missouri activities, in the confessional to prove to him I'm telling the truth. Or outside of the box so he doesn't get hung up on the seal. I don't give a God damn which. His opinion of you will drop like a rock. Probably throw your perverted ass off Cathedral's choir. You can explain that to your parents. Oh, speaking of your parents, I will tell them exactly what you were planning while they were out of town. See if you can explain that one, too. Think I'll add Sister Cecilia ... good friend of my mother's ... so you don't go around seducing naive, young girls at McKenna like Monica Matthews."

"You God damn, blackmailing, fucking son of a bitch!"

"You might see it that way. I see it as defending my sister's reputation from your sick, perverted mind. I **will do anything** to protect her! You understand Asshole, **anything**! Well, Prick, what's it going to be? Do we have a deal?"

"Nothing to the Monsignor or my parents? Or that God damn bitch nun?"

"As long as I don't hear **any of your shit** about DeForrest."

"All right Marlowe! ... You Bastard ... You motherfu—," slamming the phone in my ear.

Now I needed to talk with Mother. Hearing someone in the kitchen, I hoped it was her. While I put my Eskimo pies in the refrigerator, she glanced up from the sink, looking drained and even more exhausted than when I left. "Hey, Mother, is DeForrest here? How about Aunt Danièle?"

"No, DeeDee's over at Karen's. Danièle's taking a nap. Why?" There was panic in her voice, "Oh my God! Are you feeling worse?"

"I'm fine! We need to talk a little more about last night."

"Holy Mary, Mother of God! Now what?" She sighed deeply. Her shoulders sagged heavily, looking like fifty pounds of more shit had been dumped on her. "I thought that was over. Finished."

"**It is now**. I just made a deal with the Devil."

"Forrest, **what** in God's Name did you do?"

I told her about my telephone conversation with Bush and how I blackmailed him. She wasn't pleased at all with my method but I said at least it would protect DeeDee's reputation. Sternly, she admonished me, "The end never justifies the means."

"You forgot about the exception when dealing with the scum of the earth."

Ignoring my rationalization, she said, "DeForrest and I were truly concerned about her reputation but we just accepted she would just have to live with whatever came out. But, this ... which I don't approve of ... will greatly minimize any rumors about her. **You cannot tell her.** For her, it was over and done with last night. She is in terrible pain but she has begun to heal, especially since you forgave her so completely and so quickly. That was extremely kind, very loving of you, Forrest. And **very needed** for her. She really looks up to you." My mother stood on her tiptoes to kiss my cheek, very tenderly.

I shrugged, vowing, "She will always be My Little Dee, regardless of whatever happens. I *will always do* anything for her."

"I know you will, Forrest. For me, it's over and done *right now*. Only Danae knows everything, *every detail*. I told her the full story on our way back from the Union Station. She will never mention it. DeForrest knows not to tell **anyone** the full truth, even Karen. The story will be, 'they already had broken up as he was too domineering and you overheard his insulting comments about her, lost your temper and hit him'. Forrest, none of us are ever going to talk about this again."

"We won't. *C'est fini.*" [It is finished]

Then I broke into a big smile, but curtailed it quickly, my face still hurt. Eagerly I explained, "Remember that fabulous looking girl of my dreams I saw at Ball's Supermarket a couple of months ago? Well, I saw her again. I didn't know the next time I would, so I introduced myself, injuries and all. Her name is Autumn Knight and she's a junior at Prescott. She is incredibly beautiful with long golden brown hair and shimmering light brown eyes. Virtually as tall as I am. She's slender and just so ... so statuesque like a Greek goddess. Oooh, such a terrific smile."

"Well, Richie, she sounds wonderful. But why are you always attracted to Protestant girls? That jealous, childish one who giggled a lot ... uh, Bonnie Jo and that crude ... **so crude smoker** ... **that Charlotte** ... both Methodists. Then your summer of '62 redhead ... uh ... Janet who you called Rusty ... Congregationalist. That ... **that** Linda is Lutheran. And the quiet Ukrainian girl ... Olga ... *should have been* Russian Orthodox. I assume your Sheila of last night is something Non-Catholic. Why can't you just find a nice Catholic girl? From McKenna or Sagesse or some more girls from St. Catherine's or even try St. Mary Magdalene's? Just a nice, wholesome Catholic girl. That's all I ever ask."

"I didn't like any of those Missouri girls … Antoinette was stuck on another guy, Brenda was stuck on herself, Gloria was stuck with being completely crazy. Caroline is stuck with a heavy cigarette habit and a bad temper. Karen isn't stuck on anything. She's just immature. Don't worry about last night's date, who is C of E. She's stuck on being a mean, spiteful witch! And you better get use to some Protestantism … I'm going to marry Autumn."

"Maybe we should go back to Bethany and get your head checked again."

We both laughed, and my chest rebelled. Mother looked even more haggard.

"Go take a nap! Please? You have everything back on course again."

"Okay, in a bit. I'll go to bed." Ignoring her, I turned her around and prodded her out of the kitchen, kept pushing her through the living room to the stairs. I followed her up the staircase into her room. I pulled back the bedspread and covers as she removed her shoes. I covered her up, kissed her cheek, wishing her, "Sweet Dreams". As I closed her door, she said, "Thank you, my Little Forrest."

Even with the pills, I still hurt a little, so I went to my room and took a nap myself. Before I dozed off, I replayed **"the meeting"** in my mind for about the tenth time, realizing something I overlooked during the previous nine. Autumn *remembered* that the first time we saw each other, I was buying Eskimo pies. She had been seriously *watching me, too.*

****

On Monday at St. Ignatius, when I was asked what happened to me, I just varied Autumn's answer. "Just a door. A revolving door". The guys would smile knowingly.

I went to confession and told Fr. Fitz everything. He told me I was a good brother and son. He blessed me and said my beating was more than enough penance, but to say one Glory Be and be especially nice to my sister and mother.

After confession, I met Jack for lunch and only told him that three guys were making sluttish, vulgar remarks about my sister after she had broken up with one of them. This was the result. He said when I wanted to settle up with the bastards, he would be there with me — he knew the two of us could take out these three assholes. I believed we could and asked him to keep it between us. He said of course. Then I delightfully changed the subject to tell him all about Autumn.

****

I could only wait as long as Tuesday night to call her. Sunday, I had daydreamed about her constantly, especially at Mass when the priest discussed angels and their role in God's plan. I had a pretty good idea about two already — including my little sister. All day in school Monday and Tuesday, I couldn't get Autumn off my mind. I picked up the receiver to dial her number and my palms were sweaty. It was like meeting a hot, good-looking girl's parents for the first time. I dialed and the phone was picked up on the second ring. A man's voice said, "Hello, Franklin Knight here".

"Is Autumn there, please?"

A very disappointed voice said, "Yes, just a moment."

I heard a muffled 'Autumn' and about eight or ten seconds later, "Hello?"

"Hi Autumn, it's Rich Marlowe from Saturday at Ball's. How've you been?"

"Oh, Hi Rich. Look, I can only talk a sec. My father is expecting a long distance call."

"Ah, then ... would you like to meet somewhere Saturday afternoon for a coke or something?"

"Sure, I'd really love to. Let's meet at The Hangout at 2 o'clock. It's a malt and record shop at 18th and Central, real close to Ball's. Oh, I hope you are feeling much better."

"Oh yeah, I'm a lot better."

"Glad to hear *that*. Look, I'm sorry I have to hang up so quickly. But I'll see you Saturday."

"Till Saturday at two."

"Great! Bye."

"Bye." ... ... *Saturday! ... Saturday! ... Saat tuur-daay! OOOHHH WWWOOOWWW!*

****

With the Quarter ending last week, I knew I would be receiving my grades soon. When I walked in the front door and past my mother in her study, I yelled hello. Then saw she was waving an envelope in her hand.

"Your grades came today."

"So how did I do?"

"You tell me," and handed it to me to open.

My grades were almost excellent, but Latin had cost me dearly:

Religion	85	English	92
Français	89	Advanced Algebra	92
Ancient Civilizations	96	Latin III	80

I gave the machine printed sheet back to my mother and within seconds, she said, "An 89.0, excellent except for Latin. Why so much trouble?"

"I just don't understand it that well, certainly not like DeeDee."

"And speaking of my lovely linguistic lady, here she is."

"Hi Mother," and she went over to her, kissed her cheek and picked up her grade envelope. "I know they are all excellent, well, except for Geometry."

She quickly scanned it and handed it to our mother who said after another quick interval, "Well done Angel, 91.4 ... First Honors. Your Achilles heel is Geometry, just like Richie's is Latin."

"How do you calculate those averages so quickly?"

"I will show you my trick, but not today. We are going out to dinner and will meet Danae at the Indian Head to celebrate. Oh, I am going out with Rex ... Friday night. He had to reschedule last week's date."

"Is he going to manage your money, Mother?" I asked.

She smiled and said, "Only some of it. He thinks he is getting a much larger portion than he really is. We won't tell anybody, though," and she winked.

****

Mother was running a little late. Aunt Danae had already left with some girlfriends. DeeDee was going to stay in her room until either Hell had frozen over or thirty minutes after Rex and my mother left. He and I sat in the living room and I said my mother had got caught up in pats and culls. Something like that.

Rex laughed, then said condescendingly, "They're 'puts and calls'. You wouldn't understand how they work."

Well, Hell no ... if no one explains it to you. Dee has the right idea. YOU ARE AN ASSHOLE!

Then he started bragging about Kansas City Chiefs football and on the "hush-hush," he might have had a silent but effective part in their move here from Dallas last May. He had season tickets close to the fifty-yard line. When I didn't bite on that, Rex moved on. "I assume your good-looking, fashion conscious sister is already on a date."

"Nope, she's here. Upstairs in her room."

"I'm surprised! A girl as attractive as she is with no date on Friday night. It's **too bad** for such a gorgeous girl to be home! But I'd certainly like to say hi to her."

"She's studying for an exam." I easily lied to the jerk, "Said no interruptions." ... ... *What's* **too bad** *is that you're here.*

My mother finally came in, apologizing for being late. She was dressed in a shamrock green suit which I was sure was new, looking wonderful as always. She laughed, saying, "You children don't wait up for me."

As I went upstairs, I thought about teasing DeeDee concerning Rex's comments, but quickly realized they wouldn't be funny. So seriously, I did tell her about what Rex had said about her, especially wanting to see her. She gagged and mimicked like she was going to vomit, ranting, "Barf! Barf! Yuck! Double Yuck!"

The next morning Mother said she had had a good time with Rex and they were going to go out again sometime soon. I had joined DeeDee. I didn't like the guy's attitude and she didn't like his 'etiquette'. Maybe the date would be later than sooner. It turned out it was for two weeks later.

****

I arrived at The Hangout about 1:45 and spotted an empty corner booth. I had on one of my best sweaters — a navy cashmere crewneck over a blue button-down dress shirt, my best jeans and polished loafers. About ten minutes later, Autumn came in with two other girls and I stood up out of politeness and to get her attention. All three started walking towards me, I noticed the other two were really checking me over. They were the best-looking trio of girls I had ever seen in my life. A redhead, a blonde, and a golden brown-haired one named Autumn. The blonde said something to her, giggled, while the redhead smiled pleasantly at me and waved which I gladly returned. They parted and went to join some other girls and guys.

Oh God, does she look fantastic!

As Autumn approached, I paid close attention to what she was wearing — a caramel-colored turtleneck sweater which modestly displayed her wonderfully shaped medium breasts with matching long slacks and a slight kitten heel on her T-strap shoes. A memory flash of Professor DeForrest's lecture on ladies' shoes with demonstrations had crossed through my mind. When she stopped about a foot away, I gazed into those light-brown eyes, accented by light-brown eyeshadow and peach lipstick.

"Hi, Autumn. You look really great."

"Well, thank you, Rich. You look much better than you did last Saturday. Are you feeling much better too, I hope?"

As we sat down, I said, "Oh yeah, much. It wasn't that bad. My chest and the place on the back of my head are still a little sore. Got the stitches out of my eyebrow yesterday and it's Tuesday for my head. At least it's not baseball season."

"That's great. Oh, my girlfriends wanted to see if the legend is true about St. Ignatius guys."

"Awwww ... no different than Prescott guys."

"Maybe so. But Ginny, the blonde, wanted me to ask you if all the guys at St. Nate's are as good-looking as you," she teased. I could feel my face reddening up a little. "So you're going to play baseball for the Hawks?"

"Yes, I have strong hopes of starting. Had a really good fall practice week and a great season in the A league in Omaha. That's the most competitive league in that city."

"Let me guess. I bet you played first base for the Ravens."

"Yes, I played first base. No, I played for the Cardinals **against** the Ravens. Are you psychic or something? How do you know about the A League?"

"No, I'm not psychic. A couple of years ago, a Raven named 'Nevermore' told me."

Poe makes no sense in this context. But how does she know about the A League?

Before I could quiz her more, the soda jerk/waiter came to take our orders. We both picked chocolate shakes.

"Are you able to dance?"

"Only slow dances."

"I'll be right back." She went over to the jukebox, made a selection and put a nickel in the slot.

An oldie, *Moon River,* began to play and I moved out of the booth to a waiting Autumn on the dance floor section of the shop. I put my arm around to bring her in close but not too close, and we began to dance.

"You're a good dancer, even with your injuries."

"It's really about who your partner is." She giggled.

We drank our shakes, talked mostly about school and the courses we were taking. Autumn was enrolled in the Arts & Science track, taking English, Advanced Algebra & Trig, U. S. History, Accounting I, Study Hall and a new class, Interior Design which she thought was terrific. She made the honor roll with a 1.4 average. I told her I had just missed First Honors because of Latin but still had an 89 average. In converting to a common measure, we decided hers was an A- and mine was a B+, but she insisted mine was harder since I was taking a sixth course. We talked about what college plans we had after high school, some of our dreams, our likes and dislikes and a lot more. We finished our shakes and danced twice more — *In Dreams* by Roy Orbison and The Beach Boys' *Surfer Girl.*

"Rich, these two and half hours were terrific. The time went by so quickly. But I've got to leave."

"Sure," I said deflated. "I'll drive you home, if you give me directions. You probably have a lot to do before tonight."

She laughed delightfully, "Oh yeah, after I help make dinner tonight, I'm washing my hair. Maybe working on my term paper."

"You mean you don't have a date? On a Saturday night? I can't believe that! No guy asked you?"

"Well, two guys did, but I was waiting for this one guy to ask me. Never did."

"Wow, that guy sure is a king-size idiot."

She widely grinned, "That 'king-size idiot' is *you*."

"**Me**? Really? You would go out with **me**? **Tonight**?"

"Of course."

"Where do want to go? I'll take you anywhere. Anywhere at all!"

"How about the movies? *Tom Jones* is playing at the Electric and I would love to see it."

"Great, what time should I pick you up?"

"How about six-thirty?"

"Six-thirty it is and I can take you home now if you would like."

"I would like *later*," she snickered, "but I should go now."

****

When she answered the door, I immediately gushed, "You look wonderful."

"Silly, it's the same outfit I had on two hours ago."

"Oh, I know it is and *you still look wonderful*."

It was now her turn to slightly blush. "Well, thank you. Again. C'mon into the living room. I want you to meet my parents."

"Mom, Dad, this is Rich Marlowe. Rich, these are my parents."

I shook hands with Mr. Knight and smiled at Mrs. Knight who remained seated. I said, "It's very nice to meet both of you." He was tall and medium build, nice-looking. Had a confident demeanor. She looked like once she could have been attractive but had let herself go. She was overweight, wore very little makeup, frumpily dressed, out-of-style hairdo. A stark contrast to my mother and aunt.

Mr. Knight asked, "Are you Forrest Marlowe's son?"

"Yes sir, he was my father."

"Married a Wyandotte girl, Genevieve Richelieu, I believe."

"Yes sir, my mother. We moved here from Omaha about three months ago."

"I was very sorry to hear about your father. He was top drawer. None better. I knew him a little from my business. We do some work for the government as a defense contractor. My company is Sunflower Industries."

"Thank you, sir, for kindly remembering him."

"How is your mother? Val, you remember her, everyone called her GeeGee. Very pretty, had a cute younger sister. Uh … Deirdre."

"Oh yes, the Richelieus who lived over on Tauromee. Are they all doing well?"

"My grandparents have retired to Naples in Florida. My mother is doing fine and my Aunt Danièle is living with us, doing fine also, working at Ellis and Mullins. Thank you for asking. There is my younger sister, DeForrest Danièle or DeeDee. She is a sophomore at Notre Dame de Sagesse. I go to St. Ignatius College Prep."

"Oh we know of St. Ignatius, it's a *very good* Catholic school," said Mrs. Knight. "And you live in the Hoel edition, correct?"

"Yes, it's a great school and we live on the west side of the subdivision." … … *But it's Jesuit Catholic.*

"Mom and Dad, we really need to leave to go to the show."

"Sure, of course you do." Her mother stood, then moved towards the TV.

"Certainly nice to meet both of you."

"You too Rich. Have fun tonight kids," her father concluded. Her mother just smiled and turned on the TV set.

"We will. Good night, ma'am, sir."

As we walked to the car, Autumn said, "I had heard your father was dead. I'm so very sorry."

"Thanks for saying that. He was an Air Force major. A military advisor in Viet Nam."

"That makes life pretty difficult at times, I would imagine."

I didn't say anything in response. She was also quiet for a few long moments and finally asked, "Hey, you said at The Hangout this afternoon you would take me anywhere I wanted to go."

"I sure did."

"I would like to go to your house and meet your Three Graces ... as you called them then ... if that's okay with you."

"Sure, it's great. What about the movie?"

"Oh, it will be playing next weekend and you can take me then, that is ... if you want to."

"Of course I do! Friday or Saturday night?"

"Both nights!" and she laughed.

"Let me get this straight. You will go out with me on both Friday **and** Saturday nights?"

"Of course. I knew there was a reason you were in the A class at St. Nate's."

"Now how did you know that?"

"I know Claudia Carson."

"Wait a minute! *You've* done some homework on me."

"Why wouldn't I? During which, I also found out a little about your injuries."

Maybe I can find out how much shit is floating around about DeeDee.

"Last Monday morning, Judy and I *just happen* to eavesdrop on Sheila Rhodes ... your date for that previous Friday ... telling some of her clique all about 'a brawl' her 'Neanderthal date from St. Ignatius started over some fast and easy girl—' "

I interrupted, quickly flaring, "**My sister's** not some— "

"Oh, I know, I know." Autumn cut back in, good-naturedly, "After her date 'obscenely' flirted and danced with '*that* chain smoking ... uh ... uh "tramp" Caroline Cunningham.' So I dug a little deeper after school on Monday by talking with Pamela Parker and I found out this guy was dating your sister, made some very nasty comments about her so you decked him. There were three of them. You know Rich, those are really bad odds."

"Nah, if one hadn't hit me with a bottle, I would have won. I pretty much had taken care of one of them." Hoping for the best, I warily asked, "What kind of comments about my sister?"

"Oh, the usual garbage guys put out after they get shot down or the girl breaks up with them. Of course, only very little of it is ever true. You know ... like she's a lifeless make out or cold or she's stuck on herself or she's a big tease or not that interesting or smart and on and on ... ad nauseam. Twice, I've even heard some stuff about me and I just laughed it off. Anybody that knows me, certainly knows none of it's true. Oh, and I don't think smoking and flirting make your dance partner, Caroline Cunningham, a so-called 'tramp'."

Fairly inaccurate on the facts ... but so far, so good for Dee. Poor Caroline ... completely forgot about her. ... ... "But what about baseball in Omaha, the A league? How did you know about that? You couldn't have checked on me with someone from there."

"Remember I told you my sister Summer is semi-betrothed ... whatever *that* means ... to a St. Ignatius's alum?"

"Sure, I remember."

"He played first base in your A league for the Ravens three summers ago. He liked Poe's *The Raven* so much, he was nicknamed 'Nevermore'. So I guessed first base, because you have that same cocky baseball attitude that he has which says, 'I can catch anything'. My second guess was outfielder. I could only remember the Ravens, so that had to be my choice."

"Well, Miss Sherlocka Holmes, you make it sound so easy. Great, both Friday and Saturday night, it is. Could I ask you a personal question?"

"You can ask me anything. I just may or may not answer it."

"You said last Saturday afternoon you *won't* go steady. Correct?"

"Yes, I said that. All my girlfriends go steady constantly, almost always after only one date. It lasts anywhere from three weeks to maybe a month or so. Then they break up to start all over again, continually switching from one guy to the next. I would rather play the field, you know, date a whole bunch of guys to decide if I like any of them enough to go on a second or even a third date."

"And this works out?"

"So far, I have dated mostly seniors, one sophomore ... ugh, some juniors, but lately college freshmen. Never has been interesting enough to date beyond a second or third one."

"Was The Hangout this afternoon a date?"

"Yes."

"Tonight makes two. So next Friday **and** Saturday would be three **and** four."

"You, Rich, are such a mathematical wiz. Is Rich short for Richard?"

"Rich is short for Richelieu, a middle name, but everyone calls me Rich, except at St. Nate's. It's Lou there. I hate asking this for fear of jinxing myself completely, but we haven't had two full dates, yet you know I will make it past the three date threshold of failure where every other guy has washed out."

"Sometimes it just takes a longer time to figure out there is nothing really substantial there." She grinned, "Or perhaps, only rarely ... *very rarely*, it takes an extremely short time for one to know there is something exceptionally worthwhile pursuing."

"I love your logic. Here we are."

I parked, turned to face her to ask, "Autumn Knight, will you go steady with me?"

"Yes, Richelieu Marlowe, I will most definitely go steady with you."

"About 2:30 on September 14th, you were in Ball's Supermarket wearing a red and white polka dot blouse and red, nearly short shorts. You with your wondrous long legs were out of this world. I absolutely wanted to do this then, but I will certainly do it now ... if you let me." So I leaned over and kissed her, then I kissed her again. A lot longer. I was not on the planet Earth anymore.

"Thank you, Rich. Did that hurt?"

"Maybe a little, but you can kiss it later and make it better." We both laughed as I pulled out my handkerchief and wiped her enticing lipstick from my lips as she redid hers.

I unlocked the door and there were DeForrest and Karen in the living room listening to records, practicing their dance moves and giggling. When they saw me with Helen of Troy, they became instantly silent, even turning off the record player. My mother came into the living room from the kitchen, saw the two of us and said, "You must be Autumn. I am Rich's mother, Mrs. Marlowe." She was followed closely by Aunt Danièle, who was really giving Autumn the once-over, then the twice-over.

"Hello Mrs. Marlowe. It is very nice to meet you."

I finally rebounded saying, "This is my Aunt, Danièle Richelieu. The tall, smiling one is my sister, DeForrest. The short, smiling one is her best friend Karen Reynolds."

The girls both said virtually in unison, "Hi, Autumn."

"Hi to both of you, DeForrest and Karen," and Autumn sort of waved at them, followed by, "Hello Miss Richelieu, it is very nice to meet you also."

"Nice to meet you too, Autumn. Well, Richie," my Aunt said, "you certainly made us wait long enough to meet her."

That slightly embarrassed me and I started to say we only had our first date this afternoon but didn't.

"I thought you two were going to the movies?" my mother added curiously.

"Oh we were, but I asked Rich to bring me here to meet all of you. I think you know my parents from some time ago … Franklin and Valentina Knight, oh … her maiden name was Jefferies."

My aunt answered, "Sure, I remember them. Don't you, Gi Gi? Frank lived over on 14th Street. The Jefferies were on Elizabeth."

"Sure, sure Danae. I remember now."

"Well Autumn, would you like to see the rest of the house? It's only messy in Richie's room where we aren't allowed without permission."

"Oh, that would be wonderful, I would love to. The Tudor exterior looks splendid."

Richie! From both of them? All I need now is for DeeDee to chip in. Oh God, Autumn probably thinks that name is for a five-year-old.

This is unbelievable … like a dream. I'm going steady with Helen of Troy.

Yep, Helen of Troy … H-O-T … yes she's so hot, she's scorching.

I know exactly what I am going to do.

As all five of them continued touring the second floor, I held back in my room, went to my antique box and found what I needed under some old ticket stubs.

When we all went back to sit in the living room, Autumn said, "You have a very lovely, wonderful house, Mrs. Marlowe. You have decorated so well in such a short time. Your color schemes are brilliant. I especially love your study. It is very functional, but certainly creative in its design."

"Why thank you, Autumn."

"I have always loved the houses in the Hoel edition. I'm going to major in interior design and architecture in college."

For the next hour, the conversation was like Autumn had known my girls for years. I knew DeeDee was completely enthralled with her. Rarely she would encounter a girl taller than she is. None had ever possessed the looks, the air of total self-confidence and charm, *that* authentic ultra-coolness of Autumn's. Karen joined her in her admiration. My aunt was enjoying her company immensely. Even my Mother was quite friendly, warmer to her than she had ever been with any of my girlfriends — first or following times.

This was not exactly what I envisioned our first evening date would be like at all, but then again, I never dreamt I would end up going steady with this dazzling girl after less than one hour of this date coupled with the two hour and forty minute one this afternoon. She simply seemed to think and see things so much differently from all the rest of any girls, even ones I liked a lot. Just so different, so unique. I sure never saw the "going steady" as even a slight possibility in one day. If I were lucky, maybe in about three to four weeks — probably longer.

About 8 o'clock, Autumn said, "It's been so wonderful to meet and talk with each of you, but Rich is probably feeling we should go to one of the hang-outs." She particularly said individual good-byes with variations of how nice to meet you to each as we left, especially my mother.

We drove over to Zesto's to get a couple of cokes, some burgers and fries. Luckily, a couple in a beautiful red and white '57 Vette was just pulling out from a great parking space. I backed in and we watched the continuous Saturday night parade of cars which cruised through, all wanting to see and be seen. Judging by the colors attached to some of the antennas, most were from Prescott or McKenna, but some were from Wellington. Quite a few prom garters and pairs of fuzzy dice — usually in school colors — would hang from guys' rearview mirrors, sometimes a necklace, even an occasional St. Christopher's medal or a rare white wedding garter.

More than a few times, Autumn leaned over to honk the horn and wave at friends and acquaintances with their dates. I recognized Ginny, the gorgeous blonde who had come into The Hangout with Autumn. She waved wildly, made her hand into a phone, held it up to her ear, then plainly mouthed, 'call me'. Another time, it was a car with a double date — the two girls were in Autumn's clique. When they saw us, they started laughing and made kissing gestures. While we ate and watched the cavalcade, we simply laughed and talked.

After about an hour, we decided to go. As I flipped my lights on to indicate we were leaving, a couple of girls in a cherry '56 black Ford Fairlane convertible signaled they wanted our spot. The driver was an extremely good-looking, black-haired girl — probably twenty or so. The blonde was terrifically gorgeous too.

Earlier, I had noticed on the island opposite us, there were a bunch of older guys either standing around or leaning on the trunk or up against the doors of two 1950s Chevies — a red Deluxe Coupe and a brown Business Coupe. Two of the guys had really been giving Autumn the eye for the last five or ten minutes, obviously talking about her. She was quickly forgotten as the whole gang hastily moved toward the two girls.

Each guy yelling excitingly, each trying be noticed and to be acknowledged.

"Hey Carlotta! Heard you were back."

"Sure missed you! Still a knockout."

"Yowza Teri! You beautiful blonde! You're back too?"

"The wind's caressing that blond hair ... like I'd do."

A nearby carhop quickly picked up our tray. As I slowly pulled out, both girls were smiling appealingly at them. The black-haired Carlotta loudly encouraged them, "Oh you marvelous sweet talkers! Only until Christmas! Back west to Hays, then the real west ... LA! Until then, you've got me."

Teri, the blonde, seductively added, "Ooohh boys! It's been way *too long* since we've seen you! Just here on some weekends this semester until Christmas vacation. Definitely for semester break after those last two weeks and finals. When I'm in town, I'll look for you."

The guys, still talking and shouting over each other, swarmed the waiting convertible which slowed me considerably, otherwise I could have easily tapped one of them since their attention was definitely not on an exiting Galaxie.

"When are the Ladies of the Lake going to dance for us again?"

"God, when you two did your act to *The Stripper*! The crowning moment of the summer before last! The Lake will never be the same!"

"But you kept your clothes **ON**! That was a **shame**!" They all laughed bawdily and the girls agreed with alluring grins.

Autumn, however, didn't see any of this as she was laughing and talking, saying a long goodbye to both couples in the DeSoto Adventurer parked next to us. The girls, Melody and Wendy, were the ones from Autumn's clique who had passed through twice earlier.

No wonder those two babes attracted a crowd of guys. Both are drop dead gorgeous. Those two will become 'The Legends of the Lake'. Built up by those guys' memories and recollections ... either exaggerated or truthful.

※※※※※※※※※※※※※※※※※※※※※※※※※※

As I was taking her home, Autumn asked, "Are you familiar with these streets around Prescott and McKenna?"

"Not really. Until today, I never had a reason to come this way."

"Summer told me about a place. Think it's down this street. Oh yeah, Sandusky. Take a right here, please."

I drove slowly for about a block down a fairly dark street, then I said, "It's a dead end. What exactly are we looking for?"

"There should be a little parking area off to one side. Think we found it, here ... on my side."

This was an ideal parking spot, and I pulled over. I said kiddingly, trying to suppress my extreme jealously, "Do you come here often?"

She explained, in a matter-of-fact tone, "Never been here before. Summer told me she and Jake would come here. She suggested it. Told me it was reasonably dark and a quiet place. Certainly, *certainly* not in front of our house ... too much light and way too many nosey neighbors."

"Well, Summer was right, this is a great place. An even better place to give you something. It's a little dark, and you won't be able to see it very well even with the dash lights, but ..." I reached in my pocket and pulled out an oval gold locket, about an inch by an inch and a half. "Since we are going steady, I thought you should have a piece of jewelry that says we are together. It was my grandmother's and I always told my great grandmother I really liked it, so she gave it to me before she died."

"O Richelieu! This is a beautiful locket!" She exclaimed and turned it over, "It's quite ornate. With three, no, four diamonds, set in a wonderfully engraved design." She tried the catch. "And it opens easily. I can't see if there are any pictures in it. Are there?"

"Not yet, fill it as you wish."

"I'll need a picture of you. Is some of the engraving personalized?"

"It is. The letter M for Muccy or Marlowe. No one's quite sure."

"Oh, Rich, this is the greatest. Better than all those *rings* that get passed around at Prescott. I'm going to wear it as soon as I find a really nice gold chain."

"Your wish is my command." Its companion medium length gold chain appeared.

"Oooh, you Magician, you really do belong in the A class at St. Nate's. These are just wonderful. Just terrific. Yew-weeee, *I love this locket and chain.*"

Then she leaned over to give me a surprising long and passionate open mouth kiss. She pulled her long hair to one side and waited impatiently for me to put it on her. With the minimal lighting, I was having trouble putting the chain thru the locket's slide.

"Hurry up, hurry up. I want to see how it looks on me. Come on! Come on! Sometime tonight!" she teased but excited like a little girl.

I finally threaded it and placed it around her neck, locked the clasp tightly and tucked it under the roll of her turtleneck sweater. She beamed. The locket hung down close to the top of her heart. Even in the poor lighting, she was checking it out with the mirror from her compact.

She happily squealed, almost like she was back in grade school, "Oh, this is perfect! *So perfect*! **So wonderfully perfect**! I can't wait until I show all the girls at school on Monday! Oh goody great! They will be oh, oh sooo en-veee-us. This is so cool ... so ultra-cool ... so **super ultra-cool**!"

Underneath the outward appearance of sophistication and ultra-cool combined with her natural, instinctive friendliness ... she's just a thrilled, happy little girl.

She kissed me again, followed with one of mine. Then we begin to talk.

"How did you come up with the locket? You had no clue we would be going steady before you picked me up tonight. Or are you the psychic one? Oh wait! Now I know where you disappeared after the inspection of your room."

"You're right. They've been waiting in my antique box for the right girl since I inherited them. You know, this is the **best day** of my life. Twelve hours ago, I was nervous about just meeting and talking with you and now, we're going steady."

She grinned, "Not just bad things happen quickly, good things can occur just as quickly and without any warning. I would like a favor from you."

"Anything, 'your wish is ...' and you know the rest."

"Be careful. You may not want to grant this."

"This sounds ominous," I said in a faked dramatic tone.

"When we are alone, I want to call you Richie," quickly adding, "only then."

"Sure, I guess. Why?"

"Obviously it's a special name which implies a certain degree of intimacy. Like when your aunt and mother use it, and probably your sister. I want to be able to use it too."

"Sure, it's fine with me."

"What is your first name? And the M for Macey or Marlowe?"

"Forrest, after my father. Étienne Richelieu is my grandfather ... Étienne translates to Stephen. So, I am Forrest Étienne Richelieu Marlowe. Macey is my paternal grandmother's maiden name. Both grandmothers' married names, obviously, Marlowe. What's your middle name?"

"Victoria. And you better *never* call me Vic or Vickie! Autumn Victoria Knight."

"Wow! Really? I have always *loved* the name Victoria, the Roman goddess of Victory. Well, you sure have conquered me, I surrender completely to you." I took her hands and kissed both of her opened palms as a sign of mock capitulation. We both laughed. "When we are alone, could I call you Victoria? I would *never* call you Vic or Vickie. I like the name Victoria way too much. It is so cool of a name."

She laughed, then agreed, "Richie, you certainly may."

Then I realized something, "Well, this is strangely coincidental! Grandmother Macey Marlowe's name was Victoria. So this locket and chain return to Victoria."

"Wow, that's weird. I'll love it as much as she did. You can tell by the care taken to maintain its beautiful condition. Oh, it's terrific. It's wonderful. I'm sorry Richie, but I probably should be getting home."

"Soon, Victoria, soon." I leaned over to kiss her again, thinking what a great place to park this is. After we kissed some more, I took her home. She had to turn off the porch light otherwise our kiss goodnight would have been on display for the entire neighborhood. She was still ecstatic about the locket and affectionately held it as I told her I always wanted her to be happy and I knew I certainly was. We passionately kissed good night. I told her I would call her tomorrow night. She gave me a short last kiss and quickly went inside.

****

As I walked into the house, the three of them were sitting in the living room, just talking casually. Or as I knew — waiting for me.

"Well?" My aunt immediately began the interrogation.

Quickly followed by DeForrest begging, "Tell us, Richie! *Please* tell us!"

My mother just smiled.

"Tell my Three Graces exactly what?"

"After you two left, Karen and I called Georgia Elms. She lives down the curve and around the corner. Goes to Prescott, a sophomore like us."

"Good for the three of you. I'm kinda tired. I'm going to bed," I teased.

"No-no-no! Not yet. Georgia says Autumn's really, really popular with everybody, especially the guys. She won't go steady with any of them. When a guy tries and fails, he's called one of 'Autumn's Fallen Leaves'. But they keep trying. She's like some kinda legend. Must date at least two or three new guys a month. So how didja do? Are you going out with her again?"

"Guess I did okay. We're going out next weekend."

"Richie, that's really good. She is so ultra-cool. Moves so gracefully, just like a model does."

I was slowing making my exit to the stairs. I could tell Aunt Danièle and DeForrest wanted to know a lot more about the date. So did my mother but she just continued to smile. My aunt couldn't contain herself anymore and jumped in, "She's a wonderful girl, so just be yourself with her. Take it slow. You'll do fine."

I couldn't hold it in any longer. I started to laugh, but my chest hurt.

"What's so funny?" demanded my aunt.

"Yeah, why are you laughing?" wondered my sister.

"Remember the gold locket and chain Grandma Marlowe left me? That was Grandmother Victoria Macey Marlowe's?"

My mother's smile widen. "Of course I remember. An exquisite piece, 18-karat with very fine engraving work of an M. Has excellent quality diamonds. The companion chain is Italian gold."

Bombardier to Captain ... 'dropping the A-bomb now, sir'. ... ... "Well, Little Auntie, it's a little late to take it slow. Mother, I hope it's all right with you, because I gave it to Autumn. DeeDee, your brother is going steady with that statuesque girl named Autumn."

All three, almost at the same time, "You're what?"

"What did you do?"

"How did you do it?"

"Yep, going steady with Autumn. St. Ignatius' guys don't mess around. Just like our reputations. We're fast. **But I'm one of the fastest!**"

"But ... but ... but how? Georgia says only some guys have a second date and she loses all interest after a third."

I laughed and thought of Autumn's comment of earlier this evening and so I quoted, "Rarely, it only takes a very, very short time for one to know there is something exceptionally worthwhile pursuing." Continuing with my arrogant attitude, I said, "That 'something worthwhile' would be me."

Aunt Danae said, "Wasn't this afternoon just your first date?"

"Yep, the coke date this afternoon was our first. The second was two hours later. After we left here, we went to Zesto's, cruised around, then I took her home where we talked. And both happily decided to go steady. Good thing I took the locket and chain with me. Good night, girls." They certainly didn't need to know the true sequence of events, especially the spot on Sandusky.

I went over and kissed each one of them good night. Only my mother was not in shock. I started to climb the stairs two at a time but my chest rebelled. So I backed off and took the stairs slowly, still smiling all the way up.

Until twelve hours ago, only two very short conversations with her. And now ... Wowzer!

I faintly heard Aunt Danae say, "Oh Gi Gi, who does he remind you of?"

I pictured my mother smiling happily as I heard her say, "More and more."

I couldn't fall asleep. Couldn't quit thinking about HER. She was so different from other girls. So wonderfully, magnificently different.

Each girl of "My Love List" — the ones I had seriously liked — began to frolic through my mind, smiling.

Bonnie Jo, my freshman fun ... first time touching a girl ... wondrous ... despite being small ... she insisting steadfastly 'only on the outside of my sweater'.

'Red-Hot' Rusty ... Of fiery red hair & navel rub fame ... her incredible blood red glider butterfly tattoo to completely cover her nasty hip burn ... cheated on, then dumped me for that senior prick. 'Crudely' challenged him ... rewarded by getting the shit beaten out of me.

'Scarlett' Charlotte, my older, so risqué talking, cigarette smoking, 'Frenching teacher' ... absolute stunner ... broke my sophomore heart, dumped me for that college bozo.

Olga, my cute Ukrainian babe, great personality, helped me get over Charlotte ... that tongue could fabulously French or tie cherry stems in a knot ... only able to touch her slightly with my hand partially in her bra for never more than a quick moment in those so brief semi-private times ... returned to Belgium when her father's tour ended early.

Linda, my senior of last summer ... the pleasure-seeking girl of partying, drive-in drinking, fabulous making-out and beautiful 'baseballs'.

Caroline, of 'bewitching butt and beckoning breasts' fame ... burned me with her hot temper and fiery cigarette habit.

Antoinette, of 'best French kiss' stardom ... glorious skimming of her aroused peak and the rest of that medium grapefruit ... beautiful queen of style ... returned to her idiot boyfriend.

'Girls, WAY too late now for each one of you!' Each one frowned at me as she was mentally struck through on The Love List.

I looked over at my father's picture on my desk. As usual, he remained stoic.

All the girls on My Love List differed in looks and shapes, mannerisms and attitudes, yet all seemed to be essentially from the same crowd. Every one of them lacked something. Something **SHE** has. Her demeanor, her personality, her style, her charm, her intelligence — so statuesque, so beautiful, so unique, so Autumn Victoria Knight.

※※※※※※※※※※※※※※※※※※※※※※※※※※※※※

I thanked God profusely during the entire Mass for the second coincidental meeting in Ball's, for the coke date, for hanging out with my Graces, for Zesto's, for the parking spot, for starting to go steady — lastly but certainly the most — for her.

On Monday, I told Jack all about Saturday, especially the locket as we parked. He congratulated me on a job well-done. Now his job was done. Said Autumn was fabulous, that I was crazy about her after just two dates in one day. Remarkably, instead of Jack razzing me, he simply said he knew exactly what I meant. He was sincerely happy for me.

Later, when I pulled in the driveway, Mick was already waiting for me on my front steps. "What the hell dija do? Howja do it? The whole school cannot believe it. Well, at least a ton of the girls in the junior class. A bunch of Autumn's Fallen Leaves too."

"It's pretty simple. We had an afternoon date and an evening date. During the evening date, we decided to go steady."

"Shit, nobody can believe it. Girls *just had* to see the locket. Ginny Foster ran all over school telling all the girls how 'terrifically handsome' you are with Judy Kingsley confirming it."

"Yeah, that would be me all right," I arrogantly said and started to laugh. "Not bad for 'a Neanderthal' as that fat-assed Bitch called me."

"Yeah, your old date, Sheila said you must have hit her over the head and dragged her away to your cave or something like that."

"No shit! She said that? She's definitely The Wicked Bitch of the West. Why in God's name did you fix me up with that fat-assed broad? Beefy thighs too."

"She's not always like that. C'mon, she's really smart, good looking, really nice knockers ... and well ... ok ... a big butt with stocky thighs. Now embarrassed as hell. Really screwed up with you at that hall dance last week. Made herself look stupid. And foolish. The *word* going around is you were having a lot more fun with Caroline. Pam and I saw you two ... how you kept smiling at her and laughing and how she was hanging on your arm. Then the way she twitched her butt towards the door as she waved oddly at you. We figured it was a 'See you outside' ... you were getting ready to ditch Whopping Ass and Beefy Thighs, but instead ended up in the fight. So the aspiring actress flubbed up her 'partial' date with the guy who is now Autumn Knight's steady. Every time Ole Whopping Ass opened her mouth to save face, she said something dumber." We joked about her "whopper ass and beefy thighs" with a couple nastier slams.

"But with Autumn ... you pulled off something that at least 25 or 30 guys, probably more, never could do. And a *locket*! Do you realize what you've done? Every girl at Prescott will want a locket, not a ring, from her boyfriend. Hey, why don't we double sometime," asked Mick. "Pam and Autumn know each other somewhat from Whittier but they don't hangout. You know, different cliques."

"Sure, be great with me. Pam's really nice, but you're just OK." We laughed and kidded each other some more. Mick and I had become good friends.

༺༺༺༺༺༺༺༺༺༺༺༺༺༺༺༺༺༺༺༺

During our nightly call on Wednesday, I had asked Autumn if she wanted to go to Prescott's game on Friday, but she said she would rather see *Tom Jones*. When I picked her up, I said hi to her mother. She was intently watching TV and only waved at me. Her father didn't seem to be home.

Autumn looked great again tonight, wearing a mint green wool sweater and matching slacks with some muted green eyeshadow. As we walked to the car, I said, "You look nice tonight, as always."

"You have only seen me twice now for dates."

"I know these things." She snickered, sliding into the middle of the seat. I got behind the wheel, turned and asked, "May I kiss you now?" She answered by leaning over to kiss me much longer than I hoped for. "Thank you. I've been thinking about you all week in school. When I look around, I see nothing but other guys, and well..."

"I missed you too. I do the same and when I look around, I see other girls ... but then also some guys." We laughed then she continued, "But I don't see **you**. That's why the movies tonight instead of the game. I don't feel like sharing you."

"Fine with me." I wanted to be with only her tonight too.

We both liked the movie a lot even though it was considered by some as "bawdy" — like her mother — who had never seen it, only heard about it. We held hands throughout it and all the way to the car. As soon as we got in the car, we kissed. Then again.

"Blender's or Zesto's?"

"Zesto's, I still don't feel like sharing."

We had to pull into the elongated island in the middle on the entrance side and could only see others in the steady stream of cars cruising through by looking over and around the cars across from us. Autumn pointed out a bunch of guys and gals, however, rarely would we be seen. But when we were, she enthusiastically waved to them.

After we ordered, Autumn said, "Keep forgetting to tell you a couple things. Roland Bush ... the guy you decked at that McKenna hall party ... met him briefly at a Lake party in early September. Danced with him only once ... I had a date."

Lying asshole prick! 'Don't know her name' and 'Wellington'.

"In fact, at Best Cleaners, maybe three or four weeks later, he asked me to go out with him. I already had a date for that Friday and Saturday ... besides I had to check him out."

Add cheating as Dee was going steady with him. The communion fast 'oops' and start of the escalating petting. ... ... "What do you mean, 'check him out'?"

"Suppose a girl from Prescott, like me, would be asked out by a guy from McKenna, like Bush. The girl would call her contacts at McKenna to check him out. See what kind of a guy he is. Smart? Athletic? Does he try to move fast? Drink? Smoke? Other stuff. I have contacts at McKenna and Wellington, even Wyandotte Junior College. St. Maggie's and obviously, Sagesse for St. Nate's."

"Well, I'll be damned. Oh, sorry."

"It's okay, Richie, just please don't use any of the real bad ones."

"I won't. Promise. So you girls have a network of spies to check us poor guys out."

"Tell me guys don't do the same."

"Well, yeah, if we can. Other than Jack and Mick, I don't have anybody. And look what Mick came up with." ... ... *Plus the tempting but so hot-tempered, heavy smoker. Jack came up with three St. Cat's mistakes.*

"It's one of the few ways a girl would know what she is getting into for that evening."

"So how did Bush check out?"

"His report was 'really good-looking,' ... which I knew ... 'very smart, sings in a church choir, a good pitcher.' Okay so far. However, Amy Hughes from McKenna went out with him a few times, thus knowingly told me 'likes to control the dates ... and quickly ... *you*.' **Certainly** not what I want in a boyfriend. So the next time he called, I was busy."

The next time? What the shit! Poor DeeDee ... SO USED by that Prick. ... ... I grinned, "So, how did I check out with Claudia Carson?"

"Terrible! It's going to take a lot of time to rehabilitate you." After we laughed a little, she took a curious pose, "Oh, I was going to ask you something else about Bush. Do you know a sophomore named Monica?"

"No, I don't think so."

"She's fairly attractive, has a good shape ... actually *terrifically* good ... dark-haired, terribly smart. I only know her by name. Oddly, she came up to me yesterday, said to give *to you* 'her infinite thanks for slugging that slimy, blank-ing B-a-s—'." She stopped, began to turn red, finally continued, "The blank is for a word I rarely have ever heard, only twice from girls, but they were vulgar, low-class girls. A word I would absolutely never, never use. This Monica then just turned, walked away. She was going *seriously* steady with Bush this summer, then he just suddenly broke up with her. Just like that ... no more Monica Matthews."

Monica Matthews! Prescott, not McKenna. Poor, miserable girl. Betrayed into losing her virginity ... the identical fate DeeDee was being deceived and set up for ... and neither will be his last seduction try or unfortunately his success ... The Bastard!

I truthfully replied after a moment, "Nope, never met her ... name's familiar though."

"Maybe your punch was hers ... vicariously. Ginny thinks she was terribly crushed by their breakup. Wendy said she has dated hardly at all since. Hopefully more now. Anyway, back to us. Do you feel like being shared tomorrow night?"

I puffed up, "Absolutely not, *I am* in control of tomorrow night's date! And you!" We laughed again. "Of course, what's the plan?"

"Judy is having a couples only party, all Prescott. Eight couples. Girls from our group and their steadies," she giggled a little, "or at least they still were at school this afternoon. What do you think?"

"Sure. Of course."

"Thank you and for being such a good guy, you deserve a reward. Please, please, take me to the Spot right now." She kissed my cheek. Then again.

"Your wish is my command." I quickly obeyed.

****

Every inch of Autumn's six foot plus looked superb. Light red eye shadow. Cherry red sweater. A pair of wonderfully, form-fitting jeans with red, medium-heeled Mary Jane shoes to accent her derrière perfectly! I had to learn how to quit drooling. I wore a black cashmere sweater with a white shirt, jeans and best loafers.

As we settled in the car, Autumn begged, "Richie, please kiss me now." She seemingly exuded a strong desire to be kissed and cuddled as she nestled into me eagerly. I only had to turn slightly and was rewarded with an intense kiss. As we broke apart, she kissed me a short one.

While she checked her lipstick, I kidded, "Hey, your mother actually talked a little with me tonight."

"Don't get too excited. It was a commercial break." She slightly laughed, but obviously forced. Driving to the party, I recalled they didn't say goodbye to each other. While I blew it off as a small mother-daughter tiff, I realized her father was nowhere to be seen again.

****

Judy Kingsley was the best-looking redhead I had ever seen in my life and one of the best-looking girls *period*. She was about five and a half foot tall, a gorgeously featured face with soft, medium green eyes, and a terrific shape. She had a lively personality, one of only two junior class cheerleaders on the varsity squad and a rare junior to be elected homecoming queen last month. Her hair — oh her hair — splendidly rich, copper tones which were reminiscent to me of a summer sunset. She was truly beautiful — especially when the light accented her hair perfectly.

Judy's steady was Terry Massey, the senior quarterback who was reliving last night's game when we entered the recreation room. "Those clowns at Southwest thought it was a run. I drop back and see Tim five yards behind the safety. Big Carl takes out the guy chasing me. POW! And I threw the ball 35 yards to Tim who hauls it in easily. A 72-yard touchdown to beat those yahoos."

"Yeah, you were great Terry," came from a guy off to one side.

"Man, just a terrific spiral to me."

"Yeah, it sure was. Well, well, well, look who showed up ... the elusive Autumn Knight."

The guy off to the side scoffed, "Elusive for you Massey, two dates, then a fumble and you tumble. A fallen Autumn leaf."

"Ha! Ha! Guess what, Coz? It's a new game 'cause I'm with **Queen** Judith," expressing himself like he had moved up a rung or two on the dating ladder scale.

Terry Massey? He's the guy Caroline's messing with on the side. Why, in God's Name, would this idiot cheat on this Copper Red-Haired Dream? What an incredible Dumb Ass!

Well, Shit, I'm the Dumb Ass. Oh Caroline, what are you doing ... that Judy won't?

Autumn introduced me to everyone, especially to the beautiful, red-haired Judy and Ginny, the attractive blonde with striking blue-grey eyes.

The guys were friendly, asking me about St. Ignatius football. I told them we had won seven, lost only two and always did well for a medium-size school. Tim, the end who scored the touchdown, said we should be consider large since the school was all guys. I said yeah, we were — in Class L, although the total four-year enrollment was only 600 guys. He said Prescott was 2400 for only three years. I quickly figured — excluding girls, of course — they were still over two and half times our size. I knew we could still beat their asses but didn't say anything.

Then the girls were after us to dance. Autumn grabbed me and we began to dance to an old one, *A Thousand Stars*.

"Thanks for rescuing me."

"Did you already use your fifty word allotment for the evening?" she teased.

"Pretty much. I was all talked out. I see guys all week. I don't need or want to be with them on weekends. Besides you are much softer" as I gently squeezed around her waist, "infinitely better looking. Even smell a little better." That earned me a playful push to the shoulder.

Ten minutes later, Judy stopped the record player and announced, "This dance is a couple's swap." Judy tagged Autumn and the other girls followed. This simply meant I danced with Judy and Autumn danced with her old boyfriend Terry. A slow song, *Angel Baby,* one of my favorite oldies.

As we were dancing fairly close with some talking, Judy's wonderful red hair kept getting in my face, so I kept blowing it out of the way.

"Oh, sorry about my hair. I thought you were trying to blow in my ear," she teased.

I became a little embarrassed and simply explained, "Not my style. But your hair certainly is. It's the most beautiful red I've ever seen. An incredible *vivid,* coppery red!"

"Now Rich ... I've heard so many variations of *that line.*"

"Sure, Judy ... I know you have. But it's not a line. A line is a compliment given to a girl to impress her or influence her. I want to do neither. The truth is the truth. Beauty is beauty." ... ... *Take that Lo Bianco, MY Catullian style.*

"Oooh Rich, I definitely see why it took Autumn only a day to decide to go steady with you."

After the dance, I told Autumn what I had said, starting with Judy teasing about me blowing in her ear. Not my style at all. Now kissing an ear, that's a different story. But she seemed to be more than a little jealous after the 'beauty is beauty' comment. I realized I was jealous too — dancing with an old boyfriend.

"She *does* have gorgeous red hair and she *is* great looking. She likes quarterbacks. I am a mere first baseman who is totally nuts over tall, long-legged, incredibly beautiful, highly intelligent girls with golden-brown hair. Know anyone like that?" She smiled, playfully punched me again, then kissed me on my cheek. The mutual insecurities had vanished.

During an hour or so of dancing with more couples' swap dances, I met extremely nice but fairly plain partners in Autumn's clique — Connie, Mary Ann, then Wendy again from last weekend.

Lastly, there was Joan Marie or Joanie. Far from plain, she was a quite cute brunette who, during our slow dance became increasingly friendly, exemplified by her inching closer to me — even more than Autumn would. So much so her medium bust would graze momentarily yet firmly against my chest. Vivacious, about five foot five or six, had a nice curved butt on a slender build. Oh, she was flirtatious and quite a lot. I found myself flirting back. It was too easy with her.

There was some talk about Prescott basketball, but much more about Prescott football. Then the lights began going off one by one. Time for the make out session to begin. I told Autumn I would like to leave, whispering to her that more than anything, I wanted to make out, just not in public. She looked pleasantly relieved and said she not only understood but totally agreed, thinking it too personal. So we found Judy and said goodnight and thanks for having us and she thanked me for the special compliment about her hair. On our way out, we saw Ginny who was in a solid clinch with her steady, Vince Something, but broke away to say she was sorry we didn't get to dance and talk. Definitely next time we would, swap or no swap. She then smiled and winked flirtatiously at me, waiting until Autumn's back was turned so neither she nor her date could see. A great party to meet Autumn's girlfriends, especially the copper-haired Judy, a teasing Ginny, and a flirtatious, inviting Joanie — whom I *knew* wanted a date.

On our way to Sandusky, Autumn teased, "I know guys from St. Ignatius, two in particular. Both are absolute charmers. One is loud and openly funny. The other is quiet yet full of tricks and subtly mischievous. Both my kind of guys." She teasingly blew in my ear off and on for a block or two, progressed to kissing it, then grazed my cheek with the back of her hand. I couldn't get to the spot fast enough.

****

After Mass and brunch, DeeDee and I re-joined my other two Graces who were still sitting around the dining table. Mother was talking about her date last night with Rex. "I'm not sure why he felt it necessary to tell me. My side of the relationship certainly isn't serious."

Aunt Danae questioned, "So what'd he say?"

"Well, we were having dessert. Rex began to discuss his marital status since he wanted to explain it to me. He was never baptized since it had something to do with one of his parents which, of course, I already knew ... and for which, Momma only called him by her name for him ... '*Le Païen*' [The Heathen]. After he was married for six years, he decided to become a Catholic but his wife would not be baptized under any circumstances as she was an avowed atheist. If he converted, she was unwilling to continue in the marriage compounded by the fact they were not getting along anyway. During his separation, he was baptized, then applied to the Diocese for the Pauline Privilege so he could marry in the Church. He had met a wonderful Catholic girl and they planned on marriage. During the long wait for his dissolution to be granted, the divorce began to get ugly and drawn out with numerous delays. Then the fiancée started to have doubts about moving away from her family and finally the marriage idea withered and died. However, he was now free to marry a likewise eligible Catholic ... ... or Protestant."

"Sounds like he's very serious. Hoping you will become too."

"Oh well, time will tell." My mother smiled one of her conjuring smiles. She had an idea or two up those lady magician's sleeves.

And coincidences do really happen. After we finished discussing divorce and remarriage in Religion class on that previous Friday, we were assigned to write a term paper. Given this turn of events, I chose to write about The Pauline Privilege. My grade was a 96, the only time I scored above 90 in that class.

****

One of the clients at Ellis and Mullins was in the movie distribution business for Warner Brothers and Paramount Pictures with the Kansas City office on Film Row. When he was at the law firm, he would always seriously flirt with Aunt Danae. Being Danièle Richelieu, she would flirt back in her own "come hither" fashion but he was, unfortunately, married. He did give

Aunt Danae two tickets for *Cleopatra* on Friday night which was showing at the Capri. She thought I might want to take my new girl to impress her. I thanked my Auntie but told her Autumn had a few dates with me thus she was totally, thoroughly impressed. She whispered to me, "You always try to bullshit me and I never buy your crap at all," smiled, kissed me on my cheek and handed me the tickets for some great seats — right center in the orchestra section. When I told Autumn, she couldn't believe it, saying it was like magic. She always figured it would be a while before it would be showing in a regular theatre because of the ticket cost. Even if she was lucky enough to see it during the special engagement run, it would never be with such great seats. We talked just a little as I had a big Latin test which I was sweating blood over.

****

Jack and I were eating lunch when some seniors came into the cafeteria telling everyone President Kennedy had been shot from some grassy knoll in Dallas. Just when we were going to tell them what a dumb ass, lame joke they were making and what Assholes they were, the PA came on and Walter Cronkite was talking. The office must have hooked into a TV or placed the microphone up close to it. Immediately, there was complete silence in the cafeteria as everybody began listening intently to the broadcast. When we quickly went to Math class, Father Hoyle simply told us to listen and pray silently. At 1:38 Cronkite made the statement Kennedy had died at 1:00. About five minutes later, Father Carroll told everyone to go home and pray for the President's soul and his grieving family. And the country.

My mother was watching the coverage, saying how horrific it all was. They had closed the stock market since it was out of control, spiraling downward. I'm sure thoughts of my father's murder crossed her mind more than once this afternoon. They certainly had mine. She had called and cancelled her date with Big Rex. DeeDee and I were glad about that.

I called Autumn and said I would be picking her up at 7:15. We both wondered if they would cancel the showing. I wore my navy double-breasted blazer, blue and grey tie to match the grey dress pants with my dress shoes. Autumn looked terrific, dressed in a wheat-colored wool suit and dyed-to-match high heels. The manager came on the stage and said they were going to show the film as some people in the audience had come from out of town. Anybody wanting to exchange tickets could certainly do so for another night. The film was good and made us forget today's catastrophic, tragic events. The sets and scenery were unbelievably elaborate, yet the movie was only minimally historically accurate, but at least it had Elizabeth Taylor. Autumn and I held hands throughout the movie. Neither of us felt like going anywhere afterwards so I took her home.

****

Saturday night I picked Autumn up and brought her to my house where we watched more coverage of the assassination's aftermath. Both Mother and Autumn had agreed how gruesome it was to have seen Bobby Kennedy with Jackie, still in her bloodstained pink suit.

Mother woefully moaned, "Good bye, O beautiful Camelot."

Autumn sadly agreed, saying with an Irish lilt, "Johnny, we hardly knew ye." My mother nodded and warmly patted her on the shoulder, telling her that was a wonderful accent. Autumn merely replied, "My wonderful Grandmother Knight ... a true angel ... my loving Nanna ... from Belfast."

Only by accident would Mother be in close proximity to any of my girlfriends. Certainly never consciously touched them much less in such a friendly manner.

Later, I asked Autumn what she would be doing for Thanksgiving with Summer home. She said Summer would be going with Jake to spend the day and evening at his Aunt Genie's. She guessed she would be going with her parents to one of her mother's church friends like last year.

"Boy, **that** doesn't sound like any fun."

"It isn't. It's so blah! In capitals ... B—L—A—H!"

"Why don't you come over here, spend the day and eat dinner with my Three Graces and me?"

"Oh no, no! I couldn't. It would be too big an imposition."

"We would love to have you. I wasn't eavesdropping on you two, just passing through. Need my stock reports on Merck and Coca-Cola. **I would** sincerely love to have you, Honey."

What? Mother never calls anyone 'Honey'. Never!

Autumn was stunned, then gushed, "Thank you, Mrs. Marlowe. What could I bring?"

"Oh, nothing, just yourself."

"At least let me help you in the kitchen. Please?"

"That sounds like a fair offer since Richie is worthless there. You could come over about ten, ten-thirty ... if that's convenient."

"Who's coming over at ten-thirty?" It was DeeDee now "passing through". We would have more privacy in the middle of State Avenue.

"Oh Angel, we will have a guest Thursday. Autumn is coming for Thanksgiving dinner and its preparation beforehand."

"Wow, that's fab! Terrific! Outta sight! Oh Autumn, **I'm so glad** you'll be here."

"Now all we need is Aunt Danae to make it unanimous," I said sarcastically.

Promptly paid back with, "Did I hear my name mentioned?"

"Guess what, Aunt Danae? Autumn is going to help with dinner and spend all day Thanksgiving with us. That will be *so ultra-cool*."

"Well, it will be terrific to have you Autumn. You certainly do move fast Richie ... living right up to that St. Ignatius reputation."

That completely embarrassed the shit out of me. This was our on-going game which either one would start. My aunt would try to embarrass me or I would give her some of my lines of bull shit, interspersed with "Little Auntie" or just "Auntie". She certainly won this one.

I quickly collected Autumn's coat and hurried her out the door. "Good. Unanimous vote. See you later. Going to Blender's. Night all." However, we didn't go to Blender's, instead we went to Zesto's to talk, then to our Spot to talk some and make out a lot.

****

We didn't have school on the National Day of Mourning for President Kennedy. During lunch on Tuesday, Jack and I talked intently about Jack Ruby killing Oswald on national TV and the evolving conspiracy theories. Finally, I changed the subject by saying I was going to meet Jake Ford this weekend. Jack said seriously I would be hard pressed to replace him at first base as he was an incredibly good ballplayer, actually the best he had ever played with. He was the captain of last year's championship team, then got a full-ride scholarship to Missouri.

****

Later that afternoon, DeForrest came rushing into the house, yelling "Mother! Mother!" She saw me and pleaded, "*Where's Mother*? I need Mother!"

"Think she went to the grocery store. Why? What the hell is wrong?"

"Some **real bad shit** happened to me at school!"

She was now visibly shaken and I thought she would cry. However, she continued anxiously, "Big Rex 'accidentally' ran into me in the school library after he had finished some business at Sagesse. I was coming out of the stacks, having found a book for a paper. Told me how 'particularly lovely I looked'! How could I look 'particularly lovely'? With only *some* makeup on and in this shitty school uniform? Then he offered to give me a ride home. There was no way I was going to get in any car with that creep."

"Where were your carpool buddies?'

"Claudia and Karen both had club meetings, so I was studying there, waiting for them. Who knows where those two seniors went ... probably smoking somewhere off campus. I lied, told him after the meeting, we girls were going shopping on the Plaza. He says okay, maybe another time."

Tears started to run down her cheeks. "Then the **Son of a Bitch** pats my shoulder, quickly brushes his hand over my neck to start caressing my cheek and jaw. It shocked me! Stunned me! After only a couple moments, I yanked his hand away. Christ, him fondling me like that was repulsive. So humiliating. Suddenly, I was wetting myself! Couldn't stop it! Rushed like hell into the library bathroom, locked the door, jumped on a toilet. All the while, I felt him stroking me, touching me ... ... over and over again which caused me to start crying pitifully. When I finally could finish urinating, I wiped down my legs, dried up the places on my slip and socks as best I could, then wrung out the soaked area of my panties in the stool. During all this time, I cried. And it was a while before I could finish sobbing and blubbering. After I did, I went to the sink, took off my blazer and blouse to scrub my face and neck then my shoulder area until they were red. Even wiped down the entire shoulder area on those clothes. Then dressed, grabbed my books and purse and went to find Karen or Claudia."

She noticeably shuddered, "The whole damn thing was so traumatic … him **feeling me, rubbing me**. Oh God, so damn disgusting! **Don't** want him near me! Ever! **Don't** want to see him! Never again! THAT DEGENERATE COCK SUCKING CREEP BASTARD!"

I put my arm around her to reassuredly hold and hug her, "Tell Mother **all of it**. **Everything**. **Every detail**. Bag your swearing, though. Oh, you can bet she'll take care of Rex. Thoroughly."

After Mother finishes him off …… God, please grant me my turn.

※※※※※※※※※※※※※※※※※※※※※※※※※

Thanksgiving holidays finally started at Wednesday noon, so I picked up Autumn at Prescott and we went to The Hangout for some shakes and fries. While we ate, she talked about Summer and Jake coming home today and I would get to finally meet both of them. I told her about what Jack had said about Jake's ability in baseball and leadership of the team.

"Oh, you'll like Jake when you meet him this week." She happily continued, "When I was in the 7th grade, I had the **biggest** crush on him **forever**. Actually, over half the school year. I flirted with him **all** the time, every chance I got. Yet he could only see me as Summer's cute, friendly little sister." Her smile widened, "Still does," then sourly concluded, "But he was with a black-haired beauty named Carlotta."

Was that the same 'Carlotta' who took our spot at Zesto's? That absolute stunner?

"He's Disney's Shaggy Dog, incredibly funny and lovable, extremely smart … just a lot of fun."

Our conversation shifted from going steady like Jake and Summer had been for over three years to going steady then to dating in general to its related problems for girls. Autumn confessed, "Unfortunately, there are kinds of 'unwanted situations' which happen to girls on dates."

"Anything ever happen to you ... on a date?" I started to fume a little as immediately I thought of the Prick's plan of seduction for DeeDee and the assaults on my poor Aunt by that dead Bastard.

"Yeah, twice. Both on second dates. I just pushed the jerk away, then quickly left without saying a word. I couldn't ... I just couldn't slap either guy, even though they both fully deserved even more! Summer told me I should have smacked the s-h-i-t out of them. She would have. That girl has big, sharp, well-hidden claws. Summer always has protected me against anybody ... *anybody*. Both times, she told Joe to make each one fully apologize to me. Each did. Immediately! Oh, Joe is Jake's best buddy and a golden glove winner. Tough as they come."

We talked a little while more, then left. As she got out of the car, I offered, "I'll pick you up at 10 o'clock tomorrow morning and my mother told me to be sure to tell you we dress informally for Thanksgiving. Jeans would be fine."

Autumn wore a navy blue turtleneck, that pair of super-snug dress jeans she wore to Judy's party with two-inch heel blue T-straps. Solidly accenting her legs and derrière wonderfully! Bright red lipstick and navy blue eyeshadow, tapering down halfway across her lids. So fabulously tall, looking so gorgeous. I still had not learn how to quit drooling.

I parked in the garage and we went into the kitchen where the Three Graces were. They stopped working to welcome and talk to Autumn for a short while before putting her to work. When they gave her an apron, *they* actually told *me* to leave. I went to my room to read my Old Civs' assignment about the Etruscans.

About two hours later, Autumn came into my room, gave me a chaste kiss, "Dinner will be ready in about an hour. Like to see what is in **my** locket?"

"Of course."

She opened it to show two facing pictures, both recent photos of each of us. We both were smiling happily, ecstatic to be looking at, almost kissing each other. "That **is so cool**, Victoria!"

"Guess who set the table, peeled and mashed the white potatoes? Your Mother and Aunt let DeeDee and me do the sweet potatoes with a recipe using maple syrup. I kept it from Home Ec last year and brought it along with the syrup. After we had finished everything that needed immediate attention, we took a break and your mother got out a photo album. Then the four of us sat around the breakfast table and looked at old pictures. Oh, you were a cute little boy. Your aunt said to tell you that you still are."

"Cute?" ... ... *God, could 'Auntie' embarrass me further!*

"No, little boy," she teased me. "There was one of DeForrest and you when you were about six or seven. Now that one **is** really cute. On the back, your father had written 'Richey Rue & My Little Dee.' "

I smiled broadly. "Our childhood nicknames for each other." I thought of that Saturday morning of All Souls in the kitchen when DeeDee and I used them as we completely and firmly reconciled from that blow-up at the hospital.

"Then I saw a few pictures of your father. Wow, do you resemble him ... very strongly ... except for the brown hair. He was quite handsome, especially in the one taken in his military dress. There was your mother's incredibly beautiful engagement picture and your parents' wedding picture at St. Patrick's Cathedral. After those last two pictures, I could tell your mother had become uncomfortable. I quickly asked if she had any smaller pictures of you. Your mother seemed relieved by my request, went over to the buffet, pulled out a group of pictures, and said, 'You need a nice one to go in your locket. You choose.' I picked this one and everyone agreed it was a perfect match to my picture. I cut it very carefully to fit. And here it is ... with me."

"Yeah, we look happy, like we belong together there. I'm sure Vintage Victoria would be happy to see Modern Victoria with her grandson in the locket." She laughed. Accordingly, I was given something more than a chaste kiss. While we talked more, DeeDee walked by — certainly on purpose. Regardless of the reason, Autumn happily invited her to join us. About an hour later, my aunt called the three of us to dinner.

If there were guests for dinner, one of the traditions of my house would be to have one of them say grace, forewarned of course, and only if they were comfortable saying it.

Autumn began, "God, bless this wonderful meal which we are about to partake in through the hard work and love that made it possible. God, also please bless this exceptional family for inviting me here to take part in its preparation and sharing, especially Mrs. Marlowe. Amen."

"Why thank you Honey. I have never been included in a dinner blessing." We all laughed.

There was Honey again. ... Mother really likes her. ... Boy, does she.

Dinner was incredibly delicious as always. I was drafted into drying the dishes as Autumn and my mother washed. DeeDee went to talk with my Aunt while she dressed for a date, then was so excited when Autumn asked her to go cruising with us. However, the three of us knew full well there would not be many cars on State, especially with the hangouts closed. But DeeDee did get her chance — once — to wave and yell at some guys. After dropping my sister back at the house, we drove over to the Spot.

That night I had the nightmare which was more intense. I woke up with profuse sweating, heart racing, but most importantly, the feeling of helplessness and loss. Desperately, I needed to figure out what to do as I tossed and turned, trying to get back to sleep.

****

On Friday, just my mother and I were eating dinner in the kitchen. DeeDee had gone to Karen's and my aunt was upstairs getting ready for a dinner and dancing date with the same guy from last night. After we finished eating, Mother handed me a letter, "Danae had a little research done for me on Rex when he was living in North Carolina. Here, you should read it."

The typed letter spoke volumes:

Randolph County, North Carolina, Department of Public Record

Miss Daniele Richelieu
Ellis and Mullins, Inc
501 Minnesota
Wyandotte, Kansas 66101

November 22, 1963

Dear Miss Richelieu,
Public information on one Mr. Rex Reagan Finnegan, et al. as per your request of November 10, 1963:

Marriage License granted on this day of June 12, 1952 to Rex Reagan Finnegan, age 27, and Louise Marie English, age 19

Divorce filed on this day of November 30, 1959 between Rex Reagan Finnegan and Louise Marie English Finnegan Divorce granted on this day of September 7, 1960

Alienation of Affections Suit filed February 2, 1960 Louise Marie English Finnegan vs. Belinda Jo Cummings Settled without court proceedings, May 10, 1960

Yours truly,
Miss Geraldine Regnier

M. Richelieu, please note — Miss B. J. Cummings born 2/1/1939 — GR
Rex moved to KC in Aug 1960 for current position at bank — DMR

"Does this mean he was involved with this Belinda Jo Cummings before she was twenty-one?"

"Yes, he was ... I'd guess two years earlier, probably when she was nineteen. Certainly it's a telling document. I'll show it to DeeDee sometime later when she has calmed down sufficiently from her ugly encounter with **Mister** Rex Finnegan."

※※※※※※※※※※※※※※※※※※※※※※※※※※※※※※

Autumn and I were invited to Jake's Aunt Regina's for dessert. I started to go up to the front door and Autumn told me that was for regular people. So to the "secret" back door entrance. Autumn didn't even knock, just walked in, so I followed her. She first introduced me to Jake's aunt and uncle. His Uncle Charley was tall and lean, well-dressed, naturally friendly. Aunt Regina was a striking, stylish woman with affectionate light grey eyes and silver hair which had a beautiful luster. I knew she was at least ten years older than my mother but she certainly didn't look her age. She had this presence of independence, of someone who was their own person and knew it.

I met Summer. Having seen pictures of her, I knew she and Autumn shared a likeness, certainly the same beautiful golden brown hair and light brown eyes. Seeing the two sisters together now, a reasonable facial resemblance was evident, especially as Summer didn't have her glasses on. Their figures were also very similar except Autumn was a good four inches taller. And better looking. Jake would certainly disagree about the looks, but he couldn't on the height.

Jake, himself, was a couple inches taller than me, broad shouldered, and probably outweighed me by a good twenty pounds. We shook hands and he jovially commented, "So this is the guy who finally snagged our 'Little Autumn'. Of course, it had to be another St. Nate guy to do it." Everyone laughed.

When we all sat down to talk, Aunt Regina began to serve tea, Coke, or 7-Up. While everyone else had a soft drink, I opted for tea. "A very good choice, Richelieu. Would you like sugar?"

"No ma'am. That ruins it."

"Oh so true. You can never make tea too strong."

"I certainly agree, ma'am."

My only contribution to the general conversation was to tell Jake I had Moose, Hoyle, Fitzgerald and Lo Bianco — the ones he would know.

His advice was as expected, "Stay alert for 'Monotonous Moose' and stay prepped for Lo Bianco. Fitzgerald is a real bear but underneath he's probably a good guy. Ya know he was a cop before he became a Jesuit."

Not good guy ... a remarkable guy! And still a first-class detective.

"Hoyle is a sweetheart. I really, really like him. Had him all three years for math. Geometry, Advanced Algebra, Calc and Advanced Calc. He is the one who persuaded me to major in Math at MU. And of course, Miss Sörensen at Whittier, put the idea in my head and he encouraged and developed it. Very sad about her. Turned sixty-five and was forced into mandatory retirement last spring, so she moved to Salina to live with her widowed sister. Got a letter from her last week. She's doing volunteer tutoring at Salina Central where those lucky students will learn more in one session with her than a week or two in a regular classroom. Oh, but Father Hoyle ... I love that man. In fact, Summer and I went to visit him this afternoon. Still wonderfully eccentric, still great to talk to."

"I didn't know there was a class beyond Basic Calc?"

"Not exactly," Jake said a little embarrassed, "I skipped Algebra II until senior year and instead of a study hall, Father Hoyle taught three guys Advanced Calc last year. Terrific, wonderful class."

"If you like math."

"If you **love** math." And we laughed.

Later, I was standing next to Jake and his aunt was remarking about how it was going to be tough on the Kennedy children, growing up without a father, especially with him being assassinated.

Jake calmly said, "They'll make it."

I said to Jake, "Maybe ... but it'll still be hard."

"Oh, they'll adapt somehow."

"Really? What would you know about it?" A weak retort, but I had become a little steamed. He wouldn't know shit about it. Peripherally, I saw Summer nudge Autumn.

In a quiet voice, he said, "Let's *talk* outside." Then loudly teased his aunt, "Hey Aunt Genie, Rich and I are going outside for a smoke. Back in a bit." As we were walking out the side door, Jake said, "That is the only, only thing she will not tolerate. You don't smoke, do you?"

"Oh God, no." And thought of my father's painful lesson.

"Good. Never have I."

Outside on the open porch he began, "Look, we both know what it's like to not have a father. You are luckier. You had yours until eighteen months ago. It can be worse. Believe me ... much worse!"

"I find that hard to believe. You **still** have a father."

"Oh yeah, the Premier Asshole. Shit, if he were dead at least I would get some sympathy like you do."

"I don't *need* anybody's sympathy! Don't *want* anybody's sympathy! Do just fine without any."

"Yes, you do need some because you are still in pain."

"No, I'm not! I'm doing great with all of it."

"Maybe *you think* you are. Hopefully you will be able to accept what has happened and move on. When you do, it will be bearable."

"Why, do you still hurt?"

"Yeah, a little. It never entirely goes away. Oh God, but nothing like when I was in Junior High. But thank God, I always had my Aunt Genie and I finally realized Summer had always been there too. At least, when your father was alive, he loved your mother and sister, you had great experiences with him, you went places, you had fun with him, he wanted you, **he loved** you and **you** loved him. You truly miss him. **That is tragic**. Yet, nonetheless, wonderful."

Jake took a deep breath, "Well, you see, mine is still alive. After he moved out, all he could do was break promise after promise to me. Seven years ago, he disappeared completely to California except for one three-hour visit and now only the occasional birthday or Christmas check. He did not want me anymore or certainly didn't love me, so I know all about pain ... the pain of rejection. Do you know one of the reasons the Knights don't like me is because of that. Yeah, my mother and father separated eleven years ago. How in Hell is that my fault?"

Then both Autumn and Summer were at the door. Autumn had a worried tone to her voice, "Rich? Jake? You've been out here awhile. Aren't you both getting cold? Is everything okay?"

Jake jokingly said, "Never better. Guy stuff, you know, maybe like who's the better first baseman, which, of course, is me."

Summer scolded, "Okay, little boys, you have to come in from playtime now. You can continue your bragging later. We're about to have Aunt Genie's chocolate angel food cake and ice cream."

"Be there in a minute," Jake said loudly. Then quieter to me, "And there's another thing, Autumn is very special to me. She likes you a lot an awful lot. Your family too. You better not hurt her. They *say* you can function with one testicle, but—"

I interrupted, "You have no worry on that. While we have been going together only for three weeks, she means infinitely more to me than any girl I have ever dated. Hell, I almost took out an entire display stack of Tide at Ball's trying to meet her."

Jake laughed loudly. "Let's go inside. Please ... just take care of Autumn. She's the little sister I never had. You are lucky there too."

"That I know. I **will** do anything for my sister."

"So I heard. Three guys! You idiot! Next time, pull a Julius Caesar ... divide and conquer. Anyway, how can you **possibly** think you are better than me?"

He laughed loudly again and extended his hand and I gladly shook it. We had gone outside merely as acquaintances and now as we turned to go back inside, we had become friends, as he shared some of his private suffering, trying to help me through, what he thought, was my lingering, residual pain.

However, it was still as big as a whale.

As we turned to walk back in, we saw two figures coming up the drive. "Giuseppe! Sunny! You made it just in time for dessert. The great Giuseppe! And the ever beautiful Sunny, how have you been?" Jake ran down the steps, quickly moving to them and partially embraced both of them at the same time. As they retraced his steps, he confessed, "Oh, I'm forgetting my manners. This is Asunción Bustamante, the terrific looking girlfriend of the ugly guy next to her ... Joe Sorrentino. And this is Richelieu Marlowe." Under his breath, I faintly heard Jake say, "God, I've missed you Giuseppe."

Joe was widely smiling as he and I shook hands. I said to both of them, "Please call me Rich."

Even in the dim light, I could tell Asunción had jet black hair and dark eyes, a good figure, quite pretty with a matching smile. "Everyone calls me Sunny."

Jake announced, "Rich is Autumn's *steady* boyfriend."

Joe exclaimed, "What, I don't believe this! Little Autumn finally found a guy she would go steady with. Wow, Rich, you must be something else."

"Oh, he is. He's at St. Ignatius and going to inherit my first base. Sunny, **you are** better looking every time I see you. Must be those *inviting* ebony eyes, highlighting those high cheekbones." He teasingly whispered but all could hear, "If Summer wasn't around, weeell ... Hey, is the new job agreeing with you?"

Where have I seen this girl? I know I have. I don't forget good-looking chicks.

"Oh it's great, the men at the law firm are very nice to me."

That's where ... Ellis and Mullins.

"So are all the support staff. I am going to start training to be a legal secretary right after Thanksgiving. This wonderfully, nice lady is going to teach me."

"Then you know Danièle Richelieu. She's my aunt."

Sunny smiled, "Danae's the lead who is going to train me. She's just incredible."

Autumn barked at us, "Hey little first base boys, the party is inside, so get in here. **Now**! ... Joe? ... Sunny? And Autumn came rushing out the door to hug each one. Little Autumn — a grade school nickname used now by only a very few — was three inches taller than Joe and probably an additional four more than Sunny. As they exchanged greetings in the light, I took a real good look at Joe. He appeared to be about twice as broad as me and built like a tank. I *might* spar with the guy but sure as hell wouldn't step into the ring for a match.

"This is great ... oh, *just* terrific. Summer is inside with Jake's aunt and uncle. Wait till they see you two. C'mon, everybody in the house. Now? Please?"

I was the last one in and Autumn handed me two plates, each with a piece of cake and ice cream, asking me to sit by the fireplace. She would be there in a minute with fresh drinks. And she was. Their reunion talk was lively about Missouri University, how Jake was majoring in Mathematics and Summer and her best friend, Wynne White, were rooming together. Both in Journalism and thought maybe they would use it for pre-law. Their other roommate — Wynne's cousin — Sofia Savich from St. Maggie's was majoring in chemistry.

Both Joe and Sunny were going to Wyandotte Junior College for night classes. Joe continued his summer job, working at Macek's Mobil and Garage as an attendant/junior mechanic. The conversation drifted to their old classmates. Autumn knew all of them. Carlotta, the black-haired beauty, or Teri, the blond honey, were never mentioned. Probably a good reason so I didn't bring it up.

As the empty plates were being collected, Jake's aunt came over to me and smiled, "Richelieu, there is no need to be quiet or reserved here. Or maybe you're introspective by nature?"

"Yes ma'am, sometimes I am. But certainly not reticent when it comes to your cake and chocolate frosting. Excellent! I'll bet it's an old family recipe."

"Thank you. And yes, it is ... my grandmother's. Speaking of relatives, do you think one of yours posed for Rodin's *The Thinker?*"

"No, ma'am, but I would like to have been the guy who did for *The Kiss.*"

She laughed deeply. "You, Thinker, are smart, charming and a lot more than a pinch wicked. *I like you.* Please call me Aunt Genie."

Her laughter had attracted Autumn's attention, "Okay, just how are you entertaining our hostess?"

"Discussion of Art, specifically French sculpture."

Autumn looked quizzical as Aunt Genie laughed again. "Oh, Thinker!" and winked at me as she took some of the plates to the kitchen. I could see why everyone adored the woman. Always on the top of her game and the ultimate hostess making everyone feel they were needed at her party.

After the party, we went to the Spot where I told Autumn about my conversation on Rodin, she laughed heartily and alluringly purred we should be that couple as she passionately began *The Kiss*.

Later, Autumn said she and Summer were going shopping in downtown Kansas City all Saturday and just spend some time together — just the two of them. I told her my mother and I were going to Houston's Christmas Tree Farm and cut down a tree while DeeDee and Aunt Danae were going to get out the decorations and lights and do the outside lighting. She begged to come over and help decorate the tree that night. Summer was going over to Genie's to help in the annual extravaganza set-up which was always nothing short of fabulous. I knew my Graces would love to have her help as they did on Thanksgiving.

****

Late Saturday afternoon I picked Autumn up for dinner. Afterwards, she and DeeDee cleaned up the dishes while I put up the tree *by myself* — not wanting *or* needing any help. After I got the tree set up in the stand with all four females *finally* concurring on its straightness, I disappeared to my room to let them decorate both the tree and living room and just continue yakking.

When they finished, Autumn came to my room, inviting me to see the finished presentation. I told them they had done it beautifully. They had used our old-fashioned Angel hair on the tree, but with the lights and ornaments interspersed according to a new design scheme Autumn had researched at school. The base was covered with the family tree skirt and the antique manger scene was placed in front. The Santa Clauses of our family collection acquired from all over the world were strategically placed throughout the room. I told Autumn it would be great to find another for Mother.

As Autumn and I took a needed detour to the Spot before I dropped her home. I told her she was extremely good help and my mother greatly appreciated it.

"Please tell her thank you. You have such a *wonderful, fabulous mother*."

"Are you going to work your magic again by helping your parents put up and decorate a tree?"

"No, that only happens when it's my mother's turn to entertain her semi-monthly bridge club during the Thanksgiving to New Year's holidays or if she hosts the annual Christmas party with husbands."

Autumn's voice had suddenly turned harsh. "But neither one this year. And my father doesn't give a damn one way or the other." Her tone was always cheerful and upbeat, but she continued, sounding like I had never heard her before. "Regarding almost anything, my mother only cares about what others think. Her only interest is doing what is necessary and required to make her look 'so wonderful' to her damn bridge club, the damn neighbors and her damn church group. That's why she likes Summer and me to be dating Jake and you. It's the prestige of both her daughters dating St. Ignatius guys, which even overrides the fact you are both Catholic. Then there is Jake's full baseball scholarship and your family being affluent enough to live in the Hoel edition. Summer and I think it's *nothing but affectation.* **Just Bull Shit**!"

"However, not having a father is shameful. Your situation is acceptable, because your father died in serving our country. But Jake ... and I like Jake ... an awful lot. I **always** have. However, Jake's situation is unforgivable. His parents have been separated for ten years or so. That's terrible and somehow his fault. That's

Bull Shit too! You know, I don't want to talk about this damn stupid shit anymore!"

She didn't spell out damn or shit. Deeply, visibly upset ... the little girl inside her is hurting ... badly.

She pulled me to her for a tight embrace and began to kiss me passionately which she turned into our first French kiss.

DECEMBER

At Monday night's dinner, my mother announced she and Rex Finnegan would not be seeing each other in the future, either for business or dating.

I clapped and cheered, "Alright, alright … *alright!*"

DeeDee yipped emphatically, "Thank You God! Thank You! I'll say a rosary in thanksgiving." Her voice trailed off quickly, "Got you … you pervert pric…"

Aunt Danae just smiled. She already knew.

My mother had finished the putting pieces of her "Rex puzzle" together, confirming Rex was a pretty slick operator. I always knew she was smart, incredibly so. I also knew it was best never to try to deceive her.

"As you know I was letting him manage some of my money, but only about a fifth of the assets. And, give this devil his due, he is good. Then I found out through Margery Jones at Paine Webber that Rex was making subtle inquiries to some of his buddies there how much my two accounts at the brokerage office were worth. I told Margery to tell him about half of what was really there. She told me that was a terrible breach of their ethics. She could be fired. So I wrote a letter to indemnify Paine Webber, signed, had it notarized, specifically defining what I wanted disclosed. Following my instructions, the next time he came in, she quietly pulled him aside and told him what he thought was the full truth. She said he seemed extremely interested and, in a strange way, happily pleased, like the proverbial miser who is always rubbing his hands together with a glint in his eye. He quickly recovered to say he only wanted to know so he could help me improve my income by placing more of my money under his management through Paine Webber. Afterwards, she called to tell me about his fake reaction. It confirmed this puzzle piece."

"However, the grotesque, ugly part of this mystery is extremely damning and disturbingly **sick**. Rex Finnegan's **preference** is for young ladies of ages 15 to 19 or so. No, not just some level of sexual

attraction for them ... the actual desire for them as **definite sexual partners.** This condition is called 'Ephebophilia' which I found discussed in a Medical article after doing some research at the Library. His first marriage was to a nineteen-year-old and his proposed second marriage was to, at most, a twenty-year-old who supposedly looked more like sixteen. I hired Adam Harrison again to investigate like he briefly did on Harry Brooks. Found out that and a few more other items last week. The details are murky, but it seems as his engagement was falling apart, he began having a 'torrid' affair with an eighteen-year-old in the spring of 1960. His new 'situation' wasn't working out for him either as it appeared this new girl wanted marriage. Obviously, he didn't. So he takes the position in Kansas City quickly. He meets and becomes seriously involved with the highly enticing Christy Taylor. One date he had to reschedule with me because ... after her performance ... they spent *that* night together. *Another* such occasion before the end of her show's run. At the Hilton. Undoubtably, there were more such 'episodes'. **Additionally**, she spent the night during her regular run with the owner, Fred Reed, in a suite at the Muehlebach. And what a big surprise ... her show was subsequently held over for two weeks. All these 'performances' by that eighteen-year-old, I'm sure, were 'highly entertaining'."

"Finnegan was already having an affair with this Belinda Jo before the divorce was filed from his wife who was becoming too old at an ancient age of twenty-six or seven. Since Belinda Jo is Catholic, he checks with a priest to see what can be done and finds out about The Pauline Privilege. All it requires is approval by the Diocese, but it still takes an inordinate amount of time and in the interim, the two break up. The lawsuit brought against this fiancée by this Louise was probably the last straw in their future relationship. Adam said the ex-wife was highly vindictive."

My mother sighed, "So he makes sure I know he is marriage eligible and will continue to date him. Thus he will beguile and charm me into marrying him. It's a perfect setup for him. One, he can marry me in the church. Two, he "finds out" there is money for him to get his hands on. Probably thought I would be so smitten in love with him that this 'trusting, naive widow' would never ask for a pre-nuptial agreement. Ha! What a *sot*! [fool] Three, Danae will move out and Richelieu will go away to college. Both out of his way. Four, there are plenty of young college girls at the bank for affairs, even another marriage." She laughed slightly, "But I never could trust the Jerk after the summer with his continued conniving and lying about the Phelps and Simmons girls. But he went way too far with DeForrest as his early wanton desires kept increasing, finally touching her to see if his inappropriate action was welcomed and returned. That was it with him. My last straw. You should have heard his 'explanation' for his behavior. What a crock of unmitigated shi … crap! He was always a lot of fun but terribly untrustworthy … just like Momma always said he was."

I gasped, "Wow, you set him up royally. I'll never play poker with you."

"No Richelieu, I just gave him some opportunities to help him prove he had changed and I was completely mistaken about him. If the religious, marital and legal problems back east were all coincidence and bad luck, he would have had a much, much different approach with a quite slower pursuit of both me and subsequently my money. More interested in my desires and needs, especially for my family. He would have been polite but paid virtually no attention to DeeDee. She maybe only fifteen and a half but she has developed a very good sense of awareness and judgment with no more school girl infatuations. The charming Rex Finnegan is no more.

With a blasé shrug, Mother concluded, "The bank should watch who he hires for his summer help. Oh, and don't worry about Christy Taylor, the dancer. That girl *knows* exactly what she is doing and what it takes to get exactly what she wants. She knows how to 'promote' herself quite well … obviously. Far, far beyond those eighteen years of hers."

****

The next day, Autumn called me to tell me her grades, which were —

  English......................1 - Accounting I.............1-
  Interior Design ....1 Advanced Algebra.....2-
  U. S. History.............2

"So a 1.4 average again, excellent. But what did you get in Study Hall?"

She laughed but said, "Algebra is getting harder."

"I'll come over and help you this weekend."

"That would be great! But could we do it at your house?"

"Sure, on Saturday. We could spend the whole day together. That would be terrific. I'll bet my mother probably will want me to help DeeDee too."

"That's fine. DeeDee's fab fun to have around. And we are gonna need all the fun we can get for mathematics."

Autumn did come over, looking fabulous again with her Thanksgiving ensemble. DeeDee was told to be in attendance. I was some help to both, but I'm just fairly good at it, not a genius like Jake. Too bad he wasn't in town. DeeDee begged Autumn to stay for dinner which she did. I told her she didn't need to change for the movies since I would wear my khakis. We went downtown to the Paramount for the debut of a new movie, *Charade* with Cary Grant and Audrey Hepburn. We both really liked it a lot, especially the scenes on the Seine.

Autumn wistfully said, "One of my dreams is to honeymoon in Paris, but I don't think that one will come true."

"That would be a very romantic place for a honeymoon. Don't give up on your dream. Do you know what the French word is for 'Charade'?"

"No, I don't have a clue."

"Charade."

She laughed and softly punched me. We drove to the Spot and discussed Paris further, making out ending with, of course, some French kissing. We laughed and pretended we were on the Seine, then walked up and down the Champs Elysées. I told her my grandfather had taught me it was named after the Greek and Roman Elysian Fields. It would be pure "Elysium" or Heaven to actually be walking with Autumn there right now.

She began talking seriously about her perception of Heaven. The joys, the happiness to be experienced. To be united with God and loved ones. So totally different and more spiritual than my meager catechism and school instructions. She was way over my head. And I'm the one who still takes religion classes!

****

As I walked out of English class, Father Fitz called me back to tell me, "It has been a while since your last confession. Meet me in the chapel after school tomorrow. I still have to translate a few more pages of a text."

I had no idea what he meant, but I told the Carson brothers and my mother I needed to drive on Tuesday.

"Bless me father for I have sinned. My last confession was November 4th. I haven't done much sinning except falling completely, madly, crazy for a girl. Her name is Autumn."

"That's no sin."

"I haven't engaged in sexual activities with her … … but I admit I would like to. I have been making out a lot with her and … a little French kissing. She's wonderful. She's *incredibly smart*. Gentle, really sensitive, even has a deep spiritual side which she keeps well-hidden. Guess you'd say, kinda real ethereal. Terrific sense of humor, just gorgeous. She's really tall with oh such great looking legs. She likes my family a lot. They like her a whole lot too. My feelings are totally, completely different for her than I have ever had with any other girl. Fantastically different!"

"You have sincere, true feelings towards her, not just your carnal desires?"

"Both, either, a lot, I'm crazy about her, totally. I think about her, all the time. Well, except in English."

He smiled but only slightly, then warned me, "Watch yourself and your actions with her."

"On to business," as he pulled out a packet of papers. "I received two letters Saturday from my Jesuit brother in Saigon. The first letter is fifteen pages, dated three days previous to the second one and contains ideas and partial texts of 'sermons' he is offering for my use. These so-called homilies are written in a type of code we Jesuits use from time to time when we don't want the secular world, other religious groups or individuals to know what we are saying. You are never to say anything about this code. **Never**! The single page second letter simply states he was not able to find out anything meaningful or useful regarding my request for more information regarding your father ... other than what is common knowledge which he summarized. He sends his heartfelt regrets. The envelope containing these letters was definitely opened and its contents heavily scrutinized before it was mailed onto the United States. Look closely. There is a very faint **blue** smudge on the fifth page of the homilies which are written in **black** ink. See how some of its pages have slight wrinkles at their top? The envelope has been steamed opened and resealed. When my Brother in Christ made inquiries, the 'wrong' people certainly became aware of them, hence the admission of no knowledge uncovered was paramount. In the sermons, he never mentions the name of his source for this information but he is underworld and reliable. I have filled in some blanks in his narrative."

"The paper slips in the envelopes mean exactly what I thought they meant. The K's are kilos of heroin ... 'horse' which Harry Brooks was heard to garble up ... ready for shipment on a certain date, certain boat, certain smuggler. Duc Phan & Minh Trang were supposedly fishermen, hence the boats, but were actually known heroin runners. The drugs' delivery point was to a specified United States military plane via two U. S. military guys ... their contacts ... always having the same destination in California on the first and third Wednesdays every month. Duc Phan had been living with the girl in the picture for only three days, when she, Lis Hoa, threw him out. A top of the line, *highly* expensive call girl, Lily Bloom, as she was called by the translation of her French and Vietnamese names. Duc Phan, part-time fisherman and full-time drug smuggler, was desirous to be her one and only 'boyfriend,' thus had promised her a luxurious life, even more so than the clothes and money she is used to. Happened for only a weekend or so. She gets rid of him to resume her high-priced trade. I had sent my Brother in Christ Harry's copy of both the picture and the letter along with copies of your father's envelopes. He has burnt everything, but I still have the originals which are here in this envelope for you." The priest tapped his cassock on his chest emphatically.

"He said Lily Bloom would have undoubtedly enjoyed posing for this type of picture. She loved being sensually and provocatively photographed, and highly thrived on Caucasian male attention of any kind. Because she was a Eurasian with impressive bodily and facial features, her 'art' photographs were a lucrative sideline business in Europe and the States for her and her photographer 'manager'. He also had his legitimate photographic business as a cover. Obviously, your father was in her house at some time. This photographer must have been hiding there somewhere. Your father is smiling as he is leaving, supposedly having enjoyed her talents. She is beckoning him back for more. Hence the perfect picture for blackmail."

"Three critical side notes of mine. **My** guess is that there was some early checking on your own mother here in the States. Would she even care? Was she having her own affair? Your mother would have checked out as **extremely** vulnerable. Second, Harry did say your father paid the prostitute to set up a meeting ... at her house ... with her 'boyfriend' ... to which he never showed. Known undoubtedly from one of your father's numbered slips or in his logbook. Lastly, your father was quite smart, astute. Knew if something happened to him, all his documentation would be in a lock box. Someone from SAC would gain entry, via Harry, and figure it out. His choice of Brooks was before the unfortunate man went off the deep end."

"Back to the coded writing. The Vietnamese Drug Boss makes Lily Bloom write the letter twice and he sends both the picture and one of the copies with Trang to give to your father along with the message of lose your proof and stop your investigation or an identical picture from the negative and the same exact letter of pregnancy goes to your wife. Your father probably told him to go have sexual relations with himself. The Boss went nuts when he was told about his elaborate blackmail scheme being thwarted.

My Jesuit brother's source stated your father did not take any crap from anyone and that certainly created a major concern. Thus the Boss uses Phan as a pawn. He was shown the second letter and another picture made off the negative. Phan went crazy as he was passionately in love with Lily who, obviously, is having sexual relations with this Major and who wants her, according to the Boss, to be his private whore. This is the same guy who is trying to put him in jail, even get him executed. The Boss tells him if he kills Major Marlowe, there will be no more investigation. After he 'lays low' for a while, he will get a big bonus and a high place in the Da Nang operation, a much bigger cut of the drug money which he will be very happy with. His Lily, too, so much so, she'll willingly move to Da Nang with him. He instructs Phan to tell your father that he, Phan, will give him the lacking evidence your father needs and another beautiful Eurasian whore but only if he guarantees money and passage to the United States for Lily and himself. Remember the last envelope with words 'deal' in caps and 'for $$$ & 2 Am Pass'? I believe the contents of the entire collection of envelopes and other information ... only God knows exactly how many ... forty more or less ... were his back-up 'logbook'. When your father came to Lily's house to discuss the details with them, Phan was hiding in the vacant house across the street and shoots your father in the back twice."

I suddenly gasped, then loudly rasped out, "O God! O Jesus!" An instant coldness struck throughout my body, causing me to uncontrollably shiver.

"Are you okay? Should we continue? We can finish this another time."

"No, no Father! Just a bad jolt! Even though ... he's been dead ... almost nineteen months ... now."

"Only if you're sure."

I nodded after a few moments, "I'm sure. Please continue Father."

"The second set of 'suggested sermons' tells of the Saigon Police immediately arresting Hoa for the Air Force Military Police to interrogate her and uncover her role in all of this. Lily is questioned for six hours, during which she's intermittently slapped and beaten, resulting in some facial bruising, a black eye and split lip. However, she steadfastly maintains she was the Major's private whore and he frequently 'visited' her, as he was doing that morning. She is now about three months pregnant with *his* child. She was asked how she knew it is his? She's a whore. She always insists every client wear a 'sheath' with her. After a few times, she wouldn't let him as she wanted to show him that she loved him by letting him be the only one. She repeatedly said she knew nothing and cried repeatedly, stating she was 'his flower' and she misses her lover ... her 'tall, black eyes'. Why would she be a party to his murder? She loved him. The examining Air Force doctor's opinion was 'a definite pregnancy'. The prostitute angrily yelled at the MP's that Duc Phan is the bastard they should arrest. He was so insanely jealous and hated her Major and wanted him dead. He begged her to meet him in Da Nang where he would have a bigger job with more money. She vehemently told the investigators, roughly translated, 'don't give a good shit if I ever see the lying, worthless little turd ever again'."

"After her release, Lily Bloom was paid off for her performance and quickly left for Hanoi to live with relatives. Not being able to find Duc Phan, the Saigon Police simply kept the murder charge of your father against the four known Viet Cong radicals since they already had claimed credit for the act. Additionally, they had been arrested for conspiracy and treason for the writing, printing, and distribution of their literature to undermine the repressive Diem government. They were quietly and swiftly executed. Duc Phan was found dead four days later in a Saigon slum district. Determined a robbery. The day before, the photographer pimp dies in a chemical fire in his darkroom which destroyed it and part of his shop. Its cause is ruled accidental, due to the mishandling of flammable chemicals. Minh Trang was assumed to have had an accident at sea as his empty boat is found during that week. His body was never recovered. Then Lily Bloom, now Lis Hoa again, is killed in a hit-and-run accident shortly after her arrival in Hanoi. Ironic ... on her way to have an abortion. The drug operation is thus closed in Saigon but most probably moved to another city ... at least temporarily. These are the supposed homilies from my Brother in Christ."

"My God, what a colossal mess! My father and four other people dead because of this drug operation."

"Seven. Don't forget Harry and the fetus. I believe the Air Force at a high level decides to tell your mother the version of the Viet Cong sniper story, which the VC fabricated to use in their propaganda. That is far, far better than telling your family that your father was killed by a now deceased, insanely jealous, drug smuggling 'boyfriend' because his expensive call girl 'sweetheart' scorned him for her Major. They had been sleeping together, possibly for months. And she was pregnant, supposedly by him. All compounded by the fact your father was going to put the wishful boyfriend in jail, even possibly have executed for the drug smuggling. The Major's death shuts down the operation and the Viet Cong happily take credit for his killing, probably at the strong suggestion of the Drug Boss. The Air Force closed their investigation after Phan was found dead, but they never tried, or more likely, never knew to piece together the interconnections among the deaths of the other drug smuggler, the photographer pimp, and the whore in Hanoi. The Air Force's mission is deemed accomplished, unfortunately, at the cost of your father's life."

Then it hit me like a ton of bricks, "Oh God! What have I done? What about my family? Look at Harry!" I was going crazy with panic.

Father Fitzgerald said quietly, "Calm down, Lou. Just take it easy. There are too many people, even the Wyandotte police, who know about Harry Brooks' rantings. Most importantly, any and all proof evaporated when he was murdered and all your father's files ... those numbered envelopes, documents and any other evidence ... were removed, except the picture, letter and the three envelopes which can prove, at most, nothing but a sordid affair and cryptic notes on maybe a drug deal gone wrong. My request came back negative from Viet Nam, verified to the drug boss as the smudge and re-sealed envelope would indicate. Someone undoubtedly thoroughly searched your father's quarters ... finding nothing ... because it was all kept in his head, backed up by his files in Wyandotte ... now stolen. Lou, IT'S OVER! On both sides of the world."

While he had continued, I did calm down greatly, "However, you're adamant the picture must be a fake. I don't want to believe its authenticity either. There's a woman who just returned to the Kansas City FBI station. SuEllen is an old friend of mine, specializing in photography and counterfeiting. The best. I want to give her the original to scrutinize it completely. If there is fraud, I am missing it. I have to admit, it **looks** genuine."

"Sure, whatever you think, Father. But **it can't** be real."

"I sincerely pray you are right. Watch yourself carefully with Autumn. Say four decades of Hail Marys. One for each of the girls in your life and go hug your Three Graces. I know you will hug your girl."

"Thank you, Father, for all your help in this ... this investigation. *You're the absolute best.* Isn't there some way I can ... can pay you for all your help?"

"You could study your English more." He laughed, then became serious, "Lou, remember all Jesuits take vows of poverty. As Plato said, 'The truth is its own reward'. You are very, very welcome, my son." He patted my shoulder warmly in a paternal fashion. "I am **always** here to help you."

****

When I finally got out of bed on Saturday, I began to think about Christmas shopping. DeeDee and I would pool our money for Mother and Aunt Danae's presents. We would buy my mother's favorite — Jean Patou's Eau De Joy. My father always bought the fragrance with its various accessories for Mother. And her last bottle was almost empty. He always told me, "Never buy your wife or girl something that plugs into the wall." I would laugh. But what else for Mother? What to buy DeeDee and, more importantly, Autumn? I was going to buy her some Chanel N°5. I really loved it and I knew she would. Maybe a small bottle and still be able to buy something else for Autumn.

Last night the carpool dropped the Sagesse Sisters off at the Savoir-Faire Boutique, an expensive ladies' clothing store. When they finished shopping, they walked the block and a half to the Law Offices to ride home with Danae. DeeDee told me she had found the perfect present for our Aunt. A light grey wool suit — jacket top and pencil skirt — which would be ideal for client meetings at the law firm or going out on dates. Very gorgeous, but it cost a little more than our pooled money for her. She knew Aunt Danae had either coordinating or matching cotton or silk shells which she could wear under the suit jacket. She had already put it on lay-a-away as she figured I would agree. All I had to do was pay my half and pick it up.

Since they had some extra time, DeeDee said they shopped a little for themselves. "Karen found a pear green wool sweater and I fell in love with a fabulous black and camel sweater. We're going to wait to buy them after Christmas, hoping they'll be on sale. But neither of us think they will be."

That afternoon I drove to Savoir-Faire Boutique and asked for Mrs. Stewart, the saleslady who helped DeeDee with Aunt Danae's lay-a-away. She was older, about Mother and Aunt Danae's age — even so, very attractive facially. Further displayed an impressive style with her youthful figure, expensive suit and heels. Her accessorizing jewelry was also striking, especially her engagement and wedding ring set.

When I told her I wanted to pay the other half due on Aunt Danae's present and needed to please have it gift wrapped, she was quite helpful. Obviously displaying a sense of high-fashion combined with a pleasant nature, she would certainly be extremely helpful for Autumn and my mother.

I told her I wanted Chanel N°5 for my girlfriend. Mrs. Stewart suggested something brand new, "A two-piece set of Chanel N°5 Spray Cologne in their standard black and gold case having almost 1000 equal sprays for use at home *and* a small black perfume purse spray which your girl would carry to freshen up when she went to the ladies' room on your dates." Next time, I promised myself I would look at the price tag, but it was for Autumn. I bought both Chanel sprays and the Eau De Joy perfume.

I asked her if she remembered the black and camel sweater DeeDee was crazy about, said yes and motioned to a display case across the aisle. This time I did look at the price tag and it was much, much higher than what I should spend. DeeDee would look incredible in it and she loved it. I told myself she had had some cruel, rough times since we moved here. Maybe this could help somehow. So much for looking at the tags. Anyway, it was for My Little Dee. As I was waiting for it to also be gift wrapped, I saw a beautiful, white blouse on a mannequin. I knew Autumn would look fabulous in this, enhancing anything she would wear — a suit or a skirt and sweater, even jeans. I found Mrs. Stewart again and asked about the blouse.

"You have a very good eye. That is Crepe de Chine silk in a twill weave. A very beautiful blouse. If it's for your sister, we will need a larger size."

"No, no, for my girlfriend," I told Mrs. Stewart. "But I don't know her size. She's a couple inches taller than my sister. I'm really at a loss."

The saleslady began to bail me out, "Your sister is quite tall and very well proportioned. We know her sweater size. So, does she have a larger frame, smaller, or the same as the mannequin ... or like your sister's?"

"Same," pointing to the mannequin. "A little smaller than my sister."

"Her bust? Larger, same, or smaller than your sister or the mannequin?"

"Uhh ... well," as I mentally pictured the two together, "definitely smaller than my sister ... like the mannequin's size." This wasn't as embarrassing as I thought buying clothes for your girlfriend would be.

"This longer length blouse would work perfectly. If not, we can easily exchange it."

"Great. I'll take the blouse too."

"Wonderful. Only take a couple minutes to gift wrap it also. Your sister and you too, young man, have excellent taste. I'm one of the store's buyers ... also a saleslady at Christmas and other times. Here's my card. And please call me Claire. Ask for me when you need anything for those four, extremely lucky girls in your life." With a captivating smile of perfect teeth and her blue eyes enticingly dancing, she said, "Thank you, Richelieu."

I politely responded, "I certainly will. And you are most welcome ... Claire."

She's cool ... a definite allure about her ... even for an older lady. Bet she has a considerable male clientele that love this sex appeal of hers. And hopefully, a trusting husband.

As I left, I thanked the blue-eyed, now topless mannequin, then looked in my billfold. There was only $10 left — $5 from my Christmas saving account which I had cashed in last night at the bank and only another $5 from my allowance. Dee would figure out what else to buy for Mother and float me a loan. When I came home, I neatly placed all the presents under the tree and was pretty pleased with myself, but not with what remained in my billfold.

❋❋❋❋❋❋❋❋❋❋❋❋❋❋❋❋❋❋❋❋❋❋❋❋❋❋❋❋

That night Autumn and I went to a Prescott hall party and we saw the beautiful Ginny with Fred Folkes — her third boyfriend since I had met her less than six weeks ago. The gorgeous Judy, not with Terry Massey, the quarterback, but with Sam Miller, the starting forward on the basketball team. Flirtatious Joanie gave me an overly inviting smile. Her new steady was Carlton Smith, another basketball player. After Autumn introduced me and I shook hands with the guys, we joined those six and I asked if anyone wanted a coke or anything. Autumn and Joanie said please but nobody else wanted one, so I went over to get us a few.

While waiting for the cokes, I heard over my shoulder, "**You** really embarrassed me, making me look foolish and stupid by starting that brawl. Everyone saw *my* date having to be carried out of the hall. Just so humiliating. Then a trip to the hospital. How gauche. You ruined *my* night!"

No need to turn around — the kennel door at Prescott had been left wide open. "Oh, you don't need any help looking stupid or foolish, you nail that act every day. Oh right, not an act. You *really* are foolish and stupid. Watch out for your Gen Ed buddies, they might want you back."

That struck a nerve, **totally** pissing her off. "You God damn Neanderthal! You don't know how to treat girls. Impress them. Or **anything at all** about females! Foul-mouthed little sluts, or naive, sexually embarrassed, puerile girls or good-looking, intellectual young ladies are all the same to you. Go jerk your dick off if you can find it. Or get that little whore who loves you to do it for you!"

I swirled around, now **totally** pissed off too. "Oh I don't, **do I**? Then why am I going steady with Autumn Knight, the most sophisticated *young lady at your* school?" I grabbed the cokes, snarling at her, "Your head, as usual, is way up your butterball ass. Bet your old lady girdle screams every time it tries to corral that great whopping ass with those guy thighs. You **phony, pseudo intellectual cunt**!"

Hearing the humiliating sizing of her butt and thighs combined with the insulting genitalia slur, she blew up, almost yelling, "I'll get even with you. You and your puny pecker of a prick! Swear to God I will, you dick-licking Papist! **I'll get you**!"

I began walking away, muttering loud enough for her to hear, "And my little dog too. Watch out for falling houses, you Wicked **Bitch** of the West. Go find your flying monkey minions and spray your hateful, stinking piss on them for their baptism."

SHE would easily beat Karen Reynolds for the 'Girl Spouting Most Profanity' Award. And I didn't think Protestant girls swore much. She's incredibly nasty ... a vicious cunt!

Puny pecker of a prick? Say that three times fast!

Autumn and I began to dance to the band's try at covering *Sea of Love*. I told her about my encounter with "the wicked bitch" of Prescott giving an **extremely** edited version. Among the omissions were her suggested "abuse" of my penis by me or Caroline's undoubted success, and *certainly* the name for her genitals. Did tell her about the mention of my Catholicism — somewhat, and the tongue twisting insult concerning the incorrect sizing of my penis — somewhat. Finally the correct sizing of her ass and thighs, along with her minions' baptisms. She still turned scarlet at even my chewed-up *Reader's Digest* version.

She recovered sufficiently to explain, "Sheila puts on a good act that she's nice to everyone but it's like one of her roles. She can be mean, even vicious to some girls, like to Sally Adams ... Pamela Parker's best friend and Rhodes' recent target ... the girl I was telling you about last week. She loves to spread rumors for excitement ... boosts her ego. She's always wanted to smear my girlfriends, *especially me* ever since I got the part to play *The Ghost of Christmas Past* last year. Mr. Elbert wanted 'a tall, beautiful ghost'. She had to play 'a plain, matronly' *Mrs. Cratchit*. Haha! Strange though ... even before that, she's *never really* liked me. Not a bit. Don't know why. Ginny said and Judy agreed, 'a case of **a-s-s envy** ... overweight and balloon b-u-t-t cheeks with football pad thighs versus tall, slender and curvy'. She won't try to attack me. The clique can make her look bad. She knows it. The girls would fix that Butterball B-u-t-t B-i-t-c-h Witch."

"And all along I thought you were this sweet, innocent little girl that everybody loves."

"Keep thinking that, Mister!" She said in a fake intimidating voice. We laughed and finished out the dance.

Even in these short six weeks, she has let me see not only her real talents but certain true inner feelings which no one else, except Summer, has been allowed to see. Under that remarkably friendly, carefree facade, she's incredibly creative, so innocent, so gentle and extremely sensitive, knowingly wouldn't hurt anyone. There have been more frequent intervals of spirituality, especially when talking about her Nanna.

After two hours of dancing, mixed in with listening to the other couples talk, especially the guys brag about their basketball season so far of five wins without a loss, Autumn leaned over to whisper softly in my ear, "The Spot?" I nodded in full agreement.

"We are going to leave, so I will see you all Monday. Goodnight, everyone."

"Great to see you, Ginny and Judy. And Joanie," who again smiled very flirtatiously. She was always so obvious, yet my gentle Victoria has never said a word to her. Or to the sometimes blatant Ginny.

"Good to meet you Fred. Continued good luck this season, Sam and Carlton."

Ginny laughingly called after us, "Bye Autumn and Rich-**e**-lou! *Wonder where* you two are going?"

I turned, then winked, "To St. Victoria's and pray. You know how us Catholics can be."

****

When we parked at the Spot, I solemnly said, "I hereby christen this hallowed place to be known hence forth as St. Victoria's."

"You are **so** sacrilegious. Even a Presbyterian or Reformation chick ... as you call me ... would know you are being as such."

"How can you say that? I come here to worship my Victoria as much as I am allowed."

"Therefore I christen you Richie, the Wickedly Incorrigible. There is absolutely no possible redemption for you."

We laughed and began making out.

"Richie, promise me you won't spend a lot on me for Christmas."

Means she can't afford to spend a ton on me. Don't care. ... ...
"Don't worry. Already got you something small."

Autumn and I talked more about Christmas. She had no plans for Christmas Eve. She and Summer would celebrate Christmas that morning with their parents — very low key. The girls would have picked out their own presents beforehand. Her father simply would give their mother a check and she would give him a tie and matching shirt or something else as habitually boring. The girls always bought something nice for both of them and certainly each other. Her mother would cook the special Christmas dinner after the Church's Christmas service.

"Why don't you spend Christmas Eve with us?"

"Oh thank you. I thought you would never ask. Of course I will. Do you exchange presents then?"

"Yes, with a buffet dinner around 6 o'clock followed by the presents."

"Richie ... oh Richie, I can hardly wait for the holidays. This will be so much fun. You and me. Summer and Jake. Your mother ... your aunt and DeeDee too. School will be out! Oooh, only ten more days till Christmas! Oh goody great! Oh goody, goody great!"

The little girl showing through again. Becomes so happy and excited. And her hidden side of innocence.

****

The last day before Christmas vacation!

While I was sitting in English, I was thinking about all the advice and guidance Father Fitz had given me during "The

Investigation." especially with the evidence and his unwavering support. After class, I asked, "Father, what do you Jesuits do for Christmas Eve and Day?"

"We say our three Masses and pray for our families and our students, especially certain ones who need it." He looked very pointedly at me but would not smile.

"Could you celebrate with others, outside the residence?"

"Yes, we can, however we need to receive permission ... but it's always granted."

"Why don't you spend Christmas Eve with my family? They would love to meet you. I've spoken of you not only as my teacher but also my regular confessor."

"I can go you one better, Marlowe, if you would like. Why don't I say Midnight Mass for your family? But you should check with your mother first."

"You would **do that**! **Wow**! Really! No need! My mother would be thrilled! 'Over the moon' as she and my aunt would say."

"Okay, deal, but call me Sunday or Monday to confirm your mother's approval and a Tuesday afternoon pick up time."

"And you'll get to meet my Three Graces and gorgeous girlfriend, Autumn." ... ... *School's out for two weeks. Spend much, much more time with Autumn. Father Fitz saying Midnight Mass. Christmas and Holiday parties. ... This is great!*

Now who is the little girl? Okay, I am. ... SO WHAT!

****

When I walked in the front door, I went into the study, greeted my mother with a kiss. "Hi Mother. Hope it's okay that I invited Father Fitz for Christmas Eve. He accepted by offering to be our own personal priest for a Midnight Mass."

"Father Fitzgerald? Oh Richie, that would be wonderful ... really wonderful for us. Our own family Mass. Richie, sometimes you are the magician Autumn calls you. Oooh, *what about Autumn*?"

"Well, she'll be here for dinner and presents."

"Of course, but what about Mass?"

"Oh, she'll stay. Know she will. And she'll love him and the Mass."

When I picked Autumn up to go hangout at Blender's, I told her about my plans with Father Fitz. She thought that was wonderful he would do that for my family and she "would be honored to be there". She had never been to a Catholic Mass before.

****

On Saturday, Autumn called about four o'clock and implored me, "I have a really big favor to ask. I told Jake and Summer about Midnight Mass with Father Fitzgerald. They would like to come, so would it be all right?"

"Of course, it's fine."

"Thank you, Richie, oh thank you! See you in a bit." Autumn was going to come over here and just hang out. Summer and Jake were spending the day Christmas shopping.

She called back in fifteen minutes. "Oh Richie! Richie! Now I have a tremendously big favor. Enormously big! I will owe you a ton."

"Well, we both know the foreign currency I like to be paid in. Big hint ... it's French."

She laughed, "Oh, I'll be sure to take care of you." She very seductively added, "Don't I always, big boy?"

"Yes, you certainly do. What's the new favor?"

"Jake wants his mother and brother to come and—"

"Sure," I interrupted.

"Weeel, they want to have the Mass at Aunt Genie's. Is that a problem since she is Presbyterian?"

"Oh, religion is not a factor. I need to check with my mother though, hang on." I asked her if she would agree and she said certainly we could move the Mass to Jake's aunt's, a few more like Regina would just make Christmas merrier. She knew Mass would still be personal and intimate.

When I brought Autumn back to the house, she went immediately into the study where my mother was and greeted her, then quickly apologized, "I hope this does not cause a problem with your intended Christmas plans, Mrs. Marlowe. I'm really so sorry. I will tell you exactly why—"

"Oh no, it doesn't, not a bit. Please don't worry yourself, Honey," my mother interrupted. "It's even better. I haven't seen

Regina for at least a month. She is always great fun, especially when she entertains. And Honey, you must start calling me Gi Gi. 'Mrs. Marlowe' makes me feel so old. No more Miss Richelieu either. Danièle would love you to call her simply Danae."

WHAT? I don't believe this! Gi Gi! Instead of Mrs. Marlowe! Danae too!

Later at St. Victoria's Spot, I told her to guess what Monday was, but she didn't have a clue.

"The Feast of St. Victoria. We should honor her by parking here at her hallowed place and heavily making out."

"You can be so unbelievably sacrilegious," then she laughed, but very suggestively promised, "I just might consider it for you."

I then asked Autumn why Aunt Genie wanted it at her house.

"If you tell any living soul, I will be so very, very mad at you. I might not come over Christmas Eve. Do you promise?"

"With that as a threat, I don't wanna know."

"Please, please! Just don't tell anyone. Please?"

"I promise."

"Aunt Genie gave Jake money to buy Summer an engagement ring. That's where they have been all day, looking at rings. They bought one right before I called you! Can you believe it? They are officially engaged! It's great!"

"Well, I'll be damned." I was amazed.

"Richie, I hope not, I might miss you," she teased.

"Really fab, just terrific for Jake and Summer."

"Yeah, but my parents won't like it one bit since they are only freshmen plus all the other stuff. I don't think his mother will like it either. Still they have known each other since third grade, so it's not like they just met at Columbia this semester. I think it's wonderful. I'll get to be 'maid of honor' and have Jake as a brother. So, they are going to announce it right before Mass. Also, Genie thought it would be nice to have some members of the families get together, especially, since you and Jake are 'Mackerel Snappers' and Summer and I are 'Reformation Chicks'. A very nice mixing of the religions, as she called it. Also, Joe and Sunny might be there. Sunny is trying to awaken him from being a lapsed Catholic from his grade school days. She, evidently, is quite devout. They're serious, too."

The foreign currency exchange window opened and was very accommodating as we intermittently talked more about Christmas and possible plans for New Year's Eve and the intervening days.

****

Since Christmas Eve dinner was going to be at 6 o'clock, I picked Autumn up at 4:30 to go with me to St. Ignatius. She was dressed in her Christmas present from her parents, picked out by Summer and herself. I told her she looked fantastic in her new creamy beige, rayon brocade outfit consisting of a double-breasted jacket and very long trousers, almost covering her matching stiletto heels. Her turtleneck sweater a dark brown, nicely accessorized by her locket and Nanna's gold pearl drop earrings. The sisters had gotten their hair styled into upsweeping bouffants and Autumn was probably again a couple inches taller than me. I still didn't care. She put a few nicely wrapped packages in the back seat, saying they were for someone very special and lightly gave me a kiss on the cheek, then wiped the lipstick off as I pulled away.

Autumn had never been to the new high school campus. She had been with Summer a few times last spring before the high school ended its final year as part of the college campus. I pulled up in front of the Jesuit residence and Autumn got out with me to be properly introduced to the priest. I buzzed the intercom, saying I was there for Father Fitzgerald. Within minutes he appeared with a small carrying case and I introduced him to Autumn. As we drove back to Wyandotte, I expected a totally different side of him to emerge. Certainly not his authoritarian classroom or even his counseling confessional demeanor. I was not disappointed in the least.

Autumn and Father Fitz, as he told her to call him, just chatted away like a couple of old friends. I may have said two sentences, with a couple grunts mixed in. We drove in the garage right at 5:45, then went into the kitchen to meet my Three Graces. I could tell he was impressed with their charm, style and good looks. As that trio finished the final touches for dinner, our trio went into the living room and he marveled at the tree centered among the wonderful seasonal and religious decorations, saying how magnificent it looked. I told him that Autumn had greatly helped in its design. He tersely replied he wasn't surprised in the least.

When everything was ready, my mother insisted that Father Fitz go first, followed by Autumn, then the family. We all sat down and Father said a blessing, of course not the regular run-of-the-mill catechism bore, but one thanking God for the excellent company to share Christmas dinner with and my mother in particular for her invitation. My comment was it was getting to be a habit — a pleasant one — as she was named in Autumn's Thanksgiving blessing. He said it was either a sign of Jesuit training or extremely good manners and intelligence. Autumn smiled, beaming, "You're so kind. Thank you, Father."

He was very jovial and witty and entertained all four girls who were laughing and smiling throughout the dinner. I was sure my mother was missing my father as I was, yet on a much different level. I thought about the Viet Nam cover up of its murders and drug running, but quickly put it out of my mind, telling myself Father Fitz would wrap up that area finally and *successfully* for me.

After dinner we opened presents. DeeDee, as always, played Santa's elf and passed out the presents one by one. The first one went to our guest. Two large bottles — quarts of Cutty Sark Scotch. The card said in Latin, "For my favorite of the Jesuits from Pope Paul VI". He looked at me, then smirked, "Very droll Richelieu. Thank you."

Autumn opened her present of the two Chanel sprays. She was amazed and particularly happy, especially after she sprayed some on her inner wrist to sample the fragrance. Then DeeDee gave her the gift-wrapped box containing the blouse. She was surprised for another gift. "This is beautiful and the right size. Who picked it out for you? DeeDee?"

"Nope, all by myself with only a little help from Misty and one of the store's buyers regarding the size, *confirmed* by DeeDee."

"Three presents. Rich, you said you bought me something small."

"I *did* buy you something small." I grinned, "The purse spray is small."

"There are two other presents. You, sir, are being influenced entirely too much by your Jesuits. Your contextual phrasing suggests them." Everyone laughed with the biggest one coming from the Jesuit himself. "And just *who is Misty*? A model?" she asked with a hint of real jealously.

"Of sorts. Misty the Mannequin was very helpful." We all laughed again. I thought of the mannequin episode on the *Twilight Zone* of a few years ago with Anne Francis.

Autumn gave me two shirts, one of which I had been looking for, ever since I had bought my new camel hair sweater. A button-down with a matching camel colored stripe. The other was a matching black stripe button-down for my black cashmere. Summer had picked up both for her at Puckett's in Columbia. DeeDee loved her sweater, saying she had no idea I was even listening to her when she mentioned the sweater, then came over to give me a big thank you kiss. Aunt Danae was very excited with the grey suit, saying she really needed something like this. My mother loved her emerald and gold bracelet which DeeDee picked out and for which I owe her big time for my half. She got tears in her eyes when she opened the perfume. There was a present to her from "Father Christmas" — a German antique Santa Claus which fit perfectly on the mantle and as well into the family collection. But no one took credit.

I whispered to Autumn, "Victoria, these are perfect. I'll be right back."

I went to my room and changed. Great fabric in the perfect color. I went down stairs and showed her then everyone else. We all talked over dessert with tea and coffee for a while, then Autumn asked if we could leave to go to Aunt Genie's.

I teased, "Yeah, but Mass is not until Midnight and we have the necessary and sufficient person to make that happen."

She gave me a playful slug, whispering, "Rich, you know we need to leave."

We drove both cars as Autumn and I would take Father Fitz back to the Jesuit Residence from Aunt Genie's.

All six of us went in the back door as instructed by Autumn then I made the necessary introductions. Jake with a broad smile, shook hands with Father Fitz, telling him it was great to see him again. He introduced Summer, looking fantastic like Autumn. Father Fitz, in observing their attractive resemblance, declared beauty always finds ways of replicating itself. He readily confirmed Aunt Genie's living room envisioned Christmas wonderfully, both secularly and spiritually. She and Charley hit it off right away with the priest. They decided to have Mass in the dining room where Father would use the buffet as his altar to celebrate Mass. I was introduced to Jake's mother Eleanor or "Ellie" and brother Peter and his girlfriend, Mary Jane — reasonably attractive, quite personable and extremely smart. As my mother would say, "Peter's smitten!" Joe and Sunny were also there.

It seemed like everyone was all over the house, laughing, talking, being festive and thoroughly enjoying themselves. I asked Father Fitz if he needed anything. He said no, he was having a great time just conversing with the "old" people — Ellie, Gi Gi, Danae and Regina and Charley.

Jake took a spoon and gently rang his crystal glass with it. "Everybody, it is 11:11. One weekend night last month, Summer and I were out walking around the columns at Mizzou, holding hands. I did what I had been wanting to do for a long, long time. At 11:11 on that Saturday night, I formally asked Summer to marry me. She said, 'Yes!' Thanks to Aunt Genie, we bought a ring Saturday and here it is." He held it up for everyone to see, then slipped it on Summer's finger and kissed her. Everyone cheered.

But Eleanor didn't cheer. She was in shock. However, when she composed herself, she happily exclaimed, completely surprising everyone, "Oh, thank You, my Lord Jesus Christ! This is what I have been praying for so long. Oh Jackson, Summer has always been perfect for you. A perfect daughter-in-law for me." She and Summer hugged and kissed.

Autumn, Aunt Genie and Sunny followed with kisses. My Three Graces and Mary Jane all wished her the best for their future with friendly hugs. Charley, Peter, Father Fitz and I shook hands with Jake with similar good thoughts. Autumn gave Jake a kiss on the cheek. Ellie hugged and kissed him, then Genie whispered something in his ear and kissed him. The men wished their happiness to Summer with kisses, hugs, or pats on the shoulder. The women likewise expressed their joyfulness with Jake.

I heard my mother say to Aunt Danae, "So this is why Mass is here. I knew there had to be an extremely good reason. And *it's* a great one!" Then she went over to Autumn and beamed, "Thank you Honey for Father Christmas, that perfect Santa," kissing her on her cheek and hugging her.

Autumn blushed. "You're so welcome, Gi Gi." Autumn kissed her back, confessing, "When I saw it, I instantly thought of you. I *had* to buy it." They hugged again.

Not even two months, Gi Gi is 'smitten' with her Honey ... so is Autumn with Mother. Remained so aloof, so distant, even downright haughty ... with EVERY OTHER girl.

Mass was wonderful in itself. Father Fitz's homily was about love. His words were that love transcends everything. Differences in religion as evidenced by Catholic and Protestant families joining here tonight to celebrate a joyous happening. Love doesn't see boundaries, only openings to infinite possibilities. Love doesn't see the differences, just unlimited harmony and peace. Everyone enjoyed his short but poignant homily and thanked him heartily for coming and saying Mass.

Joe went up to him with Sunny and gratefully told Father Fitz this Mass and its Christmas celebration confirmed what he was missing and should return to the Church. He would. Sunny said it was the best Christmas present she could have ever wished for and she happily thanked Father Fitz four or five times for providing the basis for it, impulsively kissing him on the cheek in her joyfulness.

There were snow showers on the drive back to the Jesuit residence, but Autumn and Father Fitz were oblivious to them, intently focused on discussing the interconnectedness of the mind and soul, then specifically on the soul. I could only focus on the driving. The snow showers stopped when we arrived, yet they continued to talk for at least another fifteen minutes. As we all got out to say good-byes and thanks, I made sure he had his case and the two bottles. Autumn said, "Oh Father, thank you so very much. Thank you for our discussion on the soul and its spiritual dimensions. I would love to further talk more about *its* essence. Ooh, so wonderful to have my Nanna's spirit there for Summer's engagement. During your beautiful celebration of the Mass, I felt as close to God as I have ever felt in my life. My soul feels so hearten tonight."

She is so POSITIVE that her Nanna's spirit was there.

"Wonderful! Could be the season. Could be all the families together. Could be the announcement. Could be all three or it could be something else. Time will tell. Certainly, certainly wonderful to meet you, my dear. You have a very special influence on this rapscallion. So extremely enjoyable to talk with you about man's spiritual aspects. You are one markedly, insightful young lady. So I promise you, the next time we shall continue in greater detail. It was great to spend my Christmas Eve with your families. One of my best. I will see you," and he looked narrowly at me, "in eleven days." Then he blessed us both, then placed a hand on each of our shoulders and in parting, "Celebrate the remainder of Our Lord's season well, my children. You made an excellent start. Thank you."

He picked up his packages and carrying case, turned away to become the gruff, authoritative Father Fitzgerald again, however I saw him grinning broadly, then slightly chuckling as he walked through the entrance door. We could hear his loud laugh's echo before the door slammed.

My best Christmas I ever had too. Except Dad wasn't here. Really missed him in its celebration. But like Jake said, 'The pain never really leaves'.

As we drove back to Wyandotte, Autumn gushed, "This is the best date we have had, Richie. Your priest is a fabulously good man. I'm so glad he enjoyed it ... 'one of his best'. It's definitely been my best!"

"He is a good man ... more than you know, Victoria, more than you know. My best Christmas too."

"Richelieu, you spent a lot of money on me!"

"Not really, everything was 75% off."

"I'm being serious. I didn't spend a third of that on you."

"Victoria, I love the shirts. That's what is important. I am wearing a shirt I have been trying to find for five months. Now I have a charcoal stripe one which matches perfectly to my second favorite sweater. I love that one too. If I could, I would wear both shirts at once." She laughed. "All you got was a bland, white blouse and a tiny bottle of perfume with its purse spray."

"That blouse is far from being bland. That is an extremely lovely, very expensive silk blouse. It's definitely the best one I have and very versatile. It will even look cool with dress jeans. And here," as she turned her head to spritz herself and I could smell the N°5 on her neck.

"Oooh wonderful! That combination of Spray Cologne and Purse Perfume is brand new. No other girl at Prescott will have that purse spray."

"Richelieu, sometimes you are so utterly, d-a-m-n dense. It's Chanel N°5! It's d-a-m-n expensive perfume! Most assuredly NO girl will have it. Period!"

"If you love it, that's all that's important to me."

"I love all three." She kissed my cheek three times. I wanted to go to St. Victoria's, but it was almost 3:00 am. We did talk some and make out a bit in front of her house for the first time. No neighbors would be up to gawk.

I held her tightly as we walked slowly to her door. "Could we do something tomorrow afternoon or night?"

"Both, if *you* are lucky! Merry Christmas, Richie!" We Frenched goodnight.

"Merry Christmas, Victoria!" A short last kiss and she went inside.

****

The next seven days passed in a whirl. Autumn spent as much time as she could with Summer, however we were still able to be together most nights and the two afternoons Jake and Summer visited Sister Cecilia. Autumn told me there was a New Year's Eve dinner/dance party sponsored by the Wyandotte Junior College Tri Delta sorority at the old Grinter House with the best area band, The Silvertones. Admission was by a couples only ticket of $10.00. Summer had called her old friend, Maggie Johansson with whom she had gone to junior and senior high about the tickets. Her given name was Margreta Annika and went by Greta

Ann until Jake christen her with the nickname from *Cat on a Hot Tin Roof*. Everyone followed and began calling her Maggie when high school started. As Treasurer, she had the few remaining tickets with her, so Summer ask her to hold two of them for a day. Both Autumn and I thought it was a great idea, so we drove over to Maggie's house on that Friday and I bought the tickets. Mother had given DeeDee and me our allowances early with a nice increase, yet I was still deeply in debt to my sister.

Autumn was dressed again in her outfit she had worn Christmas Eve, but with her caramel sweater, shorter heels and a varied bouffant style. I told her she looked her natural fabulous self. Jake was already there with Summer who had asked Autumn earlier if we would follow them to the party. Earlier in the week she told me the announcement at the Knight house Christmas Day had met with the expected negative reviews. Her parents both wanted to know when they would be getting married which the couple said would be upon graduation. Her mother was a little hesitant to announce it to her bridge club and church group. Her father thought they should have waited until closer to the marriage date. Jake, in true form, simply said the time was now. Still neither parent was pleased. Jake figured the Knights thought if they married before graduation, they would move in with them for a while, further exacerbated by Jake being Catholic. Summer told Autumn Hell would freeze over before she and Jake slept together one night in that house. If they needed to stay overnight in Wyandotte, they would go to Aunt Genie's, where they would always be greatly welcomed with open arms.

I had never been to a college party and this one had been limited to about fifty couples. The fried chicken dinner was excellent. The band, which I had heard once at the Broadmoor, was in great form. We danced for about an hour, then Summer and Autumn decided to go to the ladies' room to freshen up.

Right after they left, Maggie came over and sat close to Jake, trying to make herself look sexy by French inhaling her cigarette. They hadn't seen each other since last summer and they talked and laughed about old times at Whittier, some high school stuff, but virtually nothing about the engagement or Summer. Maggie frequently touched Jake's arm, giggling and snickering during their banter, but stroked it when he said she was "still incredibly cute, hadn't changed". When she pulled out another Salem, she held Jake's hand a moment or two longer after he finished lighting it for her. Maggie said she heard Carlotta was back in town from Hays and looked even better. She had danced as Christy Taylor in some Starlight productions and now at some bar downtown. Jake said that made sense as Christina was Carlotta's middle name. Maybe she was staying for good.

Carlotta of Zesto's IS The Inferno's Christy. Rex's budding protégée ...both as an entertainer and a calculating, amoral slut! But a damn sexy, beautiful one!

So I finally contributed to the conversation, "No, she was leaving before Christmas to go to California after stopping off in Hays. And it's not a 'bar'. It's a very popular and fashionable nightclub ... 'The Inferno'."

"Who told you that? Where did you hear this news?" demanded Maggie.

"Do *you* know who *she* is?" asked Jake.

"Seven weeks ago, Autumn and I had just begun dating that day and this Carlotta or Christy came through Zesto's in a black Fairlane convertible, top down, black hair blowin' in the wind. She yelled that at a bunch of older guys who were shouting some real flattering come-ons to her. The great-looking blonde with her ... Teri ... was an accomplished teaser too, enjoying herself as she caught her own compliments and returned some hi-powered flirting.

Jake chuckled, "*That's* Carlotta, all right! Still hanging out with her good-looking buddy, Teri. Sure sounds like *they* haven't changed."

"When my mother was at the nightclub, she met the owner and Christy. She was a terrifically good dancer but just a fair singer. Exuded tons of sex appeal in her skimpy outfit. The engagement was for four weeks, but her act got held over." ... ... *Gee whiz, wonder why?*

Jake smiled, "Good for her. Always was a terrific dancer ... and sexy. Very!"

When the sisters returned, both greeted Maggie warmly. Summer thanked her for holding the tickets, and said to Jake and me she was sorry they were gone for so long. They had seen and talked with a few girls she and Maggie had graduated with — Marsha, Penelope, and Frances Parke who is now Mrs. Dan Driscoll. Maggie asked to see the ring, only saying it was nice. After briefly continuing to talk, Maggie lit up her own cigarette, got up to leave, saying, "Happy New Year everyone, and Best Wishes to you Summer, Congratulations and best of luck, Jake, **as always**." She kissed him on the lips, lasting entirely much longer than a friendly, 'best of luck' kiss should.

Evidently, Summer thought so too. She twirled her ringed hand, calling out angrily to Maggie's back who had to hear her, even as she walked away, "All mine ... **forever**! You perpetually Jake-horny lit...." The band began to play *Midnight Thunder* so I didn't hear the obscene name she undoubtably called her. Summer proceeded to wipe "little whatever's" lipstick off Jake to quickly replace with hers.

❆❆❆❆❆❆❆❆❆❆❆❆❆❆❆❆❆❆❆❆❆❆

Margreta — Maggie — Annika Johansson graduated from Washburn University with a degree in business; her friendly personality and ability to recognize and satisfy her customers' needs paved the way to a highly successful sales career at The TRW Credit Bureau as she became their Central Region's VP; Maggie and Janice O'Shay rekindled their teenage friendship during a cold call — before long, Janice or J. J.'s bank became an exclusive client of TRW;

Maggie never dated much, committed to only three relationships; The last one turned into marriage to a younger widower when she was thirty-three; Unfortunately, she never was able to conceive;

However, she became a wonderful wife and excellent 'Mummy' to his two small children, loving the son and daughter as if they were her very own; As she continued her successful career, she constantly helped to solve their problems, rejoiced in their successes & gave solace in their failures, insuring both did well in high school and graduated from college;

**Still happily married & a loving,
exceptional 'Grams' to her six grandchildren**

❈❈❈❈❈❈❈❈❈❈❈❈❈❈❈❈❈❈❈❈❈❈❈❈❈❈❈❈❈❈❈❈

Autumn teased, "Jake, you always were utterly oblivious when it came to girls."

"What do you mean?"

"Your saucy Maggie for instance. She has always 'had a thing' for you as far back as Whittier and you never could see it. Jake, she **still** does!"

No Shit!

"Oh, no, no, it was just like brother and sister, nothing was ever there," and he looked at a somewhat cooled down Summer, appealing to her for confirmation.

She shook her head, "Autumn's right. Maggie the Cat-bitch has always wanted you for-ev-ver. You just never could figure it out. You never made a move. She told me she had hinted very strongly quite a few times. Thought the only way you would ever do something is if she strutted stark naked in front of you. I think she really would have done it in high school ... maybe even tonight if she had the chance! It's okay, Slugger. Really." She patted his hand with her ring-hand condescendingly. Jake was dumbfounded.

"It's a malady first basemen suffer from," laughed Autumn, "Rich has it too."

"How? Who?"

"Ginny Foster. Most definitely that first-class flirt ... Joan Marie Myers."

"Naw, no way," I said disbelieving.

"It's okay, Slugger. Really." She patted my hand in the same teasing fashion. I was the one now dumbfounded about Ginny. I thought it was just some innocent flirting. But Joanie's smiles and teases aren't so innocent. Not one bit. She would even go out with me on the sly. Once, she very strongly hinted, virtually asking me out.

Marsha McCabe and Penelope Evers came over to see Jake and meet me. Marsha was medium height, nice blue eyes, lengthy straight brown hair, good-looking, likewise good-looking set of knockers. After the introductions, she didn't say much, but certainly looked me over and I guardedly did her too, especially *that* pair. When she turn sideways, I noticed a nice butt too. Oddly, her glances turned into intermittent staring for moments at a time. Penny, also attractive with brown hair and eyes, was doing all the talking and all to Jake, ending with a laugh, "Well, guess we'll never have **that** date." Both smiled and left to search for their dates whom they didn't seem too much in a hurry to find.

Summer followed with the facts of Marsha was Jake's eighth grade steady, Joe's senior love, and from the girls' recent Tag, dating *the* basketball star at St. Benedict's College. [I now called it a 'Tag' — tinkle and gossip.]

Summer explained, "Penny had the off and on high school hots for Jake, wanting to date him. But I was always going steady with him, so she thought she would just wait on a back burner for him.

Jake smirked, "Hell, she wasn't even on the stove. Oh, she's good-looking but can't shut-up. A nice gal ... really ... but yaks on and on, mostly about nothing."

Tonight, Penny's guy was from Washburn, who liked to drink and doing a lot of it. Hopefully, he would let her drive when he took her home. Weeks later, however, Autumn heard Penny's date ran his car off the road into a tree. He suffered only cuts, a broken wrist and minor bruises. Unfortunately Penny sustained a broken leg and pelvis. She had to take delayed grades for the semester, missing the next term completely.

Later, a guy named Dan Driscoll came over with his rather pregnant wife, Frances. He and Jake talked briefly and Jake told Frances her sea blue eyes sparkled even more now that she was pregnant. She told Jake he hadn't changed at all, "**stillll** the ir-resis-tea-bill charmer" just like in high school, even when they were at Whittier and Park. She congratulated him, kissed him on his right cheek, his forehead, left cheek, finally on his lips, laughing loudly, saying she wanted to **cover** all the bases, **especially home plate** and quickly kissed his mouth again. She was more than slightly blitzed. Summer merely laughed at her display. However, Dan was not amused with her behavior and he pulled her away to leave. Autumn explained to me later that at Whittier, Frances, Maggie and Summer were all best friends — part of "The Charmed Circle". Marsha and her smart cousin, Carol Sue, were kind of in that group, frequently hanging out with them. Both Jake and Danny, as Jake still called him, were two of "The Seven Wonders" from those days.

After they left, Summer sadly related, "In the Ladies' room, she was having a couple or three Lucky Strikes ... can you believe ... smoking non-filters! During which the poor girl downed a few easily hidden drinks of vodka from under that god-awful looking maternity outfit. She became so talkative. Poor, poor Frances. Kept talking about 'the good old days' of high school and now ... pregnant. Knows she 'got knocked up on our drunken graduation night'. They eloped to Miami, Oklahoma in mid-August, three days after she turned eighteen and a month before Dan had to go to school at Emporia. Frances said she was too afraid to tell the Parkes about the pregnancy. She thought they wouldn't let her marry him. Guess they didn't like the idea of Danny as a son-in-law and father of their grandchild at all. The couple are trying to sort out the living arrangements. Jake, you remember she's always had this 'thing' for him ... always. Like Maggie with you, but far worse. Even at Whittier, she wanted him back with him more than going with Sam 'The Stud' Fuller. Danny was always with blondes. Eighth grade was her year, but freshman year, it was Teri Carter ... then as sophomores ... Joyce Hart, but junior year was Frances' year again. They broke up for a while in the fall last year, but got back together at Christmas. She made *damn* sure she would keep him the third time."

"Yeah, Danny always had a thing for blondes. Still a great guy. He told me his full basketball scholarship at Kansas State Teachers College is terrific as he doesn't have to pay for anything ... like mine. Frances continues to live at home with her parents and he tries to come home every weekend and other times when he's not playing ball. Some things do have a way of changing, don't they?"

The band began their cover of Elvis' hit slow song, *Can't Help Falling In Love*. Jake suggested we switch sisters. I happily agreed.

Summer said, "Autumn really likes your 'Three Graces' as you call them. She sincerely enjoys being with them at your house."

"Yeah, the only reason she dates me is to hang out with them."

Summer laughed then became serious, "Rich, you know she really likes you. I mean **really** likes you. You should have heard the long distance call I had that Sunday morning after your first dates when she started going steady with you. I have never heard her talk like that about a guy before."

"She is the most amazing girl I have ever known. I like her incredibly so much. Far, far more than any girl I have ever dated. After she spent only an hour with my Three Graces, they all acted like they were old friends which, of course, they are now. You should have seen her with Father Fitz when we brought him to my house and the trip back to the Jesuit residence. Like they had known each other for years, talking about the soul's spirituality in a deeply religious discussion."

"Autumn can do that with people. Ha ... but me? I am a little shy with people, especially when I first meet them, but, oh no, no, not our Autumn. She has this natural charm. Reminds me of both Aunt Genie and Nanna ... our Irish grandmother ... she and Autumn were terribly close. She would always go talk to her or me, rather than our mother. Autumn was totally devastated when she died. A week later, she said Nanna appeared in her bedroom ... like she use to when she would come to see Autumn to help cheer her up or talk to her about some problem. Told her she had no pain anymore and in a wonderful, beautiful place, somewhere close. She would always be with her Little Audie when she was needed."

"Autumn says she strongly felt your Nanna's spirit for your engagement announcement. In fact, she says your Nanna still talks to her. Only very rarely though."

"She said you are the only other one she has told about Nanna's 'presence'. She really believes Nanna does 'communicate' with her. I really don't know if she does, but Autumn just sees and experiences some things differently, *so very much so*." Summer quickly changed the subject, "She says you are quiet around others, almost secretive, like you were Thanksgiving. But you aren't tonight."

"In larger groups I always am. I just listen. Sometimes it's not so great or it is fun like it was at Thanksgiving ... or tonight ... to hear you and your old high school friends talk. But with you and Jake, it's different. You're both genuine, real smart. Simply a lot of fun to hang out with. A lot of guys like to brag, talking about how great they were in last week's game. Some girls talk about the latest skirt or sweater they bought and how much it cost or who's dating or not dating who. Autumn and I have been to small parties like that which turn into a couples make-out session. When Autumn and I are going to make-out, we do it privately." I smirked then began to laugh playfully. "We make good use of your place on Sandusky."

She laughed, "Good, hate to see it going to waste. Speaking of girls and clothes, that was some blouse you bought for her. The Chanel N°5 is wonderful. Especially that spray! She let me use some for tonight." She added a little sheepishly, "I hope that was okay with you."

"Of course. Anytime. It's my job to keep her looking and smelling wonderfully. Maybe you too." We both laughed. "Smells nice on you too." I added.

"Well, Jake said he likes L'Interdit on me better. Oh, she also says you are always plotting something, never giving anyone a clue then, 'Poof!', something just magically happens. Like when the locket just happened to appear and its companion chain materialized from nowhere. She really treasures and loves that locket and chain. They mean a great deal to her."

I said very seriously, "She means an extremely great deal to me."

"I know she does. I know you mean an extremely great deal to her too. I also know you are incredibly considerate with her. She needs that warmth, that caring so, so much. She's *so vulnerable*." Summer became more serious. "I will protect her against *anyone*. It's my 'maternal instinct' for her, since our mother certainly doesn't have it, want it or even knows what it is."

I remembered Autumn talking about how Summer enlisted Joe to make those two guys apologize. I still wasn't exactly sure, but sure enough to think she meant 'the innocent little girl' in Autumn. I just let it alone. Fortunately, the song ended.

As we rejoined Jake and Autumn, he kidded, "Hey Magician, Autumn told me all your secrets."

I smiled, kissed her hand which I had begun to hold, "Oh, she can try. It's about 11:30. I'll be right back."

As I headed towards the door, I heard Autumn say, "Uh-oh, Jake, now you did it! You stirred him up. He's already up to something new."

I went to the car and opened the trunk. There was my tenth of Moët et Chandon champagne. Since the temperature was slightly above freezing, it was still properly chilled. I popped the cork using the screw I brought with me, made the four plastic cups into two sets of two, pouring half of the bottle in each. Then I walked back through the door with my song and dance bullshit ready for whoever was manning the door, but there wasn't anyone there. At the table, I easily split the two halves, equalizing into four cups, thus giving each of us about three ounces to drink. Enough for a couple of toasts.

"This," alluding to the drinks, "my mystified audience, is some very nice champagne for toasting the New Year and more importantly, the engaged couple ... so drink some now and save the rest for Midnight." My toast was short, as I thought about our two fathers, "I wish you two the very best in your long, long life together." We all touched our cups and drank.

"Whoa, this **is** really great champagne. You really are a magician, Rich," exclaimed Summer. "Far, far better than that pink champagne crap we drink at Mizzou. Or the cheap stuff ... Gallo Thunderbird or White Port ... even Mad Dog 20/20.

When the band was beginning the countdown to midnight, we toasted for a great 1964 as Jake added, "I propose that the four of us get together every New Year's Eve to celebrate." We happily agreed, clicked our cups again and drank our remaining champagne.

****

Jackson Ford had no idea of the complexity of events which would unfold as the seed of his simple suggestion for the future germinated, starting sometime later that night

****

Moments later, I kissed Autumn tenderly for a long time as Jake did with Summer. Then Summer gave me a nice sisterly hug and kiss on the lips and Autumn kissed Jake likewise. Our girls traded us back, Autumn giving me an open mouth kiss, quickly flicking my tongue with hers, then whispered, 'to start the year right'. I was sure Jake received something very similar, as I heard him adoringly say, "My beautiful Radiant Summer. Now my Radiant Fiancée. My once and forever Love. Once and forever."

Summer whispered something, making him smile broadly. She revealed, "Jake and I are leaving now to celebrate our beautiful engagement," and gave Autumn a look of pure happiness as the two sisters kissed goodnight, exchanging whispers with each other. Jake and I shook hands. Summer kissed me again in thanks for the toast while Jake and Autumn exchanged goodbye kisses. While we said our goodnights and Happy New Years, it became obvious where Summer and Jake were heading and for what glorious purpose. Even wrapped together tightly as one, they still were able to hurriedly exit out the ballroom door. Autumn was smiling, hardly blushing. And she was oh so happy for both of them, especially Summer. Jake never broke a promise and he had just professed his solemn marriage vow to Summer.

JANUARY

Although the public schools were back in session on Thursday, most private and all Catholic schools weren't. I tried doing some homework — even for Old Civs — but couldn't keep my mind off of Autumn. I decided to drive over to Prescott, wait for her in their large social commons area which was a massive square room — thirty by thirty yards — with a beamed ceiling and two huge fireplaces with a large painting hanging above each — one a scene of massive cliffs and the other of trees and a lake. The artist, Birger Sandzén, was exceptionally good. I was early so I leaned up against one of the fireplaces to wait and marvel at more of the room's architecture.

A short man came walking through the area and saw me. As he rapidly approached, he said in a loud, hostile voice, "What are you doing here?"

"Waiting for someone," I replied, mentally adding "You Asshole".

"Who?" in an acidic, challenging tone. The Asshole's rude manner had now pissed me off.

"A student," I flipped back as disrespectful as I could.

"What is *your name* and where do you *go to school*?" he demanded quickly, harshly.

Instantly I thought to give him Bush's name but figured that could come back to bite me in the ass. Cockily I said, "Kevin Corcoran from McKenna."

"Corcoran, **you** will leave immediately. This school is only for Prescott students."

I turned and walked towards the door calling him a prick, chicken shit son-of-a-bitch and worse under my breath. I wasn't causing any trouble, not interfering with anything or anybody. Just waiting for my girl.

When Autumn finally came out her usual side door exit, she was with a tall, blond-haired guy — smiling and laughing with him. I was immediately jealous and pissed off at her. What else did she do when I wasn't around? I went to confront her. The guy saw me and disappeared.

"Richie, what a wonderful surprise!"

"Yeah, Autumn, bet it is. It looked like I was interrupting something between you and that guy," I said jealously.

"No, no, that's just Mike Warner."

"Well, it looked like you and Warner were enormously enjoying each other's company."

"Richie, you're *jealous*. Oh, please don't be. Let me explain. Mike wanted some ideas for Joanie since she and Carlton Smith just broke up. He's been trying to date her for the longest time. I was only being friendly and helpful. That's all."

"I'm sorry," I contritely said. "If I see you with another guy, I can't help it."

"Even if the guy is 5 foot 4 and homely?" she teased.

"Yeah, probably. I'm really sorry. I missed you."

"Since just yesterday. Richie, that's soooo sweet."

"No, I'm just a dumb dip shit."

"No, you aren't. But you can make it up by taking me to Zesto's. And we'll start over."

As the temperature was unseasonably warm in the 60s, we slowly strolled to the car. I carried her books in one hand and held hers with my other. We laughed and teased each other. There was certainly no hurry.

When we pulled into Zesto's, I told her about the Gestapo from the social commons. "Well, you have met the A-s-s-h-o-l-e of Prescott High School, little *Mister* Robert Walters. He's the only person I don't like ... ever since the summer after my seventh grade year at Whittier ... his last there ... then he came here." She smirked, "That was quick thinking. If you had told the truth, he certainly would call St. Nate's, especially, since he despises the only other guy from there he knows. He **IS** a Gestapo! But who is Kevin Corcoran? Won't he get in trouble at McKenna?"

I laughed, telling her, "Oh no, he's Moochie in the TV series and the Shaggy Dog movie."

She began laughing loudly and mischievously for a time. When she could finish, she said she **really** had to use the drive-in's restroom. As I helped her out of the car, she started heartily giggling again, "Ya got him! Ya got that jerk! Dumb little twit will never know it. ... ... Uh-ooooh! Now reeeally gotta goooooo!" She scampered very quickly to the drive-in's entrance door, laughing and yelling, "My magician! Ya got him!"

When Autumn returned, she was still smiling. Before I opened the car door for her, I apologize again, telling her I was still sorry. She told me she would always be talking and laughing with other guys, even some flirting, but that was her nature. There was only one Richie for her. In the broad daylight of Zesto's Drive-In, we kissed, then a few more times.

****

Here I was — back in school, back in Religion class, back thinking of Autumn's long, shapely legs. Oh God, how magnificent they are.

Moose drone on about some sin, maybe even dealing with girls' long, shapely legs. My peripheral vision picked up Moose walking down an aisle, two over from mine. Suddenly Moose yelled, "**Isn't that right Davidson**?" with a simultaneous loud whack. Davidson flew about a foot out of his chair, taking it with him into Geoff Harding in the next aisle. "You had two weeks for that! And I'll be there to 'wake you' after tonight's Jug*!"

Translated from Moose language, this meant Davidson would be there until its completion at 6 o'clock. Davidson always had First Honors, once even Class Honors last year. It was said Moose never played favorites and this certainly proved he didn't. As I became more attentively, Autumn's beautiful legs vanished.

****

Notre Dame de Sagesse had their annual Snow Ball on Saturday night. Karen had set up DeeDee and herself for the double date with the McEwen twins from St. Ignatius. Both girls were looking forward to the dance, additionally hoping to meet some "senior studs" or "junior hunks".

*****JUG** is from the Latin *'sub jugum'* — **under the burden or yoke**; although some believe it is *'**Justice under God**'*; whatever its meaning, it is, almost always, a harsh punishment

When we arrived at the house, Autumn announced to the Three Graces she had been voted to be one of the five candidates for Queen of The Winter Wonderland Ball to be held in two weeks on the 25th of January. They all congratulated her and wished her the best and good luck to win.

DeeDee was unbelievably happy when Autumn asked her if she could help her get ready for her big dance. Our aunt was going to help, but quickly stepped aside, endorsing Autumn as "definitely the right girl for the job."

Later, DeForrest came down the stairs with Autumn following. She looked absolutely striking in her forest green gown, hair done in a bouffant style, and wearing some of Mother's best jewelry. I took her aside and told her, "DeForrest, you look *stunning*." She appeared sophisticated, very elegant, looking every bit a senior. She smiled, "Thank you, Richie," and kissed me carefully on my cheek. She went into the living room to show my aunt and mother who began to rave about her. Autumn had done a great job, saying it was terrific to help DeeDee.

The trio arrived and a lot of pictures were taken, then they left for the dance. My mother was worried because it was forecasted to snow and the twins had just passed their driving tests.

Autumn and I went to Blender's then the Spot, and as I drove her home, it did begin to snow. Aunt Danae was not feeling too well and had already gone to bed with her heating pad — translated "painful cramps" — so I sat with my anxious mother. We talked about Autumn and I told her again how she really enjoyed Christmas with us, especially the Mass. One Sunday, she would tag along with us. I told her it might not be as special or intimate and she responded if it wasn't, I would just have to recruit Father Fitz again. We talked about college. Then back to Autumn at which time the front door opened and our "older" sophisticate walked in.

DeeDee had "a really fab, outta sight time," so did Karen and their dates. They would probably double again. But the high point of her Dance was when she was asked to dance by **both** Thomas Rush and Chris Ewell, the St. Ignatius' senior star basketball players. I'd guess during their dates' Tag.

DeeDee happily gushed, "It was just sooooo cool ... first Thomas ... immediately after him, Chris ... who asked during that slow dance for my phone number. So exciting, so ultra-cool. Both guys thought they knew you". Oh, they certainly **will** — this Spring. The driving was not bad although they did slide once and yelled like they were on a carnival ride. My mother said this was why she was getting grey hair.

****

The next weekend was 'at the movies' weekend, as Friday night we saw Steve McQueen and Natalie Wood in *Love with the Proper Stranger,* followed by tonight's *The Cardinal* with Tom Tryon and Romy Schneider. I had read the book this past summer and knew it should be a good movie. During St. Victoria's, Autumn thought it coincidental while both movies were totally different — tonight's being a drama and last night's was kind of a romantic type comedy — both dealt with abortion. We began to talk about teen pregnancy. The more we did, the more she seemed to tense up, starting to become visibly upset. I was able to "skillfully" change the subject back to the movies themselves. She laughed shakily, saying she had been hanging around Catholics too much as they were beginning to rub off on her. She became very serious, commenting she believed, like Catholics, abortion was wrong. I couldn't argue. I felt the same.

"Do you remember Frances Parke ... err, Driscoll?"

"Sure, the very pregnant blonde with the beautiful blue eyes. Wow, a real smoker though! I got a big whiff of her at the table." Caroline came to mind but was gone instantly. "Really soused. Odd, she seemed kinda unhappy ... sadly wishing for 'the good old days' when she was talking with Jake and Summer. Maybe it was the pregnancy?"

"No, she was *terribly* unhappy. I think the pregnancy was only part of it. But dreadful news about that ... their baby was stillborn last week."

"Oh God! Do they know why? What happened?"

"No, I don't know any other information. Summer firmly believes **she** intended to get pregnant. If that's the case, then the reason he married her doesn't exist any-more. Look at the way they were living together or should I say **not** living together when he went off to school! That arrangement doesn't appear to have love as its priority. Unfortunately, I'm sure they won't stay married. But I would never wish anyone heartaches or problems." With her compassionate, gentle soul, she couldn't do that. I told her so.

****

Before those '63 Holidays began, Daniel Alan Driscoll had secretly started seeing a cute, lively sophomore *blond* cheerleader, Anne Renée West, a Salina Central grad;
Returning to the Dorm one January afternoon, he was notified to immediately call Bethany Hospital; He did & his father in-law informed him of the stillbirth; Frances wouldn't talk to 'the cheating SOB'; Ironically, he had just left Renée's apartment house — they had had sexual intercourse for the first time, certainly repeating;

The two began to live together off campus while Dan continued to play on his basketball scholarship; they married upon her graduation, Renée secured a teaching position in nearby Osage City; After his graduation, they happily moved to Salina for his coaching position and hers in Social Studies;

During the next few years, Dan suppressed his feelings of guilt & remorse, compounded by sadly finding out Renée was unable to conceive; He slipped into being a 'functioning alcoholic'; At a party one night, Dan tried to slap the hostess; Disgusted by this last straw, Renée delivered an ultimatum: 'Me or your bottle';
Renée is still lovingly with him
as he continues in Alcoholics Anonymous

****

Frances Driscoll was bedridden for six weeks during her extreme depression; So deeply ill, the hospital took care of the 'funeral'; The family attorney filed for her divorce the day after the stillbirth, granted quickly with more irony — the baby's due date; She and Dan have never spoken since the death;

> Frances Jayne Parke went on to graduate from Wyandotte Junior College; Almost a year later, the girl with the wonderful 'sea blue eyes' married an electrician; They had two girls, but divorced after eight years when his long time infidelity with a neighbor was finally discovered;
> Oddly, Frances didn't care that much;
> While she and the girls moved in with her parents, she started as a Door Greeter at Foley Chevrolet, obtained a degree in Accounting at St. Ignatius College's night school; There she found her soul mate, who happened to be her adjunct professor of Financial Investments, they married and remain very happy together;
> Professionally she rose rapidly to become the Controller of Foley's four dealerships

****

On Monday morning, Moose showed up a little late to class with a new guy in tow. He barked loudly, "This is Bartlett Sanders—Jones the Third. He will be joining this class." No one dared make a whispered comment or wisecrack about his first name, his implied hyphen, or his being number three.

Moose told him to take the only vacant chair which was in the last one in the last row. When I came back into the room for Ancient Civs class, he was sitting there and remained there for English class. Both Mr. Bannister and Father Fitzgerald acknowledged him for joining each class. After English, I started to walk out for lunch, and Father Fitzgerald stopped me and gruffly directed, "Marlowe, ask the new guy to eat lunch with you," turned and walked away.

Jack and I went over to him and invited him to join us. He smiled, "Sure, thanks. As you probably heard, I'm Bartlett Sanders—Jones. But I go by Bart."

We both chuckled, then Jack said, "Well, I'm John Nelson. I go by Jack. This is Richelieu Marlowe. He goes by Lou." Bart joined our laughter as we all shook hands. He was about our height and weight but had *blond* hair and green eyes. He wouldn't have any trouble attracting girls.

As we walked to the cafeteria, Jack asked, "So Bart, where did you transfer from?"

"Gonzaga in Chicago. Before that was an American grade school in Germany ... Frankfurt. My Dad works for TWA and was transferred to Kansas City. We moved this past weekend into a town across the state line ... Leawood."

I said, "Great area."

"Yeah, seems to be."

Jack continued his interrogation, finding out he had two sisters — one already a fashion buyer for Rich's in Atlanta and another a freshman at Sagesse — his father is British and mother was originally from Kansas City and had graduated from Sagesse.

"Does St. Ignatius have a decent baseball team?"

"You are talking to the stars of said team."

I faked choking, then asked, "What position do you play?"

"I do some pitching and play second base. What about you guys?"

"Well, meet the first baseman," Jack pointed to me, "and I'm the third baseman."

"Jack means hopefully. I just transferred in from Loyola in Omaha at the beginning of the year and Jack just started regularly at the end of last year."

"You're just in time. Practice, I think, starts around mid-March. Ya any good?"

"I was the relief pitcher last year for Gonzaga. Played summer ball and had a damn good season. I can hold my own. *But* are you guys any good?"

"I am. He isn't," Jack said, pointing at me again. We all laughed.

****

On the night before the big dance, Autumn and I went to a party at Fifth Street Hall sponsored by a group from McKenna. The band was good, and there were quite a few Prescott guys and girls there whom she, of course, knew. McKenna was in the majority and she knew some of the guys, having dated them. I saw the Bastard Bush and his two shit-for-brains accomplices leaning up against the same post where I overheard his plan for DeeDee and the subsequent fight. I had never told Autumn the full story, even a censored version would have her blushing for at least the rest of the night. Someday, I would.

I bought us a few cokes and when I came back, Autumn said, "Strangest thing, I saw Bush and Rhodes talking together. I had heard they were dating occasionally or sometimes just meet up ... like tonight. Looked over here a few times ... I know they were talking about us. *Just know it*. When they began slow dancing, she whispered something in his ear. He grinned and they hurriedly left."

*And I bet I know what they are going to **exactly** do*! ... ... I sarcastically said, "Probably think what a 'cute couple' we make and they're happy for us." Then my tone became pissed, "That giant-assed, mouthy Bitch and that lying, cheating Prick are at the top of my Shit List. I know you don't have one. Ahhh Victoria, to hell with them."

****

My mother had insisted I buy the tuxedo. "There will be a few dances like this one, proms, and of course, your graduation since St. Ignatius does not use cap and gown. It's much cheaper in the long run and you don't have to go in for a fitting every time you need one to rent. We'll only need to have it tailored as you grow."

I walked up to Autumn's front door like so many times before, yet this time I felt older, more mature. Must be the tux. As she had requested, I had her white orchid wrist corsage trimmed in light blue. I figured we would take a few pictures here, immediately go to my house for more pictures, then to the dance.

I knocked and Mrs. Knight opened the door and she and I exchanged the required pleasantries of saying "Hello Mrs. Knight" and "Hi Rich" and "You look nice tonight" and "Thank you, ma'am". Thankfully, the clichéd conversation continued only for a few moments as it was interrupted by the ringing phone.

She went to it, answering "Hello ... ... Hi Bea."

When Autumn walked into the living room, I stood up in total, complete amazement, almost speechless, "Uh ... Hi." ... ... *A Goddess — my beautiful Goddess. Sent from The Elysian Fields. Ahhhhh.*

She smiled, waved, and said, "Hi Rich."

I finally regained my composure — at least I thought I did — but I spoke like it was a first date, blurting out, "Oh, here is your orchid."

Autumn looked like a model straight off the cover of a teenage Vogue. She was wearing a strapless Empire waist silk-like dress in azure blue with matching elbow length blue gloves. She had her hair done up in what I found out later was called a French twist style which showed off her pearl drop earrings in gold and perfectly accentuated her locket. I was captivatingly focused on her bare neck and shoulders.

She took the orchid from my statue-like hand and easily slipped it over her gloved right wrist. "I'll be right back with your boutonnière." As she glided into the kitchen, my mesmerized eyes followed her beautiful backside, starting with her styled hair, neck and shoulders, then sliding down her gown which fairly shrouded her terrific derrière and shapely thighs, but not her curvaceous calves concluding with those great ankles and feet encased by large, dyed-to-match stilettos.

A moment later, Autumn came over to deftly pinned my single light blue rose boutonnière to my lapel. I finally, finally regained my normal speech pattern from my brain. "I have never seen you more beautiful than tonight. You look incredible, fantastic, wonderful." ... ... *I'm happy ... excited ... pleased ... proud ... incredibly damned lucky. I'm going to the Dance with the most beautiful, the most amazing, the most remarkable girl there is. Now I completely understand why Paris HAD to abduct Helen.*

When Mr. Knight came in, I wished him a good evening. Evidently that was Mrs. Knight's cue to tell Bea she would call her back shortly. He had already taken some pictures of Autumn by herself and now was going to take pictures of both of us. Even though I finally had made it to a smidge over six feet, Autumn in her heels and upswept hair, as usual, would still be taller than me.

I helped her with her coat and we said our good-byes. As we drove off, I repeated softly, "I have never seen you more beautiful than tonight. Absolutely never."

"Thank you. And you look more handsome yourself in that stylish tuxedo."

"Only because I'm with you."

Autumn had draped her arm on the top of the driver's side seat with her hand close to my neck. She easily leaned into me and kissed me lightly on my cheek then my ear. After she wiped off the lipstick with a Kleenex from her purse, she began to caress my ear, neck and cheek slowly with the back of her gloved hand. I was totally aroused in record time, but there was no way we could go to St. Victoria's place. And just how would going to St. Victoria's calm an erection?

I blurted out, "Guess I'll meet a lot of new girls tonight. All the guys will be standing in line to get on your dance card. They can brag they danced with the Queen."

She teased, "Don't get ideas with any of them, especially Ginny." And then seriously, "But I won't be the Queen ... maybe a Princess though."

"How can you say that? You will win. Regardless of what happens, you will always be my Queen."

"I know I am, Richelieu," she agreed intently, seriously. "I know I am."

As we crossed Minnesota Avenue, I began thinking about her comment about Ginny. "What do you mean 'especially Ginny'?"

"Oh, she has had a crush on you since the day we walked in The Hangout. Like I told you on New Year's Eve and you laughed it off."

"Naw. She's just always really friendly."

"Un-huh. But you watch yourself with her, my oblivious little first base-*boy*," she kidded. "You will have a dance with her since we have already secretly traded you and Cliff. Still I have another surprise trade for you. Don't even think about asking. Because ... I ... won't ... tell you."

When we walked in the front door, The Three Graces were lying in wait. They pounced on Autumn and began gushing over her saying how "beautiful" from my aunt, how "incredibly fabulous, just terrific" came from my sister and my mother raved she looked "so wonderfully sophisticated".

DeeDee exclaimed, "I love your French twist. Take very long at Silvestri's?"

"A couple of hours, but I had a trim, too."

My sister continued to gush, "I love the way its style embellishes your beautiful gold pearl drop earrings and, of course, **the** locket."

"The earrings were my Grandmother's. My Nanna's. I love them so much."

Aunt Danièle raved on, "You two always make such a lovely couple, but tonight, you are spectacular."

Mother had tears in her eyes, hopefully of joy and happiness, maybe mixed with memories of my father and her.

DeForrest buzzed again, "You will be Queen tonight! I know it! I know it!"

Autumn smiled and simply said, "We'll see."

We took a lot of pictures and left for the short drive to Prescott.

The gym had been transformed into the Ball's theme of a winter wonderland. A very nice job. The band was, as usual, one my mother and aunt would like. They couldn't play rock and roll, so we had to deal with their 'swing' songs. The slow songs were done well though.

I was right. Autumn's dance card filled up immediately with the five guy allotment. I was a little jealous and didn't know why.

First, I danced with Connie Renner who I had met and danced with at Judy's party. Smart and always friendly.

Next was Cathy Winters, the Zesto carhop whom I only half-assedly had looked for until I was finally told she was going seriously steady. After that I occasionally saw her, but I would be with Autumn and would only briefly talk to her. We now had time to continue our little flirt of the summer. She was an *exceptionally* good dancer, smart, witty and looked pretty in her lime green formal accented in navy, instead of her drab carhop hat, shirt and shorts. I teasingly told her that. Then seriously, I told her she looked especially nice. I liked her. She was ultra-cool. However, three weeks before, her boyfriend had broken up with her. **He** was here tonight with some haughty foreign exchange student who still acts likes she just got off the boat which she probably owns. Cathy was jealous and really hurting. Obviously, still had very strong feelings for him.

After a time, the third card dance was called and the music started again, I looked around for my next dance card partner. Donnie Somebody had already taken Autumn over by the football players' tables to dance there. There standing and grinning, waiting for me on the ill-lighted and now less populated side of the floor was Little Caroline Cunningham, unsteadily taking her stiletto high heels off. I had only seen her in passing a few times in the last couple of months. Mick told me she was *extremely* popular with the football players. Farris the tackle and she had broken up right before football season ended when she had been messing around with Massey the quarterback while he was going steady with Judy. Then she and the center Todd Teller started going together, finally this Donnie, the senior halfback, before Christmas.

Not surprisingly, she reeked of cigarette smoke as I put my arm around her waist to slow dance. She eagerly embraced me, tightly pressing her breasts against my shirt as my tux jacket was unbuttoned.

Is she wearing ANYTHING under this thin gown? Did she ever wear anything firm?

She said, "Well, Stranger, how have you been? You look gooorrrrgeous tonight. Good enough to eat. Yum, yum."

"You look very dazzling yourself, Caroline, in your blue chiffon." Her dress was very fashionable yet she was wearing way too much blue eyeshadow and black eyeliner, but at least no white lipstick, just light pink.

Still looks kinda cheap ... even so there's that animal magnetism of hers. How can it still be there ... even now?

"Flattery will get **YOU annnywhere**," she giggled and tried to snuggled in even tighter. When that failed, she started to steadily move from side to side, intently kneading her breasts against me.

Oh shit, a hard-on! She ALWAYS lights me up. Every damn time!

I pulled away from her to talk, "Caroline, you've been drinking. A lot?"

"Sure, in the parking **lot**, with Don-knee in his car. Heee brought a pint of my favorite. Chat...toe orange vod-kaa. Dija know he's the best senior halfback in the cittty?"

"No, I didn't know that."

"I really misssed you." She pulled me back into her, arms tight around my rib cage. She moaned slightly, "Ooooh, FEEELS like you missssed me, too." Caroline began slowly rubbing her lower midriff rhythmically against my erection. Immediately, I panicked.

Oh God! If she keeps moving like this, I'll—

"Ooooh Richeeeee ..."

I had to quickly walk away, go back to the table, but I couldn't let Caroline's volcanic temper explode, followed by God only knows what she would say to Autumn. I distracted her with, "I heard Carl the tackle broke up with you."

That stopped her slow grind on me and she looked up at me with pure resentment in those brown eyes, "**Lying Shiiitt! I'm the one** who broke up with Dumb Fare Ass. But get thisss. **Me,** *the rauncheee mouth Gen Eddddy dummeee* was sneaking around with the boyfriend of that stuck-up red-haired Homecoming **Queenie Bitch**. Haaa! Haa! But Massey ... the Assey Hooole ... turns out was a lyyying sonuvabitch purr-rick. After almost a month of our cheeeting fun, she dumps him. He blamed my sorrriee ass. Tells his jockstrappping buddies he was the **first** guy to screw me. Banged me a bunch of times. Shee—it, he wishes ... **even ONCE**. Couldn't get a beeeer open or my braaa off without my help. Some hands on that shit-star worthless quarterback! Sure don't miss that shit Dumb Ass Fare Ass either. **Knowwhyy**?"

Her face flushed with anger while her breathing quicken. That notorious volcanic temper was ready to erupt.

"Ah—"

"Took me somewhere nice ... so I would wear a dress. Afterwards the asshole kept shoving his hands up my legs like he was going after a fummbled fooootball. That was his caveman style to get a girl all hot and turned on! Stupid Shit. Sooo after the thirddy-third time of 'No,' he said I *owed* it to him to screw him. Aye *oweeed it to him*! Said, '**Hell No**! I don't owe you **Shee— it**!' Said I was nothing but a stuuupid sluuut. So Aye said, 'Never let you passss second base. How can Aye be a slut?' Yells at me, 'You're nothing but a Prick-teasing Pussssy, you Catholic Cunt!'

Oops, I know. Bad words. I reeeallly lost my temper. **Nooo Boddee calls meee that Shee-it**! Slugged him in hiss balls. Got 'em gooood. Real goood! He could ooonly bend over. Slapped the fool's face. A bunch. Hard! Fine ... finally abe-belle to grabbb my hands and wrists. Held 'em ooo-ver my head, while he slugged a tit, then my snatch. Twice ... hard ... almost made me puke. Wish I could have ... all over the prick. Hurt like hell ... got home ... both swollen and bruised up real badly. Yannnked me out of the car by my hair. Threw me on the ground. Drove off. Acted like Aye wasss a white trashed hoar. Purr-rick Bass-turd!"

She then calmed down considerably to ask, "Sooooo, how about you? What naked naughtee—ness have you been up to with ... uh, uh, Fall? Ooh wee, how far ya gotten with that fake ... that ... that phon-eee Princess of pure and purr-fect?"

"Caroline, I think you're really very drunk. Regardless, you still have your very distinctive alliterations."

"Yeaaahhhh, my very *ample* appealing apples with jum-bow nip-pees. Aye get so hellisshhhornee near yooou. Aye wish you would, would fine ... finally feel me up. Oh pleeeease? Just tell me where and when. 'Cuz Aye want this hand in my pant-teees. These two fingers buried beee—low my furry bush ... **in meee**!" She looked at me very imploringly as she held up my left hand by grabbing my index and middle fingers. "I want them to mess with me a lot more than this one did," as she moved to my thumb.

My only response to her shameless invitation was, "I truly like you Caroline. I always have. And while your 'apples' and your 'bush' are so tempting, I'm incredibly crazy about Autumn. We are unbelievably happy together. I'm not going to do **anything** to screw it up." Her light pink lips were even paler and she was starting to lose color in her face. "There can't be anything between us. Where's your table? **You** need to sit down!"

Caroline threw my hand down. She looked immensely hurt as tears began to well up in her eyes. She wailed, "You *always* get me so turned on ... so hot and horny ... 'cause my ... my ... gets ... gets sooo ... ... Ooooooh **Shit**!" She suddenly began a mad dash towards the girls' toilet, screaming "**NOOooo**ooo!", instantly clamping both hands over her mouth.

Thankfully, it was only about twenty feet away into the well-lighted area. I sincerely hoped she made it because I heard loud, on-going retching noises. Orange flavored vodka vomit does not go well with blue chiffon. But what does?

A girl coming out, as Caroline ran past her, unconsciously kept holding the door open. Probably from her shock of seeing a shoeless girl in an attractive blue formal, on her knees, clinging to the "porcelain throne," puking her guts out into it. Unfortunately, the toilet's tile walls and floor acted like a band's loud speaker, greatly resonated the sounds of her throwing up. If it wasn't so terribly pathetic, it would have been funny.

Mick and Pamela heard her yell, then saw her bolt into the girls' restroom. Both came over to me as I was now standing fairly close to its now closed door and Mick laughingly said, "Do you always make your exes sick?"

"Only on special occasions," I shot back. "But two dates in one weekend doesn't constitute an 'ex'."

Pamela was ignoring both of us, sympathizing, "Oh that poor, poor girl! She's changed so much! Right after school started. She's *always* smoked and been somewhat crude. Lotsa girls smoke and swear. That's no big deal. But then she began hanging with a *very different* group of girls. And that's when her drinking started. A lot. *Waaay too much* at parties and on dates. And that makeup! Some nights ... looked like a real tramp on the make."

She stopped to point out, "Good. There goes her best friend Lorraine into the toilet ... to help her ... if she can. That girl is so vulgar when she dresses to flaunt those big ... uh. ... But she is considerate and sweet."

Pamela returned to talking about their group, "Well, then the rumors started flying about this fast bunch of girls. There are six in all ... Caroline even named 'em ... *The Stray Pussycats*. All have pretty bad reps, especially those seniors Rhonda Fox and Phyllis Prince ... the absolute worst two. *That* duo call themselves The Two Stray ... purposely forgetting the "cat" part. In those places Mick," she nodded her head towards the toilet where the miserable, sick little girl was, "where those *sluts* have an exclusive female audience, they brag and gloat. Once, when I was in there, those two even 'matched up' David Kinsey — that rich guy, thinks he's a stud. Fox said he was pathetic. Prince agreed, said even a Lesbo would be better to—."

She stopped herself, realizing she was talking to not just Mick but me also. Then switched the subject back to Caroline's transformation, "Oh, Caroline and I just don't hang around anymore. I really miss her. She *was* a whole lot of fun ... damn good fun."

"Know what you mean," I sorrowfully agreed. "She was an awful lotta damn good fun."

After the long number had finished, Donnie and Autumn came over and I told them Caroline had become ill and was in the girls' room. Pamela added that Lorraine was in there with her. Donnie, her halfback drinking partner, said he would get her purse, find her shoes and coat then take her home when she came out. I wanted to say, "Don't forget the orange vodka," but it was probably already stashed away in her purse. He seemed very disappointed. After *her* blatant proposition of third base for me anytime — and doubtlessly stealing home — I could easily imagine what *his* plans were for *her* later tonight, especially since he had gotten her drunk on her favorite booze. Now the Prick knows her limit to get her drunk enough. Just not sick.

As we went back to our table, Autumn said, "Can you believe this? That Donnie Wilson just asked me to go out with him. Told him, thanks, but I was going steady with you. He said that it didn't matter, we could just sneak around. So I said, 'What about your steady, Caroline?' and he said, 'Oh, she's nothing really'. How can she be nothing? Why did I accept a dance with him? What a jerk! Just a real shhii ...! Oh, never mind!"

God, I feel sorry for her. Poor Caroline! Doesn't she know she's become the football team's 'Mascot'. They keep trading her around, getting her drunk, wearing down her inhibitions and her resolve until one of them ... unless it's already happened. Followed by the rest of them.

Just then, Vice-Principal Walters took the stage to announce the Court of the Dance.

"Welcome Prescott students to your Winter Wonderland Ball of 1964. Without further ado, I will announce the Ladies-in-

Waiting, the Princesses and lastly, the Winter Wonderland Queen. Girls, as I call your names, please stand and your escort will come to your table and accompany you to the podium. The boys are all members of our excellent basketball team ... ten straight wins in our 18 and 2 record." Shouts and applause fill the gym. They had lost two out of four games when Autumn's escort was injured.

"Our first lady-in-waiting is Senior Miss Holland Crandall." There was a lot of cheering and whistling. "Holly, please meet your escort, Carlton Smith, one of our star forwards."

"A junior is our next lady-in-waiting, Miss Autumn Knight." More cheers and whistling, but there were loud boos. "She is being escorted by this year's certain to be the all-city center, maybe all-state too ... Mark Fielding."

As Autumn started to get up from the table, I quickly stood and pulled her chair away for her. She was smiling at everyone. Fielding was sitting at the next table so he was quickly there to escort her to the podium. I was shocked. I didn't care who the Princesses would be or even the Queen. Regardless, none could look as fantastic as Autumn does tonight and her warm and friendly demeanor all the time. When the Court was complete — Ginny did make princess — the band played *Memories Are Made of This* for the customary Court Dance. Next, that group went to the special area to have their pictures taken for the yearbook as the rest of the crowd danced to *Moments to Remember*. During that time I sat at our table alone and thought about this damn popularity contest.

She's very popular in her class. But she's a junior ... seniors almost always win. But I cost her being a princess, maybe even queen. If she wasn't dating AN OUTSIDER ... ... ME!

After Fielding walked her back to our table, she introduced us. He simply towered over me, must be at least 6 foot 8. He said good night and thanks for the dance. She thanked him also and said to score a lot of points against McKenna next Friday night in the Regionals. I started to tell her my feelings concerning her not winning but she said she would be right back after she made a much needed trip to the powder room with Princess Ginny who waved enthusiastically and brightly smiled at me, whooping, "See

you later." After at least a thirty minute Tag, Autumn finally rejoined me at our empty table. She apologized it took so long, but they had to talk to some of the girls about the Queen's Court and the dance itself.

She then quipped Caroline evidently had made it to a toilet bowl in time. "I heard that girl still has the serious hots for you." She jealously said, "**You** do know **that**, don't you?" alluding to me being blind to Ginny's crush.

Does Caroline beginning a stand-up dry-dock constitute 'serious hots'? Or her slut's invitation to feel her up and finger her anytime I want? Then probably easily screw her.

I leaned over and took her hand in mine and squeezed her forearm with my other a few times. I scoffed, "Yeah, so what? Doesn't matter one bit to me. I've got the serious **red** hots for you." Autumn was smiling contentedly.

Thank God, Autumn did not see her drunken seduction act. Hopefully when Caroline wakes up tomorrow, she won't remember half of the things she said and none of what she offered to me. God, she's so depressingly changed. Never saw a girl act so much like a REAL whore.

I made up my mind to quit thinking about Caroline's slutty act and said seriously, "I'm so sorry you didn't win. You know it's my fault."

"Richie, how could it be your fault?"

"I'm an outsider. It had to cost you votes. Because you're not going with or dating one of Prescott's own. How could Ginny be a princess but not you?"

"Oh Richie, you are just being silly. Ginny is really popular with the girls but especially the *guys*." As she said this, she touched the locket reassuringly. Nonetheless, I knew I had blocked her from placing higher.

The band began to play *Moon River*. When we started dancing, I held her so wonderfully close. Dancing cheek to cheek, I could smell her perfume from behind her ear.

Chanel. I love that fragrance on her. Oh God, this feels so great with her. ... ... "Do you remember the first time we danced, we danced to this?"

"Of course I do. Why Richie, you're a romantic!"

"Victoria, I wish this moment would never end. When I am with you, I don't see any other girls, or anyone else for that matter. Only you. I daydream about you during Religion class every morning and can't wait for weekends. My last thought at night is you. You are so unbelievably beautiful tonight and every night with you is terrific."

She kissed me lightly on my cheek. Then she whispered in my ear, "I know, Richie, I know. The phone calls during the week just aren't enough. I daydream about us an awful lot too. Oooh," she moaned, "sometimes, I miss you so terribly. Oooh, Richie," as she pulled me to her as tightly as we could be and caressed my neck and my ear.

This must be what heaven is like!

Our euphoria only lasted for about fifteen seconds as Vice-Principal Walters tapped Autumn on her shoulder and growled, "Autumn Knight! Girls, especially our Ladies-in-Waiting, do not make out on the dance floor! Please refrain from doing so or you will have to leave the Ball."

Autumn started to say something to him. I actually believed she was going to swear, calling him something quite profane, but she just sharply glared at him then spun me so I faced him. I thought he might recognize me from my escapade earlier in the month. He didn't, merely walked away with a big smirk on his face.

She began ranting vehemently, "He's such a Butt Hole! Such a horrid, **mean shit**! I so dislike that hateful, horrible little Turd! Nasty **Asshole! The Shit**!" She did calm down a little but still continued to fume, "Damn that stinking piece of vermin shit to Hell! He can rot there ... in his eternal stench!"

She is really upset. But what a litany for excrement! ... ... "You're right, a jumbo extra-large turd. But Vice Principal Asshole is gone. Where were we?" We resumed tightly embracing each other, but our Elysian Fields had vanished.

My next card dance, as promised, was the blonde with the fantastic blue-grey eyes, Princess Ginny Foster. While Cliff Jones took Autumn to the middle of the dance floor, she headed for a fringe area of the dance floor where they were only some dancers.

I put my arm around her to hold her reasonably close, but she moved in even closer. I could easily feel her as she pressed against me.

"Congratulations on becoming a princess."

"Thank you. Autumn should have been the other princess. She was robbed. You heard all those boos." I thought about my idea that I was the one who did the robbing.

We talked about piddling stuff, so I asked, "Are you going steady with Cliff?"

A couple glided past us, wishing her success next year as she would definitely be Queen. She thanked them and finally responded to me, "Not exactly ... well kinda ... yeah. I am thinking about adopting the Autumn Knight school of thought for dating. Look how well it worked for her." She smiled, "All the girls were jealous of Autumn and your stroke of genius ... that locket of yours. So, you cool stud, where *did* you get these good looks ... sultry black eyes ... all this wonderful black hair?" She affectionately tousled it some, like Autumn would do.

I only complimented her, "But your looks are remarkably better. Very regal and beautiful tonight, Princess Virginia, in your scarlet and cream gown."

Her blue-grey eyes looked directly into mine with more than an inviting hint, "Thank **you** very much. Your St. Ignatius manners match **your** looks. Ultra-cool." The way she smiled merely enhanced her continuing strong flirting.

"Naw, you just think that since I'm the new kid on the block. When the novelty wears off, I'll be just another one of the guys."

"Oh, I *really* doubt that. But how did you get Autumn to go steady with you in just one day? What *is your* secret?" She teased in an enticing fashion.

"It's because I play first base." Then ramping up my arrogance, "We are known for our ability to charm beautiful, sophisticated, ultra-hard-to-get girls. Since I play my position very well, *I know how to get there quickly.*"

She chuckled and muttered under her breath, "...other bases, too," or something similar. Before I could ask her to repeat it, she continued in her regular voice, "Funny, there was this mystery about you. Every one of the girls in our clique, Autumn included, would occasionally see you, appearing like magic, cruising up and down State in this cool Galaxie. Seemed like only for a single lap.

"Once with this real good-looking, auburn-haired honey. Some figured she was your girl. I disagreed." Ginny grinned suggestively, "She wasn't sitting close to you ... like *I certainly would do* ... with *your* hand on *my leg*. But you would always just disappear. Maybe you went to McKenna ... that didn't check out. Possibly Wellington, maybe Silver City. Nothing. Even tried to find out about her. We thought it must be one of the smaller schools in the county, like Townsend. Nobody ever thought about St. Ignatius. We found out later Pam Parker knew you but no one ever thought to ask her and certainly not that *drunken little slu* ... er ... tramp."

She hurriedly changed the subject again, "You know when Judy, Autumn and I walked into The Hangout, I told her if you ended up being another one of 'Autumn's Fallen Leaves', to give me your phone number. Judy thought you were **really** good-looking too but she was going with Terry Massey. Remember him? At her party?"

"Judith of gorgeous, coppery red hair fame," I reminisced. "It's really unfortunate she has the flu this weekend and well, Joanie too. I was looking forward to seeing and talking with both of them. You know they were going to be the other couples at our table. A few have sat with us to talk for a while, like Mick and Pamela." ... ... *That would have been a challenge I would have failed miserably. Trying to keep my eyes off Judy. Trying to hide my smiling mouth from Joanie's twinkling eyes and inviting grins.*

She sniffed, "Sure did, the eight ... or six of us since tonight Wendy and *her Roger* along with Melody and *that* Royce went to the Fairview Hills' dance ... divvied up the two tables with our dates in mind. Anyway, Judy's still taken. Sam Miller, one of the forwards ... you remember him ... met him at that hall dance. Joanie now is going steady with drab Larry Freeman. But I don't know why or what she sees in him. All he's ever done for her is give her the flu. Ha Ha. But it's nice some other couples have kept you company. We will too, my *St. Ignatius' partner*."

"Well, thanks. For Judy, it's a different season, so a different sport, so a different ballplayer?" She laughed, but I don't think she caught the humor in my fractured logic. "But I don't know Freeman."

"No matter. Didja know Judy, Autumn and I are 'The Rainbow Girls'?"

I smiled, "Yes, I did. But you need one more, one with black hair. I'll give you my mother."

She laughed, "Unfortunately, you have to be a Prescott junior and ultra— Oh, so that's where the *black hair* comes from." She flicked mine again.

"Well, I hope your new dating strategy works for you."

She smiled broadly, "Oooh, I do like guys from St. Ignatius."

The song ended and I started to emphatically ask, "Like who?" But another couple came by to congratulate her. Autumn and Cliff followed them. We traded partners and I thanked her for the dance. She smiled greatly with a big "you're welcome". As promised, she and Cliff joined us at our empty table until the next and last card partner dance was called.

"Well, was I right?" Autumn questioned a few moments after they left.

"About what?"

"Her crush and all."

"Oh, I think she's always being just extra nice, because you're best friends."

I was sure I didn't convince her one bit. After the overt flirting, Autumn was most certainly right.

I only want Autumn. Not Ginny, not Judy, or Cathy or Joanie — not Linda or Rusty — or even Antoinette. No one else. I need just her. ONLY HER!

The surprise Autumn wouldn't even give me a hint about was my final dance card partner for the night. She was Jacqueline Cartier, a senior foreign exchange student from Paris. Had brown hair, quite tall — only slightly shorter than Autumn. Definitely good-looking, downplayed as she was wearing only minimal makeup, the size of her breasts definitely met Jack's standard of an "absolute killer chest" helping to promote her hourglass shape.

She was graceful and statuesque which I immediately noticed as she and her date walked towards us. The guy was Harold "Hal" Fleming — another senior football player. I wasn't sure where they were sitting but it wasn't with his teammates at one of their tables. Then it dawned on me. So **Hal**, not a Mel or a Malcom, had been the fullback for Prescott. The guy who had recently broken up with Cathy Winters for good. The one she was still heartsick over. And Jacqueline was the foreign exchange student. Possibly the cause?

During the introductions, she and I spoke only French to each other. I happily surprised her when I told her my full name, emphasizing 'Étienne Richelieu'. I continued speaking Français to see how well I could hold up. She thought she was having a fairly good time in the states but guessed she was still homesick. "Everyone thinks I'm a little aloof and reserved."

I countered, "Impossible".

"I haven't accepted many dates. Most of the ones I did, were just so-so or plain horrid, like two of them. One brute said 'gorgeous French girls were all hot to trot' and wanted to find out. Another jerk said I had great 'jugs', wanted to 'go for a romp in the hay'. Their American slang sayings did not sound a bit polite, so I said no to whatever they were suggesting and ended the dates quite early and quite quickly. I asked Autumn about them and she blushed terribly, but *explicitly* told me. Most American boys think all French girls are loose. No morals. So I am 'stuck-up'. Even though this is our first date, I like Harold the best … by far. He is so different! Such a gentleman. Very mannerly and respectful. Right before this dance, he asked me out for next Saturday night. I accepted gladly. Still, I am seriously thinking about going home to Paris. My parents will be disappointed in me."

"But you can't! You are naturally cool, you know, French savoir-faire. Your poise, your elegance."

"Oh Richelieu, you are incredibly sweet, so kind. Well, my English has improved in the last few months. I still feel self-conscious and nervous about myself, especially my height. I am as tall or taller than more than half the boys. American boys are supposed to be tall. Very tall."

"Rubbish, no, no," I told her, "you have a wonderful sense of style. I could certainly tell when you walked over here with Hal. Like a Parisian fashion model. Autumn is even taller than you, sometimes me, like tonight. **I** don't give a damn and **you** shouldn't either. Models, like you and Autumn, are *meant* to be **tall**. *Meant* to be **cool**. *Meant* to be highly **attractive**."

She thanked me and continued to talk about her experiences since school started, a few good, others not so good. When the dance ended, she apologized for monopolizing the entire dance by talking about herself and her problems. Maybe because she could speak about everything with me in French. I just smiled my best smile and told her I was glad she did because she was my most interesting and coolest card partner of my evening.

She doubted my compliment, "Oh Richelieu, even Virginia? The princess?"

"Definitely, far and away, the absolute best! You can talk to me anytime, about anything ... but only in French." ...... *She's wonderful ... damn, there is something truly extra ordinary about her. I really like this girl. Oh, she certainly defines 'glamour' ... like Autumn does.*

She laughed and was still laughing when we saw Autumn and Hal Fleming coming to join us. She said Autumn was '*très* beau'. I agreed, "*Oui, très, très* beau. Vous êtes 'cool'. *Vous avez votre propre beauté, trop. Merci, Jacqueline.*"

"*Merci, Merci,* Étienne *Richelieu*. *Vous êtes un gars très doux. Au revoir,*" she smiled very happily, turned and glided away with Hal. Only then could I check out her derrière — which appeared to be nicely curved atop well-formed thighs, even if they were all covered by her straight gown. Great shaped calves and ankles. My assessment of a wonderfully topped hourglass shape was perfect for that French girl! No wonder those two assholes and more than a few others hit on her.

I was sure Autumn caught me checking out her backside. However, she only said, but with more than a little jealousy, "Well Frenchie, what did you two just say to each other. I heard a lot of beaus and trèses?"

"She said you were beautiful and I said very much so. Then I thanked her and told her she was cool as she had her own beauty. She said I was a very sweet guy."

"Sounds like I should be jealous," she teased, but with a definite air of possessiveness.

"No, don't be," and I was truly serious, "she's homesick, lonely. Insecure about her looks, especially her height, her English, herself. Guys, even girls, have tried to take advantage of her because she's foreign. I feel sorry for her. She's a loner. People misjudge loners. I think she's nice. Real nice."

"Mmmm, you never take to others quickly ... if at all. So you like her?"

"Sure, I like her. Definitely the best girl of these card dances tonight. Why?"

"Good, 'very sweet guy,' because we are going to double with them next Saturday night. You are driving, so my Magician, please figure everything out and call Hal."

I laughed, "That's great. You know you have the strangest knack for finding poor misfits and making them very happy."

"Just you and stray puppies."

When the Dance ended, we met up with Mick and Pamela and drove to the Plaza for our 11 o'clock dinner reservation at Fedora's, an Italian restaurant. We got the usual "must be the big dance night" glances from the few remaining guests as they looked us up and down, especially Autumn with her height, dress and beautiful facial features. The food was excellent. Strangely, when Autumn and I continued to try each other's dishes, I overheard the woman at the next table say to her husband, "They act like a married couple," and snickered.

After we dropped Mick and Pamela off at Mick's car, I said, "You know it will soon be Valentine's Day. It's on a Friday, would you like to go to the Plaza III for dinner? We could go early to avoid the crowds."

"Oh let's do. That sounds romantic."

"Would you like to go to St. Victoria's now?"

"Very much."

"Great, because I have been looking at your creamy shoulders all night with unmitigated lust."

We both laughed. I couldn't wait. At the first stop sign, I turned, peeled back her coat, kissed the crown of her shoulder and her collarbone next to the locket a few times. Then I headed to St. Victoria as quickly as I could.

Surprisingly, Mother was waiting up for me and asked if Autumn could begin her reign as Queen. I told her no, just a Lady-in-Waiting. She was clearly disappointed and still frowning when I kissed her good night.

As I laid in bed, I thought about my dance card partners and Autumn.

Wow, what a Dance! All the girls …… such a different experience with each!

The always friendly Connie. Nice, considerate girl. Would have sat with us longer but her date, Johnny, and the other guys wanted to sit together as planned.

Renewed a little flirting with vivacious Cathy. Cute, still a great butt, still a minimal chest. Still a terrifically fun girl with a great sense of humor. Be great to date.

Explicit third base invitation from drunk Caroline. So damn sleazy, so damn desperate, so like a true WHORE. Hopelessly different from last August or even November. What a terrible, damn shame!

Received some intense flirting from Ginny. Autumn was right. But SO attractive with those beautiful eyes. Can't go steady with a guy for even three or four weeks.

Oh Jacqueline! Wonderful, fabulously French, good-looking, tall, shapely. Yeah, what a bod! Those great knockers! Loaded with style and grace, so smart, brilliant personality. Could use some well-placed makeup though.

Ah Victoria, my beautiful Victoria. An absolute goddess, in her gown and gloves, hair done up with Grandmother Macey's locket between those naked, heavenly shoulders.

A Dream … My Dream! What we told each other during Moon River. Holding each other like neither one would ever let go. Doesn't get any better than that. Never ever!

I looked at the photograph of my father on my desk. He was silent.

****

The Quarter at St. Ignatius and the third six weeks at Prescott coincided on the previous Friday. That Wednesday, I called Autumn to tell I had received my grades. She said she did too, so I told her, "Ladies, first."

"Well, they are not much different. Thank goodness."

English	1	Advanced Algebra	2-
Accounting I	2+	Interior Design	1
U. S. History	1-		

"Still, a 1.4 average, which is good. Sure glad you helped me those times in algebra, especially that one Saturday afternoon when DeeDee was with us. Otherwise, it would have been a d-a-m-n 3. I traded my 1 in Accounting for the 1 in History. So how did you do, math wiz?"

"A little better, a little worse. Latin is just killing me … it and the rest are:

Religion	87	English	92
Français	90	Algebra & Trig	93
Ancient Civilizations	96	Latin III	79

So, a smidge better with an overall 89.5. Get this, DeeDee has a 94 in Latin. **A 94**! She made first honors again with a 91.7."

"Good for her. I can hardly wait to see you for the game Friday."

"Me, too. In 48 hours."

****

In the Regional play-offs, McKenna upset Prescott 47 — 46 as their forward, a guy named Tobias, hit a twenty-five foot jump shot with about four seconds left. McKenna students went nuts and, of course, the Prescott ones were totally dejected. I understood how the players on each team felt. I had been on both sides.

As I held the door, Autumn slid into the driver's side to the middle of the seat. After I got in, I said, "Blender's or Zesto's?"

"Neither. I don't feel like all the moaning from my school or loud cheering from McKenna. To St. Victoria, if you please.

"Oh, I please," and couldn't get there fast enough. As soon as we parked, Autumn immediately started lightly French kissing me but I wasn't going to stop right then and ask why. How else were the windows going to get fogged up?

Even before her Ball, her breasts were the focus of my daily Religion class daydream. My visions and desires continued to intensify. So enticing, oh so tempting. I was convinced those perfect, medium-sized breasts would feel exquisitely soft, be creamy white with their light golden brown nipples and areolae matching the color of her beautiful hair. I envisioned strands cascading down, touching those dream tips and halos as she smiled invitingly for me to caress them.

As we continue to French, touching her became my sole obsession. Finally, I got up enough courage to slightly squeeze her right breast. However, the wool sweater's thickness combined with the fabric of her bra greatly minimized my intense desire. Surprisingly, Autumn pressed her hand on mine, however I could feel her breast only slightly more. When our cheeks and lips had touched, her face was unusually warm, no doubt flushed.

She suddenly removed her hand, taking mine with it, quickly straightened her back, placing both hands behind her. Within two or three seconds of some behind the back fumbling, she panted in a low whisper, "Now."

Urgently, we returned to Frenching with my hand instantly under her sweater and the loose bra. I gently caressed her bare right breast, gliding upwards to smoothly rub across and back over the peak. Then sliding down the curve of her breast. So steadily, so slowly, softly stroking, lightly squeez—

IT happened. An explosion!

My Roman Candle was shooting its salvo after salvo of fireballs into my pants. When the bursts finished, I broke off the kiss. Autumn sighed softly.

Those initial wonderful sensations of exhilaration and gratification were almost immediately overridden by awkwardness and disappointment, ending just as it was starting. Autumn had to know something happened. You can't be going sixty miles an hour then suddenly stop.

I quietly confessed, "I'm sorry. I didn't think I would ..."

Even by the dim light, I could see she had full redness in her cheeks. Regardless, she tried to console me, saying, "It's okay. It's natural, Richie. I think it just sort of happens **like that** the first few times." I began to smolder with colossal jealously while she reassuredly explained, "Richelieu, you know I have no experience with guys. Well, at least **this** kind. This is exactly where an older sister's experience comes in handy. Summer told me a few things about sex before she left for college. She **very explicitly** detailed them! And this is just one. She told me when the time was right, I would know the perfect guy to be the first one to touch me. The time is right and you are the perfect guy." She kissed me softly on my cheek.

"Oh Victoria, you are incredibly the perfect girl. You feel so wonderful. So soft. They're heaven. Pure perfection. I couldn't stop it from happening. I ... I..." and drifted off.

"Don't think about that happening. At least you don't get so embarrassed that you turn a deep scarlet for these things like this. Like now. *I still am! Just look at me!* After I get used to those things, whether it's hearing about some stuff or I guess like now ... doing them ... then the blushing will almost always stop. I just have to become accustomed to it. Takes a while, most often."

"Please don't be embarrassed about anything like this with me. I'm the one who ought to be embarrassed." She kicked off her loafers, pull her long legs up on the seat and eagerly begged, "I've only one wish. Please hold me."

"That's exactly what I wanted to do. To hold you for a while."

Without waiting, she turned around and started to move her back towards my chest and shoulder. I quickly pulled my handkerchief out. I didn't want her slacks possibly stained. While she deftly adjusted her bra then cupped back in her breasts, I strategically placed the cloth over myself. When I put my arms over her stomach, she snuggled against me, overlapping my arms with hers, but never asking me to hook her. I nuzzled her warm neck and kissed it. I was flying so high, so happy to hold her after fulfilling my dream of caressing that glorious, phenomenal breast. Even the touch and feel of her bare stomach felt magnificent as I continued to hold her. While we quietly continued our embrace, I noticed we had successfully fogged up the windows.

After about ten minutes later of minimal talking, we began French kissing again and I was able to ecstatically touch and caress her while the roman candle remained silent — well, at least for a much longer time. Afterwards, she immediately turned to be held. She said she didn't blush as much this time. I said I was only a little embarrassed and it was fantastic to hold her like this again. She tightened my embrace as I nuzzled her neck and ear. After some more whispered talking for a while, she asked me to hook her.

We kissed a long goodnight on her front porch. Before I got back into the car, I looked at her bedroom window. She had pulled back the curtains, saw me watching and waved. I waved back to her shadowy form, already missing her. A ton.

I alternated thinking about Autumn and 'it' all the way home. Then I thought about Linda for the first time in over a month. After washing out my underwear, I began to diligently sponge the inside and outside my jeans around the zipper and front, knowing I was going to need a washcloth for my pants in the future.

I laid in bed and compared my experiences with the two girls.

Drive-in dates with Linda would follow the same pattern — a Smirnoff shot in our 7-Ups, interspersed with watching the movie and talking, then another 1/2 shot for me and her usual second shot. After the first movie ended, she always made her quick trek to the Drive-in's restroom. When she returned, we would start making out, then Frenching, mixed with some talking and a little movie watching.

That last night, Linda urged the back row* as there would be no foot traffic to watch us make out like occasionally had happened. She was tired of being gawked at. We had our drinks but she had more than her usual second shot. She made her typical brisk run to the restroom. But when she came back that time, she announced she had an amazing going away present for me.

"Surprise! My Beautiful Twins!" She had quickly lifted her summer sweater to her armpits. Her bra had disappeared. I **was** thoroughly astonished! Two superb objects of curved beauty — jutting out with the tops of both slopes well-tanned but the remaining so much larger rounded shapes were pure white with tips resembling small Hershey kisses. Oh, what amazing baseballs.

---

*A **drive-in's back row** was *the* best place to park for *all* stages of sexual activity since no one would be behind a couple to observe what they were engaging in plus there would be only rare pedestrian traffic

When I thought about it over the subsequent months, I figured being felt up was her present too, judging by her gratifying moans. Plus she had to know she got my rocks off — twice. I never could remember if I was even a little embarrassed. After the first time, she sure had fun brandishing her bra, whooping "beautiful, bewitching, bare boobs" as she kept slurring, fumbling over, laughing at her every failed attempt to say it. During her spree, those naked mounds lightly bounced up and down in an intoxicating rhythm. I was thoroughly mesmerized by her show — positively convinced this was not her first "performance". Linda was too proud of their shape and appearance, not to have shared those amazing twin baseballs before. She wanted them fondled, thoroughly loving to be felt up.

When Linda finally stopped, she simply cupped her breasts, offering them to me for another whirl, sarcastically scoffing, "Eeeww ... Strait-Laced Grace can't know a Catholic boy rubbed and squeezed these fabulous beauties. These *supposedly virgin Lutheran* titties. Heehee ... in **her** car ... in the **very back row** at a **drive-in** ... just so sinful. Heehee. Ooooh me! What would they say at Immanuel Lutheran? Who cares? I say **rub 'em more** ... lots more ... keep these little nips hard." And I did.

In front of my house, there were final rubs on her baseballs and petite "Hershey kisses" as we Frenched, mixed with longing good-byes. Later in bed, I wondered how many guys had kept those chocolate "little nips hard." Like Gregory Latham, her longtime boyfriend whose family moved away the last day of school. We had strongly flirted at the Officer's Club Pool all the next day, resulting in our first date that night. Oddly, I didn't care about him or what others had done with her. I had my innings. And they were damn good innings.

I looked up at the ceiling and the light fixture, but only saw the faces of Bonnie Jo and Olga instead. Bonnie Jo and I liked each other well enough. So too with Olga yet certainly more sexually. With both, I desperately tried to satisfy my unrelenting desire to feel up a girl completely bare without any hindrances — my success thwarted every time either by clothing or people or both.

Twice rubbing Bonnie Jo's small ones. Only the outside of her sweater... wouldn't let me under it. No matter how I begged. Still wonder if she wears falsies. Still her same small size last July when I last saw her.

Three times with Olga ... always happily encouraging my hand to navigate down her dress or blouse then her slip so I could somehow maneuver into her bra. Yielding only a single hasty squeeze each time. ALWAYS, always other girls and guys reappearing way too quickly, almost thwarting me completely.

Their smiling faces disappeared to be replaced by the half-naked, laughing Linda exhibiting her twin mounds.

Linda ... attractive, always a fun girl to be with ... at the pool or to kiss and French. I really liked her during those seven weeks in summer. Seeing and playing with her bare tits was an unexpected, fantabulous bonus. Her feelings? Didn't care. They didn't matter.

Linda faded as I realized we never held each other after either time.

With ALL three girls, it was NEVER intimate. It was all mutual desire and good solid lust. Right Moose? What I wanted and craved. AND what each girl wanted and craved

I thought about Autumn and sighed heavily. I rolled over on my side and saw the photograph of my father on my desk. He didn't say anything. He just looked at me. I rolled back.

I DO care about her feelings. About OUR feelings of being together, talking, kissing, and now touching. She realized my embarrassment for shooting prematurely. I realized her great embarrassment of her breasts being touched for the first time. As we talked about our mutual awkwardness afterwards, I felt my affection and a closeness to her growing, even more as I held her tightly both times.

A true intimacy ...... I never experienced before.

Oh God, it's great just TO BE with her. When I'm walking to the car after kissing her good night, I already miss her. Especially tonight, waving at me from her bedroom and me waving back.

She's beautiful. Smart and funny. Clever and sophisticated. A creative, sensitive soul. So spiritual too with such a gentle nature. My statuesque model who I adore, who I......

O MY GOD! I AM IN LOVE WITH HER!
TOTALLY, COMPLETELY IN LOVE WITH HER!

As soon as I saw my Helen of Troy in that blue strapless dress. Especially during our Moon River euphoria. Why couldn't I have figured it out then?

Is she in love with me? She has to be!
I have to tell her!
When?
How?

I rolled over to get some advice from my father. I swear he smiled if only for the blink of an eye.

FEBRUARY

I called Hal earlier in the week to suggest my plan for he and Jacqueline on Saturday night. I may have virtually not known the guy, but he was totally committed to make this an important date for Jacqueline. I quickly picked up he seriously liked her. A lot. So where to go? She loved rock and roll. And loved even more to dance to it. There was a hall dance but they weren't great places to make an outstanding or lasting impression on a girl. Thus, a superior place — The Broadmoor. Hal had never been, but he said it sounded perfect when I described it to him. After I hung up, I wasn't sure if Autumn had ever been there.

Although we arrived fairly early, it was beginning to get crowded with not many tables available. We each paid our $2 per couple cover charge, then I went up to the hostess to give her my name and tell her we wished a booth. As she bent over her scheduling book, I leaned over next to her like I was ensuring the correct spelling of my name, effortlessly laid a folded five-dollar bill next to her pen. She smiled and assured me an excellent booth would be available quickly. I thanked her and went over to wait with my trio. No sooner than I rejoined them, my name was called and the hostess escorted us to one of the best booths in the club. I smiled my best and thanked her for the prompt service. She returned my smile pleasantly, "You and your party enjoy yourselves tonight, Mr. Marlowe."

Jacqueline wondered, "How did we get such a wonderful spot?"

"Just lucky, I guess."

After we settled in, Hal and Jacqueline immediately took to the dance floor and I thought we would join them but Autumn pulled me back and whispered, "Rich, how did you do this? *I know* you made this happen."

"Must be good luck, fortunately this booth was available. You know ... right place, right time."

"*You know* I don't believe you. You just pulled off another one of your magic tricks. '*Mr. Marlowe*' who can entice a darn good-looking hostess, at least ten years older, to immediately seat his party in one of the prime spots in the club."

"I was very polite and well-mannered in my request. The Jesuits teach us that at St. Ignatius."

"Oh, Bull Shit! **You're** going to make me barf! You're already making me swear! More and more! I know you, Richelieu Marlowe. Better than you think!"

Especially after last night. ... ... I'm 'ruining' her ... forgot to spell. ... ... "A magician never tells his secrets."

"He does to his assistant."

"Later, I promise ... girl scout's honor."

"Obviously, you can't ever have been a girl scout!"

"Oh sure! Most of the guys at St. Nate's are girl scouts."

"You are always so wicked." She giggled, "But it's one of the things I've always liked about you." She took my hand and squeezed it tightly, quickly kissed me on my cheek then looked longingly at me. I kissed her hand, ecstatic that I loved her. And not some "puppy love" crap. I wanted to tell her, but it had to be when we were completely alone in a quiet place.

Later, the band played a slow dance and Jacqueline asked, "Autumn, could I steal Richelieu for a dance?"

"Of course. Hal, would you like to dance with me?"

Jacqueline and I began speaking in French again. She looked much prettier tonight than the dance as she had asked Autumn for some more makeup tips. Jacqueline applied her suggestions, now looking more attractive. I told her that. Her expensive, tailored pencil skirt of her short jacketed suit confirmed my speculation regarding her derrière — a great tush. But I didn't tell her that one.

"Thank you, Richelieu ... you are *such* an incredibly sweet guy. Thank you for setting up this hang-out with Harold and me. This is a very nice place. You and Autumn have been simply wonderful to me, especially for Harold. He is a very sweet guy too."

"For Hal?" I didn't understand.

"Sure! Autumn set up the date with Harold to the Winter Wonderland Ball. She knew I did not get asked for the

Homecoming by a truly nice guy. However, three 'of the other kind' did. Autumn said I was right to assume they had the wrong intentions ... each would "want something sexual" in return. She said this would not happen again and did a wonderful job in her making the match. I really like Harold. So kind and understanding. Fun and handsome," she giggled. "And thank you for giving me my confidence back during the Ball. I really needed those words of encouragement. In my native tongue. Like they came straight from my family in Paris. A very crucial time. I was ready to go home. Oh, Richelieu, everything is so much improved, thanks to you and Autumn. I am happy again."

"I didn't do much. You simply couldn't quit and go home. You are too much French model cool. But don't forget Hal though."

She giggled, "I certainly cannot forget Harold. I like him. *Really, really* like him. Oh, and I like you too ... ... differently, I believe."

The girls decided to "go powder their noses" or their Tag, and Autumn said we could talk sports. Hal smirked, "Not about our pathetic football team." Then to me, "Thanks for picking this place Rich. It's perfect for Jacqueline. For us."

During the next slow dance, I whispered to Autumn, "I hear the Magician's assistant has been working her magic during her time."

"How?"

"Rescuing Jacqueline by fixing her up with Hal. She was ready to leave for Paris."

"She was becoming depressed, so I hoped Hal would be the answer, not knowing, of course, the magician would strike also. Right before Christmas, he finally had broken up with Cathy Winters for good. *I'm sure he wanted* to date Jacqueline, because his timing was just a little too perfect after he kept dropping less than subtle hints about her to me. Whatever you said plus her date with Hal changed her whole mental outlook. This is a great place for Jacqueline and Hal tonight. And us. You know, you are a good guy, Forrest Étienne Richelieu Marlowe. Now look."

"So I've been told ... many times," I smirked, then glanced at them in a tight embrace, slowly moving to the music. "Hal, you fast working devil."

Autumn teasingly punched me, "You really are bad, so bad. What am I going to do with you?"

"Oh, I can think of a few things."

She merely winked at me devilishly.

We dropped them off at Hal's where he said he wanted to introduce Jacqueline to his parents and he would then take her home. They were night owls and would be still awake. Sure enough, the house was brightly lit up. We all got out of the car to say good night to them. I shook hands with Hal and gave him a knowing smile. Jacqueline said to me, "*Au revoir, mon gars merveilleux,*" then to Autumn, "*Au revoir, mon ami delà de la mesure,*". Autumn, knowing it was a compliment, kissed her on her cheek as Jacqueline simultaneously responded likewise. Her comments pleasantly surprised me.

"Well, Frenchie, what did she say?" Autumn asked as we drove away.

"Wow! 'Goodbye, my wonderful brother'. To you, 'Goodbye, my friend beyond measure'." Actually it was "guy" not "brother". I wasn't sure how she meant it, but Autumn would have been jealous and hurt if I had told her the correct one.

"Wow! I started hanging around with her a lot more this week. She is so funny and talks much more now with her self-confidence back. Judy likes her but I don't think Ginny cares for her very much." Autumn mockingly scoffed, "Like 'she's foreign.' Well, that's her d-a-m-n problem. I really like her a lot. So tell the magician's assistant one thing, how did we get seated so quickly, in a booth no less?"

"Like I said earlier, I asked politely ... along with my friend Abraham Lincoln."

"*Oh Richie.*"

"*Oh Victoria,*" I countered in a slightly mocking voice. "If I didn't, we would have waited at least a half hour or more. Then been seated so near the band, we wouldn't be able to hear ourselves talk. I wanted something nice for them ... well, to be honest, for us too."

"Have you been there before? With a date?"

"Yes, and a second yes. The dates were two of the worst of my life. You've had bad dates, haven't you?"

"Of course I have. More than I could count. Some were simply awful ones."

My mind quickly moved to a vastly more important thing as we continued to the Spot. ... ... *How am I going to be able to touch her bare breasts like last night? O God, do I WANT TO! There's the suit jacket to unbutton and remove. The Christmas blouse to unzip down the back and remove. Ease the shoulder straps off then take the slip down to her waist. Put her jacket back on. Finally unhook her bra. Her breasts could be somewhat exposed even with the jacket.*

Autumn must have figured out the clothes removal sequence going through my mind. "We can't, Richie. I have ... uh ... too many layers of clothes on. I couldn't be ... be comfortable. You ... uh ... understand."

I'll finish ... ... 'You ... uh ... understand .... you might see my breasts bare.' ***That's*** *what she's not comfortable with.*

"It's fine, Victoria," as I ignored her hesitating words. In the few passing streetlights, I noticed her face was flushed which just confirmed my thought. I had trouble hiding my overwhelming disappointment, but did by suggesting, "Let's go to Lafayette's ... for dessert. Nobody will be there to talk to. I don't feel like sharing you one damn bit."

"Thank you, Richie, I'd like that. Especially about not sharing."

Later, over our pieces of chocolate cheesecake and cokes, Autumn coyly and quietly suggested, "I have an idea ... what if you picked me up for **a study date** tomorrow at four or so, **but** go to Zesto's instead. When it's pitch dark, we can..."

****

As the three of us were eating lunch on Monday, Jack said, "Lou, you remember meeting one of Camille's two best friends ... Elizabeth Campbell ... Libby ... right before Christmas vacation?"

I nodded, "Yeah, sure ... super smart, seemed really nice, has long, dark brown hair ... a little pudgy but still has an *absolute killer chest* ... as you would call it. Unfortunately really plain-looking, even when she loses the glasses." I kidded, "I'm not taking her out ... she's Bart's."

Jack ignored me as he continued, "And her father is President of First National Bank ... owns most of it."

"Yeah, sure."

"She told Camille and Marybeth Fawkes she's been dating a guy who works at the Bank. We thought he was some after-school courier or clerk. Turns out the guy is a junior bank officer and older. Libby doesn't want her parents to meet him just yet, so when they go out, she meets him somewhere. She confessed this to the two of them since she wanted them to cover for her ... be able to say Camille and Marybeth were all out together. And of course, they said yes."

Bart said, "Hell, that guy has got to be mid-twenties and a hot-shot on the rise to be a junior officer."

"Yeah, exactly what we figured and that he's only dating her to move up quicker in the bank. Guess they think that's exactly what it would look like to her parents, too. But Libby says it isn't that at all. This guy really likes her a lot and she is nuts over him. Met at the Bank's Christmas gala. Camille knows it's been pretty strong since mid-January, yet thinks something else is going on other than the old story of playing hide and seek with the parents."

※※※※※※※※※※※※※※※※※※※※※※※※

The following Friday night, Autumn softly mentioned as we were walking to the car, "Richie, I don't feel like doing much tonight."

"Okay, you pick. What would you like?"

After she got into the car to sit close to me, she continued in a quiet voice, "I don't feel like going to St. Victoria ... now or even later." As I pulled out, the light from the street lamp illuminated her face sufficiently to tell she was beginning to color up noticeably. "I'm just ... well, I am just not **in the mood**." Driving by Triangle Park, I glanced at her and could see she was starting to tear up as well. I pulled over to the curb. I saw a single park bench, thinking we could talk there if she wanted to.

"Victoria, what's wrong?"

She started to sniffle some and a tear fell down her glowing cheek. In the three months we had been going steady, she was always so happy and cheerful. I had never seen her sad, let alone crying.

"Autumn, please tell me what's wrong? Please? I will fix whatever is bothering you. Did something happen at school? **Tell me! Did some asshole—**"

"No, nothing at school," she interrupted. "I want to tell you. **Can't** do it."

"Is it something I did or maybe didn't do last Friday or Sunday night when we …? Whatever I did, I'm sorry. The absolute last thing I want to do is hurt you."

"Oh no, no, no. You would never hurt me. It's not you, it's *me*." She moved over as close as she could and laid her head on my shoulder, wrapping her arms around my upper right arm. "Oh Richie … … shit. Just shit," she sniffed heavily. "Damn it, I'm so embarrassed," and hesitated again, face now fully red. Finally, bracing herself, "I'm sure I'm going to have a really painful … oh damn … *damn it* … just an awful menstruation. I'm so … I'm so very tender. My breasts are sore, hurting. They are so swollen that I'm wearing a larger brassiere than usual. I bought the silly thing by mistake, but once or twice a year, it has its uses."

"I'm really sorry. What can I do?"

"Just let me stay like this for a while."

"All night if you wish."

She sniffed, "If we went to St. Victoria, it would be unbearable for me and probably not very pleasant for you, rather than wonderful like it was both times last weekend. In spite of my embarrassment, I really loved it … … your excitable touches then the heavenly feeling when you hold me."

"I'm glad. I wanted us to enjoy it together, in spite of our *mutual* embarrassments. I love holding you afterwards. So much."

Having finished her confession, she began to cry softly. She squeezed my arm a little tighter then tried to hide her burning face between my shoulder and the seat. I moved my arm around her and she buried her head on my chest. I stroked her hair until she stopped crying a few minutes later, then I kissed each one of her wet cheeks. Like the boy scout motto, I pulled out my handkerchief, dried her cheeks and offered it to her.

Whether she's the ultra-cool and elegant sophisticate or the fragile, vulnerable, innocent little girl, I love her.

She dried her eyes and dabbed at her nose, still kept sniveling so she finally blew it. A totally surprising noise. A very loud sound. From Autumn.

"See, more of my secrets are out, I sound like a foghorn when I blow my nose," she sniffed.

I seriously said, "When you are having your period, please tell me. It's only me. I'm sorry that you aren't feeling well. But you look good, as always. Should we just go back to your house? Watch TV or something? Or I could leave—"

"**Nooo! I need** to be out of that house tonight. It's so depressing. Thank you for saying that I look nice." She kissed my cheek. "Could we please go to your house? I would feel comfortable there. Your family is always wonderful to me. But I really have to fix my makeup and re-cover these two ugly red blemishes. Damn things!"

"Well, they like you more than they like me," and that made her smile warmly. "Ya know something? You taste salty," I teased. Her smile widen.

"Oh Richie, I will get embarrassed if I tell you about my feminine problems, like now. Or engaging in our wonderful touching, like last weekend, until I become accustomed to it. In the girls' restrooms at school or hall parties, the girls' jokes with dirty innuendoes or some of the trashy girls even talking about their actual escapades would always embarrass me. Still does some. And the girls would tease me about my blushing. Like, 'Autumn's colors are changing, the leaves will be falling next'. You have seen me turn red more than a few times, but you have never teased or joked about it. In fact, you've never even mentioned it. You accept me, my red face and all. Richie, you are an exceptionally sweet guy." She softly caressed my cheek a few times with the palm of her hand like she's begun to do.

"Each of us can be embarrassed in front of the other and it doesn't matter one iota to either one of us. It's us, only us. Talking about personal stuff just feels so natural with you."

As we began the seven-minute ride, I thought maybe she was in the mood to share some more secrets about herself.

"You know you said once I could ask you anything."

Her mood was improving since she bantered back, "But I might not answer. Sure. Shoot."

"This has been killing me ever since the first time I saw you in those red almost short shorts. What *are* your measurements?"

Now she was giggling. "After telling you all about my tormenting oncoming menstruation and breast tenderness, there's no reason to keep that information a mystery. You know I am five foot ten and a half inches tall. What you don't know is that I weigh 123 pounds, **but not tonight**. I have on a quite firm panty girdle to hold in all this damn bloating. Oh, my measurements are 34¼ — 23½ — 35¼ and my **normal** bra size is 32C, my panty size is a 3. My sweater is a 38. My shoe size is confidential. Awww, not really, my feet are just big ... real big, 10½. Dress size is a 7. That should get you going."

"Nice measurements of a nice body. Yours! You have the same shoe size as one the biggest stars in Hollywood. Guess which one?"

She leaned over to kiss me, "Thank you again for complimenting me. I'll guess Rock Hudson." We both laughed.

"Remember *Charade*?"

"Cary Grant?"

"No, no Victoria! You have the same shoe size as Audrey Hepburn."

"Wow! I'm a lot taller than she is. Maybe not so bad!"

"DeeDee's right, you are built like a model. Move with all the grace of one. You know she really idolizes you."

"I really like that girl an awful lot. You have a great sister ... just like I do. Hey, let's take her with us to Zesto's. I am **so ultra** d-a-m-n hungry."

"The magician's assistant's wish is easily granted."

After we went in and said hi to the three Graces, I flippantly said to DeForrest, "Hey DeeDee, we're going to Zesto's." I playfully taunted her, "Bet you wish you could to go to Zesto's. Well, you're in—"

She snapped at me, "Richelieu, you're not **a damn bit** funny." Her countenance showed a deep hurt. I'd forgotten she was supposed to have gone to a St. John V's mixer with her "might be my steady" Herb Travis but instead, she had broken up with him last weekend. Adding to her anguish, I remembered before I left tonight, she and Aunt Danae were coming out of their bathroom and DeeDee was tensely groaning, "...damn cramps. Wish my red river—" only to suddenly fall silent when she saw me coming up the stairs.

Shit, what have I gotten into tonight? Female Hormone Hell?

"Oh DeeDee, *he really wants you* to come with us. *I want you* to come with us. Are you hungry? I know I'm starving. As my Nanna would say, 'It is pleasant with company at the table. Woe to him who eats alone'. Come on, grab your coat. Go with us. Pleaaase?"

"Oh, Autumn, you're always so wonderful. Sure I want to go with you guys," and she smiled. "Do I have time to fix myself up a little bit?"

I started to say something teasingly to try to make her laugh but Autumn cut me off, "Take all the time you need. I know what ... we can help each other if you want to. C'mon, be like before your dance, only both of us helping each other."

"Really?" DeeDee smiled from ear to ear. "Oh Autumn, you're so fab." The girls walked up the stairs and started chattering about some new lipstick color.

Teasing thwarted for my sister, deserted by my girlfriend, I turned on my mother and aunt, "So, are you two going bar hopping?"

Aunt Danièle answered for them, "No, we are going to the Benedictine Monastery and find some good-looking monks."

"You two are probably too bright for those boys. Try the Jesuits."

My mother gladly dismissed me, "Good bye, Richelieu."

I headed into the kitchen. I didn't know why — maybe no female hormones were in there, maybe for solitude. Or both.

Can't tell her tonight either. So wished we would be celebrating my declaration later, but she needs to feel better, to feel like herself. She's definitely not now. She must love me too. Damn! I have to know for sure. **Soon***. Can't keep telling myself 'she must'. Need to have* **her tell me***.*

☼☼☼☼☼☼☼☼☼☼☼☼☼☼☼☼☼☼☼☼☼☼☼☼☼

"Richie, that was really nice to take your sister with you and Autumn, especially since I'm sure you know she isn't feeling quite herself."

"Mother, it really wasn't my idea, it was Autumn's. You know, she really likes DeeDee a lot. She's really wonderful."

"Autumn is the epitome of 'cool' to DeForrest. You're getting serious with her, aren't you? You know there is a year and a half of high school, then five years of college ahead of you."

It was a little late for this talk, so I slightly altered the subject, "I know you and Dad met at KU. How long before you both knew you were serious?"

"Your father always insisted it was the moment that I walked into Economics 101 in old Fraser Hall that he knew he had seen 'the girl of his dreams' and he made sure he introduced himself right after class before any other boy could. He said he would protect me from any masonry which had been falling off that seventy-year-old building, then walked me to my next class across the Campus and asked me for a date. I found out later his next class was in Fraser Hall, the same decrepit building we had just left." She laughed, then said, "But that was your father. Oh, and it did have chunks of rock falling off the facade." She changed her tone, "Richelieu, I just remembered that you told me you were going to marry Autumn after only a three minute conversation with her. You **were** serious! I can see my Forrest from twenty years ago looking at me right now. How does she feel?"

"I don't know for sure. But I know she likes me an awful lot."

"Oh, I can tell she does. Certainly more than 'an awful lot'. I would tell you to be careful, but it's much too late for that. I don't want to see my Little Forrest get hurt." She touched my cheek lovingly. "Or Honey. She's *such* a wonderfully talented, sweet, sweet girl."

****

Autumn was appropriately dressed for Valentine's Day in her red dyed-to-match cherry sweater and pencil skirt with color coordinated Mary Jane pumps. Accessorized with a red and black scarf and light red eyeshadow. Oh God, did she look beautiful tonight. Of course, I complemented her on her appearance, as I always did when we were walking to the car. We celebrated at the Plaza III where we both enjoyed a great steak dinner since the Missouri diocese granted a Friday dispensation. [Kansas had not.] As we drove back to Wyandotte, we decided to go for a walk since it was still warm then to St. Victoria later. We parked in front of her house and we begin to stroll, holding hands, to Triangle Park, the small park we had stopped at last week.

"I really like my Canoe cologne. I will definitely wear some tomorrow night. Thanks again, Victoria." I stopped and kissed her on her cheek.

Autumn said, "I reeeeeally love the sweater. It is the perfect size. The size for the slacks should work but I probably will have to take the cuffs down some. Did you have help? DeeDee?" She teased, "Misty again?"

"Yes and no ... Claire Stewart at Savoir-Faire earlier this week. I told her I wanted a blue cashmere sweater and matching slacks for my most beautiful girl from Christmas. You said your sweater size is a 38 last weekend. Claire thought a 38L would probably be better since you were so tall and Misty demonstrated the difference. The slacks are on order and should be in within a couple weeks. The baby blue color reminds me of your fantastic blue Winter Wonderland dress which I will get to see tomorrow night again. OH YEAH!!"

"I guess giving you all that personal information last week paid off." And she laughed and kissed my cheek. "Thank you, Richie. I'm sorry that I am going to wear that same dress again. It is just too expensive to buy another one. I don't have enough money saved so I could afford a new one. I don't want to ask my parents since they already told me the blue one was way too expensive."

"So what! I'm wearing the same thing again ... my black tux. You would be really hard pressed to top that look with ten new ones. Besides, you never looked more beautiful than you did in that blue dress. You will have the St. Nate guys slobbering white, then red with desire while their dates are green with envy. I can't wait to see you in it again."

"You are spending a lot of money on me lately. Dinner tonight, the cashmere sweater and slacks. A corsage tomorrow night and dinner again."

"I've been saving my allowance. Besides, it's you." ... ... *Maybe I borrowed some more from The Bank of DeForrest.* **That girl** *always has money.*

We entered the very small triangularly shaped public park and went over to an extremely old, weather beaten wooden bench and sat down. "This is really great. Sitting on a bench in an empty park on a warm Valentine's Day night with my girl. Just us, nobody else. It doesn't get any better."

"Richie, you are a loner. A real lone wolf. *Who* are your friends?"

"You're my **best** friend," I answered without even having to think about it. "Certainly a *lonely* wolf when I moved here but not so much anymore. Jack Nelson who you will meet tomorrow night. Bart Sanders-Jones. And Mick Hayden. I should probably include Father Fitzgerald, but on a different level. Of course, DeForrest ... I just wished she could find and date some nice guy. Tonight, it's another new guy from St. John V's. Usually it's one and done, sometimes two. Like your old philosophy. Even with that senior stud Chris Ewell. Says he was drinking during the party, bragging about all his basketball shit, then spewing some really lame lines at her. Says most guys are interested in only one thing."

"Aren't you, too?" she said teasing.

"You always look fantastic. You're beautiful with a great figure. Oh those long legs and that terrific butt of yours. Yes, your entire physical look is incredible, but that's certainly not the **only** thing that attracts me to you. You are the kindest, gentlest and most considerate person I know. Sophisticated. Highly spiritual. Clever. Smart. Oh God, I can't wait to see you ... **to be with you**."

... ... *Just SAY it, you idiot!*

"*I love you,* Victoria, more than anything. I mean it completely."

"Oh Richie, *I love you* ... **very** much. So totally, so completely!"

We French kissed. Finally we realized we were in that very small triangular park.

"Richie, don't you think we should continue this at St. Victoria, where it's more private?"

"I'm going to yell it out for everyone to hear that **we love each other**."

She giggled, "There's no one 'here' to 'hear'." Then she became serious, "It's heavenly to hear you say it, especially for the first time. I have positively known that you have loved me for some weeks and I waited and waited for you to tell me, especially after we were intimate those two nights. There is absolutely no way I would let **any** guy ever touch my ... my breasts ... unless I was completely in love with him **and** he was truly in love with me. During *Moon River* I knew you were." She kissed my cheek lovingly, then caressed it, sighing, "Oh Richie."

"When you came out in that beautiful blue strapless dress, my feelings completely soared off the charts and went all over the place. I'm sure now I knew I was in love with you at the Winter Ball, but I couldn't sort it out. Tried like hell. But after two weeks ago when we ... uh, well, it was so obvious. I was afraid you might think I was only saying 'it' because everything that Friday and Sunday night was sexual. God, it was incredible and wonderful to touch and feel you so intimately. Since then, I wanted to say it a couple of times, especially after last Friday when you told me some of your private stuff, but the ... uh, well, the timing didn't seem quite right. But tonight, I had to tell you. **It had** to be tonight."

We kissed a long and lasting French kiss. We didn't care who saw us.

"You do know it's the bench?" I looked at her quizzically. "If you sit on the bench with the one you love, you must profess your love. The bench is magical."

"Is that The Legend of Triangle Park?"

"Yes, The Wooden Love Bench of Triangle Park, as it's called, has been around for thirty years or more."

"Well, it's a good one. On to St. Victoria?"

We both laughed, got up off the 'magic' bench to leave the park, tightly holding each other. However, after we walked about twenty feet, I turned around, stopped and suspiciously looked at it. Then I called after her, teasing, "Was it the first *Moon River* or the second one?" She stuck out her tongue at me then told me to hurry up as she couldn't wait to get to St. Victoria. Even after I easily caught up with her, I still wasn't sure if it wasn't the *first* time.

****

Possibly Autumn looked more radiant and beautiful than she did for her Ball. When she swept into her living room, I stood up, smiled happily at my angel from the Elysian Fields.

Her father was working late at the office. Regardless, we didn't need to take any pictures since we were dressed the same for her dance. I was helping her into the car, and said, "You look just as fantastic and beautiful as you did a couple of weeks ago. Even more so."

"Why Richie?"

"Because I *know* I love you and you know I love you too." I felt ecstatic.

As we drove to my house, she kissed my cheek then wiped it with a Kleenex but continued to intermittently caress my neck and cheek with her gloved hand as she did a few weeks ago. I got a quick erection exactly like then, which was no surprise. In religion class, all I had to do was daydream about making out and French kissing her — I would harden up with very little delay. Replaced now by my imagination of caressing those heavenly breasts. Instantaneous twanger.

My only thought and comment was, "Thank God, I love Eskimo pies, too."

We both laughed happily.

We went into my house for more pictures. That afternoon, I asked my Three Graces to please dress nicely. I wanted various combination of pictures with all five of us. There was one shot of me in the middle flanked by Autumn then DeeDee on my left, and my Mother on my right, offset with Aunt Danae. A shot of just my girls. More combinations. Then a picture of only me. One was with Autumn in the middle, with my mother and me on each side. Mother knew why I wanted all these pictures. I could never get anything by her.

Autumn wished to have a picture solely with each Grace. The **one** she really wanted was with my mother. As we walked to the car, she asked specifically for a copy of that picture. I gave her various size copies of all the shots, but that wallet-sized one was laminated to join pictures of me, Summer, Jake and Summer, and, of course, her Nanna. But not one of either parent. Those pictures "with Gi Gi" and "with Nanna" are her favorites.

The Sweethearts Dance was being held in the cafeteria and as we walked in, I immediately saw Jack who motioned us over to a four person table. Bart had gone to Chicago to be with his girlfriend for Valentine's weekend. I introduced Camille and Jack to Autumn. Camille, like Autumn, always looked good. But tonight, also like Autumn, she looked exceptionally enticing in her lavender strapless gown and matching gloves.

Jack looked at Autumn and mouthed "WOW!"

I added, nodding at Camille, "WOW squared, Jack!"

Within a short time, Autumn made both of them feel quickly at ease with her. Our little table became popular as guys would come by, either to or from the refreshment area, to seriously check out our girls. Some would linger for the niceties of introductions and small talk. Jack and I could tell the girls were certainly enjoying all the male attention. I even met the basketball boys, Rush and Ewell, who had both charmed DeeDee at *her* dance. Of course, they didn't know me, but they *certainly* remembered her. Ewell more so, having totally blown his date with her. DeeDee said she would *never* go out with "that shit head prick" again.

We weren't in mood to keep sharing, so Jack and I asked the girls to dance. The band was light years more rock and roll than the Winter Wonderland Geezers. However, after six or eight dances, we retreated back to the table. It wasn't too hard for the girls in their formals and heels to do The Twist and The Mashed Potato but any variation of The West Coast Swing was somewhat difficult. We would do another set later and, of course, slow dances would be mixed in soon.

Autumn asked Camille if she would like to join her to go to the ladies' room. We both got up when they started to leave and Jack and I looked at each other. We had no clue where the girls' toilets were. Our dates quickly figured it out. They would just follow a departing twosome and a threesome out of the cafeteria to the desired destination. As I watched them stroll out across the floor, heads turned to follow their progress to the exit. They were a singular pair, Autumn was more than a half foot taller than Camille, but regardless of height, both were beautiful and elegant. Jack said the same thing. As the other couples danced, we checked the guys' dates or girlfriends, comparing and commenting for some time. Some looked good, some not so much. We decided we absolutely had the best-looking and most ultra-cool girls at the dance.

Jack interrupted our bragging, "Wait a minute! Is that crazy Gloria?"

"**Oh no no no! Oh Shit**, Jack, tell me you're kidding. Please!"

"I am," he chuckled, then said, "However, I did see Antoinette earlier. *That's* not a joke."

"Ah, poor Teddy ... the dumb ass idiot. Who's she here with?"

"Didn't see for sure ... think Thompson Briggs ... the *super* rich jerk. Well, anyway, it was her. Oh damn! **There** she is. She's walking back in **with Camille! Autumn too**! See them? Wow! Now that, my friend, is a total picture of beauty!"

Oh God, she looks fabulous! In the stair-step of beauty. Antoinette in the middle of Camille and Autumn. Certainly as good as The Hangout Trio. Two blondes and my golden brown-haired girl.

When they were about fifteen feet away, Antoinette waved enthusiastically at me. She looked fantastic with her hair and makeup perfect, wearing a very expensive grey and black, fairly low-cut formal. I didn't remember her pair quite *that* big, but there they were, creating some highly enticing cleavage. I quickly thought of our extremely passionate make out and her stopping me from going further. I smiled my most irresistible grin and waved back.

Jack snickered, "Wonder what those *three* talked about while they all took a nice, long, relaxing *tinkle*. Hopefully didn't make a puddle ... ... on the stall floor."

"Shit, I don't want to know." Her continued walk with our girls was intercepted by Briggs who quickly took her to the middle of the dance floor. Obviously, he was in no mood for letting her make or renew our acquaintances.

The girls slowly approached with Camille finishing, "...that alone, had to cost at least $100 ... probably more!" Autumn agreed wholeheartedly.

We stood up, Jack saying, "Welcome back to our humble table, no one has stop to talk to us while you have been gone. It's only you girls the guys want to see. We're shocked and hurt."

Camille and I laughed but Autumn looked straight at me with a stern face, "Well, Richelieu, I just met one of your old flames. Antoinette."

"Yeah, she's extremely attractive, a good personality. Hardly a girlfriend. It was only one date which ended with her real boyfriend showing up." ... ... *Damn you Jack. You're enjoying seeing me squirm.*

"She was very candid about your date."

Oh God no! Nooo!

"She said you were very good-looking so she flirted to tempt you. While both of you talked about fashion ... her mostly ... you seriously flirted back, enticing her even more, hopefully you had become greatly interested in her. All proved correct. Some nice making-out in the car with a certainly long kiss goodnight. You were a perfect gentleman. Then her old boyfriend showed up."

The intense make out, THE French Kiss, my 'such damn tantalizing fingers' are still secret. But calling THE French Kiss a 'certainly long kiss goodnight' is like saying Mickey Mantle is just an OK ballplayer.

Camille added, "After Thanksgiving she finally broke up with Teddy Burrows for good. Antoinette begged me to arrange a date immediately ... she wanted you as her steady ... couldn't wait. I plainly told her that you were completely infatuated with your 'Helen of Troy'. She was *too late*. She pouted, saying the timing for you two was **still** regrettably out of sync, but certainly let her know when you and **she** had broken up. Antoinette would *call you* for a date."

※※※※※※※※※※※※※※※※※※※※※※※※※

Antoinette Flavia Faber graduated from Parsons School of Design in NYC, became a solid fashion designer for Anne Klein; Earned the nickname 'Toni Fab' after she went to work for Donna

Karen, her classmate at Parsons; then her own label/company of
'The Artisan Blonde' [translation of the Latin Flavia Faber]

Her personal life was virtually the opposite — Antoinette married
three times, ended by an annulment, a suicide, and an ugly divorce
as she was caught 'in flagrante delicto', resulting in her being
hospitalize after a brutal beating; She didn't care about hers or the
male's marital status when an 'affair' started, These flings would
only last a few weeks to perhaps four or five;

Antoinette was described as terribly driven, a definite workaholic;
While straining to meet the deadline for her new 1998
Fall Collection, she complained early one morning of a
burning sensation in her left shoulder; Told her assistants
she was not to be bothered under any circumstances
Long after lunch, she was found slumped on the floor
next to the pillows used to muffle her phone
Antoinette was dead from a heart attack; She was only 51

****

I tried to deflect away anything more about Antoinette by asking, "But *where* is the ladies' room? I've never seen one."

Camille teased, "Actually, there are two ... ... one close to the President's Office and the other near the General Office. You two little boys should really take a tour of your own school."

"Well, that explains it. Since the building opened last fall, we never had a reason to go to Father Mattingly's Office. Or the Main Office." Jack finished with a wide smirk, "**Or use** a girl's toilet."

"Well, well, well. Two of the three musketeers. Where's Porthos?" boomed a voice. There was Father Sean Fitzgerald, standing behind Jack and Camille about six or eight feet from the table.

We were all shocked, except Autumn, "Father Fitz. It's soooo great to see you again. How have you been? You're looking well," exclaimed the Reformation girl as she had already jumped up, moved quickly to him. She grabbed his arm, "Won't you join us for a while?" Autumn pulled him over without waiting for an answer.

The three Catholics remained dumbfounded as the priest smiled, "Autumn, just for a little while. Wonderful to see you again, my Christmas Angel."

"Yes, Father, please join us," as Jack recovered. "Father, this is Camille Forsythe, and Camille, this is Father Fitzgerald, our English teacher. Porthos is in Chicago with his girl, Father."

As Camille and Father Fitz exchanged pleasant greetings, he pulled up a chair to sit between the girls. "Best seat in the house, between two of the most attractive Sweethearts of the Dance."

Camille intensely blushed, but Autumn simply voiced, in her Irish lilt, a quote of one of that country's proverbs, "The older the fiddle, the sweeter the tune." We all laughed, especially the priest.

Father Fitz stayed about fifteen minutes, but long enough to entertain and tease both girls who, in turn, held their own and certainly charmed him.

"Good night to you Camille, certainly wonderful to meet you, my dear. Good night, Autumn, very enjoyable to see my *spiritual* Christmas Angel again. Good night Musketeers, see *you* and *your* smiling faces on Monday morning."

"Good night, Father," the three Catholics virtually said in unison, immediately reminding me of grade school, saying goodbye to a priest as he walked out of a classroom. Autumn, however, stood and waved, calling, "Hope to see you soon, Father Fitz. To continue our talk."

While he smiled and nodded agreement, a few guys at two nearby tables looked strangely at Autumn. Nobody, but nobody called him 'Father Fitz' to his face. Rarely did anyone see him smile.

"You already knew him? But how?" inquired Camille, then quickly became embarrassed, "Oh, sorry, maybe that's personal."

"Oh, no, no, no, not at all Camille." Autumn touched her forearm reassuringly. "My sister Summer and Jake Ford announced their engagement right before Father Fitz said Midnight Mass on Christmas Eve at Jake's aunt's house for his family and Richelieu's. It was the best spiritual experience I have *ever* had. Such an extremely nice priest and *he's still very handsome* too." Both girls giggled at the latter comment and nodded in conspiratorial agreement.

Jack mouthed, "Nice priest? Handsome?" and made a face.

Both Jack and I could tell that Autumn and Camille were

getting along famously. But that is simply Autumn's way and actually Camille's, too, who had always been helpful in my attempts with the St. Cat's girls.

The last dance just happened to be *Moon River*. Autumn's expression was of utter disbelief and happiness when we took to the floor as the band began playing the song. Autumn was hugging me tightly and said in my ear, "This is not a coincidence. I know you. You made this happen. You always have something going on in that head of yours under all this black hair." And she ran a hand up and down the hair on the back of my head. "*You are always plotting*. But the Magician always makes it perfect for his Assistant."

During their second Tag, I had gone over to the band to ask what the song for the last dance would be. The leader said he had a few in mind. I had asked if *Moon River* was possibly one of them. He grinned and said possibly. Abraham Lincoln convinced him. Worth every penny and more.

"Richie, I hope it didn't cost too much."

"The look on your face was priceless." I laughed and was becoming stimulated by her Chanel scent. I would kiss her but it would earn me a Jug if I were caught. A special Jug — beginning with a Mass, then spending tomorrow afternoon cleaning up the cafeteria, the grounds and anything else the Jesuits deemed necessary. No, I would wait until the car.

As we drove to meet Jack and Camille at Fedora's, I asked, "Victoria, it appears you really like Jack and Camille."

"Oh yeah, sure do. I can see why you're best buddies with Jack. He has a devilish, terribly independent streak in him which is why girls, especially Camille, are terribly attracted to him. Camille is **so** good-looking, nice and witty. She really likes you—"

I interrupted, "Oh no, not another one of your so called 'crushes'!"

"No, no! She thinks you are handsome and a terrifically nice guy who doesn't talk a lot." She leaned over and kissed my ear. "I like her. She is funny ... should have heard her in the powder room. **And your Antoinette is definitely** more than **a little risqué**. I only blushed once, hmmm, about her ... err ... cleavage

... how she made herself appear bigger. Won't tell you ... well, okay, it's some fashion trick with tape and brushing bronzer on your cleavage. Told me I could easily 'make my **smaller** t-i-t-s look a lot more tempting'. **Her** comparative emphasis of hers to mine ... just to stress she's **bigger**. But I'm going to remember how to do it ... if I ever have the nerve to buy something low-cut ... like *that* one of hers. They must use *that* language and get those naughty ideas because they attend an *all girls' Catholic school*! And have contests comparing whose are bigger! She's probably not *all that* bigger than me, but she sure looks it tonight."

Yeah, and I know every time what Looney-Tune would win the contest and what Yakety-Yak would come in last place. ... ... "Your t-i-t-s are extremely tempting exactly the way they are. Perfect size and shape." Striking an indecent look at them, "Oooh ... just trust me."

"Why thank you." She smiled happily, then became serious, "One thing is for sure, Camille really, and I mean **really**, likes Jack, in fact, I'm sure she is in love with him. But her parents really dislike him. They think he is too arrogant, too independent, and definitely too rich. His family has money, like yours. Hers doesn't, like mine. They think he will break her heart when he starts running around on her next year when she's at Mizzou or when he goes off to some expensive university after he graduates."

"I know **he** won't. I know he's in love with her."

"I don't care about money, Richie. I only care about us." She was clutching the locket.

I was starting to detect worries in Autumn about the money disparateness. Jack had told me once that Camille expressed concerns about it to him and he just laughed it off, telling her he didn't give a damn, he was totally crazy about her and there would never be a choice between her and 'some hot-looking moneyed chick' like Antoinette. He's right. I don't give a damn either.

"Autumn Victoria, I certainly don't give a damn if your family doesn't have money. Let me give you a comparison. Antoinette lives in an extremely beautiful, large house in Mission Hills close to the Russell Stover mansion. She has **a lot** of money, even her own T-bird and is an extremely attractive girl. She has probably been to quite a few dances already this year and would wear a new dress to each one. She wore stylish, *very* expensive clothes for my date with her."

"I don't give a damn about how fab a girl's car is, how many new formals a girl has or how big or luxurious her wardrobe closet is. What I care about is the captivating and delightful spirit of the **girl in** the solitary formal dress or the **girl in** those same splendid clothes during regular dates. Yes, money certainly helps to go to nicer restaurants, but it's being in the girl's company. Yes, money can buy the last dance, but it's the astounded, happy expression on the girl's face that makes it worthwhile. Yes, money can purchase expensive perfume, but it's the intoxicating scent the girl exudes only for him. And yes, money might buy the girl a new sweater and slacks, but it's to see how beautiful she will look when she wears them for him. That girl is definitely you. The rest is all just meaningless crap."

"Oh Richelieu, you always, always know how to reassure me everything will be fine and you make everything perfect for me again. You are my Magician. I love you so much." Since I was driving thru the Plaza's traffic, she turned and had to kiss my lips both times at an angle. Peripherally, I could see she was still clasping the locket like it was a talisman.

"You know Rich, I never heard you talk so much all at one time," she snickered as she wiped her lipstick off my lips and chin, then she stroked my cheek.

"But getting back to the subject of parents, what do yours think of me? I'm pretty sure *they* aren't particularly fond of me. My mother and aunt think the world of you and would probably trade *me for you* and DeeDee ... well, DeeDee really thinks you are Helen of Troy reincarnated."

"Your mother has always treated me incredibly ... always in a very special way, Rich ... like tonight with the pictures. Danae is wonderful to me also. I feel a particular bond with DeeDee. With my parents, it's hard to tell. I don't talk with my mother a lot other than routine everyday stuff. Never really have. I always went to Nanna or Summer for advice and help, *especially* about girl stuff. Oh, my mother is a very busy woman. There are her 'girls' from her bridge club and church groups or her Soaps, her

Detective and Variety Shows on TV. My father is also too busy. He is gone quite a bit to all his conventions and sales calls with dinners to socialize and schmooze. I really don't give a s-h-i-t what they think."

I slightly changed the subject. "How did you and Summer get your names? I have often wondered but never asked."

She laughed, "It's one of my mother's naming quirks. Like our middle names. Had to be four syllables, starting with a V, like hers, Valentina. Summer's is Veronica. Our first names are when we were conceived. I'm born in June, so conceived in the fall, hence Autumn. Summer is a little different. Her birthday is early January so conception was in the Spring, but my mother didn't like the name Spring, so the next season … Summer."

"I guess she could have named you by month instead, Summer would be then April or May, maybe even June but I can't see you as September, although I would love to see you as *Miss September*. Oh yeah!"

"**Richie**! You are absolutely incorrigible! So, so wicked." She laughed, redden up only slightly, slugging me playfully, then said, "Oh, there they are, waiting for us."

※※※※※※※※※※※※※※※※※※※※※※※

On the short trip to the cafeteria after English, I asked, "So, Bart, how was Chicago and Janie?"

He didn't answer at first but then said, "Janie broke up with me Friday afternoon. I called her before I left for Municipal Airport to see where she wanted to go for both Valentine's and Saturday night. She said long distance relationships don't work well. I tried to explain to her I would continue to fly there every other weekend on my Dad's pass and stay with my aunt and uncle. Then she A-bombed me by saying she already had another date for Valentine's Day. Didn't seem to matter to her how I felt about her, how I wanted to see her, how I wanted to … Awww, what the shit! She doesn't care about me like I care about her."

"This won't be a problem, my boy. Camille knows tons of hot chicks from St. Cat's and we will fix you up with two or ten. I will personally get a hot, foxy, Kansas City girlfriend for you."

I rolled my eyes at Jack, thinking of the trio of "chicks" I was fixed up with. Only Antoinette might work. I said I would ask Autumn about Ginny or Judy. Joanie would certainly work. Maybe someone else. We would take care of our brother musketeer.

"One for All!"

"And all for One."

Jack and Camille fixed him up four different times in the coming weeks. Nothing worked for him. Camille swore she would not give up. I knew he missed Janie. A lot. I wasn't any help either. All three of my picks were going steady — for a time.

※※※※※※※※※※※※※※※※※※※※※※※※※

On Friday, Jack was slightly excited and suggested the three of us eat in my car for privacy. "Okay, why all the cloak and dagger shit? It's not that warm out here."

"So turn the car on, Dummy." As I did, Jack eagerly continued, "Look, remember a couple weeks ago, I was telling you guys about Libby Campbell and her love life? Well, things have gotten really weird. Camille said, like before, she's been acting really different ... now kinda nervous, especially this week. Marybeth agrees wholeheartedly, 'cause yesterday, she saw a sales receipt from Farrar's sticking out of Libby's Religion book."

"Shit, Jack," as I shivered, "the girl just bought a set of matching undies at that expensive lingerie store. So what. We're out here freezing our asses for **that**?"

"Not at that price. And she covered it quickly, never explained it. Marybeth claims it was more than enough for some really, **really** nice lingerie."

Bart sided with me, "What the hell Jack. So they're going to ... as Moose would put it ... do a little 'consummating'. Why is that our concern?"

"Both Marybeth and Camille say there are things that don't add up. Those girls are real tight ... all three are not just the only girl, they are also the *only child*. But *they've* never met the guy. In a month! Libby's really modest, even prudish and shy. Hasn't dated much since she's ordinary looking, even with that great set of knockers. So she depends on Camille and Marybeth, like she's their little sister. Libby's always open, now she's being secretive. Something is just off in this relationship ... *really wrong*. Camille wants to follow her tonight. You guys wanna go instead?"

"Well, I got nothing going. What my father would call 'the signs thereof'... first time nerves, the expensive fancies. Probably heading to a motel."

"Well shit, I know Autumn would love being with my three Graces for a while. I'll be there since it won't be all night. But this better be worth it."

"Great, thanks guys. It's damn cold out here. Let's go eat inside."

****

I drove to Bart's, then we picked up Jack and went to the address and description Camille had given him, drove past and parked down the block and waited. Libby pulled out in her '63 red Impala SS and we easily followed her. Even before she got off the Interstate, we knew she was going to the Hilton. She valet parked, taking only an overnight case with her.

We valet parked also, but Jack and I hung outside since she would undoubtedly recognize us. After at least ten minutes, Bart hastily came out to get us and said, "Shit, if that guy is in his mid-twenties, then I'm going to kindergarten. He's older than dirt. Got to be forty." He quickly described him to us.

SON-OF-A-BITCH! It's that Pervert Prick ... REX FINNEGAN! He's going to bang the hell out of her tonight. But what's his game? Another teenage girl to screw for a while until the newness wears off? Got those terrific tits but she's a little pudgy and kinda plain.

SHIT NOOOO! A graduation marriage proposal to get his hands on a ton of bank stock. Oh, good instinct Camille. Something IS really wrong!

As we hurried to the elevators, I quickly told them about this Bastard. While he "seriously" dated my mother, he was banging Christy Taylor, the smokin' hot eighteen-year-old chick headlining at The Inferno, then finally making an ugly move on my sister. Since all three of us had younger sisters, we knew something had to be done and quickly.

"I've got a plan." Bart related what took place while we rode up to the top floor. The Bastard met Libby, kissed and hugged her in the lobby, then nodded to Mr. Mercuri, the reception desk clerk, who said to enjoy the Suite since it was one of the best with a view of the airport and river. While the couple waited for the elevator with others, Bart ran up the seven flights to barely catch the Prick picking her up to carry her into Suite 714.

We had to wait more than five minutes until a maid came to do turn down service. Jack started limping, leaning on me as we hobbled back to Suite 714 where I had placed a bucket of ice. Bart began pleading with the maid.

"My key won't work in the lock. I asked that Mr. Mercuri at the front desk who said we three boys needed to try a little harder and drink a little less." Bart pulled out a key —fairly resembled a Hilton key, even having the blue tassel — put it in the door, but of course, it didn't work. The tassel, I found out later, was from another Hilton which Bart wanted to keep on his house key as a "souvenir". Of what? Jack and I never asked, but we had a good idea.

The plump maid spoke with a heavy German accent, saying, "Not allowed".

"Bitte, fräulein, mein Freund ist verletzt und Herr Mercuri ist ein ... uh ...uh ... unhöfliches Arschloch." [Please Miss, my friend is hurt and that Mr. Mercuri is a rude arsehole.] She smiled and nodded in agreement, took the few dollars Bart nonchalantly had offered, happily opened the door as they exchanged whispered thanks in German.

We quietly entered the living room, then into the bedroom. I was first, seeing Libby anxiously sitting against the upholstered headboard where she repeatedly sucked on a Marlboro, exhaling the smoke rapidly. Her glasses were off, lipstick slightly smeared. Clad in a quite fancy, gauzy, peach lace negligée which fully exposed her "absolute killer chest". Libby saw me, squealed and instantly grabbed the bed cover and pulled it to her neck.

There was that Prick Bastard standing in boxer shorts, pulling his old man's sleeveless T-shirt over his head. I wanted to slug him, but instead threw the bucket of water and ice at him, hitting him dead center. I knew he recognized me but said nothing. Neither did I.

"You little bastards will go to jail. Breaking and Entering. Assault. For that!" He pointed to the ice and quickly starting toweling himself with his T-shirt. "Get out! **NOW**! Or I'm calling the House Dick."

Jack yelled at him, "No, you're the one who's going to jail ... for attempted **STATUTORY RAPE!**"

Rex scoffed loudly, "Oh Bull Shit. Libby's legal. Turned eighteen last month." He grinned at her, salaciously bragging, "Oh, my voluptuous Bunny is *very good* at satisfying sexual desires. Learn quickly, has **real talent.** And she'll gratify my colossal one tonight and continue with the pleasuring into the morning." His voice became harsh, "**NOW, GET THE HELL OUT!**"

Libby's countenance sharply winced, followed by a look of humiliation — like she was being groomed as Rex's sluttish private plaything. Certainly not how any guy would talk about or portray his girl or fiancée. Her shamed feelings overwhelmed her sensitive nature. Libby began to softly cry.

"The only thing **colossal** is your stupidity, Asshole! She's only seventeen."

"Bunny," he vehemently demanded of her, "tell these obnoxious, pubescent pricks you're eighteen. And **TO GET THE FUCK OUT!**"

She could only shake her head, whimpering, "I ... I'm ... **NOT!**"

The Snake spat venom at the miserable girl, "**WHAT? YOU DECEIVING LITTLE CUNT!**" Rex's face was distorted with rage, screaming, "The big socialite parents' insecure, neglected little girl! **HA!** You're nothing but an **UGLY, LYING, WORTHLESS PIECE OF ASS**! That's why no boy wants you. **Or ever will!**"

Loudly wailing, Libby threw her ashtray at him, striking his arm. She flung off all the covers, slid over and down the far side of the bed, ran to lock herself in the bathroom. Thankfully, under the lacy negligée, there were a matching pair of peach bikini panties which, although scanty, covered her decently.

"No, wait! I've got a better idea. I'll call the Campbells in New York tonight. Tell them what you've been trying on with their daughter for the last six weeks, ending up at the Hilton. So I would highly recommend, you asshole pervert prick, find yourself another job ... as far away from here as you can. You have one month ... ... then *I will cut your balls off.*"

Jack grabbed her glasses off the nightstand and went over to the bathroom, "Libby, honey, please get your things together. I'm taking you to Camille's. Marybeth's there. They'll stay the night with you." Moments later, a wildly disheveled Libby rushed by Jack, mascara and tears still flowing down her cheeks and ran out the hotel room. He grabbed her case and followed.

During this time, Finnegan was silent. Maybe he was painfully realizing his conquest lost, despite his cunning schemes leading up to and including tonight, and God knows what for the future. Or simply Jack's ultimatum had sunk in. Likely both. He finally yelled, "Get out! You Little Shits! Get out!" He seized a foot tall statue of Venus de Milo and began menacingly waving it at us.

Bart, however, decidedly taunted him with the Finger, accompanied by "Make us, you shite-laden Arsehole!".

We ran out of the bedroom, through the living room. However, just outside the room's doorway, we both turned back. Seeing Bart grab Finnegan's wrist with his hand wrapped around the statue's head and torso, I likewise seized his other forearm. Together we yanked him into the hall with us. Bart slammed the door. Finnegan swung the statue at Bart twice, each time wildly missing. We left him cursing and shaking the Venus de Milo at us while we laughingly ran down the hall to the stairs as Bart's clenched fist remained in the air, the middle finger sticking out.

****

From Camille's, the three girls went to Libby's and stayed together all weekend. Jack and Bart went to a late showing of *Seven Days in May.* I walked through the kitchen before 9:30 to find my sister teaching my mother, aunt and girlfriend how to play Baccarat. A perfect ending to our fanciful, quasi James Bond caper.

A few days later, after I told DeeDee the entire story, the secured Books of Secrets had another entry. She merely kissed my cheek, smiled hugely, and walked away.

About a month later, my aunt informed me, "Rex Finnegan is leaving the bank to take a similar position with Crocker-Citizens National Bank in LA." I only responded with my wide smile, then a broad smirk.

****

Because Elizabeth Loretta Cobb Campbell's father insisted she skip third grade, she made lifelong, close friendships with Camille Forsythe and Marybeth Fawkes;

When the 'Girls With No Siblings' Club met The Three Musketeers in St. Ignatius's parking lot after a baseball practice in late spring, Libby tearfully thanked, hugged and kissed each one;

'The Hilton' was never mentioned again;

Richard Harris, the left fielder, joined the group, and was introduced to them; Before the girls started to leave, Rich asked Libby for a date; They immediately started going steady, became engaged early in college; Libby lost her pudginess, happily her bust remained the same size, yet her ordinary looks persisted;

The couple married a week after graduation from the University of Missouri; Libby was pregnant quite a bit of the time during their first 10 years as they had three boys, followed by three girls; Richard became the First National Bank and Trust's Executive VP of Finance and eventually its youngest President;

DeForrest bought Richelieu an expensive replica of Venus de Milo for his desk, her reason was 'because of its Hellenistic artistry, renowned for its beauty'; Or, perhaps, a remembrance of a night's successful outcome by saving a girl's virginity & psychological well-being — having Three Musketeers as protective older brothers

****

On that past Wednesday, the movie distribution client made his monthly appearance at the law firm. After his usual flirting with Aunt Danae, he asked if she or anyone she knew liked foreign films. Starting her flirting, she warmly smiled, "I sure do Good-Looking," remembering Jacqueline. He had four tickets for the Saturday night showing of a two-night special engagement at the Kimo Art Theatre for a French movie musical which would open in France and Germany this same week. The English sub-titled movie, *The Umbrellas of Cherbourg*, was to be tested in four cities in America before its nationwide release in December. When she told me about the movie, I simply said, "Little Auntie, my French is impeccable, I don't need subtitles". She responded, "*Oh, bien sûr que le vôtre est. Plus de vôtre Merde de Taureau, comme d'habitude.*" [Oh, of course yours is. More of your Bullshit, as usual.] Then handed me the four tickets as I kissed her on her forehead. I called Autumn who, of course, agreed totally, then I called Hal who thought just when my ideas couldn't get any better, like magic, they do.

Hal was going to drive, so we met at Jacqueline's house. After we greeted each other, Jacqueline immediately showed Autumn and me the gold heart-shaped pendant and chain Hal had given her for Valentine's. She was greatly delighted and proud of them. Because the engraving was in French, it took longer than expected, thus Hal had to give it to her belatedly. He added he had asked her to go steady on Valentine's Day, but they would only announce it with the arrival of the gift.

So I teased, "Jacqueline, what did you say? Without the pendant?"

To answer me, she leaned over and kissed Hal on his cheek. From the rearview mirror, I could see he was smiling broadly.

The theatre was fairly packed but not many our age. As we were leaving the theatre, everyone was asked to fill out a short questionnaire about the film and to please mail it within a week. An older woman stopped the four of us, "Would you mind answering a few questions? You are a good representation of teenagers and college students."

Jacqueline unconsciously reverted to French with "*Oui, certainement,*" [Certainly yes] probably because of the movie. We readily agreed with her.

"Oh, fabulous, you're French. A true perspective."

"Did you like the movie as a musical?"

Our French girl jumped in, "Oh yes, the recitative style was very nicely done."

The three of us looked quizzical, but she was taking classes in Advanced Piano and Solo Voice, so she would sure know.

The woman interjected, "This will be greatly informative. French with a solid knowledge of music."

Jacqueline sheepishly said, "Oops ... I will explain. The big difference is while all the film's dialogue is sung, the actor or actress will adopt the rhythms of ordinary speech. Somewhat similar to our Gregorian chants, Richelieu."

Autumn loved the movie, even though it was sad. Hal agreed, still a good movie. Jacqueline talked more about the use of music in it and the cinematography. Then the lady asked me my opinion.

"Ma'am, no disrespect, but I thought it was the saddest darn movie that I have ever seen. The ending tore up part of me and yet the other part was happy for Guy and Madeleine and their son François. No coincidence how both children are named. But that little Françoise is his daughter, his flesh and blood. Yet he can't bear to meet her. So many possibilities, but a cruel ... no, not cruel ... it was a bittersweet ending. I wondered if it was tearing Geneviève's heart up. Now she has a ton of money, but does she really love Cassard? An excellent movie, but so, so melancholy."

"Wonderful opinions and perspectives. I must really thank you four youthful film critics. You helped me considerably. By the way, I am Mrs. Hardesty and overseeing the film's national December distribution. For certainly helping me, here are four passes for *Yesterday, Today, and Tomorrow* with Sophia Loren and Marcello Mastroianni. It opens here at the Kimo on March 13. Enjoy! *Merci Beaucoup.* Thank you again."

Hal and Jacqueline dropped us off at her house. As we got into the Galaxie, Autumn said, "Richie, that was incredibly nice of you to think of Jacqueline for the movie. When we went to the ladies' room ... for our 'tinkle and gossip' ... before we met that Mrs. Hardesty, she told me she had met and knew dozens of guys ... French, American, some Belgiums and Germans, a few Swiss ... but next to Hal, you were the sweetest and nicest guy she had **ever, ever** met in her life. Called you, 'a guy for any girl's dreams.' Good thing, there is Hal, otherwise, I would have some stiff competition," she said honestly yet with a slight fear of real rivalry.

"I really like 'Jacqui' a helluva lot. But there's no competition. She's terrific ... good-looking and *really built* ... stylish too ... highly intelligent. But she's only a good, close friend ... but only that. Something like ... maybe a sister."

"But I am still a little jealous. It's time to go to St. Victoria. You need a lot of love and attention after that movie made you sad. I am sure the magician's assistant has something which could appear to make her magician happy again."

❄❄❄❄❄❄❄❄❄❄❄❄❄❄❄❄❄❄❄❄❄❄❄❄❄❄❄❄

Later, as I was holding her, she wondered, "Are you still sad?"

"How could I be sad after that? Kissing and touching you, now holding you, always makes me happy."

"I'm glad Richie. Ooh, it makes me so happy too." She giggled merrily.

Then I seriously commented, "I would never let something like what happened in the movie or **anything else** separate us ... to come between us. If there was ever a problem in some terrible situation, my mother could sort it all out and make everything right."

"Is your mother a magician like you?"

"Sure, where do you think I get my magic from?" Autumn laughed.

She started kissing then Frenching me. After a few moments, I stopped and cautiously asked her, "Are you comfortable letting me see your breasts?"

She began to blush deeply, yet agreed, "Yes, of course." But only slowly did she pull her sweater and bra up, reminding me, "The magician's assistant did promise to unveil something, making a magical appearance."

Oh did her breasts wondrously appear — creamy white, so pure, so immaculate. The hue of her nipples and areolae were just as I envisioned.

"Oh God! They're **beautiful**! More than I ever imagined!" Without hesitation, I cupped my hand under one, pushed it up gently and began to kiss it, moving my tongue to its peak to brush across and around it. She sighed with a 'oooohh,' taking my other hand and kissed its palm a few times, then pressed it to her cheek. Her face felt very warm.

I stopped and looked up, "Victoria, are you okay with this? You are **red**."

"Richie, your **Miss September** is fine ... so very fine." In the faint glow of the streetlight, I could see her smiling. "I've never been happier." As I eagerly returned to my dream granted from the Elysian Fields, Autumn began to run her fingers through my hair, fondling and kissing my ear lobe and neck. She started to slightly moan, "Oooh Miss September ... loooves being ... your private centerfold. Aaahhhh."

Our newfound caressing was marvelously much longer than usual. When Autumn snuggled more tightly to me, she purred, "Oooh Richie ... Wooow-wheee. *That* created some pleasantly warm and incredibly wonderful feelings throughout my entire body. Wanna stay like this all night."

※※※※※※※※※※※※※※※※※※※※※※※※※※

Since it was Leap Day, Hal and I decided to let the girls pick out the movie. They chose the new Rock Hudson one, *'Man's Favorite Sport?'*. I picked up Autumn and we kissed hello in the car. She seemed a little down in the dumps but cheered up immediately when I said, "There is something for you in that Savoir-Faire sack. It's your Leap Day present. Sorry Victoria, I didn't have time to wrap it. I bought it just before I came to pick you up."

"What is it? What **is** it? Oh goody great! I **love** your presents."

"Well, little girl, you will have to look in the sack."

So she did, flinging the tissue paper out of the sack, like a six-year-old.

"Chanel N°5. Ooh, dusting powder. Thank you, Rich, very, very much." She kissed me on my cheek.

"So what kind do you have on now?"

Autumn faked indignation, "Well, that's a highly personal question!" She smiled and confessed, "Oh, some Prince

Matchabelli Wind Song ... from Kresge's. But I'm wearing the perfume, as always."

"Well, you have to match the fragrances. I could dust a little on you later."

"Richelieu, you are **so unbelievably wicked**," she scolded me, then grinned impishly, "I might let you." Her face wasn't tinged at all.

****

Hal and I thought the movie was just okay, however the girls liked it. Afterwards we went to Blenders' then dropped them off at Hal's.

On our way to St. Victoria's, Autumn asked, "Richie, I have a big favor to ask. Please say yes."

"Yes."

"You don't even know what it is."

"If it involves you, of course, it's yes."

"Well, I want to go to Mass with you tomorrow. Okay?"

I was a little shocked but regained quickly enough to say, "Of course, which Mass would you like to go to and which church?"

"St. Patrick's and also St. Joachim and St. Anne's have a 10:30 Mass? The girls will go to St. Patrick's as always, right? Why don't you tell them some fib that you have to go to St. Joachim and St. Anne's, then swing by, pick me up and we'll surprise your Three Graces at St. Patrick's."

"You have been hanging around with me a lot and my positive influence on you for planning surprises is beginning to show. Excellent, my Victoria, excellent. It is a date for sure. But what will your parents say?"

She startled me with painful resentment, "Who gives a **shit**? I don't give a **damn** what they think! Sure as hell won't miss me!"

Uh-Oh. She is really pissed off at them ... still. Not getting along with either one of them. Sounds like it's getting worse. She's hurting. Really hurting.

Her natural, gentle demeanor quickly returned. Before we stopped at St. Victoria's, she became passionate. When I turned onto Sandusky, she already had her bra unhooked and was kissing my cheek and ear. As soon as I put the car in Park, she took my hand off the gear selector, immediately placed it under her sweater and bra on her bare breast, then quickly began to French me. When I held her later, we laughed at her planned surprise for Mass. She went into her purse, took out her Chanel spray, spritzed herself, then invited me to dust her "to match the fragrances". I happily accommodated her request.

When I held her for the second time, she told me she didn't want me to let her go. Ever. She always gently reinforced my embrace with her own hands and arms. But this time, it was particularly tight. She began to softly cry and continued sporadically. I offered my handkerchief and to dry her eyes. She sniffed no, only wanting me to hold her. Nevertheless, I dried her tears until she finally could quit more than a quarter hour later.

Tonight, she was in a tremendous amount of pain and I could do little but hold her reassuringly. With her Nanna dead and Summer at Mizzou, I told her she should talk with my mother. She has a strong affection for Autumn and would certainly help her in any way she possibly could. Autumn surprised me when she said that is exactly what Nanna told her before our date tonight, suggesting she should confide in Gi Gi who has deeply sincere feelings for her granddaughter.

Even though Summer said New Year's Eve she just didn't know about Nanna talking to Autumn, I got the impression she thought Autumn believed their grandmother did. Maybe she didn't want Autumn to seem "kookie." Yet Father Fitz believes she sees spiritual elements and concepts so much differently — maybe Nanna is one.

Whatever way it is, I don't give a damn.

MARCH

Autumn looked just as stylish in her wheat-colored wool suit with matching high heels as when she wore them to see *Cleopatra*. "You look great in your Sunday attire, Victoria."

She laughed, "Thank you. So do you in your blazer. Do I need a hat? Sometimes I don't wear one ... irritates the hell out of the Ninny."

"Let's put it this way, Mother and Aunt Danae will be wearing some sort of hat or veil. DeeDee wouldn't be caught dead in either."

"Good."

"Where are your parents?"

"Mr. Neglectful and the Ninny are at The First Presbyterian."

"You mean nobody's home! Great, let's stay here and—"

"Richelieu, you are taking me to Mass," she said firmly, "and to be with your family." Her voice changed, "But, I'm nervous."

"Nothing to be nervous about, just stand when I stand, sit when I sit, and kneel when I kneel. That way you can make the same mistakes as me. Or just simply sit throughout Mass." I brought out the box I had hidden behind my back and gave it to her. "The second half of your Valentine's present. They just came in. I forgot to bring them last night."

She opened it and beamed happily. "Oh goody, goody great! Oh what beautiful stretch pants. The perfect size too," as she quickly examined the ankle area, "and with enough fabric to lengthen the legs and stirrups. Which I will have to do, as usual. Oh my Magician, thank you." She ran up the stairs, quickly returning, "Such a gorgeous matching set in baby blue. Your presents are so wonderful. Like you. You make me feel so much better. **But** we need to leave now."

She gave me a quick kiss. We left. I damned my rotten luck.

We arrived about five minutes before Mass and saw Aunt Danae's Chevy as we walked into St. Pat's.

"Isn't Danae teaching DeeDee how to drive? You think she drove?"

"Oh hell yes, she did! DeeDee fell in love with that four-speed manual last year. Aunt Danae started to teach her even before she got her learner's permit. But not on the street! In a big, empty parking lot, probably like the National Guard's. And she will drive just like my Little Auntie who knows only two speeds ... fast and faster. DeeDee is a lot like her in some ways. A wild streak or nicely put ... 'adventuresome' ... like my Aunt who is still some. But Dee's even more so, especially when she gets with Karen. I wouldn't put anything past those two."

"How so?"

"After she gets her license, she says the first thing she and Karen are going to do, is drive into Allen's and flirt with some bikers."

Autumn seemed a little shocked. "Oh, no ... she's just kidding, talking big. Uh ... you really think she would?"

I scoffed, "I sure do."

As soon as we went into the church, I saw them seated in the usual pew with my mother on the end. Autumn quietly stepped over to the pew and said to my mother very casually, "Excuse me, ma'am."

My mother started to slide over, then looked up at Autumn and smiled happily. She jumped up to hug her and whispered, "Oh Honey! Honey, you wonderful surprise!"

Danae and DeeDee were greatly surprised and happy to welcome her.

Mass went by quickly and the sermon was a good one on forgiveness. Autumn squirmed a little, uncomfortably. Her deepening parental problems? Given Autumn's deeply wounded feelings, I was starting to understand what Summer had said New Year's Eve about their mother. She seemingly didn't care that much about the girls, only to brag about Summer. "A smart, but a plain, thin little girl. Then **won a fabulous fashion prize** for writing in *Seventeen*. They transformed her into a talented, gorgeous genius". Yet the woman never has had much of a relationship with Summer. Only to laud her accomplishments to her "groups" and hang it over Autumn. What a fool woman. Two fantastic daughters and where is their father? Absent a lot of the time and not much of a relationship with either when he was home.

As we were leaving, my mother said, "I don't feel like cooking. Angel?"

"Not really, Mother."

Really convincing Mother and DeeDee. But to whom, I'm sure I don't know.

"Why don't you two meet us at the Indian Head, that is, if you would like to go with us Autumn?"

She quickly smiled. "Of course, I would love to join everyone. Gi Gi, it's certainly wonderful of you to invite me. **You** are always so considerate of me."

Always sophisticated. That emphasis was a shot for her absent parents and applause for Mother.

On the way to the restaurant, I'm sure my mother had given the other two strict instructions about not saying anything to Autumn. Not so subtle nuances like, 'was she thinking about converting' or 'how did you like Mass', or something similar. Unless Autumn would bring up the idea.

****

Sitting in the middle of a semicircle booth, I simply smiled to myself, realizing I was completely surrounded by females who differed by age, style, height, build, hair color and more — but each uniquely attractive. My wonderful, intelligent and beautiful girl close to me on my right and my extremely smart, great-looking sister on my left. I was further flanked by the two older girls — my elegant, still gorgeous mother and my outspoken, spirited, very cute little aunt.

I finally noticed the obvious — Autumn was always next to my mother — like now, in church, taking pictures or for dinner at our house. Just being close to her, even just talking at the house. Autumn and Mother, frequently DeeDee and even Aunt Danae would begin discussing topics of a feminine nature, like new styles of clothes, decorating or cooking and lately spirituality. I would make myself scarce by reading, except for the latter.

I looked around the restaurant for a third time, and judging by the looks and stares the table was getting, I was betting every guy in this place, regardless of age, were wishing they could trade places with me. I smirked even more.

Aunt Danae finally asked, "Richie, what are you grinning about?"

"Nothing really."

"Autumn, does he do that with you?"

"Oh, Danae, I'm so use to it. He's always plotting an overthrow of some government or his next surprise. I'll bet he's probably working on his April spectaculars now. You never know his moves until it's too late," she teased. "Something devilish is always simmering under this black mop of hair." She tousled my hair playfully.

"Autumn, a word of advice. Never play chess with him. He cheats. I know."

"If you mean winning every time, yes. Do you want me to let you win? Would you feel better then, DeeDee?"

"Ugh! I will beat you. **I will** show you how the game is meant to be played."

"Is this before or after we each have grandchildren?"

"Children, not in front of our brunch guest."

"Oh, Gi Gi, they are so funny together. You should see the two of them when the three of us have gone out together. Weeell ... maybe not. The way these two bicker, like now, and tease each other, but more importantly, how they seriously care about and love each other greatly." She nodded her head while looking directly at both of us, "Oh yes, DeeDee. For sure Rich, it's true. They even act and think like they are twins. Look at your names ... *Forrest Étienne Richelieu* and *DeForrest* Danièle *Richelieu*. Give you a better example, they will order the same food."

"No, I don't," I emphatically differed.

"I don't either. I have more taste, both literally and figuratively."

Autumn settled these denials by saying, "Ooookay then. What are *each* of you having for brunch?"

We all laughed, it was true. Eggs Benedict, hash browns, link sausage, orange juice, coffee. But only Autumn had noticed.

After we finished, Autumn said, "Thank you Gi Gi for the brunch. The company was the best as usual. Who knows, maybe I can talk this rogue into taking me to Mass again with him. It was a very nice service, even if it is in Latin."

"The Jesuits think the Mass will change substantially, even with English," I offered.

"Honey, you are welcome to go with us to Mass ... Latin or English. Come over to the house to eat with us. Or just come over and we can talk. Anytime!"

Autumn squealed, "Oh, I will, Gi Gi. I will!" as she leaned over to hug her, then kissed her cheek.

Mother was surprised yet greatly pleased as she returned the hug and kiss.

****

About an hour after dinner on Friday, DeForrest came hurriedly into my room, "Richie, wait till you hear what happened today at McKenna, Prescott and Wellington?"

"An arsonist burnt all three schools to the ground."

"No, no! Seriously! Karen and I were over at Georgia Elms' and her best friend Suzanne White came over there, told us all this just a little bit ago as just the four of us were all eating, picnic style, in her room. It's unbelievable! Completely! Totally! Have you ever heard of a Valerie Jankovich? From Wellington?"

"Nope. Any Wyandotte girls I know are mostly Prescott. Some from McKenna. Only a very few from Wellington."

"This is really nasty. I'll write her raunchy name down for you."

"Oh cut the crap, Dee. We've both heard raunchy from each other. Neither one of us shocks the other anymore. What gives?"

"Okay, you've been warned. Have you heard of a girl called Valerie 'the Vagina' or 'Valgina'?"

"Sure, I think every guy in Wyandotte has heard of her. They all want to have been with her or say they have been with her or actually have. She's supposed to be incredibly promiscuous, a real nymphomaniac."

"Oh yeah, Karen said if you look up promiscuous in the dictionary, there is her picture. Have you ever met her? Did you ever—"

"I'm sure I saw her at a Silver City hall dance," I interrupted. "She wasn't there long. Ha! That would make sense. Great set of knockers and a nice ass. Rest was just ok to look at. Kinda plain, sluttishly made-up, medium height. Definitely sleazy with long, brown stringy hair ... clothes looked kinda grubby. Like they needed a wash. Maybe she did too. Why are we talking about this Valgina?"

"Early this week, she went to the City's Health Department at the very strong recommendation, almost an order, by her doctor. She has rather virulent cases of both gonorrhea and syphilis. Her symptoms are disgusting. Do you want to know them?"

"I'm sure you'll tell me anyway."

"Naturally. She started having sores just inside ... oh damn it ... the lips to her ... her vulva ... ... not painful though, went away after four or five weeks. Lately, an occasional yellowish discharge would ooze from there. Said it burned like hell when she pissed, and she was having to piss a lot more. Has butt bleeding. As Suzanne put it, 'Painful just to take a shit.' Sore throat, hurts to swallow. She has a slight fever and some kind of a rash on her feet and a little bit on her hands which is getting worse. Finally goes to the doctor."

"Okay, that's **all** disgusting. But I'm still waiting."

"The doctor at the Health Department asks her how many different guys she has been with recently, maybe in the last four to six months ... he's thinking maybe ten at the most. She takes a little time, then says four or five **dozen ... maybe more**. The doctor almost falls out of his chair. He says there could be an epidemic with those kinds of numbers. This Valgina tells him she believes almost all of the guys are from the three large Wyandotte schools ... Wellington, Prescott and McKenna. The doctor calls the principals at those public schools and Sister Cecilia at McKenna. They all agree on a school line-up."

"What's a line-up?"

"This! First thing this morning, the doctor *and* four nurses meet Valgina at Wellington. All males are told to assemble in the gym. They all line up, single file, then Valgina passes down the line. If she recognized one that she has been with, they are told to go sit in the bleachers. The 'Clap Trap' then goes to Prescott, finally to McKenna. Nailed about twenty at both Prescott and Wellington, but only maybe ten at McKenna."

"My God! Wow! That's fifty guys! Guess she didn't like Mackerel Snappers that much. Or they're too slow on the trigger to get their 'date'. Bet Karen named it The Clap Trap."

"All the guys in the bleachers were given high dose shots of penicillin. A whole bunch refused, saying they had never been with her. *Those guys* all had to submit to immediate urine testing, maybe blood work. Can you imagine the fallout from this? Having to explain to your girlfriend why you are being tested or given shots for Syph and Clap. Yep, that's what Karen named it ... The Clap Trap. I called it The Syph Scythe."

"Yours is just as good, maybe better. So how do you know all the particulars and her symptoms?"

"Suzanne's mother is the head nurse. This Valerie told Mrs. White she didn't give a shit about patient confidentiality, certainly not after she just pointed out about 50 guys in front of three male student bodies. Why would she care who knows her symptoms? She was, she said very proudly, the 'most talked about and most sought after high school girl in Wyandotte, because I am the *absolute best* at satisfying whatever guys wanted. I've often been told I was *fantabulous* in my whoring! Why should I care now? What difference would it make'?"

"While Mrs. White was giving her a ride back to Wellington, she told her the difference is between herself now and the self that she could be. First, she should practice much better personal hygiene, like bathing daily, wearing clean, mended clothes. Get rid of her slovenly physical appearance. Second, if she thought she was popular with boys, she was deceiving herself terribly. She was being deliberately and miserably used. Third, if she wanted to continue having sexual intercourse freely, she should go to Nevada where it's legal and regulated. She would have an income instead of giving herself away, only being rewarded with frequently recurring diseases and a diminishing opinion of herself."

"She had quit school this morning, much to the great relief of the administration and probably the few guys who had missed being tagged. Mrs. White went into the school with her while she cleaned out her locker. However, the nurse's presence didn't stop the jeers and catcalls. She was called the usual offensive names bestowed on girls ... slut, nympho, whore, and so on. Also 'a poxed piece' and 'tainted twat' ... two dandy alliterations ... never heard *those* ones before."

"As they exited for the parking lot, she was yelled at, told **SHE** was solely responsible for a few breakups between her 'tagged companions' and their girlfriends thus ruining the lives of some of her male partners. She was even spit on by a guy ... it turned out ... who had been with her a few times. In the parking lot, she finally began to cry pitifully. Mrs. White put her arms around her and held her tightly to calm her. When she felt better, she insisted Valerie go with her for something to eat. They talked for quite a long while and she then took Valerie home. The nurse was told she was the only one who cared enough to help and try to understand her. She really didn't care if everyone knew her symptoms. Maybe it could help some of those girls who had been with infected guys to check if they had caught something. Mrs. White is positive some girls have become diseased and also will need quick and immediate treatment. And any of the girls' new partners too. That's how an epidemic starts."

Then DeeDee became pissed — really pissed, as only she could get. "I don't care what she did, Richelieu, she didn't deserve that terrible kind of treatment. Just damn cruel and mean. Guys are so chicken shit hypocritical. You lie to her, telling her how wonderful she is and any other crap you can think of, so you can bang the hell outta her like there's no tomorrow. When you see her again, like at a dance hall with nice girls around, you act like she has leprosy or she doesn't exist. You're such sanctimonious sacks of shit! Just Shit Holes! Like the one guy who **spit on** her. Bet he was acting soooo differently during the times he **'spit in'** her."

"God, Dee, you are so cynical. But you're right. That's the way things are. It's easier to put all the blame on girls like Valerie. Might be '64, but ..."

✽✽✽✽✽✽✽✽✽✽✽✽✽✽✽✽✽✽✽✽✽✽✽✽✽✽✽✽

Curiously, Autumn was already waiting for me on the porch. Before I could ask her why, she exclaimed, "I've got a really good story to tell you."

"Before your story ... that dyed-to-match looks fantabulous on you."

"Oh Richie, it's certainly one of my nicer ones. I know it was expensive because it fits so extremely well, especially the sweater's length. I just love the light blue color. Thank you again." She kissed my cheek very affectionately.

As we drove away to Blender's, I said, "Damn it, I forgot to grab some money. We'll have to make a pit-stop."

"Great, 'cause I need to make one too. Much rather use your great guest bathroom rather than go at Blender's public one. And I real-eee gotta go."

"Okay, now your story. Let me guess, it involves sex, VD and line-ups."

"Wow, that *was* fast. They couldn't have had a line-up at St. Ignatius that quick."

"No, but when the word spreads there over the weekend, I bet some guys will be thinking about their little forays into Wyandotte. Maybe getting some shots." I summarized how DeeDee came to get the entire scoop.

"Just hurry up. I gotta go. Badly. There's more ... I'll tell you everything, give you the full scoop. Oh hurry! It's definitely not gonna be a tinkle ... it's gonna be a torrent."

✽✽✽✽✽✽✽✽✽✽✽✽✽✽✽✽✽✽✽✽✽✽✽✽✽✽✽✽

After we got back into the car she continued, "Well, Judy was going steady with Sam Miller until this afternoon when he was pulled out of the line-up before lunch. She said, and I quote, 'I don't want to hear all his lying shit anymore'."

"Well, baseball and track seasons are starting very soon. Time for her to make a change anyway." I told her about my joke at the Prescott dance that I made to Ginny regarding changing seasons and sports and hence boyfriends. She laughed. Of course Autumn got it.

"Speaking of Ginny, her steady, Terry Massey... you remember, Judy's quarterback boyfriend of the fall. Well, not anymore, he had kinda of a 'special' place in the bleachers. Did you ever meet or talk to **that girl**?" Autumn asked cautiously.

"Not really, I did see her at a Silver City hall dance once before I met you. Camille was busy with relatives, so Jack and I went there one night, messing around, looking for a girl for me. She looked like she was in need of a shampoo. Good-looking body though ... *great* set of knockers. Nice ass too. Only fair-looking. Real slovenly but invitingly *slutty*. Anyway, the next time I looked in her direction, she was leaving with two guys ... must have been her idea of a 'double date'. Later that night, we found out her nickname and her 'talent'. A lot of guys supposedly lost their virginity with her or got laid by her a few times. Hmmm, looks like almost fifty did, just since I moved here. I still love beautiful girls with long shapely legs and stylishly combed golden-brown hair who bathe daily."

I received a slight punch and a kiss on the cheek. She changed the subject, "I got my grades today. They are the same as before except I traded back my 1 in U. S. History for a 1 in Accounting. Still sitting at a 1.4 average."

"That's always good news. Bet almost all of your classmates would trade you. I will probably get mine right before Easter vacation starts. Speaking of which, what are you doing for Easter?"

"Waiting for you to ask me to go to Mass and dinner afterwards. I hope."

"Well, uh, gee whiz, uh, golly," acting silly, then, "would you like to go to Mass with my family and have dinner afterwards?"

"Well, uh, gee whiz, uh, golly, of course."

"Great, Victoria, I know my mother would *love* to have you go to Easter Mass with then come over for dinner. Bring a change of clothes if you want to, then we can go out later that night."

"It's an all day Sunday date, then," she smiled. At the stop light on 22nd Street, I leaned over and kissed her on her cheek.

We met Hal and Jacqueline and talked about how shocked we all were at the day's set of events. The girls couldn't believe it was so widespread. Hal previously thought most of the guys were only saying they had been with her, so they could brag and sound like big studs. He heard two guys didn't get caught because they were able to hide in a john. While the girls were engrossed about what movies were coming out and maybe what we would go see next weekend, I noticed Hal closed his eyes for a few moments, subtly smiling, seemingly to reminisce.

More than a few times, I wondered about gentlemanly, mannerly Hal. After a couple of dates with Jacqueline, Mick told me about a quiet, secretive senior — Anna "The Fair" Colburn — fair body with fairly good tits, fair hair, fair smarts, fair looks. She had the *burning red* hots so badly for Hal that she steadily tempted him to cheat on Cathy Winters. They were seen at the distant Leawood Drive-in, going at it hot and heavy in the back row on a *Sunday* night in October. Mick thought there might have been a few other times Hal cheated again. Moreover, the two girls despised each other. Something that happened at Vance Junior High. For a month or so, Anna always had a smug look on her face when she saw Cathy. Of course, he denied it all. Mick thought Anna was one of the reasons for their terrible fight and break-up. I told him Jacqueline knew how to take care of herself very well when it came to guys. He said he was positive Jacqueline was certainly another reason. He didn't think Hal tried to deny that one.

※※※※※※※※※※※※※※※※※※※※※

At St. Victoria's Place, I asked Autumn if she was feeling okay, she just didn't seem like herself tonight. She said she had a lot of trouble falling asleep last night and was tired tonight. But she was fine. We had started kissing a little when Autumn stopped to ask me, "Do guys talk about what *they do*? You know, with their girlfriends."

"If it's a serious girlfriend, absolutely never. Take Jack, you *know* he and Camille have done *at least* what we do, yet Jack *never* hints about anything whatsoever. I most emphatically **never** say a word. Bart never said anything about Janie even though she broke up with him. But not true of all guys. Remember you said on our first date, some guys fabricate crap or even tell what is true just to get even."

"I did hear something in the girl's room late this afternoon from Judy about what Terry has been saying since Ginny froze him totally."

"Well, like you said, maybe he's just trying to get even."

"No, this is true. I'm going to get red telling you this ... well, maybe not. Here goes ... Ginny, Judy and I were in a corner of the girl's restroom during school about three or four weeks ago and Ginny was telling us about this new *novelty* pair of panties she had on. She pivots her b-u-t-t towards us, pulls up her skirt and slip to her waist, lowers her panty girdle to show them to us. They had little furry cats all over them. She called them her **blank-ee** panties. Naturally, I turn d-a— oh hell, damn red."

She paused briefly, tightly scrunching up her face, "You know, I'm going to quit spelling my crudities and coarseness. It's just childish." She continued rather testily, "If I want to say shit, then I will say, '*Shit*!' If I want to say somebody is an asshole then I will call them an '*asshole*'! Either I'm going to say the word or if I think it's way too vulgar, I'll substitute a clean word or simply say, 'blank.' No more kiddie crap spelling."

And what the Hell brought that tirade on?

"Anyway, the other girls in the stalls and at the mirror heard her what she called them and everyone was laughing, some loudly, even tinged faced me which is what I am now beginning to be. So anyway, these suggestive panties are known to exist, she can't get out of that."

"Okay, but I'm not following?"

"Judy said that Terry is spreading around that he and Ginny parked and they began drinking. A ton. They started making out real heavily. While he is playing with her ... her tits, **she** supposedly takes his hand and moves it under her full skirt so he can slide it up her leg to those panties which **she** had unsnapped, thus inviting him to slip his finger in—. Okay, now I'm beet red. I can't finish."

"Never mind, Victoria. You don't need to explain it further. I sure have the visual, except for what she unsnapped."

"Uh, the 'cat' snaps! He could describe them and their location on her panties."

"Maybe Ginny told him all about them to tease him. What are cat snaps?"

"Oh, sorry. This pair of undies have two small snaps with the head of a cat on each. When unfastened, they split wide ... oh damn it, they become crotchless. Making a very *huge opening*. Wide enough, 'cause Ginny bragged, 'I can easily piddle through the split space, not wetting myself one bit.' I call them 'cat' snaps but everyone called **blank-ee** snaps. Judy tells Ginny, just bring the panties and show some of the girls there are no snaps and everyone will know he's lying. Ginny tells her unfortunately, there's snaps just like he describes. Much worse, he autographed them on—"

"**He did what**?" I interrupted.

"According to Terry, after they finished their 'activities', he had a magic marker in the glove box and she let him sign them."

"**Oh no shit**! Now who in hell carries a magic marker in their car's glove box?"

"Supposedly the signature begins on the left side of her hip and goes around onto her left butt cheek. Richie, why would she do that all that?"

"Because she's an idiot when she drinks too much. Remember that night a couple weeks ago? She was stupidly drinking, hanging all over the obnoxious Massey ... kept trying to match him drink for drink. Had to run outside and throw up. Then he had to take her home. She maybe gorgeous *all the time*, but she's conceited and vain *most of the time* and just downright stupid *some of the time*."

I continued with my idea of what happened, "Who knows, she obviously had a scheme beforehand since she wore them. I'm just guessing, but maybe she planned on showing them to him, like she did with you and Judy as a funny, risqué tease. Sounds like they got really plastered. Oh, you can bet **that jerk** took the initiative. Probably she was so blitzed, she lost her inhibition to stop him from unsnapping them. Or maybe didn't care or didn't even know it until he was through its opening and in her. After they finished, like an artist, he signs his work. Something tangible to remember their exploratory fun night. Something she can now curse him because the guy decides to be an asshole. He's trying to damage her reputation by telling everyone they were intensely making out, moved into some heavy petting, first fondles her tits then she welcomes his fingers into her vagina— ... Oops sorry, Victoria, I shouldn't ha—"

She interrupted, "Oh, it's fine, Rich. You just said what I couldn't. Like you always say ... it's just us. Thank you though for not using those real vulgar words. I **don't** like to hear them. At least now when I hear the formal terms or even mildly crude descriptions, I don't blush like I use to ... **before I met you.** You're **definitely** ruining me."

She immediately had an idea, "I think I've figured out how she can conceal this. How does this sound? 'It was a stupid, vulgar prank, I brought them with me on a date for him to autograph as we both thought it would be hilarious and I would keep them as a fake souvenir'. And adding your point, 'Besides, who has a magic marker in their car's glove box'." She yawned sleepily and covered her mouth. "Oh sorry, I'm just so tired."

"Might work. His word against hers, but unfortunately, everybody likes to believe the worse."

"Right. Forgot to tell you this though. The big senior sports star has lost his dazzle with the Prescott girls because of what that Valerie said when she pointed him out, 'Yea, Terry ... we get together every couple of weeks. He always gives me nice stuff like perfume'."

"Oh God. That sure as hell makes him look pretty sleazy and quite poxed since she gave him some 'nice stuff' in return. Perfume probably 'cause she had an odor."

"Good, I will call Ginny tomorrow and tell her to say all that. Now what are *we* going to *doooo*?"

I flippantly teased, "Since the topic is panties, let's talk about **your** marvelous ones. I'm going to guess a nice light blue with the motif of something lacy.

She paused, then curiously said, "Richelieu, how do you know I'm wearing **light blue lace** panties? Just bought them after school yesterday with Judy." Suddenly Autumn became uncharacteristically livid, "Had to piss so unbelievably badly!

But that pocket door ... jammed. Pissed anyway ... so incredibly much ... with it only halfway closed! **You knew about the jam! Planned to peep**!"

A grenade exploded. "Just **WHAT ELSE** did you see? **My Kotex pad? MY ... MY...? Damn you! God damn you!**"

She quickly moved towards the passenger door and stared out the window, deeply upset and furious with me. Her cheeks were burning scarlet from her anger, hurt and embarrassment. Her eyes now had tears in them.

Those mood swings, fatigue ... seen her upset before but never seen this ... this fierce anger. This pre-period time ... much worse than last month. Just cried and was tit tender.

Two tears fell down her inflamed cheeks, followed quickly by two more.

"Autumn, please, just let me explain! *Please!*"

"**Nothing to Explain!** Take me home **NOW**! I don't want to talk to **you**!   You ... **you spying PERVERT! YOU ... YOU Peeping PRICK**!"

I reached my limit, completely losing my temper, "**You BITCH! You God damn BITCH! I wasn't even close to that God damn toilet to gawk at you pissing OR drool over your PRECIOUS PUSSY and rag.**"

During the long, silent moments which followed, I cooled down slightly to continue, "**Remember**, I had to get some money, so I was **upstairs**. Regardless, you have on the **light blue** sweater and the matching **light blue** slacks. You color coordinate **everything** you wear. You once said you **always** try to buy undies with a design and lacy trim or, at least, some lace. When they start making **light blue** bras, I'll buy you one to go with these **UNSEEN light blue LACY panties**."

Her mouth fell wide opened. She could only stare at me as two more tears fell. Then she burst out wailing and sobbing loudly. I moved towards her, taking out my handkerchief and wiping her eyes. She fell into my arms, bawling fitfully, "Sor ... sorry ... a cue ... sing ... you. Not ... like you ... at all. O ... for ... give ... me! Pleeeze!" After a minute or two, she confessed, as she continued to blubber, "Rich ... eee, obbbviously I ... I'm going to start ... my period ... soon. Just so terribly on edge. Took it out on you." She kissed me on my neck and cheek in rapid succession. "Never blow up. The last time was junior high. Yelled and screamed at another cheerleader during a cheer at a basketball game. Most months I cry, sometimes a lot, like now ... like last month. You deserve to know, especially if I'm going to ... to tear your head off. I'm so damn terrrrrible! If you want to take me home now, I understand. Shouldn't treat you like this. Like shit! Ever! Oohhh, oohhhhhh!" Then she broke down completely, crying heavily into my shoulder.

"Victoria, you are easily forgiven. Please don't cry. Please. It's just us, only us. I'm sorry for the names I called you and language used. Deeply sorry."

She pulled her head back only for a moment to nod in forgiveness, but it was only after an acutely long five minutes — probably longer — of continued crying, sometimes intensely hard, was she able to finally quit. She dried her eyes, made her foghorn sound when she blew her nose both times.

"Thank you, Richie. I feel better now. Tonight, I got into a big, really shitty fight with my mother. Nothing about you, just started with her usual crap about being inferior to Summer. I ignored her. Not tonight! She just kept on me and **on me**. Piled on the shit! Pissed me off so much I couldn't take it anymore. She really hurt me. More than she ever has. Said I was an embarrassment to her **and** my father ... missing again ... because I was such 'a lanky beanpole'. Said it was Nanna's fault the way I am. She spoiled me, ruined me ... made me too sensitive. **NOBODY on this damn planet** says a damn word against my Nanna. NOBODY! I screamed at her, 'You're just a damn nasty, hateful bitch! You've always hated Nanna! Now me. Because I look like her, act like her. You have two daughters! Not your damn TV, not your damn neighbors, not your damn church crap'. She tried to slap me, but missed. Taunted me with 'Summer would never talk to me like that, you gangling hussy.' Stomped off to watch her stupid TV. Grabbed my purse, yelled she was still a mean bitch and waited for you on the porch."

"You're not! No way! You're smart! You're creative as Hell and a lot smarter than Summer is in a bunch of ways! Your mother is a

God damn idiot. She needs to pay more attention to you and less to her damn stupid TV, the neighborhood and church shit. Your Dad does too if he ever tried to stay home from his work. But they don't. And I'm sorry. One of the things that really attracted me to you was your height, your statuesque bearing. Your mother's a complete fool. She's jealous of you. Unbelievably ... her own daughter. And undoubtably, Summer too."

"Richie, I think my father stays at the office to work and goes to all those dinners and overnight trips just so he won't have to come home to her, like tonight. Summer says she knows for sure ... he's ... screwing his secretary ... that big busted Trashy Flashy Phoebe. And the spiteful bitch must think he's with his tramp tonight. That's why she's so pissed and took it out on me. **Your** mother pays an awful lot more attention to me than damn Ninny does. An awful lot! She is so loving, so caring with me. She understands me!"

"I know. She tries to be father and mother to both DeeDee and me. She has been extraordinary since my Dad was killed. It's rough on her. Really rough. She refuses to let it show. She is just so incredibly strong."

Out of nowhere my perpetual pain struck me. Severely. More than usual.

"Oh God, I really miss my father so desperately. It hurts ... painfully so! My nightmare! My God damn nightmare! It **won't** leave me alone!"

I detailed my recurring nightmare to Autumn with its growing intensity. And when I told my mother about its occurrence that first time. While I was beginning to describe it, she took on that same terrible, distressed look when the military officers appeared at our front door before they told her of his death. She wanted to take me to a shrink. So I never told her when I had more of them. It crushes me to see my father die again and again. Bleeding more and more. Mother shrieking in pain, over and over, louder and louder.

The torment describing the nightmare completely overwhelmed me. I had no control of anything. I began to wail, "Oh God! God! They're getting worse! A lot worse! Can't do anything. Nothing! I can't take this anymore. I can't!" I tried to fight back my own tears, but couldn't. I was all over the place. In pieces.

Autumn pulled me to her, lightly cradling my head to her chest as she stroked my head and neck, trying to calm me, "Oh Richie, I'm sorry. Tell me how to help you."

I burrowed my head between her breasts, yelling "Oh Dad! God damn it!" Then I began to cry intensely against her, tightly embracing her.

Oh Dad, come back ... Come back to me .... to us ... Please!
Oh God! I miss you!
Oh God, please .... SOMEBODY help me!

How long I continuously implored God and my father for his return, how long I cried, how long she held me — I'll never know. After I finally could quit crying, I began to experience a feeling of relief as she continued to hold me, stroking my hair and neck, humming softly and soothingly. When I finally sat upright, she wiped my residual tears and kissed my cheeks.

"Richelieu, I've only heard you mentioned, in the barest minimum of words, about your father's death to anyone. Certainly, you never have with me. When anything about him comes up, you quit talking altogether. You clam up. Like the night of our first date. Did you ever talk with your mother? Maybe DeeDee? Even your Aunt? Anyone?"

I confessed, "No, my mother's pain is too great. Only that once ... the nightmare and I curtailed it, not even the full dream. Too painful for her. Never with Dee or Danae. I clam up with them, too. The only thing I told Father Fitz, was that I had 'bad dreams' about my father and ... well, Mother too. But **nothing** about it. And Jake ... but not the dreams ... only telling him I didn't need or want anybody's sympathy. I was doing fine with his death."

I admitted, "This is the first time I've ever cried since we were notified of his death. And it's the first time I had any semblance of peace since those two damn officers came, sending my mother into unimaginable hysterics. Wailing as her heart shattered. Inconsolable moaning. I was fourteen. I didn't know what to do. How to help. How to console her. So I ran outside and all the way to my Dad's facility on the base. Why? I don't know ... maybe not believing it ... maybe looking for him ... I don't know. I can't remember what I did there. Anything at all! Hours later I finally walked home. Mrs. Newton, Mrs. LaPlace and Mrs. Leibniz were there. Mother had calmed down considerably, yet part of her seemed to be missing, lost. I've never seen that exclusive light burn again. Extinguished. Mrs. Leibniz saw the two officers and was there immediately, even seeing me run out. She told me later when DeeDee came home, she and my mother had an intense cry, holding each other. My only consolation was DeeDee didn't see our mother in that terrible, horrible state of emotional chaos. This is the first time too I've really needed to ... ... really had to talk about it other than blowing it off by simply stating an obvious fact or two. I was becoming smothered, choked."

During the next hour or so, I told her all about my fabulous memories of my Dad and me; the great times we had or the very few and not so great — like the smoking. Autumn and I even laughed a few times. My wonderful life with him. Then his wretched death. But I didn't mention the drug running which got him killed and that scheming, lying bitch of a Eurasian whore, pregnant by some son-of-a-bitch, being corrupted to blame my Father.

I said yearningly, "Victoria, I felt like he was always there for me, even when he was on a foreign assignment."

"Richie, you need to realize your father is still here for you ... yet on a different plane ... **but he is here.** The spirit of his being will still guide you, if you ask him. Like my Nanna does ... she is with **me** ... like I've told you. You need to have complete peace in that part of your life. I will always be with you to help you when you need me. Even if it goes against my nature, I'll sacrifice whatever it takes for you."

Autumn was right. I was feeling a calm which I hadn't felt before *that day*. She leaned over and kissed my forehead, "You're the one who always does something magical to make my hurt vanish or me laugh. You're the one who is so understanding and patience with **me**. I love you so very much."

We began to only lightly kiss and talk a little for quite a while as we held each other. Her firestorm had completely dissipated.

My intense breakdown was over and I felt light years better, so relieved. I begin teasing, "Yeah, let's start over by checking the color of your bra since I know it's not any shade of blue ... but your panties are. And lacy too."

She was herself again, serene and happy as she returned my tease with her own, "You'll see soon enough, you *smart ass* magician! And just for the record ..." She carefully pulled down the side of her jeans, exposing enough of the top of her panties to show a lacey border of blue. Then, using her forefinger as a wand, she lightly tapped each breast repeating, "Brassiere, be blue". The magician's assistant gave a very devilishly laugh as she began to slowly — teasingly — lift her sweater.

****

The bra was a kind of a washed out blue. Autumn had taken a moderately worn, flowery white one and dyed it. She freely admitted the result of her experiment was just okay — not the warm, vibrant light blue like she wanted. Still better than plain white.

On Monday, after I dropped off both Carsons, I went to Savoir-Faire and asked for the always classy and helpful Claire. A large group of French-import bra and panties sets — expensive and elegantly patterned in colors of pale azure, maize and cranberry had come into the store last week. When she began to write up my ticket, I saw my old girlfriend Misty modeling a burgundy boudoir lingerie set, complete with a nightgown. She told me to add a real nice pair of navy blue panties for when Autumn wore those dress jeans. So I did.

While Claire went to get them, a good-looking girl, came into the store, saw me and came straight over. She flirtatiously gushed out, "Hiya, Rich ... long time, no see," moving close enough for her shoulder to rub against mine. The curves of her good-sized chest were firmly emphasized by her tight peach sweater. Her lustrous, golden caramel-colored hair streamed to the middle of her back, calling attention to her great shapely butt.

I smiled widely, not shrugging off her contact, "Weell, hey *there* Marsha. How've *you* been?" She immediately escalated her flirting — her enticing blue eyes staying centered on my face, a few quick compliments and repeatedly touching my hand.

Claire returned some minutes later, saying, "I finally found a great pair in navy ... terrific design, too," as she held them up, then scooted the expensive bra and panty set down the long counter, placing everything in front of me.

Marsha, realizing the fancy lingerie set joining the added panties were **my** purchase, stammered out, "Oh Mom ... uh ... I'll talk to you after you finish." She moved, suddenly changed her voice inflection to me, blandly saying, "Bye, Rich."

When I picked up the gift wrapped items, Marsha was still talking to her mother. I could see the distinct resemblance in both facial features and body shapes between mother and daughter. I waved good-bye to both. Each returned my wave, but only Claire was smiling. On my way out, I thanked Misty for the great idea, musing to her that I couldn't remember when such a mushrooming "come-on" went south so swiftly.

****

Marsha Jane McCabe became an anesthetist nurse; Dr. Robert McGraw would always request her for surgeries; her high level of competency was not his only reason; They began intensely dating and married quickly on her 28th birthday; Shortly after, a pregnancy was announced, the first of three — twin girls then two boys; They happily and successfully reared their children; now are grandparents of nine;

Marsha's father had abandoned her and her mother during 3rd grade; After an ugly, painful visit when she was a high school junior, Marsha told him she would never see or talk to him again;
In 1973, her father and his long-time girlfriend supposedly entered the Federal Witness Security Program — neither have been seen or heard from since; However, quite a few believe that both are buried somewhere in the Nevada desert;

Her devoted relationship with her mother only ended with Claire's death in 1994; She was 69 — Marsha took the loss extremely hard

****

At the end of class on Monday, Father Fitz called me to the teacher's desk and said, "Time for your confession. Tomorrow after class looks good for me. I will have the final piece."

"Yes, Father. Thank you, Father." ... ... *Oh shit, now I've got to tell him about Autumn and me. He can't think badly of her. He can't ... ... just can't.*

AAAW SHIT! ... ... JUST SHIT!

That night I didn't sleep well, thinking how to tell Father Fitz about Autumn and me. How his opinion of Autumn would go in the toilet and be flushed like so much stinking shit. The next day I told Bart and Jack I would meet them later in the cafeteria.

Father Fitzgerald wondered, "You seem anxious, so you go first."

"Bless me father for I have sinned. But I don't think it's sinning. It's been since the beginning of February since my last confession. Autumn and I have been ... I have been caressing and ... and ... kissing her ... breasts, Father. We sometimes we dry ... er, uh ... she lets me move my legs between hers and we move tightly against each other. Regardless, I always have an ejaculation, sometimes twice during these times we are together. **Father**, you can't think less of her because of this. Oh God, please, you can't. She's a good, moral girl and has the gentlest, most sensitive, loving heart. She is the most wonderful girl I have ever met in my life. I respect her totally, completely. I love her, she loves me. How can this be a sin?"

"I sincerely think no less of Autumn. She is full of personality, quick-witted, *extremely* smart and a very positive influence on you. This was bound to happen between you two. I observed the pair of you at Christmas and the Sweethearts' Dance. The looks between you, at times the total obliviousness to others around you, even the way you hold hands, especially when you would dance. You know, I haven't been a priest that long. When I made detective, I had learned how to observe people and became a pretty fair judge of human nature."

He returned back to our activities, continuing, "Is it a sin? Generally, YES. You two are **not** married. That type of intimacy along with its subsequent act of sexual intercourse is reserved for marriage. Any uncontrollable or frivolous behavior of that nature with a 'pick-up' or casual date, where there is only lust and no love is definitely, completely wrong."

Bonnie Jo and Olga flashed through my mind. Linda was there too, lingering a little longer.

"However, you two have a strong, **possibly** a long enduring commitment of love to each other, completely excluding all others. You are getting into a gray area. I don't have the answers for you. Oh, I'm sure you both are in love. But what can you do about it? Get married? No, far too young, but you can grow up together and grow together. Lou, you have only been dating for about what? ... Four months? But I can tell you how to **not** ruin your relationship with Autumn. Keep your pants zipped ... completely. Consequences of pre-marital intercourse kills more love in ways that you can't begin to imagine. You can always come back to confession to talk. I gladly will discuss your feelings and actions. You can always meditate or pray. For penance, say the Holy Ghost's third decade of the Glorious Mysteries, dwelling on that segment's meaning, and praying that He will descend upon you at this time with knowledge and guidance. Do you have other questions regarding this or other sins not of the flesh?"

"No, Father, I just know I love her. **Please Father** ... **please** don't think badly about her."

"Richelieu, **believe me**, I don't think badly about her. She's a terrific, highly intelligent, truly spiritual girl. You are very, very lucky. Hold on to her. Tightly!"

"Now, I have excellent news about the blackmail picture. **Fake! 100% Fake!** My friend, SuEllen Chambers at the FBI, confirmed it this weekend. She looked at the picture from Gestalt principles, something about proximity, similarity, continuation, and ... and closure. Don't ask me about them, she's the pro with the microscope. She said it was an extremely excellent, fraudulent piece of work ... possibly the best she has ever seen ... a consummate professional job. Probably needed at least two or three dozen pictures of the prostitute to match like this. On background walls, there are different shadings of light which you would naturally expect a continuous blending flow, from light to dark, dark to light. Like a lamp turned on or another light throwing a shadow across an object. However there is one small place where there is a very faint, very slight, virtually indiscernible partial line of shadow, not visible to the naked eye unless called attention to. Not possible, especially so close to the critical junction separating your father and the woman. She cannot prove anything else regarding the picture, only its total lack of authenticity."

He continued triumphantly, "And a final point ... she confirmed that there are *four* sets of fingerprints on the sermons ... obviously mine and my Jesuit brother *and* two other sets. Which confirms the 'sermons' were opened and reviewed."

"I am proud of you Richelieu. Very proud! You had this certainty of your faith in your father's fidelity and of the picture's deceit. You were *not* a Doubting Thomas. You were right. But now the big question ... are you going to disclose what really happened? Explain the 'sermons,' show the picture, the letter, how the Air Force neatly covered it up and everything else including the Wyandotte Lake murder to your Three Graces, even Autumn?"

"Father, I have thought about this quite a bit, asking the Holy Ghost for help. No, I am never telling anyone about it. The truth has been verified, confirming my faith with your resourceful help and your friend's ingenuity. It would be terribly upsetting ... even cruel to my mother all over again. My father will still be dead, maybe for different reasons. More heroic reasons. **But he's still dead**. Brooks would still be dead too, for opposite reasons ... his greed and blackmail. How can I rip open my Mother's heart? And my Aunt's, just as she's virtually over all the hideous atrocities that bastard inflicted on her. My problem is I don't want to burn the proof and I certainly don't want to keep it in my room as someone could find—".

Father Fitzgerald interrupted, "There is a special place in the Jesuit vault that I could have this fraudulent picture, its analysis, the prostitute's letter and the 'homily' letters, my notes, everything would be stored."

"That would be great. You are the best, Father Fitz ... er ... gerald."

Lastly, I told him about the terrible, ugly fight with Autumn thinking I had spied on her while she was relieving herself in the guest bathroom. I explained to him about my nightmare and its subsequent increasing intensity. After I painfully explained the entire recurring bad dream to her, it was the first time I cried since his death, crying for a long time and deeply, praying for help as she soothingly tried calming me. That I told her about my father and me — our great times. She told me my Rock had not vanished, but was in a different sphere, still watching over me. He would still guide me, as I wanted and needed.

He wholeheartedly agreed with her about my father and said to tell Autumn he inquired about her, "She is changing you, greatly dissipating your menacing storm clouds. Putting this lock on Viet Nam will help you greatly, but you still have a lot of pain to work through regarding your father. Autumn will help, simply by being Autumn and being with you. She is a very unique, remarkable girl. She has a strong, almost transcendental religious spirit. She has intimately found God and sees Him and the spiritual world most differently than others do or even can."

"You have a very strong spiritual influence on her, Father. She seriously holds you in the highest regard. She invited herself to Mass with me a week ago and she really loved it. It's great to have your girl with you at church and great to have Autumn with you anytime."

He smiled again, "She may want to convert, especially if **we** don't try to force it. Let her find her own way. **Should there be one**! Catholic or Presbyterian, she will always have that deep, strong spirituality. Now make a good Act of Contrition." He emphatically pointed at my groin. "And keep it **zipped**, Richelieu."

Before I said my penance that night, I looked up the third decade of the Glorious Mysteries and found it to be The Descent Of The Holy Ghost, and prayed to Him to descend upon me for guidance and help with Autumn to keep our relationship strong and us growing in love and growing together. I begin to pray this nightly. I need her to be with me. If not physically near me, then mentally to imagine and see her and spiritually to feel our love.

****

Thank God! Baseball was finally beginning today, and of course, there was a cold rain all day. Still there was the usual kick-off team meeting, and Coach Bannister outlined how we will conduct each practice — warm-ups, batting practice, then infield with outfield practices. We would also have probably two intra-squad games. The season for The Border League would start Thursday, April 2 and we would play twelve games over the eight week season. The Coach said that it would be OK to play catch in the gym but absolutely no "ground balls". Everybody fragmented into groups. Outfielders throwing short "fly" balls. Two pitchers and Mike Thomas, the first-string catcher from last year. Bart, Jack and I got into a very elongated triangle which mimicked third, second and first base. Bannister made some notes on his clipboard, intently watching the entire group of hopefuls.

****

That Friday night, when we were at St. Victoria, I told Autumn about Father Fitz sending his greetings to her, hoping she was doing well in school. That she was certainly helping me through my problems. He thought she had an extremely strong, positive influence on me.

"Even though I have only seen and talked with him twice, I feel strongly about that priest. I loved my discussion with him on the soul. I can tell he is from God. What an extraordinary man! Maybe this summer, you know, after school is over, maybe Mother ... uh ... *your* Mother would have him over for dinner? Or we could see a movie with him? Or both! Something, anything? Please, Richie, please?"

"Your wish is my command. We'll definitely do it. I promise."

... ... And 'Mother' was not merely a slip of the tongue ... it's how Autumn feels about her.

That night I had "The Nightmare" again. But it was diametrically different. My father was standing in front of the white picket fence. But this time he saluted me, smiling broadly and said, "Good *something?*" Work? Job? Luck? I was sure it was "LIFE!" He then slowly began dissipating into the air. I yelled for him to stop, come back, please talk to me. He was gone. My mother then came out, looking for him. I told her that he had just left and she said she would wait for him until he returned for her. She was smiling and very happy. When I woke up, I felt very relieved and peaceful.

At St. Victoria's place on Saturday night, I told Autumn of the dream's happy ending and she must have obliterated my subconscious pain simply by holding me, comforting me as I cried, then listening to me talk about him. I added, "And just being my incredible Victoria." She smiled, said she was extremely happy she was able to rid me of my pain, reminding me she was always here to help me or do what was needed, regardless of her feelings. At my next confession I thanked Father Fitz profusely for his help in destroying the nightmare. The 'sermon' letters and the FBI analysis of the picture had both finally dissolved my anxieties and torment.

****

Richelieu never had the dream or any variations of it again;
His conscious pain diminished with the passage of time
as he rejoiced in his own family as it grew and flourished; However,
Jake was correct in saying, 'It never completely goes away.'

****

On Friday, we were walking to the car to go pick up Hal and Jacqueline and Autumn told me, "Remember that the semi-formal Spring Fling Dance is April 11 The court of royalty nominees were announced today."

"Terrific! You were nominated for Queen again, right? Since you weren't a Homecoming or Winter Wonderland Princess or Queen."

I opened the door and she scooted in, "No, Rich, close but no. Just missed the last spot. I found out from Judy who peeked at the results when she was in the Main Office. However, Jacqueline has been. Isn't that great! We will be sitting with her and Hal. We will be right there to support and root for her."

"Yeah, that's great for her. I'm very happy for her. But you weren't. I know it's my fault, just like you didn't make princess or even queen at the Ball. Do you think she was nominated because of Hal?"

"Well, it certainly helped that Hal is really popular ... ... good-looking, quite smart, class VP this year and lettered three years in football. But really because all the kids at school finally have made an effort to get to know what a talented, sweet girl she is. Everyone likes her. **Not** just the horny pricks who want to find out if there are any limits of French girls' morals."

I laughed, then said, "Yeah, she's really ter-rif." Naughtily, I visualize her absolute killer chest in my mind. "And I sure hopes she wins." ... ... *Now that girl wouldn't need any tricks for a fantabulous cleavage.*

"Richelieu, you remember after your Sweethearts' Dance, you told me you didn't give a shit about the differences in money between our families. You wanted **that girl** who had a *captivating and delightful spirit*, money was immaterial." Autumn uncharacteristically spoke very sternly and strongly, "Damn you, just damn you, Richelieu, this time **you** are the one now who certainly needs to be straightened out. Quit your damn girly whining about it! **I** don't give **a shit** about all the high drama for a couple hours, the well-wishers for a week or two afterwards, and having a picture as a Princess or even the Queen in some yearbook which eventually just gathers dust. Just ask my sister, the Winter Wonderland Queen of 1963! What I **do care** very deeply about is the guy who treats me like I am a Queen **all the time**, who can wonderfully, magically surprise me, who can always find the remedy when I hurt or need comforting. You are **that guy**."

"Thank you, my beautiful, fabulous Victoria."

I kissed her passionately but only for a short time, as she broke it off by saying, "More later. Much more. We need to get to Hal's and the movie."

"Really nice of that Mrs. Hardesty to give us those passes. Sophia Loren! Oh yeah!"

※※※※※※※※※※※※※※※※※※※※※※※※

While Autumn had Sunday dinner with us quite a bit, Sister Cecilia had been able to only come rarely. This was the first time both were here together. This afternoon's dinner was a sumptuous chicken cordon bleu with Caesar salad, asparagus and potatoes lyonnaise. As always, I was at the head of the table and my mother at the foot. On one side, Autumn was seated next to me, then DeeDee. On the opposite side, Sister was sitting next to Mother and Danae between her and me. Sister Cecilia had finished talking about the way her first year was progressing to its end. Dinner was also coming to a successful close.

Autumn had been intensely focused on the nun for some minutes, then in a soft tone, said to her, "Sister Cecilia, when Kenneth Jr. crimped his tiny fingers and hand in a wave to you, I know that had to make you so euphoric, so joyful in happiness. You are so blessed from that beautiful sign. To beckon you."

Sister Cecilia dropped her fork mid-air and her mouth fell wide open. She sputtered out after a moment of shock, "How ... how ... did you... How could you know ... that? I only told Mother Superior during my novice interview and evaluation. **No one else knows**."

Autumn was now vividly embarrassed, "Oooh, I'm sorry. I'm so sorry. I didn't know." Tears instantly welled up in her eyes. "Please excuse me." She immediately left, heading into the living room.

I got up to follow her as did my mother, but Sister Cecilia strongly said, "**Please, let me**." As she followed Autumn out of the dining room, we sat down. The remaining four of us looked at each other in amazement.

After at least fifteen long minutes, the nun returned and I heard Autumn making a detour through the kitchen to the guest half-bath.

Sister Cecelia smiled, saying, "Another benefit to being a nun ... we don't have 'to fix our faces'. Autumn is making 'adjustments' to her beautiful one." However, it was obvious, the nun had been crying. "Don't worry. She's fine now. So am I. Such an intelligent, incredibly ethereal girl. With a holy gift bestowed upon her from our Almighty God."

Soon Autumn rejoined us, going quickly to my mother. She said, "Everyone ... especially you Gi Gi, I am truly sorry for stopping this wonderful dinner and to cause—"

My mother stood up, interrupting her, "Oh, Honey, you did nothing wrong. **Nothing at all!**" She hugged Autumn for a long moment or two, whispering, "You're fine, Honey. Everything's fine." Then kissed her on her cheek. Mother immediately announced, "We have Profiteroles and Macarons for dessert. Made by my two Danièles. So they will be marvelous ... like them."

Autumn never mentioned what she and the nun discussed. Those two always inquire more than just the health of the other when their name comes up in conversation. When the two happen to meet, they hug then join the conversation, yet occasionally they excuse themselves for a private one. When I mentioned this bizarre occurrence to Father Fitz in confession, he said he wasn't surprised. But I should never ask Autumn regarding their shared vision or her talks with Sister Cecilia. I never did, nor did my family mention this to any outsiders.

※※※※※※※※※※※※※※※※※※※※※※※※※※※※

On Tuesday, the roster of sixteen guys was posted along with tentative positions. The three of us knew we had starting positions as we each had an exceptional try-out. Bart was also considered as a relief pitcher. During this intra-squad game, Coach Bannister played second base and Fr. La Croix was in right field on the B team. Richard Trent, the first line pitcher, played for the B team and LaFleur for the A team. I had a pretty decent game with a double and a single. Bart went 0 for 1 with 2 walks and a sacrifice fly and Jack crushed a home run and a single. Evidently the rest of the team had caught on to Fr. Fitz's Valentine tag of 'The Three Musketeers' as we began to find those kinds of candy wrappers stuck in our uniforms, in our lockers, and hidden in our books.

When I walked in the front door, my mother called me into her study then handed me my grades to be opened. They were very good, except Latin. *Still* dragging me down:

Religion	85	English	93
Français III	91	Algebra & Trig	90
Ancient Civilizations	95	Latin III	80

My mother looked at them and said, "An 89.0 again. Still good grades, Richelieu. If it wasn't for Latin, you would have a 90.8

average. You don't have to take it next year, unless, of course, you want to."

"Oh no, no no, no. But there is a new course going to be offered ... Finance. Also, I think I want to take the Accounting class instead of a study hall. Ugh, Latin IV. No. No way! But it will move me out of the Latin Course into the English Course Path."

"I certainly wouldn't disagree one bit with you on those selections. Latin Course or not, I think you've had enough of that language."

****

The next day, the tentative starting line-up was posted along with The Border League Schedule, with the reminder that although there were no classes on Thursday, we would practice at 9:00.

TENTATIVE STARTING LINE-UP

Harris, Rich	LF	Miller, Phil	RF
Sanders—Jones, B	2B, RP	Trent, Rich	P
Thomas, Mike	C	LaFleur, Todd	P
Nelson, Jack	3B	Hawkins, Rick	CF
Marlowe, Lou	1B	De La Rosa, Francisco	SS

BORDER LEAGUE SCHEDULE

April 2	Home	Wellington	April 27	Away	Fairview Hills
April 7	Away	Northwest	April 30	Home	Fairview Hills
April 10	Home	McKenna	May 5	Away	Wellington
April 14	Home	Prescott	May 8	Away	Prescott
April 16	Away	St. J. Vianney	May 15	Away	McKenna
April 23	Home	Northwest	May 19	Home	St. J. Vianney

****

Later that night DeeDee popped into my room, "Guess what I heard from Suzanne White about Valerie Jankovich." She didn't wait for a response. "That Monday night ... after the line-ups ... she called Mrs. White to tell her she firmly decided to take her advice and change her sleazy appearance and shitty life. Hearing her commitment, Mrs. White invited her to come stay with her and her daughter as she could monitor her infections as they healed. Valerie could have some time to make a few hard decisions about her life. She gave Suzanne some money to buy her some new underwear and a few tops, a sweater, jeans and loafers. She then burnt **every piece** of her old clothes and even her shoes. The two girls then went to Savoir-Faire for a makeup make-over for Valerie."

"During those weeks, some old guy in his thirties had heard about her, somehow located her and offered her a job to be their 'junior hostess' for The Stanley-Frobst Chemical's hospitality suite at a four-day industrial convention in Chicago. She was 'to entertain *only specific* attendees' and did so well, she was asked to work a second convention for some Minneapolis paper company the following week. She now has the latest hairstyle, new clothes ... two dresses, a sweater and skirt set, hose, shoes. As a bonus, she got to keep her 'uniform'. According to Suzanne, she looked nice ... respectable. So when she came into the Clinic, Mrs. White almost didn't recognize her. They went into an examination room to talk. Valerie said to Suzanne's mother, 'I wasn't going to leave until I could see and talk with you. I will be taking the train for Reno later tonight. I wanted you to know, you are the only one who ever truly cared about me. Thank you for advice on my looks and hygiene but most importantly your compassion and understanding.' However, she stayed three days with the Whites and Suzanne took her to the Union Station today. She's gone for good. I hope things work out for her."

"Could not be any worse than the shit life she was living and where it was going to end up." I couldn't resist teasing, "DeeDee, just what are the *duties* and *uniform* of a 'junior hostess' at an industrial company's convention?"

My sister simply responded by taking a few steps towards me and playfully punching me on my arm, "Hitting dumb ass, older brothers who wise off to me in my *sexy uniform*," laughed, kissed me on my cheek and walked out of my room. Those hideous, voluminous pink robes would put *any* guy off.

****

Valerie Julie Jankovich never told her severely alcoholic father and her physically and emotionally abusive mother she left for the

Whites; For some time, the mother searched for Valerie to inflict her daily abuse, finally figuring out 'Her Huge Embarrassment' had left for good; She lamented missing the opportunity 'to throw the grubby, smelly, worthless little whore in the street';

Over the years, Valerie continued to stay in touch with the nurse and daughter, meeting and treating them for some long weekends in Las Vegas;

She was good in her profession at the Wild Stallion Ranch; In 1988 with her savings combined with a loan from one of her regular clients, she opened her own 'Ranch' called European Delights, having a 'foreign flavor';

In 1997 she returned to Wyandotte to attend Nurse White's funeral, Valerie was warmly greeted by the divorced Suzanne Fells, introduced as a distant cousin, and stayed with Suzanne and her two girls during her short time in Wyandotte;

Five years later, Valerie sold her Ranch and retired to France, a well-to-do woman; She fell in love and married an artist of slight renown; A gift of a beautiful nude painting of a 'reclining young Valerie hangs in Suzanne's hallway;

Valerie and Suzanne still remain in close touch

****

On Holy Thursday, after I came home from morning baseball practice, I went to talk to my mother about Autumn joining us for Mass then dinner on Sunday. "Such a gentle, caring girl and *so very* smart. Obviously, I feel strongly about that girl. Very, very much."

"Not according to her parents. She only has a 1.4 average, unlike Summer who had a straight 1.0 average virtually every time. She hears that's why Summer got a partial scholarship to Missouri in Journalism. Her father does pay some attention to both girls when he is home. Autumn's not her mother's favorite. What bothers her is the numerous times she's ignored or compared as inferior to Summer that hurts her. Oddly, 'Val' doesn't seem to care a lot more about Summer."

"It's unfortunate that her parents don't see she is an incredibly creative and sensitive girl? And outgoing too, I don't think I have ever seen someone like her who can make a person or people feel so greatly comfortable with her in a matter of minutes."

She paused for a moment or two, then continued, "We have talked about God, it is obvious that she is highly spiritual … … … and much more." Her hesitation was probably due to Autumn's "vision" last Sunday. "Greatly more than any girl, Catholic or not, around her age whom I have known … my college self also included. I feel privileged to discuss some of her problems with her. *I think* she is a completely magnificent daughter. Her mother, unfortunately, is *exceedingly jealous* of Autumn's model's appearance with height, looks and grace, her personality and more. And her beloved Nanna."

My mother smiled cryptically. The type of smile that occasionally crossed my lips. Rarely did my Mother plot something but when she did, it was always something very involved, way more than any of my antics. Just ask that pervert Rex.

****

"I really liked the Mass today. Its pageantry, the symbolism mixing with the spiritual feeling and atmosphere. Thank you for taking me, Rich. Thank you Gi Gi for inviting me to be with your family for the sumptuous feast."

"Honey, you are always welcome for both eating and talking. And anything else. I heard you tell Rich some time ago that you had to start your important Interior Design semester project by Tuesday. Do you know what you are going to do?"

"Oh Gi Gi, I am really concerned about it. I was supposed to pick something for a project last week and I haven't yet come up with anything. Most girls are just choosing, 'How I would redecorate my room' which I think is too easy, so trite. I want something that makes mine stand out in lights, really have pizzazz. But I'm going nowhere. I suppose I'll end up looking at my room and join the boring, monotonous crowd."

"Well, Honey, why don't you take your clothes and change in the master bedroom and I will meet you up there in ten minutes. Okay? Richelieu, you can entertain yourself somewhere else."

I could certainly 'entertain' myself helping 'Honey' change her clothes. But I would need much more than ten minutes ... say a couple hours. OK, make it a week. A month?

About ninety minutes later, Autumn came rushing into my room where I was reading my Ancient Civs book, dutifully trying to entertain myself.

"Your mother is the absolute most ultra-cool lady there is in the world. She is a true magician. Now I see you weren't kidding about inheriting your magical talents from her. Your mother wants **me**! **me**! ME! to completely redecorate her entire Master Suite. Oh and not 'How I *would* do it?'. Really and truly do it. The project will have everything, painting, drapes, carpeting, furniture, tile and painting in the bath area and especially, working with Gi Gi, the client. We are going to take photos, before, during and after. It's all real, not supposition or guesswork how the client would react. She is even going to talk to Mrs. Wallace ... first thing tomorrow ... to confirm everything with a scheduled client start-up meeting for the three of us this week to work out preliminary plans with a deadline for the project and my grade. Of course, Mrs. Wallace will give me tons of guidance throughout the whole process. This is fabulous! Your mother is so fab! Oh goody great! Oh the goody greatest! Richie, **this is real**! Not some damn popularity contest for some damn dance. Your mother picked me! She could have chosen an established designer. Gi Gi and I are going to start shopping Saturday morning. DeeDee might come along. Richie, your mother has made me so happy. Truly a wonderful, fabulous lady."

Knowing Mother, she wasn't finished:
Point One   — Mother really did want to redo her Suite.
Point Two   Mother really did want to help Autumn and just as importantly, Autumn to help her.
Point Three — Only Mother and the Holy Ghost know.

APRIL

First game of the season. I was keyed up. Could not quit thinking about it all day. While Richard Trent loosened up with Mike Thomas, we waited and watched as Wellington took their infield warm-up. Jack said they had not been very good in the past, but it's a new year. We took our infield and stayed on the field to start the game. Trent put them down 1—2—3. In our half of the inning, Harris grounded out, but Bart walked, Thomas had an infield single, then Jack hit the first pitch over the left field fence. I had a single but died on first. In the third, Bart led off with another walk and Thomas hit a rocket over the fence to left center. Wellington changed pitchers to a left hander. Jack doubled and I doubled him home. We had more chances to score but could only get two more runs. Coach Bannister made a few substitutions in the sixth and two more in the seventh. The final score was 8 — 0. Jack and I both went 2 —4, Bart was 0 — 1 with three walks and a ground out, but scored 3 runs. We kidded him that he should keep his bat on his shoulder since when he swings it, he makes an out. Otherwise, he scores.

****

When I pulled up in front of Autumn's house for Friday night's coke date, she was already sitting on the porch swing. Seeing me, she stood up, then almost ran to the car. I had only gotten five feet from the curb when she passed by me. Her eyes were red and puffy, makeup uneven with a streak of black eyeliner that had run down a cheek. Crying. A lot. Dressed in an old St. Nate's sweat shirt with cutoff sleeves and a pair of beat-up jeans.

"Richelieu ... I need to tell you something. Just damn bad shit!" She opened the door on the passenger side to sit next to the window.

What the hell is going on?

"You know I'm the co-chairman on the Music Committee and we selected 'The Del-Fi's,' the same band that played the

Sweethearts' Dance at St. Ignatius. They were really good. At our final meeting at lunch today, Grace Price, the senior and other co-committee chairman said there was a misprint in the program regarding the band. Right on cue, Little Walters, **The Big Asshole**, prances into our meeting, says he checked out our band last month, they were not appropriate and he wouldn't sign the contract the committee gave him. So *he* hires the same old geezer band from Christmas. Nobody said anything so I said, 'Why do we even have a committee then?' He said, 'The student committee makes the choice within guidelines. Your choice, **Little Missy**, was way outside the guidelines.' I thought about all the students with tickets promised something vastly different and better. My thought kinda slipped out ... and a little too loudly, '**Damn Gestapo**'. He heard me, took me down to the office, gave me a letter that my parents have to sign and return. Then suspended me for the rest of the day for 'complete disrespect of authority."

"You did that? Nooooo Shit!" I exclaimed.

"All I have heard since I gave my mother the paper was, 'Summer would never do anything like this.' ... 'What will my Bridge Club think?' ... 'That I have a delinquent daughter?' ... 'What will they think at Church?' ... 'When did you become so disrespectful?' ... 'Wait till your father gets home'. Just stupid shit like that. She was so upset that she couldn't watch TV. Like I gave a **shit** about that too! I went to my room. Well, when my father got home, he was really pissed off, said I needed a damn good spanking, but was too old. Said I would have to apologize to that little piece of vermin shit and I told him, 'Bull Shit! When Hell freezes over.' That's when he lost his temper, started to slap me, but stopped quickly. Instead he solidly grounded me for two weeks. Told me I can't go to the hangouts, shopping, even the grocery store, anything. Home and school, school and home. So now I'm really pissed off **at him**. I said, 'Fine, don't forget **her** church on your damn shit list. **I won't go**!' "

"Oh no, no, no! Shit! Shee-it!"

"He yelled at me for swearing. Told him I didn't give a **shit**. He pushed me down ... hard ... onto the bed. When he calmed down, he had an odd look in his eye. Said the only exception for the two weeks is the night of the dance and left. But I don't know if I feel like even going. So I have about two more minutes, then I have to go back inside. But I'm not sorry about what I said. Oh, Richie, the only thing I'm sorry about is us. Not being together. Obviously, you can't come over either. And two damn weeks in the house with *them! Mostly her*! **The crowning turd** on all this heap of shit, I just started menstruating. And no, thank You God, it's normal. So my crying, for once, is not because of **it**. But it does make me feel so much worse." Autumn leaned over, gave me a very short kiss.

"I'm sorry, Victoria. Sorry for you. You don't deserve this."

She then groaned, "It'll be fine. I'll be fine. We'll be fine. Please call me later tonight. Of course, I'll be home. The damn warden told me I'm allowed phone calls from his prison." She got out of the car, walked onto the front porch, picked up the hand towel, turned as she waved it sorrowfully and went inside. I could tell she was starting to cry again. I wanted to go hold her, to do something, but…

When I dejectedly walked in the door, my mother came out of her study, thinking Autumn was with me. When she didn't see her and I looked greatly dejected, she winced sharply, "Oh no, Richelieu! Please tell me that you and Autumn didn't have a bad argument. You *didn't*, did you?"

By this time, Danae had come out of the kitchen. DeeDee had already left on her second date with some senior from St. John Vianny's. Must be the third or fourth guy from that school. She was running through that school's list of cool guys in what must be record time.

"No, nothing like that. But she's grounded for two weeks." I related the entire incident.

Neither my mother or my aunt said anything. My mother broke the silence, "But Richelieu, what about her dance next weekend? She won't be able to go!"

"An exception. Odd … he was so strict about everything else, but I don't know if she even wants to go after all this crap. I'm going to my room."

How damn ironic ... I was to begin Milton's 'Paradise Lost' this weekend. Now I get to live it. The phone ... ha ... a joke ... just like during the damn week. God, I want to hear her talk, see her laugh, to be with her, to hold her hand. Not the spot at St. Victoria for secrets about our thoughts, our dreams, or just us. Damn it, no making out, no Frenching, no caressing and touching her, no holding her. Damn it, damn it, damn it, SHIT!

Oh well, guess it's a good thing I went to confession yesterday. Be able to go to communion for a couple of weeks.

But I am so glad she called that Bastard Asshole a 'Damn Gestapo'

Autumn called me an hour later, "Jacqui phoned me after I came back inside. She and I have definitely been hanging around with you waaay too much. She has a plan which I wholeheartedly agree with. Here's what we are going to do ..."

****

For the Northwest game, Coach shuffled the batting order. Bart was now lead-off and I was second, Harris went to sixth and Miller took over my previous spot. Northwest wasn't much of a challenge either, the score was 10 — 4 with LaFleur pitching. I went 2 — 4, both singles, with a really long fly out, but it was too high and lack power to get over the outfielder's head. Jack went 3 — 4 with two doubles and another home run. Bart also hit two singles, scoring both times. After we changed shoes, we grabbed our bats, gloves and jackets and walked to our cars to drive home. On the way, we talked how the next three games would be tough, not like these first two.

****

I wanted to win the next three games badly, especially Prescott and this one with McKenna. I was really hoping the Prick would be pitching against Richard Trent. The three of us were standing around, waiting for McKenna to finish their infield so we could take ours. Jack already knew the edited version of my history with the Prick, so I filled Bart in. Unfortunately, he was warming the bench, so I subtly pointed out the Son-of-a-Bitch to Jack and Bart, then the bottle bashing Asshole Snake Ronnie Kovac sitting next to him, who was staring right at us. Deciding to give him something to mull over while he also sat on the bench, I emphatically arched the biggest wad of spit I could muster in his direction, while giving him The Finger. He looked dumbfounded, then turned away. Immediately, the Coach called the team to huddle up, saying, "Play hard! Play your best! Play to win! Go now ... take infield!"

Some guy named Dragush was pitching this afternoon and he was fast — very fast — but his curve didn't break much. The game was scoreless until the fifth inning. When Francisco De La Rosa — "The Cisco Kid" and only sophomore in the starting line-up — was batting and thought curve. However, the inside fastball was too close and the ball hit him in the ribs. Bart walked on four straight pitches. On a 2 — 2 count, I figured he would come with his weak curve for a strikeout. As the pitch came, it broke only slightly towards the outside corner, so I stepped into it and hit the ball into right field. My blast was the best I had hit in my life, clearing the fence by at least twenty feet. I was triumphant and euphoric as I rounded the bases.

Too bad Victoria and my Graces weren't here to see that whooper. Dad? ... He saw it! I know he did!

Thomas doubled then Jack singled him home. But they came back in the top of the seventh, scoring a run and had runners on first and third. Bart came into pitch and walked the next guy on five pitches. Then up came Lester, their left fielder and best hitter, but Bart struck him out on three pitches, the last pitch was a terrific curve and a called strike. The guy was so pissed off that he threw his bat at their bench, yelling something to the umpire. If it wasn't the end of the game, he would have been thrown out. But he was suspended for their next game, Northwest, as I found out later. Kovac never looked at me again — that I knew of. The Prick and I never even exchanged glances. I prayed to God he would pitch the next time.

❋❋❋❋❋❋❋❋❋❋❋❋❋❋❋❋❋❋❋❋❋❋❋❋❋❋❋❋

An extremely hurt Autumn answered the door. As an added punishment, yesterday her mother returned the new ecru colored gown that her parents had paid for last month. So tonight she was wearing last year's dress — a strapless, knee length, elegant cocktail dress of rich burgundy with a quite modest V neckline. Autumn deftly accessorized with light burgundy eyeshadow, the gold pearl earrings and, of course, the locket in the V. Her hair was in a bouffant of her own styling. I told her I didn't care that it was last year's. I had never seen it and she looked fantastic. I left my boutonnière along with her corsage in the refrigerator at home. Autumn icily muttered that we were leaving and slammed the door so hard that it shook.

When I helped her in the car, I complemented her, "Victoria, you look extra beautiful tonight. Maybe because I've only seen you for five minutes and we've kissed only once in the last two weeks. I seriously missed being with you." She slightly leaned over to kiss my cheek then softly caressed it.

"Are you all ready?"

Autumn pulled back. "Can't wait. Calling me *'Little Missy,'* because I questioned him! Who in Hell does that Little Shit Hole think he is? Bastard! **And** my parents can still go to Hell and stay there. That was just hateful, just mean **shit** to return my beautiful dress. I really loved it. Last night, when I went to check and lay everything out in Summer's room, I couldn't find it in the closet. That's when the Ninny told me. I know they planned it this way. That's why my father said I could go to the dance. Punished either way. No dance and no you **or** forced to commit the inexcusable 'fashion sin' of wearing last year's formal again. I just went back to my room, slammed the door, and cried. A ton."

This hurt her already raw feelings more, deepening the rift between she and her parents. During pictures at my house, I could tell my aunt was pissed off, but nothing like Mother was. Under that calm exterior, she was seething. Yet neither said a negative word, only how beautiful and elegant Autumn looked. DeeDee happily complimented and gushed over her then ran upstairs to finish getting ready for her date with Chris Ewell who had just accepted a basketball scholarship at Villanova.

When Hal and Jacqueline joined us at our two couple table, he quietly reiterated he wasn't too happy about the scheme and was still against it. She, however, remained strongly adamant about the ensuing plan. Jacqueline looked elegant in her sleeveless, black cocktail dress with its length quite a few inches above the knee. The turtleneck collar was accented by several long, layered strands of pearls. Thus, my great disappointment of no cleavage, yet a nice show of thigh.

About an hour later, the crowning ceremony began. The two ladies-in-waiting were named and honored. Next, the two princesses would be named. Vice-Principal Walters very happily announced, "Our first princess is our wonderful exchange student from Paris, France ... senior Miss Jacqueline Cartier. Mercy bow coop, Jacqueline. She is escorted by Mr. Hal Fleming."

However, there was no Jacqueline, nor was there Hal. Prior to the start of the crowning ceremony, they had slipped out the dance. Everyone was looking around for them. There were murmurs of 'I saw them just fifteen minutes ago.' And 'Yeah, I think I just saw her in the girls' room.' During this confusion, Autumn nudged me and I stood up to help her out of her chair.

She confidently walked to the podium and up to the microphone, "Everyone, I am extremely sorry to tell you this, but Jacqueline has become ill." Murmurs and ahhhs went throughout the crowd. Autumn continued, "She thanks you heartily for your support. She wanted me to accept her tiara for her."

Loud applause. She reached over to the Asshole and took the small tiara from his hand. Speaking distinctly into the microphone, "Thank you, Vice-Principal Walters. The Music Committee wishes everyone to enjoy tonight's music."

The small amount of applause was drowned out by the loud laughter from the cries of "Next year, get Lawrence Welk." Then, "Yeah, that's what we need ... a Polka band." Followed by "Nah, the band from the Old Folks' Home. If they're still alive!" More loud laughter. "Great to dance to my parents' music! What **crap**!" The jeers and ridicule increased. I had told Autumn that when she left the podium to make sure not to look at Walters. But I looked at him. He was an extremely, totally pissed off red-faced "Damn Gestapo." After a few moments to compose himself and when the continuing jeers and laughter finally died down, he resumed the ceremony.

✲✲✲✲✲✲✲✲✲✲✲✲✲✲✲✲✲✲✲✲✲✲✲✲✲✲✲✲✲✲✲

At the beginning of eighth grade, Autumn became deeply hurt
then incensed when she found out Walters had made some
defamatory comments about her beloved Nanna, Aibreann
— 'April' — Doyle; An offhand remark had slipped out and
Autumn compelled her grandmother to tell her the entire story;

Walters had desperately tried to date April in high school,
but she wouldn't have a thing to do with him;
In retaliation, he spread rumors about her,
calling her 'that promiscuous Irish tramp';
Her new beau, Cornelius Knight,
severely 'thrashed him for his loose tongue';

When Autumn began attending Prescott,
she began to incredibly resemble the beautiful April,
acutely reminding Walters of his dating humiliation & beating;
His deep-seated hostility surfaced, aimed at Autumn who
responded in kind

✲✲✲✲✲✲✲✲✲✲✲✲✲✲✲✲✲✲✲✲✲✲✲✲✲✲✲✲✲✲✲

Autumn came back to the table, tiara in hand, and snatched up her purse to leave. As we were walking out the door, Joan Marie Myers was announced as the other princess. Ginny was wrong — dating Larry Freeman somehow paid off. Which meant my "carhop girlfriend," Cathy Winters, would be crowned Spring Fling Queen. I was happy for her. She truly deserved it. Rumors about she and Hal's break-up included Anna Colburn and his wish to date "The Foreigner". Cathy would now have her turn to gloat as she not only beat out Hal's new "fresh off the boat" girlfriend to be Queen but would also wipe the on-going smile off "The Fair" who could only dream about being as popular as Cathy.

✲✲✲✲✲✲✲✲✲✲✲✲✲✲✲✲✲✲✲✲✲✲✲✲✲✲✲✲✲✲✲

Cathryn Jean Winters graduated from Kansas State Teachers
College, was a cheerleader for three years;
obtained her degree in primary education;
She married Paul Janesko, her college sweetheart who became
an actuary; Since she loved children, she was ecstatic for each birth

of their two girls and a boy; The couple remains very happy with six grandchildren [two are HS cheerleaders]

****

We drove to the rendezvous point at the Sinclair station, near the 18th Street Expressway, to meet the new princess and her escort, then followed them to McMaster's for dinner. Bart told me about this great restaurant in Leawood where no one, of course, would be there from the Dance. Autumn crowned Princess Jacqueline to our laughter. We laughed even more when I described the look on Walters' face after the commotion and hilarity caused when Autumn told everyone to enjoy the music. I reiterated my comment, "Certainly worthy of the Jesuits. Father Fitz would be proud."

Hal wanted a picture of Jacqueline wearing the tiara for the yearbook and Autumn reassured him it would be, as a photographer would take her picture sometime in the coming week. She remembered that Summer had told her that about three years ago, a member of the court really did become sick and her picture was taken later.

Jacqueline wondered, "*Mon cherie* [My darling], you're still positive you won't get in more trouble because of the comment about the music?"

"Oh no Jacqui, I told everyone to **enjoy** the music. Ugh! Such as it was ... **Fossilized Shit**." We all joined in laughter as she strongly emphasized her crudity. "But I believe it will change how bands will be selected in the future, **otherwise** no one will come. And no, I **will not** be on a selection committee ever again. I've had my stomach full of that little **Piss-Ant**! But it's quite empty now." Everyone laughed more then decided what we would order.

After dinner Autumn and I went to St. Victoria's. As I turned onto Sandusky, I moaned, "Victoria, you know, it's been only two weeks without you, but it seems like two months. How utterly beautiful you look tonight, your ultra-cool demeanor in both accepting Jacqueline's tiara then shoving the band selection up Walters' ass. At dinner, your sense of humor and your laughter. I have missed every bit of you terribly."

"I have missed you *so much*," and she kissed my cheek, then my ear, whispering, "I must have your jacket, though."

I parked and unzipped the back of her dress. While Autumn easily slid its top down to her waist where she neatly draped and folded it, I removed my jacket and helped her into it. After we Frenched for some moments, I began to unlock her treasure chest. That front fastening, longline strapless bra had at least a thousand hooks and it took me forever to open. Finally I breached the fortress, revealing her perfect breasts, heavily tinged a wintry, snowy white with extra Chanel dusting powder. They never looked more beautiful or scented more fragrantly which I whispered to her while I began to softly caress them.

Paradise Regained! Thank you, God!

❊❊❊❊❊❊❊❊❊❊❊❊❊❊❊❊❊❊❊❊❊❊❊❊❊❊❊❊

After I came home after ball practice and dinner Monday night, Autumn called. "Well, I got my grades."

"And?"

"Excellent and awful!" and she began to recite them for me, "1- in English, 1- in U.S. History, Accounting is a 1 and, of course, a 1 in Interior Design."

"Wow, straight one's, but you forgot Algebra?"

"I wish I could forget that damn Algebra. I got a 3. **A DAMN 3**! Oh Richie, I haven't gotten a 3 since 7th grade ... in gym class. Before you ask, I'll tell you *that excruciating* embarrassing story now. Nobody's home and you won't get to watch me turn bright red. Here it is ..."

She took a deep breath, "Right after that Thanksgiving, my very, very first menstruation started during a gym class! When I started to change, I noticed there was quite a bit of dark reddish-brown blood on the thick, white cotton panty's front section which Summer had help me cut and sew into my one piece brown gym suit for ... well ... 'accidents' ... *like that*. For a month or two, Summer had told me I should expect 'it' to happen soon. I had started wearing a bra ... barely an A, but still a real cup and Nanna had gone with me to buy it. I had begun shaving my armpits and legs. Just so damn pleased with myself! I had arrived! But even so, when **it** did finally **arrive too**, I was nervous and tried to clean myself up quickly. I didn't see the suit fall off the changing room hook."

"Since the doors are only a mid-calf to head type, Hélène Marston, one of the freshman girls, saw it on the floor, reached in and pulled it out and announced to the whole locker room, 'Hey girls, looks like Autumn Knight isn't a little girl anymore'. Then she held up the damning evidence for all to see. Those damn tawdry girls laughed and made jokes, teasing me with their so crude language. Most of the others empathized with me. Naturally, I began to cry. The teacher, Mrs. Potter, didn't have any sympathy for me, just saying that was part of a girl's life, that I had to get used to it for the next forty years ... except during pregnancies which made monthly periods feel like picnics. I was so terribly embarrassed and hurt. Since it was the last class of the day, I skipped homeroom, went straight home and wouldn't go back to school for the rest of the week. The following week I went to the nurse's office instead of gym class. I was so ashamed, completely humiliated. Nanna and Summer had to talk to me a few times. The Ninny **never** did ... even once. I finally got over my embarrassment because my sister made the tormentor, this Hélène, privately apologize to me. Then this girl ... who was always kinda strange, just plain weird at times ... had to tell all the others in the gym class that it was a very mean thing to do for so personal an experience."

"Girls can be mean just like guys. How did Summer make her apologize?"

"Guys and rough girls have fights, but respectable girls take subtle measures. Summer was a freshman cheerleader, previous class officer, in the most popular clique, you know, all the important stuff. Summer has a wonderful disposition, but if she thinks someone has caused me pain ... **look out**! She told this Hélène she would make the rest of her life at Whittier as miserable as possible, insuring she would be snubbed and ignored with one exception ... there would be a ton of cruel jokes made about her weight, *especially* to the guys. Summer knew the girl couldn't take *that*. She was highly sensitive about her size and thoroughly tried to entice guys. This Hélène saw herself as only 'slightly pleasingly plump', yet she was truly overweight ... the clique girls already called her 'The Chubber'."

"Huh ... Summer did that? Well, I'll be damned. But back to your grades. It's still your constant 1.4 average, an A- . What did your parents say about the grade?"

"Ninny just jabbered on and on about Summer **never** getting a 3. Mr. Neglectful said I should spend more time studying and less time being disrespectful. Nothing about all ones in every other subject."

Her deteriorating relationship with them was hurting her more and more. All I could think to say was, "I'm really sorry about your parents. They're a pair of damn fools. I could help you on the weekends. During the week is a mess with practice or a game and my Achilles' heel ... damn Latin."

"I think I will be okay from here on. It was Trig that killed me. Even though you helped me with it, I never could really understand it. Thank God, we are done with it. Good luck tomorrow night against my Bears. I wish I could be there."

"I wish you could too. More than you know, Victoria."

※※※※※※※※※※※※※※※※※※※※※※※※※※

LaFleur was going to pitch this afternoon and I hoped he could hold them. The word was Prescott had an extremely good hitting team. Mick was on the bench. Autumn and I had briefly seen Pamela and him at the dance and he said he was going to pitch against McKenna on Thursday but he would be there to watch us lose. I laughed and told them his pitching buddy would need to be a lot better than him. As Prescott took infield, we ragged on each other behind the backstop for a few minutes.

However, the niceties were over when the game started and they quickly scored two runs in the top half of the first. Bart got his first double of the season and on the first pitch, I singled him home. But Thomas fouled out and Jack hit a wicked one hopper to the shortstop for a double play.

About the third inning, I saw Camille and Libby go into the stands. Jack said, "I promised Camille I would hit a home run for her."

I kidded, "When you get to the plate, why don't you point like Babe Ruth did."

"Yeah ... I will," he said with his natural cockiness.

They scored two more in the top of the fourth *and* the fifth. Shit! Now it was 6 — 1. We needed to get something going. De La Rosa walked and Bart swung late but hit a line drive down the right field line for a triple. Some innings before, when I was on first from my single, I tried to recall why the pitcher looked familiar — from where? Now this at bat he threw the first pitch too inside for my comfort, and Jack yelled at the guy, something like, 'Your ugly girlfriend has better control.' I decided to crowd the plate some and was rewarded with the next pitch hitting my forearm. When I was on first again, I thought about saying something to rag the guy, but maybe it was an errant pitch. After Thomas struck out, Jack got even for me by hitting one over the left field fence. As he rounded third, he taunted the pitcher, "You hit the wrong guy, Rag Arm." As I congratulated him at home plate, Jack growled, "SHIT! Forgot to point." Regardless, Jack had made good on his promise for Camille.

The pitcher was really pissed and I finally remembered who he was — the guy at Judy's clique party with Joanie. He tried to stay close to her — like some little puppy dog   must have really liked her.

We were back in the game and Bart started pitching in the top of the sixth with two out and a runner at first and retired the next batter then retired the side in order in the seventh. But we needed a run to tie. Bart was first up and ran the count full, then walked. As I walked to the plate, I looked at Coach Bannister for a sacrifice bunt sign. Instead it was "hit-away". I decided to crowd the plate again. I thought he would throw a curve, figuring that I would be gun-shy after he hit me, pull back and the pitch would break for a pure strike and I would look stupid. He served it right up and I stepped into the curve and hit it very hard into left center. My first thought was "tie" but the ball hit the top of the four foot fence and careened over.

A Home Run! We Won! Damn it, where's Autumn ... my mother, DeeDee, Aunt Danae.

My Dad saw it! I know he's proud. The Game Winner!

As I rounded second, I heard Jack yell at the dejected pitcher, "Should have hit him again!" The guy was walking off the mound but stopped to momentarily glare at Jack. Then he riveted on me, really pissed off, like I had said something too.

When I came into home to jump on the plate, I was met by the team, even the Coach.

****

Two days later, we played St. John Vianny, the other Missouri all male Catholic school. Their pitcher was Guy Frost and he wasn't good, he was **great**. The Majors were already seriously scouting him. It was said he had a fastball like a rocket and he proved it. Both Bart and Jack singled against him and Mike Thomas hit a double. And that was it. Rich Trent pitched a helluva game, but we were beaten 2 — 0. All I could do was strikeout twice and almost got a single out of an anemic ground ball that was like a bunt. The guy also had an extremely good curve, a terrific slider which he got me for both strikeouts. But he couldn't pitch every game and we were only a game behind them at 4 — 1.

****

We were at St. Victoria's and I could tell Autumn wanted to talk. She curled her legs up on the seat, laying her head on my leg, facing the dashboard. I began stroking her long, lustrous hair. After three or four minutes, she turned over to look up at me and I kept brushing her hair. "I'm glad baseball is going so well for you and the team ... well, except for last night. I want to see you play *so much* and *finally* will next month. Why didn't you save those two home runs for me?"

"I'll just hit two more," and arrogantly laughed. "Remember the party Judy, *that* pretty red-haired girl, had?" I teased her.

"Of course. When you were blowing in her ear," she countered.

I had found out during the almost six months we had been going steady, Autumn could be truly jealous regarding some girls from her own clique. Nothing with most of them. Very little with Judy, but *certainly* Joanie, and Ginny was, *most assuredly*, the one who could stir up the most. Sometimes during an off-chance meeting with Cathy Winters. But she would never say a word about it to any one of them. Definitely not Jacqueline — Jacqui, as we called her — who had become best friends with Autumn, especially after the Dance fun and games and when I told her after the French movie I thought of Jacqui as someone like a "sisterly" friend. However, I could be insanely jealous over just about any guy.

"That Terry Massey whom I met at her party and Sam Miller at that hall dance both played the outfield."

"I thought they just played around with that promiscuous sl ... ahh, girl."

I laughed, "Each one got a hit. I said 'hey' to them when they were on first. I'm sure the pitcher was at her party too ... with Joanie ... but I can't remember his name, something Cozzie ... the one saying about how Massey fumbled with his chance with you."

"Thank God! He's turned out to be *such a douche-bag*, that Shit! Oooh yuck." And she shuddered a little.

"What?"

"What he did with that **slut** ... uh ... oops ... all those times, **what** he caught from her. I **knew** he was going to try something with me ... that's why I wouldn't go out with him for a third date. What that Shit actually did with Ginny on her 'cat' panty night. I think he must have kept trying 'something' with Judy as she was the one who broke it off. She just said that they grew tired of each other or something like that. But I never really believed it. I can always read her like a book. Remember sometime later, she found out he had been cheating on her with your old dance partner, fast little Caroline Cunningham who, by the way, has gotten herself a terrible reputation. She's called the football team's 'Christmas Carol' since she's briefly gone steady with more than a half dozen or so of the senior players. Ginny told me the name is because she gives each one a present on the second date ... 'to unwrap, you unhook'. Her friends all have dirty innuendo nicknames. You said you knew two of them ... who are called 'Fast Lane Lorraine' and 'Wild Cherry Sherry'."

HA! Mick said it was now 'No Cherry Sherry'. After her wild Easter weekend at the Lake with a few guys. Now has a Park Entry **charm**

bracelet *... each charm inscribed with the partner's initials. And said she'll add to it.*

"**...vulgar**, especially what their group's name is! So gross! Okay, enough. Talking about lewd girls in my year is just going to give me a rosy tinge. They're not worth it. Anyway, your pitcher's name is Roy Cozad. He and Joanie got into a big fight after that party. She dumped him ... hard, like a rock. Told him she wanted somebody really cool ... like I had. Supposedly, he really, *really* liked her. Ancient history," she said, then changed the subject, "So, how is my client partner in design?"

"Well, speaking of my mother, how would you like to go with my mother to watch me play at McKenna and also Wellington? She could pick you up right at school. But you may want to sit with your friends for the Prescott game."

"Oh no, Richie, she is soooo good to me. I would be thrilled to have her take me to those two games and I certainly would sit with her at our game, too. I could meet her in the bleachers. You will have your private cheering section. Oh goody great! Three games to watch you play and to sit with her. Oh goody great! Speaking of Gi Gi, that brings me to an interesting point."

"Why, isn't the master suite decorating going well? One day it smells like paint, the next day there is broken tile all over, then another day two guys are taking the old tub away, and on and on."

"Oh no, that's going extremely well. The interesting point is that my parents have both taken notice of my role in the 'Suite Renovation Project'. At dinner tonight, the Ninny said, 'Agnes,' ... that's Mrs. Worth" and she began to comically mock her mother, " 'from the Bridge Club told me that it must be wonderful to have two daughters so greatly gifted, one on a Journalism scholarship and the other a real genius in Design. Her first job at Geneviève Marlowe's house! I just told Agnes that you and Rich were going steady and she says oh no, it's more than that. She heard also Mrs. Marlowe is so very particular. Agnes said you must have quite a bit of talent other than being the girlfriend. She then said maybe you could get a summer job at the Hardy Design Studio.' Mrs. Worth heard all this from Mrs. Snowden last Sunday at The Grandview Presbyterian."

And the third point of my mother's plotting was now known.

Point Three — By cleverness and stealth, the parents are made aware they have an extremely talented younger daughter.

I give you Georgie, The Lady Magician Extraordinaire, who strikes again. Wonder who goes to Mrs. Snowden's Presbyterian church? Could it be "Aunt Genie"? In a confederacy between those two ... nothing, but nothing would be impossible.

From that dinner forward, Autumn was compared as inferior to Summer a lot fewer times. The Knights began to be a little more caring, taking a little more positive notice of their younger daughter. Definitely a lot more boastful of her at Church and bridge clubs. All of which made Autumn feel a bit better at home. Mother said at least it was a solid step in the right direction.

****

With Trent on the mound, the Northwest game was never in any doubt. He shut them out 9 — 0. I went 2 — 2 with a single, a double and two walks. Bart had a great game, going 3 — 4 with a home run and a triple. Jack, on the other hand, had a bad night, 0 — 4. Everything he hit was right at someone. He was pissed off but said at least it was the weekend tomorrow night and he would spend it with Camille. She **always** knew how to make things better.

****

When I took my desk Friday morning, I glanced out the window to see the heavy downpour was continuing which meant no practice tonight. During my sorrowful weather check, I noticed Carl Landers who sits next to me in the adjoining row. He was small framed, medium height with brown hair and black glasses which were now wrapped several times with adhesive tape around their bridge. His left eye had a small cut near his nose.

"Landers, what the hell happened to you?"

"Fell."

"Bullshit! What really happened?"

His face took a pained look, "Three guys from St. John V's force me to pay each of them fifty cents every Thursday when I get off the bus. I forgot my money yesterday. The big one, Roger, tripped and pushed me down. Told me to bring the money today."

Moose came storming through the door. I hurriedly said, "You're eating lunch with us today instead of your nose in Cicero."

I knew Landers didn't have any extra money. His mother was his only parent and taught grade school somewhere. He was first honors smart and had a "quasi partial" scholarship — a grant. What Chicken Shits! That was probably his meager allowance.

I told Jack and Bart we needed to take a bus ride after school as we walked to lunch. I lied and said it was my turn to buy which would include Carl. He said thanks and he would eat his sack lunch at home tomorrow. After he explained the situation, I laid out the plan.

The rain had finally stopped when the three of us boarded the bus and Bart followed in his car. At Carl's stop, I noticed three guys waiting — medium height and builds, maybe one a little bigger. Hopefully, just bullying assholes with mouths they couldn't backup. Words from my street fighting instructor came into my mind, "You can never be sure. **Never** assume." Carl got off first and the three moved towards him.

"Ya got our money, you little piss-ant?" said the tallest prick in the middle.

Jack stepped off the bus and stood next to Carl. I could tell he was still pissed from last night's game.

A second prick sneered, "Did you take **our** money and hire a **lone** bodyguard?"

I stepped off and answered, "No asshole. And **none of you** have any money."

The third one looked at me strangely, then said, "Carl, just give us the money."

The bus pulled away and Bart appeared about six feet behind the third one, speaking in a haughty English upper-class tone, "You three Arseholes are somewhat correct. There will be a few financial transactions. There will also be a guarantee given. You have a choice on how they are to be conveyed."

The third one spoke again, "Roger, what the hell is this guy yapping about?"

"Nothing worth a damn, Kent. Just the usual arrogant shit from a usual St. Iggy piggy ... PRICK."

I addressed this Roger in my most arrogant tone, "This extortion has been going on for three weeks. That's four and a half dollars. Transaction one ... you will repay that money now. A new pair of frames cost ten dollars. Transaction two ... payable now. Pain, suffering, embarrassment of Mr. Landers' cut is valued at five dollars. Transaction three... due now. You dull-witted St. JV eunuchs probably can't add, so I will do it for you. Total bill hence, nineteen and a half dollars or rounding ... twenty dollars. Lastly, a guarantee to be given to Mr. Landers that you will never accost him for money or anything else in the future. Do you agree to these conditions?"

Roger simply scoffed, "Or what?"

Jack interjected in a menacing tone, "Each one of you will be beaten until your face is bloody and bruised. Any future assaults on Mr. Landers will result in increasingly severe beatings, starting with your balls. Assuming you have some. Clear?" It was obvious Jack wanted a fight.

Kent moved around to the second guy, saying something to him in a low voice so only the three could hear, then, "Roger?"

"Just more arrogant Jesuit bullshit! All talk ... never any action."

Jack struck like lightening — three quick steps, then blindsiding Roger with a hard punch to the stomach, then a wicked shot to his mouth. He staggered back and fell into a large puddle of water.

Bart yelled, "Who's next? Come on now! More arrogant Jesuit bullshit awaits!" He grabbed Kent to punch him, who rapidly pulled away, tearing his shirt. Kent joined the third guy to quickly pull a bloodied Roger — wet and stunned — to his feet. All three emptied their billfolds. Kent handed Carl five dollars, four in bills and one in quarters, the second guy had four singles and some change. Roger could just sputter, "I only have a five and a couple ones."

I said, "That'll be sufficient. Told you pricks a few minutes ago that none of you had any money."

Each one separately gave their word not to bother Carl ever again. They turned and hurriedly left.

Carl wouldn't quit thanking us until we dropped him off. As he got out of the car, Jack told him not to tell anyone at school. Moose would get wind of it and might not take too kindly to our methods. He promised he wouldn't.

As we drove away, Bart said, "Damn Jack, two great shots on ole mouthy Roger. All I got was a grab and a torn shirt."

"Well, it did violate your Queensberry Rules, but he had it coming. In spades!" He then smirked, "Never follow any rules anyway."

****

Saturday was Jacqueline's birthday, so the four of us all celebrated by taking her to the Plaza III for dinner on Friday, then the Broadmoor for some dancing. Hal was beaming as she took a sip of champagne and realized there was an expensive cocktail ring which he had slipped into her glass. [Hal had ordered the bottle with his fake ID.] Jacqueline teasingly said she might have "something special for him," and kissed him on the cheek.

No one ever found out or was told what it was, but since it *was* from Jacqueline, my dirty mind was sure the "something special" was definitely to do with sex, yet provided in a "virginal fashion". The more she hung around with Autumn and me, the more I was surprised and the more Autumn was shocked how much she knew about sex … … "More than Summer." She had a definite uninhibited attitude with us but evidently exhibited none of her liberated point of view with Hal.

****

We had back to back games with Fairview Hills. The school was *the* private nonsectarian boys' school in Kansas City. They were always good in football, good in basketball and damn good in track but terrible in baseball. This year, they were exceptionally bad. After five innings, the score was 11 - 0 and the game was over due to the League's 10-run rule. Coach Bannister and the Fairview Hills coach conferred with the head umpire after the last out and they decided to play two more innings as practice. The rest of the bench got to play and De La Rosa got to try his hand at pitching. I had managed two singles and a double, Bart had a double and two walks, and Jack could *only* hit two home runs in our four innings.

Thursday's game was a carbon copy with LaFleur pitching. The score was 12 — 2 after three innings and remained so until the fifth, thus there were the same two practice innings. I told Jack and Bart it felt strange to be on the bench again, earlier this time — after the second inning — and they agreed but we had a walk, a single, two doubles and a triple and a signature Nelson home run among us. But on the bench, he was uncharacteristically quiet, moody.

When the Three Musketeers walked out of the locker room, Jack admitted to us, "I can't quit thinking about Camille going to Mizzou next year without me. All those guys ... frat rats or regular bozos, all the partying, the whole university scene ... without me. I'm worried we'll somehow break up. Real worried."

Both Bart and I tried to convince nothing would change, but he remained unconvinced.

Mick called me after I got home to tell me Prescott had beaten St. John Vianney last night, 3 - 0. He had pitched a four-hitter. He and Pamela with some of his teammates and their girlfriends celebrated afterwards for quite a while. The kicker was Guy Frost didn't pitch as he had shut-out McKenna on Monday's make-up game. Thanks to Mick and Prescott, we were tied for first with St. John Vianney at 7 — 1. Prescott and McKenna were tied for third, still close, with only two losses each.

MAY

At lunch the next day, Friday, Jack seemed relieved about he and Camille when I asked him if he felt any better about the situation. He then told us that after his father was called out on an emergency last night, his mother surprisingly came into his room and shut the door. She wanted to talk about him and Camille privately.

"She told me, 'Jack, you can't keep worrying about Camille next fall at Missouri. Her club ... "Girls with No Siblings" ... are going to all be roommates. You can't insist she go to Junior College at St. Rose of Lima and split them apart. That would certainly cause a rift ... because she assuredly wouldn't. You can't insist she come home every weekend, to do what you want. She'll resent that too. Other situations would add up and finally culminate by you two breaking up. You'll see her frequently ... whether here or you could go visit her and stay in Columbia for a weekend. It's only for nine months with holiday and semester breaks, not nine years.' I wasn't convinced. Then she said, 'Would you rather break up now? No, of course not. You know that answer. Look Jack, your father and I know you are in love with her. You both need to find out if it is solid, lasting.' I started to object."

"My mother shook her head. 'She is a beautiful girl with a great personality. There will be guys flocking around her, but true love will override those temptations. She's a good girl, a smart girl, and hardworking. I really like her ... so does your father. She reminds me a little of myself when I was younger and we had very little money. But we married and we got your dad through med school. On even less money. Then you and Andrea came along and we still struggled. But we made it. What I'm trying to tell you, those nine months will be a struggle, **BUT** if it's meant to be, you will stay together through it. And you will have more struggles, but still be together.' "

"I just nodded and my mother kissed my forehead, then said, 'Oh, being a woman I know all about Camille's feelings.' Then she left with a twinkle in her eye and a smile. She's right. Camille and I will make it and get married. And we'll talk about it this weekend.

✳✳✳✳✳✳✳✳✳✳✳✳✳✳✳✳✳✳✳✳✳✳✳✳✳✳✳✳✳✳

As I pull over and parked at St. Victoria, Autumn said, "I have always meant to ask why didn't you introduce yourself the first time we saw each other at Balls' instead of waiting till you looked like death warmed over six weeks later? I **really** had been checking you out, seriously wishing you would come over."

"Oh, I really wanted to. You were the most beautiful girl I had ever seen. You still are. Fantastic long legs and a great looking butt. Still have! I couldn't quit staring when you leaned over a counter, which accentuated your legs and the curve of your wonderful derrière. I desperately was hoping for at least a momentary shot of a sliver of one of your fabulous butt cheeks. I got aroused. Really aroused. You think you get embarrassed. I'm sure it was one of the biggest erections I have ever gotten. Kept trying to hide it any way possible. In my old shorts and shorter sweater, you *couldn't* have missed it. Only after you and your mother had finished checking out and left, did it finally recede."

"Well, that explains it." She began to snicker, "Remember, Froggy the Gremlin from the Buster Brown TV show? What did Andy Devine always tell Froggy to do? 'Plunk your magic twanger'!" Now she was giggling, very mischievously. "I wondered why you stuck so close to the counters, even when you moved. So my handsome Froggy, **I'm the ONE who plunked your magic twanger!**"

"Autumn Victoria Knight! And *you* call *me* wicked. What would your mother say?"

"Even though the show was on TV, I would still have to explain it to her. About sex, Valentina only told me the very bare essentials in vague generalities, like 'you'll have a time every month' and just worthless shit like that. However, swearing and the 'wickedness' part, I simply got it from hanging around with you and Jacqui ... now I'm just like a good Catholic girl. I swear all the **damn** time with you and now I'm as bad as my teacher Jacqui. Even swear some with the other girls. Lookee Master, not even a tinge."

She began to passionately kiss then French me as she swung her leg over to straddle me, having been "newly instructed for sexual activities in this position by that nice French Catholic girl". Autumn pulled back slightly, giggling then whispered in my ear, "Feels like I *really* plunked your magic twanger again."

"Easily ... so easily with you."

※※※※※※※※※※※※※※※※※※※※※※※※※※※※

Jack parked in the lot at Wellington's field and we went over to join the guys who were already there. I looked into the stands and saw Autumn and my mother. They both waved, Autumn very excitedly and I smiled and guardedly waved back. After the infield warm-up, Coach Bannister warned us in the team huddle, "While Wellington has only won three games, they would like nothing better than to be the spoiler. So give Todd a lot of support today. We must win our remaining four games to take the championship. Play like it today! Go! Go!"

Bart started off with a walk after seven pitches. I hit the first pitch into center field for a single, Bart holding at second. I heard Autumn cheering loudly when I rounded first and stopped. I smiled. It was great to hear her yelling for me. Mike Thomas singled to left field and Coach held Bart at third. Jack stepped in the box, looking hungry. After a called strike, he hit the second pitch in deep right center for a double and cleared the bases. When their threat in their bottom half was stopped, the game was never in doubt. Todd LaFleur pitched a superb game allowing only one run on five hits. The final score was 6 — 1. Jack had the best game of the three of us with two doubles and four RBI's. Bart and I both had a single and a walk, scoring two runs each.

After the game, I introduced both Jack and Bart to my mother then Bart to Autumn. Both congratulated us on winning. Autumn inquired of Jack how Camille was doing. He smiled hugely, "Fine, very fine. The best we've ever been. Thanks for asking, Helen of Troy." Last weekend, I figured they had discussed their future, especially for the next school year, probably beyond. Bart and I figured they are now secretly engaged.

The Coach saw our little group and came over to us. I introduced him to Mother, then to Autumn. "Well, Mrs. Marlowe and Autumn, I see you have met the other two Musketeers. All three had excellent games today."

Autumn piped up, "Especially the 5 — 4 — 3 double play in the first inning to stop Wellington from coming back and the excellent back hand stop and throw by Jack with the terrific dig by Richelieu in the third to stop the run from scoring. Solid team defense, Coach, no errors."

Coach Bannister was a little surprised and smiled, "Very **good** analysis, young lady. Do you do scouting reports? I may need your advice for Prescott." We all laughed.

"Oh, we will definitely be there, Coach Bannister. Look for Mrs. Marlowe and me in the north bleachers on Friday." The Coach looked quizzical. "The north bleachers at Prescott are for the visiting team. Even though I go to Prescott, Mrs. Marlowe and I will both be cheering for St. Ignatius."

"We will need a lot of help. Your school has a good, solid team. Thank you for reminding me about our excellent team defense," he acknowledged, then saying, "Nice to meet you, Mrs. Marlowe. And you Autumn. Be sure to give your scouting report to Lou." They both smiled and he left to check that all our equipment was collected and loaded.

We said our goodbyes and that it was nice to meet everybody. Then the three of us went to the Galaxie.

"Mother, I'm glad you came to watch me. Thank you for picking Autumn up at Prescott. You're the best."

"Oh, Gi Gi, you are **definitely** the best."

This must have embarrassed my mother a little. "All right, children, what do you want?" All three of us laughed.

I parked at Autumn's house, and as she slid out the door, my mother called, "Good bye Honey. See you Friday. You're excellent company at a ball game."

Autumn bent over, looking through the driver's window, "Bye Gi Gi. So are you. Thank you for taking me to watch Richie. It meant so much to me. I will meet you in the north bleachers right after school. Thank you again."

After walking her to the door, I slid back behind the driver's wheel, my mother simply said, "I enjoyed the game much more with her there. It's really nice to have someone there with you whom you care about a great deal. She is such a sweet, sweet, gentle girl, and so well-mannered. And knows the game too."

I'll bet she's thinking about Dad, too. Autumn's right ... he's here ... at the games.

※※※※※※※※※※※※※※※※※※※※※※※※※

Jack and I rode to Prescott with Bart. Camille and Libby were coming to the game straight from St. Cat's, having been given directions from Autumn. They joined my mother and her as the game started.

Mick was warming up and definitely going to pitch this afternoon. I had met Autumn at Prescott on Holy Thursday and she went with me to watch Mick pitch a couple innings in their intra-squad game. He had an exceptional fastball and a great breaking curve. He was good. Damn good.

In the top of the first, Bart had a very rare third strike called against him. I hit the first pitch, a fastball, into right centerfield for a double. I heard Autumn yell for me and I smiled again. But I died on second and the game remained scoreless until the fourth inning when I led off. I noticed during the last inning that Mick appeared to be grimacing a little when he threw a curve. On a 2 - 1 count, he went into his wind-up, wincing during his delivery. Curve. It hung and I hit it to right center again for another double. I heard my personal cheerleader yell for me again. Thomas flied to deep right and I tagged and went to third. Jack crushed a double of his own to left center and as I scored, I heard *his* personal cheerleader holler for him. Harris singled him home, and *his* personal cheerleader yelled loudly. Miller, however, hit into a double play to end the inning.

I noticed Mick was rubbing his hand and wrist after our inning, so I mentioned to everyone about the tight grimace before a curve. Regardless of what he threw, he was now having pain and losing his stuff. In the bottom of the inning Prescott scored, making it 2 - 1. De La Rosa led off the top of the sixth, and walked on four pitches, none of which were close. Prescott's coach went to the mound to join the catcher. After a quick discussion, Mick went to the bench. He received a nice round of applause, especially from my mother and Autumn.

The relief pitcher was Cozad, the guy who Jack starting ragging after he hit me at St. Ignatius. Bart walked on five pitches. Jack yelled at the pitcher in a sarcastic voice, "Now if you hit him again, it will load the bases." He didn't hit me even though first two pitches were close. I hit his third pitch — a line drive double down the left field line and both runners scored. Jack screeched, "Should have hit him again, Rag Arm."

Mike Thomas virtually put the game out of reached by hitting a towering blast over the left fielder's head for a home run. It was now 6 - 1. Jack came to the plate. The first pitch sailed way inside, almost hitting him even as he jumped backwards. Off balance, Jack fell to the ground. Before he could charge the mound, Harris quickly grabbed him. Coach Bannister went over to Jack, and I heard only the last part, "... ... so no more shit, Nelson!" After seven pitches, Jack walked. The game ended with that score. I looked for Mick but he was gone, probably to take care of his hand or wrist.

The Three Musketeers, after quickly sharing congrats with our teammates, went over to the girls' cheering section. Harris and Libby were off to one side, privately talking, said goodbye to everyone, then hurriedly left. Camille greeted Jack with, "Wonderful game," then scolded him for the 'excessive use' of his mouth to provoke the pitcher.

Jack just shrugged it off, saying, "Yeah, probably so. But I don't like guys intentionally throwing at my best friends. Like he did the last game." While I blew it off back then, now that I thought about it, Jack was right. They *both were* intentional. Shit, it was because of Joanie and her flirting at Judy's party — well, mine too. Autumn said she "dumped him hard" afterwards, wanting somebody different, like me. He had trouble getting me out at St. Ignatius, going 2 for 3, capped by my game winning home run. No wonder he was totally pissed off when that game ended. Jack ragging him today then my two run double. Now pissed off even more!

Autumn clapped for me, "You had all doubles ... three for three, perfect game at the plate." My smiling mother patted and rubbed me on my shoulder, then told Bart and Jack they had good games also. Both thanked her.

Ginny and Judy quickly appeared. I introduced everyone and Judy was beginning to talk to Bart a little, then a lot. Porthos, chivalrous Musketeer that he is, happily responded. Ginny said to my mother that she could tell where I got my thick black hair as hers was very attractive and teasingly nudged me a bit. We all talked for a while and as they were leaving, Ginny said the legend was right, the guys from St. Ignatius were all good-looking. Bart wasn't paying attention as he had Judy's ink pen and was writing her phone number on the forearm of his long sleeve jersey. Ginny patted the long sleeve jersey on *my* forearm as they were leaving, saying, "See you Monday, Autumn. Bye Rich-e-lou. See you soon ... I hope."

Bart decided to catch up with them, after telling us he has a second date with Elke Brückner — a blonde German exchange student at St. Maggie's from Frankfurt. Jack and Camille were going to his house where she would drop him off, drive home and change out of her school uniform and wait for Jack to pick her up. Autumn and I had a similar plan after my mother and I dropped her off.

My mother said happily, "A nice game, Richie. Win one more then it's for the championship."

"Didn't he play great, especially on that high throw from 'The Cisco Kid' and the one hopper from Jack?"

"Sometimes, I think you like defensive plays the best." I changed the subject to the bevy of good-looking chicks, asking my mother, "What did you think of the assorted Miss USA candidates?"

"I really like Camille, she *is* gorgeous *and* funny. Seems like she can keep Jack in line better than your coach. That Libby is very smart and very sweet. Judy is absolutely stunning which Bart had no trouble realizing. Seems like an awfully nice girl too. Your Ginny is also gorgeous, but I don't care for her, Honey," and she patted her hand, "you win out. You have the looks, the style **and** the grace."

"Thank you, Gi Gi. You are always so complementary to me. But why don't you care for Ginny?"

"Autumn, I don't like a girl who flirts with another girl's guy right in front of her. That's not cricket. She's just waiting."

"When Hell freezes over!" The words jumped out of her mouth. She then giggled nervously, "Ooh, did I just say that? Well, she does try to make me jealous. We're not close anymore. Not like we use to be. Richie is too dense to notice her antics," she said pointing to my head. They laughed. Neither of them would have laughed at Ginny's 'antics' at the Dance. She was so blatantly obvious.

※※※※※※※※※※※※※※※※※※※※※※

Judith — Judy — Claire Kingsley decided her senior year she was going to be an international airline stewardess; She would have to wait until she turned 19 1/2 in January of '67 for her age eligibility;

During the interim, Judy went to Wyandotte Junior College year round, taking as many languages as she could for electives and graduated at the winter semester which coincided with the beginning of her proposed career; Dressed impeccably on that snowy day, she was instantly accepted at TWA;

During her eighth year, as Judith managed the three other stewardesses in a very sparsely filled first class cabin, she met and talked with a handsome British Lord as much as she could during the London flight; As he disembarked, he asked her to dinner for that evening, During dessert, she told him her return day and flight number, He re-appeared in first class on that flight with a dozen roses;

They married within a year and Judith became the Lady of Blairford Manor; Lord and Lady Blairford had a girl and two boys, Their eldest — a copper toned redheaded beauty — married a Danish prince

※※※※※※※※※※※※※※※※※※※※※※

Virginia — Ginny, then Ginger — Gail Foster went to Kansas State University, joined a sorority, was first runner up in the 1968 Homecoming Queen pageant; She gave up drinking completely at the beginning of her sophomore year after a night of 'extended boozing', resulting in her experiencing alcohol poisoning;

She and a very concerned pre-med student spent the night together in a toilet stall in a Dickens Hall women's restroom; He helped insert Dramamine suppositories in her, kept her awake and talking, giving her water throughout the night, constantly monitoring her condition;

A week later they had a 'first' date which led to their marriage upon her graduation; Ginger taught high school Home Economics and was a part-time model, putting him through Kansas University Medical School and his Internship; After his residency to be a surgeon, they moved to Leawood and she 'retired', being pregnant with the first of their three daughters; Ginger was adamant that each attend Sunset Heights, a private girls' school, the two married daughters had three girls and two boys between them, the stunning middle daughter 'came out' at KU, marrying the love of her life — her 'roommate' since college — in July 2015 when they could legally do so;

Ginny's explanation for how her 'cat' motif panties were autographed was generally accepted by the Prescott girls as 'terribly vulgar' and 'tastelessly crass', the boys thought it was 'funny' and 'hilarious'
The true version was never really believed
****

As I was holding the car door for Autumn, she said, "Gi Gi, thanks for meeting and sitting with Camille and me. And thank you for putting those jerks in their place."

"What jerks?"

"Later, Richie."

"Oh that was **my** pleasure. I certainly enjoyed all the girl company. Is 9 o'clock too early to pick you up tomorrow morning? DeeDee wants to go too."

"No, nine is perfect. It'll be really great to have DeeDee with us, too."

"Goodnight, Honey."

"Goodnight, Gi Gi."

⁂⁂⁂⁂⁂⁂⁂⁂⁂⁂⁂⁂⁂⁂⁂⁂⁂⁂⁂⁂⁂⁂⁂⁂⁂⁂⁂⁂⁂⁂

A couple of hours later, we were sitting in Blenders. I suppose I wanted to rub in winning with my cocky presence. A couple of the Prescott players temporarily left their dates to come over to talk about the game. My arrogance evaporated quickly — Fielding and Fogarty were good guys. They said Mick had slightly dinged up his hand or wrist somehow earlier in the day. As the game progressed, it worsen. Autumn remarked how odd it was that Pamela wasn't at the game. They agreed, saying it was strange as she was always there for Mick. Both guys said they hoped we would beat St. J.V. I thanked them, wanting that to happen more than anything. As they rejoined their dates, Cozad walked in with a cute girl. Fogarty motioned to the pair to join them. The girl waved enthusiastically at Autumn. As she returned the wave, she commented, "Debbie Jo Barber ... a sweet, friendly sophomore and a JV cheerleader". The look Cozad gave me was anything but sweet and friendly. Still pissed off. And a lot. Probably hopes St. J.V. beats the shit out of us.

"Oh yeah, what's this about some jerks, my mother and you?"

"Your Mother, Camille, Libby and I were in the north bleachers and after you hit your first double, these two jerks came over. One says, 'Hey Knight, why aren't you sitting in the Prescott bleachers. You go to school here.' The four of us ignored him. Then the other says, 'Hey Knight, if you're going to cheer for St. Ignatius, why don't you go to school *there?*' "

"Your mother immediately turned on the pair, to rebuke them in a greatly acidic voice, 'You male adolescents need lessons in etiquette. **Miss** Knight and the other two young ladies, **Miss** Forsythe and **Miss** Campbell are my guests. They are sitting here at my request. Your comments to **Miss** Knight are boorish and infantile. Who she cheers for is her personal business. You failed miserably in noting that she cheers quite enthusiastically for one in particular, the first baseman. Your attitude regarding young ladies also needs immense improvement. Thus, I doubt that either of you are able to obtain a date. A note to your education, **Miss** Knight could not attend St. Ignatius. It is an **all-male** high school.' After she finished, the two looked at each other a little dumbfounded and embarrassed. Ralph Beck, a couple rows from us, yelled to them, 'Hey! Translation for dummies. Go sit down and shut up. Quit acting like a couple of stupid clowns.' So they went back to the other bleacher. I smiled at Ralph who said, 'It's a better view of the infield from here.' He turned back and whooped, 'C'mon Bears, get your mojos working.' The three of us girls thought your mother really frosted those two fools."

"Yeah, she can do that. She probably would have frosted Ginny too if they had stuck around longer. She has become very protective of you. She likes you immensely and thinks in addition to your Miss USA's attributes of style, grace and looks, that you have talent ... real talent."

"Does she really, Richie? Really?"

"Why else did she pick you for *The* Design Project of the decade? She's very punctual. I'd be ready at 8:55 tomorrow morning."

"Oh, I've noticed that. Have you and Hal talked about a movie for tomorrow night?"

"How about The Broadmoor instead?"

"Ooh, goody great! I'll call Jacqueline. Mass on Sunday?"

"Sure. Could I talk you into breakfast afterwards?"

"Mass with you would be wonderful enough. I'd like that very much. You don't need to talk me into breakfast. Of course I'll go. Oh, St. Patrick's *will piss off* my parents no end. And before *you even think it*, I'm going to Mass because *I want to go to Mass.* **With you.** Has nothing to do with them. But it's their tough shit and a damn scrumptious bonus! Hee hee hee."

****

Tuesday was the two-year anniversary of my father's murder. I really didn't know what to do. After I finished breakfast, I simply went over to my mother and hugged her for a few long moments then said, "Mother, I'm so sorry. I wish I could do something."

With tears in her eyes, "Thank you Richelieu. You do. Both you and DeForrest." Then, in a happier voice, "Your little sister adamantly insisted she play hooky today, so we are having lunch, followed by an afternoon matinee of *Paris When It Sizzles* at the Paramount, capped off by some shopping," She smiled whimsically, "I don't know where that girl gets all this determination and obstinacy from. Don't worry about me. I'll be fine. Oh, there's the Carsons. We'll pick you up after practice about 5:30. Good-bye, Forrest." We hugged again and kissed good-bye. I hurried out the door. She would never "be fine". God, though, was granting her the peace and tranquility to deal with her tremendous loss.

※※※※※※※※※※※※※※※※※※※※※※※※※※※※※

On Friday, I was really charged up for the McKenna game. I wanted to beat them, beat them badly. My mother was going to pick up Autumn, then they would be joined by DeForrest when her carpool dropped her off. I had told Jack that they would certainly enjoy having Camille sitting with them again.

Well I'll be damned. The Prick is going to pitch against us.

"Wonder if he can take a little ragging?"

"Might want to be careful. Remember the Coach ... last week," I reminded him.

Bart smirked, "Or even more careful ... remember Camille." We all laughed.

I saw my mother and Autumn walk over and sit on some blankets in the bleachers so their skirts wouldn't get dirty. Camille joined them as we finished infield. Libby couldn't come as she needed to attend a bank meeting due to her large block of shares. Her custodial account had become solely hers — a year early — on her seventeenth birthday. Now without any parental supervision. Certainly Big Rex knew about the block, definitely a substantial part in his plot.

The game started with Bart hitting a single on the third pitch. I stepped into the batter's box, realizing it was the first interaction I had with him since the All Soul's Day phone call to blackmail him. The first pitch was way inside, and I fell to the ground to avoid being hit. The next two pitches were strikes then the fourth pitch was a bean ball. I hurriedly got up to charge the mound but quickly changed my mind. He wasn't worth getting thrown out of the game. The umpire called time, stepped in front of the left side batter's box, and motioned to McKenna's coach who came over. All I could hear was, "One more and … … … …!" Their coach went to the mound with their catcher, John Tobias, who I had met through Karen. The next pitch was a curve outside then another curve, also breaking outside. As I trotted down to first, I smirked, "You always needed a lot of help to hit me!"

Bart took a big lead on second, and taunted with, "Hey pitcher, looks like **you're** being ganged up on. How do **you** like it, Raggy?"

The third baseman was hugging the line and Thomas hit a one hopper to him. Within one continuous motion, he caught the ball stepped on the bag, threw to second base to double me off. The second baseman made a major league-like move — jumping up from the base as I slid in, throwing a strike right to their first baseman to barely catch Thomas. A triple play! I couldn't believe it. If the third baseman had been playing two foot over, we would have two runs and Thomas on at least at second. As I came off second base, The Prick just looked at me and gloated.

When I went to the bench to get my glove and the infield ball, the coach yelled, extremely pissed off. "Nelson! Marlowe! Sanders-Jones! Get your asses over here! Now!" We hurriedly ran to him. "I don't know what kind of shit is going on with you three and Prescott, **and** now even **more** of the same crap with McKenna. But this **shit stops here** and stops **now**. You've lost focus on the game. Any more of this kind of shit from **any one** of you three and I will bench **all three** of you. We could lose this game. And the championship! All because of your God damn mouthing off! Your lack of concentration! Want to play and keep your mouths shut?"

"Play ball Coach!" The umpire shouted.
"Choose! Now!"
"Play, Coach. Sorry, sir."
"Sorry, Coach. No more, sir."
"Yes Sir. No more, sir."

"Good. Now focus on the damn game. Go!"

The game was scoreless for the first three innings. After the triple play, we went down in six straight outs. Bart seemed like he could aggravate pitchers simply by making them throw a lot of pitches to him. This time was not an exception, he fouled off five straight pitches then finally singled. I was going to hit this son-of-a-bitch if it killed me. He ran the count to 1 - 2 then threw an inside fastball which I promptly hit in the exact same place that Thomas did in the first inning. But this time the third baseman was cheating *away from* third and Bart scored and I had a stand up double. I saw the cheering section and there was my sister standing with Autumn, yelling their heads off, my mother and Camille clapped hardily. Then it was the petite blonde's turn to be the head cheerleader as Jack doubled me home.

When our side was retired, Coach Bannister yelled at the three of us as De La Rosa brought Jack his glove, "That's right, get them with your bats, not your mouths."

Bart asked, "Who is that girl cheering next to Autumn?"

"My sister."

"You're kidding!"

"Nope," and I threw the warm-up ball to Jack.

"Oh, God, what a beau..." Bart finished with something unintelligible as he ran to second base.

We kept getting guys on base but we couldn't score again. The lead lasted until the sixth when Tobias hit a towering shot over the left fence for a two-run homer.

Bart started the seventh with a bad swing at a great breaking curve. The next pitch was too far inside, not breaking, but hitting him in the leg.

I wanted so badly to hit a home run off this asshole, but I fouled out by first base. I noticed The Prick was grinning widely to himself. Bart took a big lead and Bush should have paid more attention to him and less gloating about nailing me. Bart stole second.

Thomas singled but the Coach held Bart at third. Jack was up, only one out, *my* out. There was a ball, then a strike. Bart had taken a good lead off third and the next pitch went exceptionally wild, bouncing in the dirt off in front of the left side of the plate, ricocheting off Tobias' shin guard, hurtling to the backstop then careening around it on the first base side. Tobias quickly went after it and Bush rushed to the plate. Here came Bart. The Prick was covering with the left side of his body blocking the plate. Just as Tobias threw the ball, Bart lowered his shoulder and body, plowing into Bush, skillfully taking him down hard, the ball flying past. The Umpire yelled, "SAFE!" As Bush recovered from their tangle, he started to swing his fist at Bart, but the umpire grabbed the Prick's arm and threw him out of the game. Thomas had gone to third during everyone's attention during the action at the plate, then Jack hit a sacrifice fly off the relief pitcher. That was all we needed. We won 4 - 2.

After the final out, the team went to the bench to celebrate and congratulate Bart again on a fantastic "slide" home — more like a downfield block — and I quietly added, "Thanks for taking the Prick Bastard out". I glanced over to McKenna's bench and noticed the Son of a Bitch, all by himself, glaring right at me, making sure I saw him. He had complete hatred in his eyes. So I gave him The Finger, regardless that any of the female entourage might possibly see it.

Coach said, "Great game, fellows. Celebrate this weekend, Tuesday is going to be very tough, but we can do it." Jack, Bart and I grabbed our gloves, jackets and bats and headed to the bleachers to meet all the girls.

On the way, Bart asked hesitantly, "Lou, no bull shit, the really great-looking one is your sister?"

"No, the really great-looking one is my girl, Autumn. In the yellow dress with a white top. You met her at the Wellington game." He elbowed me in my arm.

"Oh, you mean the really great-looking *other* one. You've doubled with Camille and the only *other* one is my mother." I laughed heartily, "She's waaaay too old for you." Now he punched me.

"Okay, the only girl left there, the one with the reddish-brown hair in the blah school uniform. That **is** my sister."

I thought he was going to punch me again. Since we were fairly close to the stands, he could see her clearly and simply said,

"*Oh, God.*" He then quickly regained his composure, and jokingly added, "Thank God, she looks nothing like you."

I introduce DeeDee to Jack and Bart as the girls and my mother congratulated us on winning, especially Bart with his collision and we talked a little more about the game. I noticed Bart and DeForrest were having trouble keeping their eyes off each other. Then he said, "That's a pretty name, a very unique one."

Autumn said under her breath to me, "Is that pickup line a requirement taught at St. Nate's? Seems I heard that exact one."

I turned to Autumn with a big grin and loudly kidding, "Yes, it is ... medieval in origin, I believe, but it *works wonders*." Then I said, "Bart, why don't you, Jack and Camille come over to our house? We'll grab something to eat and have a victory party."

Saying the magic word, "party," my mother's ears perked up even while she was speaking to some other parents. Uttering the magic words, "Bart" and "house," my sister's ears perked up further.

"Excuse me," my mother said to the other mothers. "Oh, children, there's not much there. I became so engrossed in the market today that I forgot to go to the grocery."

DeForrest mouthed something to Autumn who suggested, "Why don't we all go to Blender's."

My mother bowed out immediately, and said, "Danae and I will just find something quick and, besides, we want to watch *77 Sunset Strip*."

Bart apologized, "Lou, I would like to go, but I am really dirty, especially after that fun smash-up at home plate."

Jack followed, "Yeah, I'm all hot and sweaty. Lou, *some* of us did play hard today," and he pushed me cheerfully.

DeForrest was making all sorts of facial and hand gestures, mostly in various contortions of '*Please*' and '*Do something*'.

"Guys, I have an idea, why don't you come over to our house and take a shower there. You can change back into your street clothes and the six of us can go out and celebrate. DeeDee, why don't you ride with Bart in case we get separated. Jack and Camille can follow us too."

DeForrest mouthed a big "Thank you".

Bart said to my mother, "Mrs. Marlowe, if you're sure it's not too much of an imposition."

Jack said, "Really, ma'am?"

My mother said, "Of course boys, it's fine."

I knew the arrangements for the drive home would result in a grilling from my mother. After some talk about the game, my mother waited until about four blocks from the house, laughed a little and said, "Did you set this up?"

"No, he saw her come into the bleachers during the 3rd inning and sit with Autumn, Camille and you. When we were on the bench later, he said she was very good-looking and would I introduce him after the game. I don't think he believed DeeDee was my sister."

Autumn teased, "I thought you guys always had to focus strictly on the game."

I smiled, "Yes, during any game, we always strictly focus on what is *critical*. You know Bart is my other best friend. And remember everything I've told you about him. He's *a great guy*."

"He's very good-looking, don't you think Gi Gi?"

"Autumn Honey, you're right, he is. Richelieu, you watch out for her. Oh, why am I even saying that?"

"Mother, we are just going to get something to eat with Aunt Autumn chaperoning."

"I know, I know. But I can tell he is infatuated with her already. Anyway, I barely caught his line 'that's a pretty name, very unique too.' **Who** uses that? How many times did I hear **that one** on campus?"

Autumn started laughing so hard that she could only point at me, then continued to laugh harder and harder. When my mother realized she meant me, she began to laugh very hard also. I didn't. I meant it. I bet Bart did too.

As I pulled up to the garage, Autumn said now she needed to use a bathroom *immediately* because of all her laughter. Mother told her to use the Master where she could also check on its renovation progress. She ran up the stairs faster than I ever had seen DeeDee.

After Autumn rejoined the girls, Camille suggested that DeeDee might want to change out of her school uniform. She responded,

"There's no way I'm going upstairs to change. The entire second floor will be a boys' locker room in about two minutes. We girls can take turns in the half-bath for what we want or need."

My mother smiled at her show of good manners. If DeeDee had changed, Camille would be the only girl in a horrid, midnight blue, Catholic school uniform skirt and blazer with a white blouse. She would probably look like someone's little sister since she's much shorter than the others even though she's the oldest.

The guys showered, dressed and came downstairs to meet our girls and leave. Camille said she and Jack would follow us as they would leave from Blenders to go to Missouri. Bart said he would leave his car at our house and he and DeForrest could go with us.

There were a few of McKenna players there with their dates, including John Tobias in the next booth. He said, "Great game, even though we came up short."

"Your helluva home run caused us some real nervousness."

"Thanks," and to Bart, "Sorry about that jerk. Always has his game plan, but it didn't work this afternoon. And boy, did he lose his temper completely after the collision. He was livid, went totally nuts on you. Dumb ass, got himself thrown out." I thought of the fight and my beating thwarting his vile plans for DeeDee. Had to have been livid and totally nuts then too. I knew my sister was thinking the same.

****

On Saturday, Autumn and I were back at Blender's with Hal and Jacqueline. I said, "Yeah, school is almost over. I sure will be glad." I was kicked soundly by Autumn.

Jacqueline immediately looked very sad, "I'm going to miss you two a very great bunch."

"I'm sorry Jacqueline! I meant only school, certainly not you! Why don't you apply for another student visa for college and come back to the States?"

"I would like to do that very much. I will tell you two only. My Harold already knows," and she patted his arm, "I am trying now, but it is very hard."

"If you need a character reference, don't ask me ... you better ask Autumn," and we laughed.

While we were talking, I had noticed "The Wicked Bitch of Prescott" and her flying monkey minions, Mary Lou Babson, Neva Smith and Maureen "MoMo" Modica had climbed into the booth next to us. Hopefully, she wouldn't start any shit. I was never in any mood for her after our exchange of scathing insults.

"My Mother and Aunt Danae are going to New York on Wednesday, but I told her it was just for the shopping on 5th Avenue. She said no, it was something about a financial analysts' meeting she had been wanting to go to for a long time. I said sure, uh-huh. Anyway, they come home Saturday so I was thinking about a big party Friday night but that's been vetoed in spades. DeeDee and I can't have **anyone,** except Karen and Autumn, over to the house during that time."

Jacqueline teased, "I believe your mother is very much aware of your designing and creativity in the planning department. She wants her house to be still standing when she returns!"

"Yeah, I'll just wait till they drive themselves to the airport. Then what would a very small party on Friday night hurt? A quiet band, like 'The Silvertones' and only a couple hundred guys and girls with lots and lots of booze. We could charge admission … make hundreds of dollars. I've got it! We'll make a fortune. We can get TWA airline stewardess from their Plaza compound to serve drinks. No, even better, we'll get five or six Playboy bunnies who are in training for the Club's opening next month. Okay, both."

"Oh Richelieu! How do you put up with him, Autumn? He **is** terrible!"

"I only pay attention to him when he is serious which, fortunately, is rare."

"No party on Friday. Flat nobody! No, I have a better plan. With no curfew, Autumn and I will stay out all night."

"I tell you Autumn, he is really terrible. Still so very sweet, but so terrible."

I interjected, "And the French word for 'terrible' is … *terrible*."

"Yes, he is, Jacqui, more than you can imagine." Under the table, she squeezed my leg.

"Not like my Harold." She ran her hand down his cheek fondly.

"Okay, next Friday, why don't we all go to the movies, the Broadmoor or something? I'll pick Autumn up at our usual 7 o'clock then come and get you guys around 7:15 when we can decide for sure."

They both readily agreed, with Autumn confirming, "Yeah, seven it is."

****

After Monday's practice, Jack and I took turns hitting and catching as Bart kept pitching sliders the best he could. Neither one of us were going to strike out on Frost's specialty.

As I walked in the door from the garage, DeeDee said that it was Autumn on the phone. They were still talking when I came back into the kitchen after putting my books near the stairs and she shook her head, smiling, "You are such a lucky devil," and handed me the phone.

I took it and heard, "Your mother is so, so incredible!"

"Hi to you too."

Ignoring me, she continued gushing, "Gi Gi called Mrs. Wallace this morning and said we had an appointment with a lighting expert at Endicott's. Tomorrow at 2 o'clock. Could I please be excused from school at 1:30? So Mrs. Wallace immediately cleared it with the Gestapo. Do you know what this means?"

"You get to leave school a couple hours to go shopping and work on your project."

"No, Silly, it means I will get to watch your championship game tomorrow. After a *brief* meeting at Endicott's, your mother and I are going to Sagesse to pick up DeeDee then straight to St. Ignatius. Your magician mother got me out of school to watch you play! Oh goody great! She is so wonderful. So wonderful, Richie."

Lady Georgie, the magician extraordinaire, strikes again!

"She didn't tell me this! That's great! You will bring me good luck. All three of you will bring me good luck. I'm so glad you'll be there."

We talked some more and I then told her it would be great to see her tomorrow, then told her 'I love you' and she said, 'Good luck in the game' then whispered back 'I love you very much' and we hung up.

I went to my room and prayed fervently to the Holy Ghost to help me play the absolute best I was capable of playing tomorrow. Then I prayed my nightly decade to Him for guidance with Autumn. I still didn't see any way that this situation could ever change. We were still in high school and would be for another year, then college. Then it struck me, there was something in my antique box that would make a great piece to carry for luck. Perhaps when I looked and dwelt upon it, He would, at some time, descend upon me and show me a way. There had to be one. After all, I am supposed to be the Magician.

****

As we finished infield, I noticed that my personal cheering section was already in the stands. Camille and Libby were also sitting with them. So was Father Fitz.

Frost wasn't going to get me this afternoon. He did. I struck out on a fastball that I wasn't sure I saw.

The first three innings went scoreless. We went nine up — nine down. In the bottom of the fourth, the game changed. Bart bunted down the first base side and caught St. John V's flatfooted. My turn and I looked down at the Coach at first base, and saw Bart who gestured to me 'sliders'. After my strikeout on the fastball, I thought the first pitch could be a slider and as it broke down and away from me, I stepped into it and sliced it ten feet over the first baseman's head. It landed about three feet inside the foul line and sailed quickly into foul territory. Bart scored and I had a triple. Greedy me, I wanted an inside the park home run. Autumn and DeeDee were yelling and screaming — even my mother. Camille, Libby and Father Fitz were cheering loudly. Mike Thomas struck out, but Jack got under one to center and I scored easily on his sacrifice fly.

However, they scored in the top of the fifth and sixth. I could only manage to ground out in the sixth. Nothing for either team in the seventh. Extra innings. They started hitting Trent and scored a run before Bart came in as relief with the bases loaded. Unfortunately, they got another run on a single to left and almost got a third but the throw from Harris was perfect and that ended their half of the inning.

We needed two to tie but both Hawkins and The Cisco Kid struck out. Bart singled and DeeDee was really yelling for him with everyone else cheering loudly.

My time.

A curve ball outside, a slider outside, then another fastball strike I didn't see. The fourth pitch was another fastball that I hit, and it went to the same place my triple did, only ten feet outside the line, not inside as before. Then a curve that broke downward. I swung. **I missed**.

GONE ... in less than one second, the game, the season, the championship — LOST. My dream vanished. Gone.

Faintly, I heard the other team celebrating ecstatically at the pitcher's mound. I just stood at home plate. Why? I have no clue. For another at bat? Bart came from first and said, "C'mon. It's over." I told him I had lost the championship for us. He dejectedly replied, "You didn't lose it. We all lost it ... ... Yeah, we all lost it."

I couldn't look in the stands. I just picked up my gear and went into the clubhouse. As I walked dejectedly into the locker room, I wailed loudly, "SHIT! JUST SHIT!"

Coach pulled Mike Thomas, Harris and me aside and said forcefully, "The three of you, quit feeling sorry for yourselves. There are thirteen other players on this team." He then addressed the team, "You guys had one helluva season. You won ten games, you lost only two, you came in second place. You are a young team, two thirds of you will be returning and so will I. It's a cliche, but next year is our year. Oh ... Father."

"Sorry, I didn't mean to interrupt you Coach Bannister. But I just wanted to say you men did well today as you have done all season. A good fight until the end! You never quit!"

And he blessed the whole team with a Latin benediction. Could have been in German, Chinese or Martian, I still felt like shit.

"Father Fitzgerald is right. You never, never quit. That says something about your character. And your spirit. This year was extremely *good*, next year will be great!"

"Thanks, Coach Bannister, for coaching us. And just helping us," said Mike Thomas and we all chimed in to thank him for everything.

When you lose a championship, there is nothing to say except, "Shit," which I said a few more times. Neither Bart nor Jack felt much better. We showered and dressed to meet our girls.

As the three of us were dressing, Jack's attitude had improved considerably and said to Bart and me, "We need to quit pouting like little girls. Shit, Lou, you and I got the RBI's, and Bart, you and Lou scored the runs. If the Three Musketeers didn't do anything, it would have been a seven inning shut-out. A whitewash. The big null set! Next year! Besides, I've got this beautiful, little blond babe who can hardly wait to get her hands on me. Bart has this great-looking auburn-haired chick who can't wait to see him, especially on Saturday night when he can take her out without a crowd in tow. And you, Lou, have the tallest, most gorgeous, golden brown-haired fox I have ever seen in my life who is just waiting to console you with love and kisses. Damn it! Next year! One for All!"

All three of us started to cheer up, "And All for One!"

There was Autumn and my mother waiting for me and trying to smile for encouragement. So was DeeDee for me but also Bart. And Camille for Jack. Libby was already consoling Harris.

Jack's right, the world had not ended. It was only a ball game. Right? Yeah, but the BIGGEST of my life. We lost.

I still had Autumn. And there were my Mother and DeeDee and Aunt Danae.

My father's here, telling me I had done my best. Yeah, there would be a 'next year'.

****

I ended up taking my mother and Aunt Danae to the airport after I came home from school on Wednesday as my aunt car was towed to Macek's garage with a badly leaking fuel pump. They had an early evening flight to New York.

Right before they boarded, my mother reiterated her instructions to me for about the tenth time. "Remember, we are staying at the Waldorf, Paine Webber's apartment, if there are any problems, the phone number is on my desk. Call Macek's Friday from school to see if Danae's car is ready to pick up. ... I'm sure they'll have repaired it and it will run perfectly. There will be *absolutely no parties*. Nobody can come over except Karen." Reluctantly she said, "Autumn *could* come over."

"Oh, Mother," I interrupted, "she wouldn't come over anyway … because you wouldn't be here. Don't worry."

Mother smiled, "Richie, there is money in the top right drawer of my desk in my Quo Vadis appointment book, if you need it. We return—"

"Yeah, I know. TWA Flight 192 on Saturday, arriving at 11:30. DeeDee and I have it all down. You forgot to say study hard." I kissed and hugged both, telling them to have a great time seeing the Broadway shows and shopping, and the New York Stock Exchange, Analysts Meeting and shopping and not to forget shopping. They boarded the plane and left on time.

****

"It's Friday night. Aren't you and Karen going to some big senior McKenna party?" I asked DeForrest.

"Yeah, we were. But she has some relatives she hasn't seen in years who are visiting from Ohio. They're staying until tomorrow then driving to California and Disneyland. I'm still not quite sure how we got invited. Neither of us know either of these guys, only by sight. Karen's feeling was, 'so who gives a shit, it's a great chance to meet some cool studs, *virtually* college guys. Hopefully horny too.'"

"You girls' fame and beauty has spread far and wide."

"Another one of your bullshit lines, Richie. What are you and Autumn doing tonight?"

"Going to The Broadmoor with Jacqueline and Hal."

"Well, I'm going to my room. Maybe study. Later, gator."

I went into the study to get some money for gas. I couldn't remember where my mother said she would put some extra money. I searched around. Nothing.

"Dee?" I yelled, hoping she could hear through her closed door. No luck.

Then louder. "Dee, where is the money Mother left us?"

There was a loud knock at the door. Without thinking, I opened the door to an overly made up, grinning Caroline Cunningham clad in a trench coat. "Wah-la! Heeere Eye am, Spesh Delivery."

She unfasten her coat and quickly peeled it off. Caroline's all black attire was straight out of Fredrick's of Hollywood, consisting of a rhinestone ribbon around her throat, risqué bra and panties, garter belt with hose and high heels. Utterly erotic and thoroughly arousing.

"Jesus Christ! Get in here before the neighbors see you." I pulled her inside and locked the door. Drunk, there was no telling what she might or might not do on the front lawn. "Caroline, you've been drinking again! A lot?"

"Nawww ... ... well yeeeah ... own-leee some gin-gin for the mooood. But no fags toooday. Just like you said you wanted me. ... My breath and everything else fresh soooo we can French each other allll night long. You can give me a herd of hickeys on my tantalizing tittties and my thrilling thighs. Annywhere else. 'Cause annything you want tonight is yours. Jusst take."

"OH GOD! GO IN THERE!" I pushed her towards the study then followed her, yelling, "**DEFORREST, PLEASE**!" Then to my unwanted guest, "What in God's name are you doing here? I'm still going with Autumn."

"But are ya going **with-IN** Autumn? Never will! You're not her kind. Heheheh! She wants mooore clothes and stuffff from you. But you won't give her more 'cause now ya know she's just been using you. Sooo the gold-digging bitch and you are breaking up."

What the hell is she talking about?

She flatten each hand angularly over her pubic area. "Unlike your prissy pisssy pincess, you can watch me *spread ... these ... legs*. You'll be amazed by your e—NOOORM—ous treeeat between them." She flopped on the couch, easily shifting to strike a lewd, tempting pose.

I yelled, "**WHAT**! What the hell! Who told you all this crap? It's all bullshit. We haven't broken up. We have a date in ten minutes."

"Some spesh-al friends. **They know**!"

"They don't know their ass from third base! They're full of shit." I went to the door of the study, shouted as loud as I could, "**DeForrest, help me! PLEASE! NOW!**"

I turned to a smiling and sprawling Caroline, back braced against the arm of the couch, legs spread-eagle displaying her inner thighs. The crotch of her panties was pulled sideways, fingers fluttering to fully expose herself. An image of the French-Vietnamese whore popped into my head, but instantly vanished, displaced by the **real** presence of what was spread open in front of me.

*OOOOOOOH GOD! ... ... **SHE'S SO**...*
OH GOD NO! NO!

I screamed, "**DEFORREST! NOW!**"

I shut the study door, rushed through the hallway into the living room — to get far away from "my treat". Then I heard a key in the front door and began to panic, thinking it was my mother and aunt had come home early.

No, it wasn't them. INFINITELY WORSE! Autumn and Jacqueline were coming through the doorway.

OH GOD! NO! NOOO! **OH GOD HELP ME!** *OH GOD!*
Can't talk ... ... Can't talk.

Autumn said, "Rich? Aren't you ready yet?" As both girls joined me, off to one side, she continued, "Come on, let's go to Blender's. Hal's sick, so I brought Jacqui—"

The door to the study had swung wide open. Out strutted Caroline with her breasts invitingly bared, twirling her bra as she half-pirouetted to show the back of her panties below the garter belt. Embroidered with the red wording of "Rich's ASSset". She continued to badly bump and grind while she excitedly begged, "It's all yours, now gimme..." When she completed her turn, only then did Caroline see Autumn and Jacqueline, but not before lustfully craving, "...**that big, hard—**," instantly freezing for a few seconds then quickly scampered back into the study.

"**THIS ... THIS SLUT ... HERE? Oh, I know why!**" She was screaming and she began to break down sobbing loudly. She wailed, "**She's your whore! Your WHORE!**"

Finally I was able to move towards her, but she cried out hysterically, "**Don't you touch me! Don't you ever touch** me again! I hate you! You God damn Prick! Caught with YOUR WHORE! You cruel, cheating Bastard! OHHH, I HATE YOU! HATE YOU! OOOOOW!" She ran out the door.

Can't think.

Can't breathe.

Within a few moments, there was a blur following her out the door, then another. When I dropped to my knees, I don't know. I felt like somebody had just ripped my testicles off. How long I just knelt there, I don't know either. Somebody came back into the house. Followed by someone else.

DeForrest's incensed voice shouted from the study, "Get your skanky, naked whore's ass off that couch! Put every **damn stitch** of your clothes on! **Here Bitch!** ... ... My brother will never touch you, tonight or any other night. **Stay in this room** until I come and get you!" The study door slammed loudly.

"Richelieu, what the hell is goin' on? What **is** happening?"

When I didn't respond, DeForrest continued to yell at me.

"Damn it, WHAT?"

"**WHAT?**"

I could only babble, "Dunno."

"I didn't have enough clothes on to come down. When you started shouting, I was almost undressed for my shower. I put my clothes back on in the upstairs hall, during which I saw the whole damn mess, including the bra whirling while **it** pranced around. What the hell is **that naked THING** doing in our house? Why was Autumn—"

My brain began to slowly function again. "I don't know. Honest to God, I don't know. No idea what Autumn was doing here. Jacqui too."

Jacqueline put a hand on my forearm, squeezing, "And I am still here for you, Richelieu."

"We chased after Autumn, but she was too quick and peeled out. Jacqueline grabbed that little slut's clothes out of her car and I found her trench coat and saddlebag of a purse off to the side of the porch in the bushes. I threw all her clothes at her. **And** that little whore better have **all of them on**." Turning to Jacqueline, "Do you know what in hell is going on?"

"This whole scene is not real." She pointed to the study, "Richelieu, you would never have a girl **like that** here anytime. And DeeDee, more incredibly not so … with you here **and** not after you called to tell Autumn to come over."

"**I did what**?" DeeDee was shocked.

"DeForrest, Autumn said **you** called at about 6 o'clock to tell her Richelieu was having trouble with the Galaxie. Could Autumn drive tonight and pick him up before seven? He still might not be ready, so just let yourself in with your key and yell for him. Autumn said sure. I called Autumn about 6:15 to tell her Harold has become ill. A slight 'food poisoning'? Is that not right? Anyway, Autumn says I cannot stay home by myself tonight. I must go out with Richelieu and her. She picks me up and here I am. What is happening, DeForrest?"

"A nasty, nasty, mean bucket of shit, Jacqui. First, I never called Autumn."

"Second, my brother was shocked to see that little slut! He tried to make her stay in the study 'til I could come down and get rid of her. But noooo! Shameless bitch does her topless little dance strut."

"Third, there's nothing wrong with *either car*. Rich just got Aunt Danae's car back from Macek's after school. Hmmm … but Autumn wouldn't have known that."

"Richelieu and Autumn have been set up in some sort of a terrible scheme. Jacqueline, will you stay with Rich? I'm going to get Autumn, explain everything and bring her back here."

I regained my focus. "Dee, you don't have a license. Neither does Jacqui."

"I'm going Richelieu! Don't **even think** about stopping me! She is **never** going to talk to you. Not after **that little whore's** exhibition. *I will* talk to Autumn. *I will* convince her of this scheme against you two! *I will* bring her back here! This shit is so unbelievable! Jacqueline, please go talk to that … that stripper slut. See what she knows about setting my brother up." DeForrest flew through the kitchen to the garage.

Jacqueline and I went into the study. Caroline was fully dressed, looking very sadly at a pint of Seagram's Gin on the table next to her. Even though the bottle was almost one quarter down, she seemed reasonably sober as Jacqueline started talking very sweetly with her soothing French accent, "Caroline, sweetie, would you tell me how you knew to come to see Richelieu tonight?"

"Rich and Lou? Oh, I certainly know Rich. Who is Lou?"

"No, no ... just Rich. Who told you to come here tonight?"

"I got a call last night from my friend Sheila Rhodes. She has been really nice to me this last month, especially after apologizing for all the shit she's said about me this year. Said she was sooo wrong, just so wrong about me. 'Just a wild Catholic girl, but definitely, certainly not a slut'. But really extra nice this week, telling me she wants to make amends by finding a way to help me get back together with Rich. She thinks he and I would be perfect together. So last night, she tells me there is great news. She found out a rumor that's true. *But not to say anything*! A couple nights ago, Rich was told by that bitch ... she needs more pampering ... like buying her more clothes, more gifts, going out to expensive restaurants more, doing the stuff she wants to do. He's got the money, so he can afford it. He finally figured out she was just using him, so he's going to break up with that gold-digging bitch."

She wailed, "**Which I know now was a gigantic crock of Shit! I wanted that and everything else to be true. Oooohh, so much.**"

She calmed down some, "Her Asshole boyfriend, that Roland Bush, was with her. He had found out about Rich's coming breakup with the bitch from Bush's summer ball teammate and Rich's neighborhood buddy and best friend ... Mick Hayden ... when he ran into him at the Best Cleaners yesterday afternoon. **More lying shit!**"

"God damn them! I'll cut that fucking prick's balls off! Shove them down that cock sucking cunt's throat! Watch her choke on them!"

"*Tais-toi*, **Richelieu! Ferme ta putain de bouche! À PRÉSENT!**" [Shut up, Richelieu! Shut your fucking mouth! NOW!]

She continued in her quiet voice. "Go on, Caroline."

"I should hear it straight from him, so she puts Roland on the phone. He said, 'Rich started talking to Mick about us together at the movies, the Lake party, the dance on All Saints, and the Winter Wonderland Ball."

Caroline turned and looked at me, "Remember Rich ... Oh, how I wanted you. Desperately! At the dance. Even begged you at the Ball to feel me up and finger me ... anytime, anywhere."

She continued with last night's events, "He said you miss me an awful lot. That you still wanted me badly! So badly. But you messed up by telling me I had to quit smoking. **Completely**! So you would give in ... just no smoking on dates and when we're together ... *like I told you* I did for you tonight." Caroline yelled again, "**A God damn pack of lies! All God damn lies.**"

I thought she was going to lose her volcanic temper, but Jacqueline reasonably calmed her down, soothing and rubbing her shoulder.

"Said Mick knows Rich sure wishes I could somehow magically appear at his house this weekend since his family is out of town. Mick said if I really want to get back with Rich, I should come over here tonight about quarter to seven ... 'cause about seven, he and Rich are going to a Santa Fe Trail mixer and find something slutty to pick up and play with. Roland thinks I should surprise Rich. Wear something sexy. I think nothing but black undies, right? I'll show Rich what real girls do, not fake shit like that frigid bitch only does! So I'm to call Bush, let him know everything that happened, but only after we had our first nookie. He wants to call Sheila after her play tonight to give her the news."

She paused and looked longingly at the gin bottle. "I asked why he was helping you, Rich, after your terrible fight last fall. He felt that he was really to blame. Your sister had just broken up with him and he was really pissed and wanted to get even. Baited you with some raunchy, made up shit about how he had her always under his thumb ... made her keep her pube hair shaved ... banged her all the time, rag or not ... shit like that. This was his way, thru Mick, to try to make amends. He sounded really sorry, you know, like you are when you go to confession."

"Oh Rich, I really blew my chance with you last September. I wanted to get back with you so badly. But I never saw you. Then, there you were at the All Saints' Day hall dance. I was so damn hot and horny ... ready to leave with you ... ready to do **anything** with you. But you ended up in the hospital. Unbelievably, I heard you were going steady with that frigid bitch. At Winter Wonderland Ball, I couldn't believe it. Got to dance with you, but I was so shit-faced drunk, I almost puked my guts out all over you. Tonight I made up my mind. Somehow, someway I was going to screw you so fantastically, you would want to keep screwing me not just tonight but *forever*," she wailed forlornly.

Jacqueline's face remained impassive so I spelled it out, "Good God Caroline! Couldn't you see that Bush and Rhodes just were manipulating you like the guys you date. Those damn football players. College guys you just met at some party who pick you up. They all use you! See how far they can get with you!"

Caroline ignored my comments, "When I talked to Lorraine during this week, all we talked about was you. She convinced me that I had to realize something. That ... that *I was in love with you*! I've always wanted you so badly. She said she knew it because every time I broke up with a football player, I would always talk about you ... how I wanted **you** to screw me. But not any one of them. Know she's right ... 'cause look at her and Dale, they've been screwing for *bunches of weeks*. Right before they started, he told her he loved her terribly ... so much so he said, without a doubt, he'd marry her sometime this summer. Screwing would only strengthen their love. She told me after we got back together, to bang you anytime and do anything you wanted. Said if I did, you would definitely, completely fall in love with me too like they did. Rich, I know you've always **wanted me**. Oh Rich, **I love you**!"

"Caroline, *sex by itself* isn't my idea of love!" Instantly, the impending storm clouds unleashed the tornado, striking with its fury.

"FUCK YOU! **You Fucking Bastard! You were always with that FUCKING CUNT. ALWAYS! Every fucking time I saw you**! Cruising up and down State, in Zesto's, at Blender's, the Indian Head. **Everywhere! Always with her**! When I got the guts to call you, sometimes the God damn line was busy. Probably talking **to her**! Or your General would answer and I'd hang up. I would drive by here just to see if you might be in the yard and you were ... twice ... **with her**. She could have had any God damn guy. **Any guy**! But that half-queer bitch picks **YOU**! The only guy **I** ever really wanted ... that I love."

She grabbed the gin, downing some quickly. "Those God damn holier-than-thou Rainbow Cunts! Always acting so pure, so innocent, so Blessed Virgin-eee! NONE of them are! That brown-haired cunt is AC/DC ... absolutely keeps it really, really hidden. Maybe why the bitch only dates any guy a few times. But I know Rich is incredibly wonderful so she stays on her straight side for him. Phyllis Prince claims she knows about this dyke, last summer, named Jewel or Sproule from St. Catherine's who heavily made out with her before the two did MORE! Lesbian stuff! Her queer side. Guess that makes her a Lesbyterian Presbyterian. HA! And the other two! They haveta hide being such *real* sluts! I know that for sure. That redheaded bitch is the biggest prick tease in the city, thinks she walks on water. *So la-di-da.* 'I'm only a junior but already made Homecoming Queen and a cheerleader.' And that hypocritical blonde whore thinks every time she bats her eyes at any guy, she gives him a hard-on. Which she would grab if she gets the chance. I hate them ... **every FUCKING one of them**."

Suddenly, Caroline radically changed her demeanor, acting sad and forlorn, "Running around here, Rich ... mostly naked ... talking dirty ... **showing you** what no guy's dick has ever got to taste. What do I get? A damn audience!"

Then she desperately pleaded, "Please, Rich, you can't think I'm some whore screwing every senior football player or college guy who picks me up. **I'M NOT AND I DON'T**! I know I have a rough, dirty mouth. And they've nicknamed me Christmas Carol **Cunt**-ingham because I'm supposed to be this easy piece of ass every guy on the first date feels up and within weeks, screws. **But I'm still a virgin**. You would have seen **my proof** when you broke my cherry* wide open tonight. I would have done **anything**

---

*A widespread misconception among teenagers in the '50s and early '60s was *every* girl had a **hymen** (or the vulgar slang — **cherry**) and barring some rare physical misfortune, it remained intact until her first intercourse when it would bleed very tellingly so

... anything at all to get back with you. Both that prick Bush and the mean, cock sucking cunt knew that. They set me up. **They fucked me over like I was their whore**. Sadistic Shits! **They used me**. And they ... they broke ... my heart."

She burst into tears, body shaking, chest heaving. I didn't say a word. I didn't know what to say. I **just** didn't know what to say. I felt sick to my stomach. While Caroline continued to cry pitifully, Jacqueline put her arms around her and stroked her hair, trying to soothe her.

※※※※※※※※※※※※※※※※※※※※※※※※※※※※

DeForrest told me later that night what happened when she went to Autumn's. When she came home, Autumn told her mother she was sick and going to her room to lie down. Her mother said she would be up when *Burke's Law* was over. Autumn began to cry again and couldn't quit. DeForrest said she arrived about twenty minutes later and interrupted her mother's detective show again. She went upstairs to Autumn's room, but found her in the bathroom. DeForrest closed the door and knelt beside Autumn next to the toilet bowl. She had become so emotionally distraught she was now physically ill. Retching a few times, then began to vomit. During her bouts of throwing up, DeForrest wiped her mouth off with a damp hand towel. All the while, Autumn had grasped her locket to protect it. She finally was able to quit vomiting but still continued to cry.

"I know **he** sent you here! Please go away. DeeDee, I don't want to talk to you. I never want to see **him** again!"

DeForrest implored, "Autumn Honey! It was **my** choice to come here. This was a trap designed to split you and Rich up. *And I can prove it.* I saw the whole thing.

Poor Richie was utterly clueless when it all happened. He's completely innocent. Jacqueline is grilling that little whore about her involvement."

"Oh God forgive me! I forgot all about Jacqueline. She must think I'm terrible."

"She understands you're in a lot of pain. She'll do anything to help you and Rich. Honey, we need to fix you up, go back to our house, get this sorted out."

"Rich was set-up? I was set-up? But I can't go back! *I can't face him!*"

"You have to!"

"No! No! I **can't** do it!"

"Damn it, Autumn, *you must*!"

"**I can't**. I wanna die! Just die. **Right now**!"

"**God damn you Autumn! Quit whining like some little grade school crybaby! Get off your damn ass! NOW! We will fix this.**"

"But I've lost him. Probably to that ... that slut. I told him I never wanted him to touch me ever again. Oh God! How could I? I love him to touch and hold me. I called him vicious, cruel names! Vile names! Oh God, he probably just ... just hates me. **SHIT**! Told **him I hated him! Ooooooh Shhhhit**!" And she started to cry again in heaving sobs.

DeForrest then put her hands on Autumn's shoulders, squared her up, looking her straight in the eyes, "**Enough of this sniveling little girl shit!**" She strongly shook her with firm determination. "**Enough! If you want Richelieu back, quit acting like some poor, whiny bitch! Listen to me**! He never touched that whore. Oh, I'm sure he had his chances. My brother still loves you, regardless of what you said to him. Look ... I have never told anyone this ... **anyone**. But once I said some very ugly, mean things to Richelieu and called him vile names too. They were even worse than what you said. I was cruelly hateful and vicious to him. All he was trying to do was simply protect me. He forgave me immediately. He never stopped loving me."

Autumn hugged DeForrest until she could stop her whimpering. She began to think out loud about losing me and the tremendous pain it had temporarily inflicted on her. "Even if it's not true, I have to do anything to keep him. Summer told me this ... Judy too. There are some guys who have their steadies ... good girls, nice girls ... for dates and parties, you know, for the cool, swell stuff. When they want 'something,' they find a tramp, a piece of trash, like that little *whore* or that Valgina and ... and, oh ... oh shit ... *they go all the way*."

"Honey, my brother is not one of those guys. We both know that. Let's go home. Need to change your blouse though. It's got puke on it." DeForrest picked a clean blouse from the closet and exchanged it with Autumn for the soiled one. While she cleaned up the bathroom and stuck the dirty blouse in the linens hamper, Autumn put on the new top and she began to redo her face.

When they were both ready to leave, DeForrest said, "Oh, I drove here illegally, so you have to drive back ... legally." Autumn half-laughed as her tearful bout had dissipated. On the drive back to the house, DeForrest explained the entire story to Autumn about dating the dominating Bush, their "activities," especially how she unleashed her verbal barrage at Richelieu in the hospital, her terribly arguing with their mother, being severely lectured, finally ending with a candid, explicitly intimate discussion. A harsh, yet loving mother—daughter talk.

****

Jacqueline and I were sitting in the living room trying to plot revenge. I told her I had to find a way to keep Bush home, then some way to temporarily isolate him from his two flunkies. I apologized to her for my outburst of language.

"Ha, Richelieu! I just gave you some back. I can make not only Autumn blush but sailors too. You have heard me, uh ... uh ... 'let loose' that other time, so you know. But has Harold? Only a 'damn' or a 'hell' ... and quite infrequently. **We must** keep it like that. Oh, the distraught little girl is resting now, 'sleeping it off,' I think it is called. I feel very sorry for her. She was so terribly used, so abused. They **knew** whatever they told her regarding getting back with you, she would believe and, unfortunately, she would do." She vehemently continued in French, which signaled intense profanity, "those hideous fucking monsters ... that **repulsive cunt of a poxed whore and—**"

Jacqueline stopped as we heard the front door open. DeForrest walked in the room, "There is someone who needs to talk with Rich."

Jacqueline and DeForrest left quickly as a tearful Autumn rushed in the living room, "Oh Rich ... I'm so ... sorry. Don't hate you! I love you!" She burst into tears even before I could put my arms around her, "Called you ... vicious ... names. Told you never

... touch me," and her tears fell quicker, "Love your touch ... just can't bear ... you touching ... another girl. No ... you can't ... you just can't ..." She wailed pathetically, "Ooow. I hurt, Richie. Make me ... feel better. Like you ... always do. Oooow!"

I still held her tightly and she tried to compose herself enough to continue, "You must ... take me ... back! Oh God, please tell me you'll—"

"Victoria, Victoria," I interrupted, "We never, *never* left each other." But her crying persisted, heavily for moments. "Nothing's changed. Victoria, please don't cry. You didn't mean it ... you were only reacting to this damn Charade. I still love you ... very much."

During the next few minutes, I continued to hug her tightly and kissed each cheek a couple of times. I wiped her final tears away, telling her, "Everything is fine now. With a little help, I'll fix this. *For good!* We were set up by that slut Rhodes and that prick bastard Bush ... whose dick he undoubtably shoves invitingly between those willing, hefty thighs."

"What? How?" she sniffed.

"Remember last week ... we were in Blender's and I said that my mother and aunt were going to New York this weekend? But neither Dee or I couldn't have a party or anyone over but Karen and you. Well, remember the Bitch and her toadies were sitting in the next booth, and, I guess, taking in not only all my fanciful plans for tonight but my serious ones too ... my mother and aunt driving to the airport ... your pick up time. Front door opened or locked ... didn't matter. Everyone knows you have your design project key to the house. Couple of days later, Dee and Karen get invited to a McKenna party given by two really popular senior guys who they only knew by sight ... to get her out of the house. But they didn't plan on Dee not going at the last minute. Or Hal getting sick and Jacqui coming with you."

"Thank God for Dee and Jacqui! Where is that ... that *whore*? Is she gone?"

"Not yet, we may need her."

"Shit, I don't need her. I don't want that **thing** around!" She squealed painfully, "**Not you ... especially**!"

While Jacqueline quickly filled Autumn and DeeDee in with, undoubtably, an edited version of the conversation with Caroline,

I went in to check on her. She was sleeping off the booze and hopefully, some of her mental pain. I truly felt sorry for her and thanked God for my father and mother who always immensely loved and cared about DeForrest and me. Not like her indifferent parents with their pathetically low expectations of "just don't get pregnant" and "grades good enough to graduate".

When Jacqueline finished, Autumn was still quite hurt as she explained to the three of us, "I just didn't think anything was fishy when that bitch Rhodes imitated DeForrest. It was an excellent job. However, she called Rich, 'Richelieu' which was slightly off. DeeDee rarely calls you Richelieu."

Autumn sniffed loudly, "If they could have pulled this dreadful scheme off, that Bitch would have exaggerated and lied, spreading it all over school Monday 'you won't believe what Rich Marlowe got caught doing with the football team's whore right in front of Autumn Knight.' I would have been so devastated, so horribly embarrassed. I would not have been able to finish the school year, exams or not. Rich, I never would have spoken to you again. *That Little Whore* would have gladly gone along with whatever was said to insure she would have finally gotten rid of me. Beaten me. Then made her whore's play for you repeatedly, until you..."

She started to cry softly. "Oh, thank You God, so much for DeeDee and Jacqui." Both DeForrest and Jacqueline began to hold her, calming her.

I left the three of them. It was now after 8 o'clock and I needed to go upstairs. While I was changing into some old clothes, I realized I needed to formulate a solid plan. I had to figure out how to keep the Prick home, maybe with Caroline's help. That son of a bitch had deeply hurt and messed up DeeDee months ago — her pain goes on and on — won't end. Now Autumn. Time to mess up and deeply "hurt" him. Bone-deep.

I grabbed "Little Lou" from under the bed. Little Lou came into existence when I broke my first Lou Gehrig. From the knob to where the bat had cracked in two, there were about 12 or 13 inches of solid wood. I took it to the Offutt woodworking shop and asked if someone would cut off the fragmented pieces and polish up the end. The airman knew exactly what I wanted it for and did a craftsmanship job. Next, I went to my antique box, found the felt sack under some papers, slid the set out and put them in my jeans pocket.

As I went back into the living room, worrying, "Got to figure out how to keep that piece of Shit home for maybe an hour, at least a half hour after Caroline calls him."

Jacqueline sighed heavily, "I know how to take care of that. Does anyone know his phone number?"

DeeDee reluctantly responded, "Yeah, it's Atwater 2 - 8284."

Autumn softly asked, "Rich, what are you going to do?"

"I am going to beat the shit out of him. Badly. Real badly."

I thought she would argue with me. Try to talk me out of it. She didn't.

Jacqueline dialed the phone and Bush answered immediately, probably waiting for Caroline to give him a report.

"Hello, Roll-e," she began very syrupy, "This ez Jacqueline Cartier from the choir at ze Cathedral." She continued speaking in a heavy French accent, not her normal slight one. "Unfortunately, I will be going back to Par-ree so soon. Never to see you again. I need to before I leave away. I have a very nice present for you."

Bush clearly then asked where was Hal as she faked hot anger in her voice, "***Le grand fils de la chienne***! Awww ... **Big Son of a Bitch** and I had such huge fight earlier tonight! Broke up with me because I am leaving away! That is why I am calling you." Her voice became sweet again, "I have seen how you are looking at me after choir practice. I know what will make you really sing. But I have to give it to you tonight ... very soon too, or I am afraid," as she faked giggling, "*never, ever*!"

Bush obviously wanted a hint. She replied, "Yes, I tell you what it is like. Oh, it is warm. It is nice to stroke and pet." A terrible thought raced through my head of what she was planning as she explained further, "*Ma chatte douce et soyeuse* ... my silky, soft pussy. I have learned from one of the best madams in Par-ree ... so I was skillfully taught how to pleasure your cock. Like it has never been."

Bush evidently wanted confirmation of his gift. Jacqueline quickly replied, "Ha! You will be fucked so expertly, so thoroughly.

You will never experience another girl's attempt close to mine for the rest of your life!" She laughed seductively yet falsely, "Must be tonight. I will be flowing blood shortly, maybe tomorrow. Never during blood times. Hurts too much. I cannot perform flawlessly for the full male gratification." When my shock wore off, I wondered with Jacqui talking so knowledgeable, had she really had some sort of training? Was this madam real?

I looked at Autumn. She had gone from pale coloring to a deep, full red. Her mouth had dropped wide open. I looked at DeForrest. She had even colored considerably and looked stunned.

Bush must have quickly agreed with the necessity of tonight with its assured 'activity', then asking about his buddies. "Oh no ... they can only watch." She said amusingly, "Tell your boys they will enjoy seeing my talents being displayed. But, as you Americans say, **no ganger-banger**. No one more."

She then finished in her still phony, thick accented words. "Okay, in forty-five minutes, maybe an hour? I must be home before midnight. I will be parking in front of your house. When I am ready for you, I will honk twice. All right then, until the honks."

She hung up the phone, retching some, then took some deep breaths. "I think I am going to vomit up. *Oh mon Dieu! Mon Dieu. Quel putain de salaud lubrique!* [Oh my God! My God. What a fucking lecherous bastard!] But that will keep him at his house for a while! Oh my God in Heaven, he is so sickening. You should have seen the way he would leer at me after choir practice. When I would leave ... as girls say, 'a guy looks at you and quietly is undressing you with his eyes' ... well, this pervert instantly strips you naked. I was going to quit the choir because of his indecent looks at me, especially for long times at my tits. But the singing was wonderful and I always had a ride with Marilyn Marinovich. So I put up with his few minutes of nauseating ogling. He is a nasty, nasty piece of *merde* ... er, shit! A putrid turd who bubbled up out of a smoldering, colossal heap of reeking male shit! Richelieu, go beat that Prick badly. I am sorry, but I cannot drive. No license. *Oh mon Dieu!* Harold! You cannot tell Harold **anything** about tonight! I really like him so very much. Much, too much for him to know this. He would not understand. He is so moral, so strait-laced."

"Jacqueline, not one of us will ever say anything about your involvement in this. You have our word. If that Shit says anything about you, nobody will believe him. Way, waaay too out of character for you. But my glorious French femme fatale, you have created **the perfect plan** to isolate the Bastard! That's brilliant how to get him in the car by himself."

DeForrest immediately offered, "I could drive her in Aunt Danae's car and either get out or get into the back. But, Rich, there are three of them."

"I've a better plan. Part I of this Charade, I'll call Musical Cars and thank God we have both of them. Dee, you will drive Caroline home in our car. Follow me. I will drive her car. Give Autumn your key to drive Danae's car with Jacqueline to follow you. Then Dee, you and I will hide the Galaxie on the south side of the park so they won't see us. Autumn pulls up in front of the Prick's house, switches places with Jacqueline. Then Jacqui turns the dome light on, drawing attention to herself ... like checking her makeup ... and away from a slumped over Autumn who opens the passenger door and crawls out of the Chevy by the curb, then sneaks down the park side in the shadows to stay with DeeDee in the Galaxie. Turn the light off afterwards. Whenever, you ... Jacqueline ... think it's best to start the show, honk twice and turn the dome light back on ... *keep it on as long as you can.*"

"How are you going to take out three guys?"

"That's Part II — Julius Caesar. Jacqueline, I hate to ask you this. You have to make sure when that shit Roll-e gets in the car with you, he keeps his two buddies outside and him inside. So lock the doors and keep him in there as long as you can. I will start with the one on the driver's side. Neither one of them will take long. After I get you out of the car, go to DeeDee and Autumn. I will take care of the Prick Bastard."

"It will be easy," she forced a smile, "but please be quick, I might vomit up." She began to apply extra eyeshadow and mascara, quickly transforming her distinctively attractive look into a slightly slutty, yet such an enticing one.

Shit, now I need to go wake up Caroline for her call. Hope she'll cooperate. Not lose that terrible temper of hers again.

Almost right on cue, she came out of the study smiling. "I just woke up and called Bush the Bastard. The prick who lied to trick me, so I lied to trick him. I told him you and *your goody great virgin*" and she glanced at Autumn with a venomous look, "are beyond finished. She caught us," she continued slowly, provocatively, "your hand *very lovingly* caressing one of my **lusciously large nipples**," demonstrating as she fondled one of her breasts over her blouse, "with your mouth sucking like a Hoover on the other one. My ample, so **eager beaver**, openly poised as your divine dick easily slid into me, **fucking me so gloriously**!"

Autumn had strongly flinched, then taken a couple of steps towards her, hesitated for a second, turned away and quickly ran out of the room. Unfortunately, she heard the entire detailed lewdness, especially Caroline's finish. I could tell both DeeDee and Jacqueline were utterly disgusted. Jacqui could be extremely vulgar. Autumn and I had once heard her greatly obscene retaliation to a couple guys' extremely smutty comments. That was in a manner of utter *contempt* or now a lewd, risqué *play acting of necessity to nail the sonuvabitch* not for hurtful, viciously taunting verbal porn. Dee started to follow her, but changed her mind.

"After Miss AC/DC ran out ... like now," she snickered, "you confirmed the rumor wasn't true, except the part you two are certainly, totally finished. You were going to really miss her as you still liked her an awful lot, but she never seemed to have much of a desire to do any sex stuff. Told you that my perfect pair and pleasing pussy will make you forget that switch-hitting bitch quickly. You laughed, said, 'Think you're onto something. Let's find out. Again.' Bush wanted to know where you were and I said you were fixing us something to drink while I took another piss and cleaned myself up. Needed to get my snatch spiffed up for you and our next nookie."

She continued in a bragging tone, "Then the lecherous Bastard propositions ME, 'I've always fancied your terrific tits and that splendidly firm, superbly round ass ... **bet** you're a dynamite piece in the sack'. I said, 'I'm only Rich's. Thought you liked to spread Her Royal Chubbiness' plump thighs then blow your wads into her porky muff? He said in a dirty tone, 'Yeah, I *bang her anytime* I want. Oh, and I'll *bang you* this summer. You'll love my technique. Especially **my size**. Now I've got to get ready for my treat ... a French apple tart lay,' laughed real filthy-like and hung up. Don't know exactly what he meant, but I *know exactly* what both 'a tart' and 'a lay' are." The girls continued to ignore her crude remarks. "Can I go home now? *And* I want the rest of my gin back."

"Just a little while longer, Caroline ... when I'm sure you're sober enough. And you're not driving anyway. Why don't you go lie down some more?"

"Still can't get laid," she laughed bitterly.

Five minutes later, the string of Musical Cars left. After Dee drove Caroline home, I walked her to her door, thinking about the last time I did — seemed like a hundred years ago. I gave her the car keys, told her to quit smoking, to *definitely* quit drinking. Find a guy who loved *her for herself*, not just how he could use her body. She promised me she would. She knew I was going to retaliate but she would never say a word — not to any of The Stray Pussycats, not even her best friend Lorraine — the only other virgin until the fireman came along. Since she had been so cruelly duped and exploited, she would look like a dumb, stupid broad — but above all, she wouldn't because of her "real feelings of her love" for me. She would say she figured it was all lying crap when Autumn open my front door tonight and you were telling me I was full of shit by saying those things about you two breaking up. Told me to go find a football player since I was their whore. The bitch just laughed at me.

She was terribly embarrassed since her "Nookie Plan" ended abruptly with her mostly or fully naked in front of girls and not just only me as she desired so much. She hurt a lot — all she wanted was me. I told her I knew. I was sorry. Regardless of all the shit tonight she was duped into, I still liked her a lot. She again stood on that first step of their stoop, hugged then kissed me on the lips, saying thanks and began to pitifully cry. I broke away, hurriedly leaving. I knew Autumn saw everything, but she never said a word. She wouldn't.

****

When Jacqueline turned on the car's dome light, I saw she had slightly turned and was doing something with her arms which would totally shield Autumn and opening the door. The light went off for a few moments then Jacqueline honked twice. While the gang of perverts came rushing down the hill from his house, Jacqueline again flipped the car's dome light, signaling she was ready for her show to begin.

Bush immediately hopped into the passenger side, exclaiming loudly, "**Christ**! **Knew your tits were dynamite**! **Light copper nipples**! **Oh Man**!" Then he slammed and locked the door. Only later, did I understand Bush's vulgar exclamation. She had stripped off her blouse, easily shielding Autumn while she got out of the car. Underneath was a completely transparent bra with only minimal lace edging around the cups — she was visually topless.

My assumption was correct — one shit, Billy, on the driver side window, the other shit, Ronnie, on the passenger side. Both just drooling for the action to start. Billy was completely riveted on Jacqueline as she turned past the steering wheel towards him, giving him a full view. With this enticing preview happening and anticipating an entire strip show, complete with a promised high-voltage fornication, he didn't hear me as I approached. I swung Little Lou, giving Billy two particularly hard shots to his rib cage. A split second later, I struck the side of his knee. As he was falling, I slugged him solidly in the eye with my two fingered brass knuckles. He began to moan loudly.

When I rushed around the front of the car towards Kovac, peripherally I saw a dumbfounded Bush, trying to peer out the windshield to see was happening, however the light from the dome was greatly hindering a clear view. As it went off, DeForrest swiftly appeared by the passenger door.

Kovac had figured out he was next and began to run. Suddenly, Autumn appeared from out of the shadows and tripped him. As he scrambled to get up, I squarely hit him in the nose with my left hand, blood spraying everywhere. With my right, I whacked him with Little Lou three or four times, all very solid, hard shots in the ribs. He stayed down, crying in pain.

Just as I had finished off Ronnie, I saw Bush try to unlock the passenger door and get out, but Jacqueline was pulling on him, trying to yank him away from the door on the inside and DeForrest was holding the passenger door shut with all her strength on the outside. Bush slammed Jacqueline hard with both hands, smashing her into the driver's door, yelling "fucking frog cunt". She screamed in pain. I had already yanked my keys out to unlock the door. When I jerked it open, Jacqueline halfway fell out of the car, moaning in French. I grabbed her to help her stand up, then she staggered around the back of the car to DeForrest, who helped her as they joined Autumn in the shadows and trees of the park.

The Asshole's pair of buddies were starting to slowly hobble away up the street. I shouted at him, "Quit crying and get out, you scared little Cunt! Get Out! The Douches for your rancid Pussy won't be coming to rescue you this time!"

After a few moments, he finally confronted me. His stalling had purpose. He had unscrewed the large California Custom T handle from the gear shifter on the floor and came at me with unexpected fierceness. He hit me in the chest then immediately on my left shoulder with it, both stinging like hell. However, in the same instant, I had blasted him in the leg twice with the club — a hard, direct hit on his shin and the other a glancing blow to his knee. They were enough to drop him to the concrete pavement as I fell backwards on top of the car's hood. Recovering first, I slugged him in the jaw with my left, knocking him back to the curb. He reached out and tried to hook one of my ankles with his left arm to flip me off balance and down to the street with him. That failed, giving me a few seconds edge when he started to swing the T handle to smash my kneecap. Little Lou hit his right hand very hard, knocking the gear shift handle out of his grasp, delivering a solid crack of bone, accompanied by a shriek of pain. Instantly, I struck the hand again, more viciously, wanting to hear more of his pain and was rewarded with another crack and a howl of agony.

He turned to crawl under the safety of the car. Before he could get there, I bent over him, bashing him on the left side of his chest three or four times in quick succession, bellowing, "For Jacqueline! My Mother!" He fell over on his back, cradling his smashed hand and his injured rib cage with his good hand and arm to somehow soothe his intense suffering. His face contorted in agony, whimpering.

"For my Autumn! And DeForrest!" as I dove on his chest with a knee-drop. He was still screaming in pain from it as I pounced on him for a second time.

When I got up to knee-drop him again, he choked out, pleaded, "God, no more! ... I'm sorry! Sorry! ... No more! Please!" Ignoring his begging, I started to jump on him again. Then I became aware of someone to the side of me.

Thwack!

DeForrest kicked him dead-center in his scrotum.

Sthump!

His meager reflex action didn't protect him from her rapid, vicious stomp with her boot on his genitals.

As he writhed in extreme pain, she leaned over him, screaming savagely, "**You pathetic, slimy cock sucking prick.** Think about how your balls and dick feel now the next time you plot to entice some poor, innocent girl to spread her legs so you can **rob her virginity from her**."

Like a silent spectre, Autumn suddenly materialized again from the shadows. She stomped on his mouth, then twisted her heel to grind his lip into his teeth. Shrieking hysterically at him, "**Or the filth you spew out this wretched mouth** when you think about cooking up some vile scheme **with that venomous cunt of yours**!"

As Autumn faded back into the darkness, Jacqueline immediately kicked Bush's eye, yelling, "**Filthy Bastard! Finally saw my tits naked**, **eh**?" She moved around to strike him close to the other eye, screaming, "**Fuck you! And your fucking eyes**!" She spit profusely on his face until she ran dry of saliva yet still continued trying for a few moments.

We left the pathetic weasel loudly sobbing and moaning, imploring God to help him with his pain.

❊❊❊❊❊❊❊❊❊❊❊❊❊❊❊❊❊❊❊❊❊❊❊❊❊❊❊❊❊❊

Roland Oliver Bush obtained an Accounting Degree from St. Benedict's College, upon graduation he went to work for the Archdiocese;

Ten days later, he became engaged to the delightful, good-looking Jean Haley, Lasted only two months; Jeannie caught Bush crawling back into *her* bed with the mostly nondescript Michelle Lowe, not only one of *her* roommates but also one of *her* bridesmaids; He had just stuffed Michelle's pair of black panties into his hastily thrown jeans on the floor;

He worked tirelessly for the Archdiocese for fifteen years, having become their chief accountant after ten years; On the second day of a Diocesan Mission trip to Rio de Janeiro, he disappeared; Fearing the worst, his associates notified the authorities; Before the Rio police arrived, a wire was received at the Hotel stating $173,205 in Diocesan funds were missing; The Wyandotte Police investigation later found he had obtained Brazilian citizenship and learned to speak Portuguese;

Bush was last seen during Carnival in 1995 at the Copacabana Palace's Crystal Room with a beautiful, big-busted, blond-haired thirtyish 'companion'

❊❊❊❊❊❊❊❊❊❊❊❊❊❊❊❊❊❊❊❊❊❊❊❊❊❊❊❊❊❊

DeeDee collapsed into my arms and had begun to cry softly, moaning through her tears, "Richey Rue, Richey Rue." I felt a sharp pain in my shoulder and a deep burning sensation in my chest. Hurt like hell, but she needed me badly. I needed her. Autumn more. Jacqueline too. When I put my left arm around Autumn, the chest pain heightened, yet I manage to growl at all three of them as Jacqueline came from the Chevy, having retrieved her mauve silk blouse out of the backseat. "Damn it girls! In what language does 'Go, stay by the Galaxie' mean 'C'mon, get in the God damn fight'. Any of you could have been hurt. Hurt seriously. Damn seriously."

Autumn was visibly distraught and her eyes were glistening with tears. She seemed to be on the verge of collapsing. She somehow stammered out, "The Magician ... of the Charade .... needed help." She tensely giggled but her voice quivered, "**Your girls agreed** ... give you our strength in our hands ... our feet ... our breasts."

I was astonished and thought it strange when Jacqueline made no attempt at modesty while trying to put on her blouse. After a second failure, a slightly shaking Autumn held it for her as Jacqueline happily chimed in, "*Oui*, why should you have all the fun, eh Richelieu?" But when she slowly slid her left arm into the sleeve, she noticeably grimaced. Autumn buttoned up her blouse but could only do so fumblingly.

"Yeah, you're right. I did need all your help. But it's done. Let's go home."

Autumn and Jacqueline were slow to retrieve the Galaxie, finally pulling it behind the Chevy and got out. My poor little Dee was still tightly holding onto me but was able to stop crying, telling me she was okay yet felt drained. She then joined the other two to kiss and hug. They were relieved it was over, telling themselves "they did their jobs and did them well". Jacqueline added, "Oh oui, nous étions de superbes Amazones. ... Yes, we definitely **were** superb Amazons. Such magnificent Amazons."

When I helped DeeDee into the front seat, she curled up, resting her head on Autumn's right thigh. I asked, "Autumn, are you all right? You still seem rattled. Sure you can drive? With Dee like this?"

"I'll be fine," she assured me and appeared to be recovering somewhat.

"Your '10½' did a brilliant job to stop that Kovac shit. Nice facial footwork on that Son of a Bitch."

She frowned crookedly, gently stroking DeForrest's hair, "It was the only time in my life that I have felt the overwhelming need to inflict any type of pain. I'm not pleased with myself at all about what I did. I don't like the feeling. Not at all. Not a bit. I feel tainted and dirty. ... I betrayed ... ... myself. But **you needed me** to trip that bastard. And **that prick monster** needed to be punished and ... well, hurt and humiliated. He deserved worse. So much worse. ... ... But these awful, ugly feelings of mine still persist and—"

DeeDee told me later that Autumn stroked her hair for the entire ride, quietly crying all the way to Jacqueline's and almost to our house. Evidently, it was only then did Autumn finally start to truly recover. They never spoke. DeeDee, herself, said she never felt quite right until the three of us were driving to Autumn's.

Bush had now crawled to the park sidewalk, still in agony — bleeding and crying — about forty feet from the cars. As Jacqueline and I drove past him, he looked up, hoping it was his buddies. She put her right arm out the window, hand already in a fist. As she raised her forearm, she slapped her biceps, groaned painfully, but managed to yell in French that he was "a loose, watery shit spurting from his whore of a mother's syphilitic ass". During a French class last winter, Father LaCroix had translated "The Finger" into that French gesture along with other graphic sayings. He didn't mention this one. Another Jacqueline Cartier colorful creation. The French Catholic girl contemptible insults were exceptional — just sheer, raunchy poetry.

A few minutes later she quietly said, "Richelieu, you should know this," continuing in a very serious tone, "while you were calming and soothing Autumn, DeForrest told me that this whole terrible incident with Autumn and you brought back all her agonizing memories regarding Bush. Sounded like she has been suppressing them. She told me the whole story of his controlling dates, your fight, the hospital blow-up and your mother counseling her. What the devious bastard had already enticed her to do and your telling of his plan for his conquest of her. Hopefully, stomping ... uh ... aww ... *la bitte et les couilles du trou du cul* [the cock and balls of the asshole] will wipe away all her suffering from that whole ordeal. Like the Ancient Greeks called it ... a catharsis. The poor girl started to tear up but was relieved to tell me she both admires and greatly looks up to Autumn and me. My other American sister, my little DeForrest. And Richelieu, I couldn't have kept that perverted Shit in the car without her holding the door too."

After parking in front of her house, I walked Jacqueline to her door. Autumn and especially DeeDee were too distraught to try to say good-bye again. There would be tomorrow. As she pulled her keys out of her purse, she grimaced, with a yip of pain.

"What's wrong? I **knew** you were hurting. When you tried to put your blouse on. Oh God damn it, this is my fault. What the hell happened?"

"That *Merde* grabbed my hair and yanked me into the steering wheel which severely hurt my arm. Held me there while he turned off the dome light from a knob on the dashboard. He couldn't get out the passenger side because of DeeDee. So after slapping me, he drove me terribly hard into the car door, slamming my breast straight into the door handle. Then tried to yank me out of his way but you opened the door. My breast will be fine. I hope both it and my arm aren't bruised a lot ... **OH MERDE**! Oh Shit, just SHIT! I will need to tell Harold something ... like I tripped and fell against the dresser in my room." She continued unashamed, "He would certainly notice my pain and see the bruising when he begins to touch and kiss my breasts tomorrow night."

I acted like I ignored her plans with Hal, but I had seen a deeply redden, thin rectangle on one breast. "Sorry I had to involve you. You didn't have to tart yourself up. *And taking off your blouse.* Which you virtually exposed your—"

"Oh my sweet Richelieu! Hah, my tits are exactly what that *horny, lewd Shit* wanted to see naked and to feel bare in his perverted hands. And *a lot more*!" She gestured to her genital area. "As I always say, 'When guys see something that turns them on, their cocks swell and harden up quickly to do their thinking for them.' Gave you some extra time to deal with those yearning, swollen little boys. No, Richelieu! It was my chance to help you. You needed me desperately to set the trap by being the 'bait' for that Bastard. I doubt if **my** tricking that *merde* plus the kicking and stomping **my two sisters and I** inflicted **and** the horrific beating **you** gave that disgusting bastard and his two repulsive cunts of poxed whores was worth it to see my exposed tits."

"Was your bruised area already hurting since you're going to start your ... your..."

She began to snicker, "Oh my darling Richelieu, I will not be bleeding for two more weeks. You are always *so sweet*." She leaned over to kiss my cheek. "Also, I would not know about menstrual intercourse..."

But regular intercourse? Bet so. Before America, some 'lessons from a madam'. If Hal and she go that far ... she'll make it believably 'virginal' ... complete with a fake cherry.

A moment later, I sort of laughed, "I have never met both a more tempting, convincing, yet mendacious mademoiselle with that phone call or more seductive, ensnaring movements to keep those three distracted. They positively were focused on your ... your—" Having trouble about verbalizing Jacqui's physical monthly non-occurrence and now her breasts — but certainly not visualizing them. No wonder she had those pricks' eyes riveted onto hers. Mine were too before she finally succeeded by replacing her blouse but only with Autumn's help.

God, what an absolute killer chest! Believe she wanted me to see them. Breasts so perfectly round and big ... gorgeously full with penny colored nipples ... so fabulously lovely!

Yeah, but what girl's naked breasts aren't so fabulously lovely?

After a moment, she put her hand on my forearm, and in a distraught voice, "Please, just tell Harold we had a wonderful time cruising around and stopping at Zesto's or something else." She intensified her grip, "Oh, something better! Richelieu, he **can't** find out! **I beg you, Richelieu**! Give him a bunch of monstrous bull shit! But so credible! Please?"

"Oh, he won't!" I promised. "Hal will never hear such a tale as I will spin tomorrow night. You just follow my lead. I know a great place for dinner, the French restaurant ... Lafayette's and you tell Hal it is definitely my treat ... that I lost a bet to you on some French history thing. **I promise you** with all my heart, he will **never** know anything about The Charade or how you really got bruised. You need to put some ice on ..." finally stumbling out with, "your area."

"That filthy *enculé* [cocksucker] with his lewd looks at my breasts. The times I caught him mentally salivating. Always upset me. You laid into and beat that *Merde* **for me**. Watched and heard, then *I kicked him. Cursed him. Spat on him.* It was immensely healing for me. My own catharsis. The bruise is a small price. I am fine and I will ice **'my area,'** Richelieu." She laughed after she emphasized my word choice.

Even though we lightly hugged, it still hurt my chest, certainly hers as well. I kissed her forehead. Then she kissed me as we began an unmistakably lengthier and deeper kiss than a friendly parting one should be. Our mouths were slightly open and for a brief, yet lingering moment, Jacqueline's tongue entered to touch mine. It wasn't accidental. After we mutually ended the kiss, we said goodnight.

As I walked to the car, I knew the long kiss with its "accidental" French touching would have to be considered only "heartfelt friendship," yet my thoughts begin to contemplate the what-ifs as I had done numerous times before. *What would have happened if Jacqueline had joined the choir before All Saints' Day? Would we have fallen in love? Or become 'unusually close' friends ... like now ... ... a 'friend' who French kisses? Uh-huh! Or would she just taken that fantastic bod, great personality, looks and brains back to Paris to stay?*

Only Fate knows.

But I was in love with Autumn and she probably was with Hal. I realized that when she became panic-stricken and thought he would find out about tonight — her topless show, looking every inch the wildly hot, enticing slut.

Hal, you lucky, lucky dog! But I'm definitely an incredibly luckier 'lone wolf'. ARH-WOOOOOOOOO!

We dropped off Danae's Chevy at the house and Autumn wanted DeeDee to go with us to take her home. She had her head against my arm and shoulder and DeeDee had hers likewise on Autumn's. They held hands to comfort each other. We all got out of the car and DeeDee and Autumn tightly hugged and kissed each other, telling each that they were true sisters.

At her door, I said, "This was the shittiest night of my life but everything is fine now, Victoria. I always have loved you. I believe ever since that Saturday I met you in Ball's. I just didn't know it."

"It was the shittiest night of my life too. I'm sorry I ever doubted you," but she frowned slightly and shook her head a little, "but you did have a drunken little whore ... parading in and out of your mother's study ... virtually naked, behaving like the slut she truly is. Oh Richie, she wounded me so terribly with that explicit, foul-mouthed description about you and her which she wished could have happened. Oh God! Such nasty shit. Just filth ... like she is."

She gave her head a little shake again like she was trying to toss the memory away. "I was actually going to slap her. But I didn't. I couldn't hit her. I just couldn't. I just ran out. She wanted me to smack her. That little whore truly wanted to hit me. She wanted a real fight. She's a ... a ... as Jacqui would say .... **the repulsive cunt of a poxed whore**."

She hugged me tightly which caused me a lot of pain. However, I was in the shadows and remained silent with difficulty, so she didn't notice my grimace. "Tell Dee, if she had not come over, I don't know what I would have done. She helped me through my pain, like your mother would have. Oh, I definitely saw your mother in DeForrest tonight. She was so strong, so intently focused. An excellent stand-in." She now laughed happily, "Gi Gi Junior even called me Honey. She is fine now as she has worked through *her* pain. I love her. And **I love you so much**."

"I will tell her," I promised. "Tomorrow night will be terrific ... we are going to Lafayette's with Jacqueline and Hal." She brightened up some. "I'm going make up some huge bullshit story about the three of us tonight. I'll call around noon, get some sleep. You've had a real rough, traumatic night."

Suddenly she exclaimed, "I almost forgot! This was lying in the street by the front of the car." She pulled out the T handle gearshift from her purse.

"Oh thank God! Thank **you**! I realized it was missing when I drove to Jacqui's. There's no way I could have explained to Aunt Danae how her personalized gear shifter had disappeared." I slightly tilted her head down, kissed her forehead, then on her lips. "I will always love you." She smiled and went inside.

DeeDee was curled up in the seat and on the way home, she rested her head against my arm. "Autumn has that warm, sensitive presence and wonderful outgoing personality. So spiritual, just ethereal. Jacqueline is just so cool, with that quiet way of understanding and acting. But what an absolute deceiver! I am completely in awe of that performance in her two act play ... simply fantabulous! Tonight, I separately told each of them everything about **that** night including Mother's extremely adult talk with me. After all this shit started tonight, I needed to tell someone. Those two, I knew, would understand intimately. And they did. They both were extremely warmhearted in their compassion. So were you that morning after." And she kissed my cheek affectionately.

"Rich, but why, 'Poor Caroline?' She **knew** what she was doing. She even told me when I drove to her house that had you 'wanted her on the side', she would have happily been 'your little piece of tail'. **And still** would be. Just ask! Richie, she still figures that's how she will take you from the 'Miss Goody, Goody' who she claims is **a real switch-hitter**. Repeated again … why would she only date guys for a few times and limit making out? Except you … you must really turn her straight side on. Phyllis Prince, truly the queen of sluts, says she knows she's AC/DC for sure. So I told her that she was terribly mistaken about Autumn. That pissed her off … called her "a rare occurrence" Lesbian in deep hiding, so nobody will know. Said she wouldn't be surprised if "that nice French girl and her aren't sweethearts. Always together, especially in a toilet for the longest times". I let it go. With that temper, **plus** she was drinking again, I didn't want to totally piss her off where she would somehow screw up the plan. Then she started on the Rainbow Girls. That's when the **real** raunchy crudities and coarseness began. Incredibly obscene! Made Karen sound like a nun. Oh Christ, she hates them, especially Autumn! And how!"

"That poor little girl gets lied to and fooled all the time, like in tonight's conspiracy. She was atrociously set-up, used, maltreated. In a way, she is very naive, almost like a child. When she gets passed from one football player to the next or gets picked up by some horny college pseudo-stud, she thinks it's a sign of being popular, and *it is* … for all the wrong reasons. She goes on to the next guy, hoping he will treat her much differently, believing whatever shit the jerk tells her. I really hope she finds a nice guy who will truly love her for who she is. Her parents never give her an ounce of praise or encouragement. She doesn't have any self-respect. Desperately wants to be truly popular and thought to be ultra-cool. She'll never find it in either gin bottles, cigarettes, trashy makeup, horny football players, college bull shitters, hanging out with sluts or hating the truly popular girls."

✻✻✻✻✻✻✻✻✻✻✻✻✻✻✻✻✻✻✻✻✻✻✻✻✻✻✻✻✻✻✻✻✻

Caroline Jane Cunningham fell crossing the stage at her graduation ceremony, Fortunately, she didn't hurt herself, perhaps because she was drunk;

Four days later Caroline was married in a small wedding at St. James's Church, she was three and a half months pregnant — the marriage was short-lived; Within two years, another brief marriage as a result of a second pregnancy, then another ugly divorce; She continued waitressing & drinking;

At 24, finally acting on Lorraine Jacobs' persistence and strong encouragement, she joined Alcoholics Anonymous and sought mental counseling; Becoming knowledgeable of Step 9 of the Group's tenets, Caroline contacted a newly pregnant Autumn during that Christmas season to contritely and humbly apologize; She was quickly unconditionally & completely forgiven during their long talk that one snowy afternoon — the two remained friendly thru the years;

After two years of her sobriety, she married Wesley Bauer, another recovering alcoholic, Caroline was truly happy in her third marriage, had a third girl;

She was very successful in her legal secretarial career at Ellis & Mullins, hired by Danièle Richelieu at Autumn's insistence soon after that Christmas; On her 33rd birthday, she was promoted to be the firm's Office Manager, responsible for the legal secretaries and the accounting group;

C. J. Bauer died a month after her 56th birthday from lung & pancreatic cancer; She had never quit smoking

✻✻✻✻✻✻✻✻✻✻✻✻✻✻✻✻✻✻✻✻✻✻✻✻✻✻✻✻✻✻✻✻✻

    I changed the subject as she scooted over to sit shotgun, "Are you feeling better? You've never hit anyone, let alone stomp the shit out of a guy's dork and balls."

    "That Prick was always controlling, always in charge, but I was in awe and simply amazed by him. I was a new little sophomore with a mature, smart, good-looking, athletic, cool senior. Which made me so *incredibly cool*. I was positive he was in love with me and just knew I was with him. Consequently, I did sexual stuff with him for which I am so totally, totally regretful."

She paused, then reluctantly started again, "But I did them. And **too damn many times**. Even so, I know I wouldn't have let him ... uh ... **screw me**. That long night, during Mother's talk, she made me realize how scheming he was, how cruelly vile he really was. **And still is**. Mother made me finally realize if I wouldn't go all the way willingly, he would have **raped me**."

"**WHAT**?" My blast made me inhale sharply, painfully.

"Oh yes, Richelieu, without a doubt, he certainly would have raped my virginity right out of me. And what's terribly, seriously wrong, that Bastard would have gotten away with it. There is no way in Hell I would have told **anybody**, certainly not Mother **and especially not you**. I could have only prayed fervently to the Virgin NOT to be pregnant. Then my pain and feelings of utter shame were exacerbated by that lecherous old Prick Bastard ... making that move on me ... his repulsive touching me at Sagasse."

"I felt so humiliated and ashamed, wondering why I had been so deceitfully used, then salaciously hit on ... like I caused it all to happen ... that I subconsciously welcomed both Shit Holes ... started to think I was sorta 'damaged goods'. Kept thinking what the hell is wrong with me? I've the looks, the body, and the brains. Why can't I attract some really wonderful, decent guys? And my luck ... until just recently ... didn't get a damn bit better."

She drew a deep breath, "Never told you this ... remember that Herb Travis from St. JV's? The guy I was beginning to really like? On our third date, he starts to feel me up through my sweater and I told him, 'No!' On the next date, he tries touching me again. I said, 'No, we're not doing this.' Minutes later he tried again ... his final time ... I slapped him, grabbed my stuff and ran inside the house. In bed that night I cried myself to sleep ... I was starting to feel something special for him ... but it was too soon for *that*. What really hurt was that he never made any attempt at an apology or explanation ... just hands all over my tits which I yanked off ..."

Thought my luck changed with Ewell ... a cool, good-looking St. Nate's basketball senior stud. Nope! *Worse*! My first and only date … the Prick had been drinking and bragging at the party about his scholarship to Villanova, then we parked. He stopped bragging long enough to make out. Moves his hand under my sweater. I pulled it out. Later, he moves it under again, quickly slides up my midriff, gets *almost* underneath a cup to forcibly shove it off me so he could grab and feel my breast bare. Like if **his magical basketball hand** astoundingly 'scored' my stripped breast, I'd miraculously change my mind and he could 'play ball' with my naked beauties to his dick's content. What a *conceited Shit Hole*! Slapped him as hard as I could. Yelled at him I had enough of his shit with his attempted bra invasion and **him**. Scrambled out of his car, called him 'a Pompous Prick,' hurried to Jake's Barbecue, called home on their pay phone. Aunt Danae came and got me.

"Same with that other senior basketball star jock, Carlton Smith, the Prescott Prick. Great first two dates with him, then he starts feeding me some real bullshit lines on the third one. We had only **started** making out and he went for one of my breasts. Twice! When I pulled his hand away the second time, he told me to quit being frigid. Just loosen up. He would make me feel so good. Smacked him hard, called **him** an arrogant Asshole, and stomped into the house. Another *conceited Shit Hole*."

She brightened up considerably, "So, yeah, tonight wasn't the first time I've whacked a dickhead. Haha! First time I *literally* did one though!

DeeDee became serious again, "I certainly attract guys easily, but like Autumn's philosophy … none were worth dating beyond the first or second date. And I've gone through a bunch of those. Thank God, Bartlett came along. He's such a great guy. I reeeeally like him. He *really likes* me! I can tell. He's so nice and considerate to me. My losing streak is completely broken. Oh yeah!"

"But getting back to tonight's shit. I'm glad I stomped that Prick's nuts. I hope I cracked them good. Crushed his dickie, too. Now he'll stop with those gloating looks and knowing stares, like he's given me the couple times I've seen him since *that* night. I would involuntarily cower. But no more! I've turned the final page of that sordid chapter. It's over. Feels like I just got out of a long, soapy hot shower, followed by a calming, perfumed bath."

She was laughing in her teasing fashion, "Okay, Richey Rue, what do we tell Mother and Aunt Danae?"

"My Little Dee, definitely the full truth ... all of it, in its colorful entirety ...

> One ~~ A drunk girl in a ribbon and high heels, wearing a sexy black bra, panties, garter belt with hose, poses provocatively on the couch, yanks her panties sideways, spreads herself en-tireee-lee open."

"**She did what? Jesus Christ, what an absolute whore**! I don't care how much you defend her, Rich. That's real whoring! Just **begging** for it! Oh God, **spreading open** ... your ... your ... **vul—** Ugghhh! Yuck! Makes me wanna puke."

"Well, **spreading herself wide open** certainly got my *full ... complete ... total ... undivided attention* for more than a few moments."

Shooting into my mind were the memorable images of catching a very thin fringe of Rusty's fiery red pubic hair, mistakenly thinking she had, in absolute modesty, pulled down the side of the high waist of her bikini bottom to proudly display her entire butterfly to me. The tattoo of that specimen was so unbelievably sexy. Positive she caught me gawking at those slender flames shooting from her burning bush since she hastily yanked up her high waisted bottom. That so slight, burning border and her full tattoo made me so incredibly horny for her that last week of summer and continued for weeks even after she broke up with me for that jerk during the first week of school.

Those two images quickly evaporated as I remembered Autumn and implored, "Dee, you can't tell Autumn! Book of Secrets! Swe— "

"Oh, I swear!" She quickly interrupted, "Bag poor Autumn's red faced embarrassment! Oh God! Think how it would devastate her! It's bad enough for that whore to describe her fake porno act, wishing about you and her *in front of* Autumn. It's something entirely different to actually try to 'get it goin' by showin' her...' ... uh ... **herself** to you. Ick! What a totally, totally disgusting **Slut! Yuck**!"

"But to continue Dee,

Two ~~ Breasts bared, twirling bra, display her decorated panties, saidgirl again blatantly offers self to me while unwittingly parading in front of Autumn and Jacqueline ... you from the landing

Three ~~ Autumn becomes hysterical and falls completely apart

Four ~~ I become numb, go into shock and fall completely apart

Five ~~ You put me back together

Six ~~ You drive to Autumn's without a license

Seven ~~ You put Autumn back together, bring her to the house

Eight ~~ Jacqueline's unbelievably lewd, obscene proposition of the Prick

Nine ~~ You drive to Caroline's, still without a license

Ten ~~ Jacqueline, fetchingly slutted up, strips off her blouse, exposes her breasts to entice the Prick and his little prick pals

Eleven ~~ I beat up and scare off Bush's two chicken shit buddies

Twelve ~~ I thoroughly pound the living shit out of Bush

Thirteen ~ ~ You try to insure the Prick can never have kids

Fourteen~ ~ Autumn tries some dental work on the Prick

Fifteen ~~ Jacqueline tries some eye work on the Prick then covers his face in her spit."

"Oh yeah, that works, but you can add another one ... around point Five. Your 'drunk girl' was *completely, totally naked* ... braced against an arm of the couch, legs crossed, so only her curlies were showing. Thank God for that! That skanky slut still was waiting and praying for you to show. Then I threw her clothes at her and told her to get dressed. Ugghh! Just yuck! I'm never sitting there ever. Never, *never*, **never**!" Then as an afterthought, she added, "Oh, for the record ... her 'Rich's Ass-set' panties are a big-time Yeech! Just so gauche. If you want something sexy *and* tasteful, get a pair in ivory with pearls and lace."

That was DeeDee and her clothes — even for lingerie. I laughed and shook my head. And that even hurt. Walking in the back door into the kitchen, I moaned, "Damn it, my chest and shoulder are killing me. And getting worse! The adrenaline is long gone. I need to get some ice on both places." I put the gear shift handle on the kitchen table. "Never saw this in his fist."

"Well, there's blood all over your sweatshirt, jeans and jersey. It's evidence. Give 'em to me and I'll wash 'em."

After I gingerly peeled off my old short sleeve sweatshirt and my baseball jersey, I sat at the breakfast room table and put a towel full of ice on my seriously bruising chest. DeForrest held another ice filled bath towel to my shoulder, having given me a few of the remaining painkillers from November along with a few cookies and a coke. She began to relate all Autumn's pain and suffering that had taken place at her house earlier and their subsequent drive to the house.

"Honest to God, Dee, I don't know what I would have done without you tonight. If I didn't know better, I would have thought it was Mother handling the whole situation. You were *extremely* strong and very decisive tonight, exactly like she is. Autumn said she saw her in you also. Later called you Gi Gi Junior. You softened her pain. You pulled me out of my paralysis. You helped Jacqueline hold that Bastard in the car. It would have been nearly impossible, if at all, to get back with Autumn without you taking charge, explaining everything, providing her with the right comforting for that incredibly sensitive nature. You are the best sister a guy could ever have. You have always been there for me, especially when I needed you the most."

"Saying I was strong and decisive like Mother is the best compliment you have ever given me in my entire life. Thank you, brother." She bent over to kiss my cheek.

As we walked a little slowly to the stairs, she hugged me very lightly then we kissed each other good night. DeForrest told me to remember to throw down my blood flecked jeans.

She was going to thoroughly wipe down the couch, especially the back and arm of the sofa with some soap on a warm, wet towel then check the Galaxie and the Chevy and replace the gear shifter. She would wash that towel, the other towels in the kitchen, my bloody shirts and jeans. Before I took off my jeans, I pulled out the two finger brass knuckles from my left pocket — my "graduation present" from the Drill Instructor. I put on my robe and, as ordered, threw my jeans over the railing. I rinsed the blood off the small "duster" set, dried it very meticulously, put it back in its felt pouch, then into its place in my antique box. There was some spots of blood on Little Lou, but I decided to leave the stains there as a souvenir.

The pills started to kick in and I finally felt like going to sleep. As I laid in bed, I began thinking about Jacqui. *Why the tongue touch? Why she kept her breasts fully exposed for a couple of minutes? Well,* **I sure liked both**. *There's more than a little 'something' from her side. And well, there's slightly a bit from mine too. ... ... Only slightly a bit? No, there's more. There* **can't be** *anything on* **either** *side in the future.* **This has to stop**! *I've got my Victoria. I'll lose her. ... ... I can't. I just can't lose her.*

The last thing I heard was My Little Dee running up the stairs to her room.

※※※※※※※※※※※※※※※※※※※※※※※※※

By DeForrest's sixteenth birthday, she was so much happier with a greatly improved spirit; Her combination of intelligence and good looks were maturing quite beautifully with a strong blend of determination — resembling her Mother and the occasional wild impulses — resembling her Aunt; Richelieu always said 'God help whoever fell for my sister'; Many did over the following years, starting with a Musketeer during that Summer of '64

※※※※※※※※※※※※※※※※※※※※※※※※※

After furtively looking around the hall, DeForrest came into my room the following Thursday after dinner. "I have **two** pieces of school gossip for you. Catherine Curtis from McKenna and Georgia Elms from Prescott came over to Karen's after school. First and most important ... this is the popular version for the beating of that Prick and his two asshole buddies. They drove over to Bethany Hospital to get bandaged up and the ER doctor called the police because of their injuries. They told the police that at least six or eight colored guys from the East side, came out of the park, jumped them and started beating on them, some with clubs. It all happened so quickly in the dark, that none of the three got a good look at any of them. The police thought it was probably part of some gang initiation."

"The shit Brewster has a badly bruised knee, cracked rib, a black right eye with three stitches. Guess you matched your earlier work to his left eye. Ha! Kovac has a broken nose, two broken ribs in a badly bruised chest. The Prick has a broken right hand and wrist which are all in a cast. He won't be playing summer ball. Tough shit! Three stitches for the lacerated area around his mouth. The loving couple's work ... yours and Autumn's. Two more on one eye. Jacqueline's work. Mine was not mentioned. Heh Heh! Three fractured ribs with a bruised sternum. Something to his shin." She wondered, "If they told the police it was our little party, probably that would have gotten them in trouble too?"

"What? 'Gee officers, the three of us tough studs were faked out by the promise of one of us getting laid by this really hot, tall chick with its peep show for the other two. Instead we had to go to the ER because there was one guy who separately beat up each one of us, but he had help ... from three really tall girls'. The cops would have laughed them out of the precinct house."

"Yeah, but Dee, you're right. Telling the whole, entire truth would have gotten them nothing but ridicule. And much, *much* worse ... a whole shitload of serious trouble, especially with the Monsignor and their parents. Sister Cecilia would have heavily disciplined them with a suspension and an excruciating summer punishment to allow them to graduate. She's supposedly very strict and quite creative. Or maybe simply thrown them out of school. Period. Possibly trouble from the police for pimping out Caroline since she's only seventeen. I highly doubt it, but an arrest ... surely dismissed ... would have pulled that bitch Rhodes down to the precinct house. While she would still graduate, her involvement in all this shit would cause her serious problems with acceptance to her chosen University. Besides it's always easier to blame anything bad on the Colored."

We laughed thoroughly about 'three really tall girls', then I joked, "Maybe they should tell everyone it was the punishing angel Uriel with his fire in his hands and his three beautiful Angels of Vengeance by his side." DeeDee laughed loudly and went to study for exams.

※※※※※※※※※※※※※※※※※※※※※※※※※※※※

No one ever found out or was told about DeForrest's part as The Strong-Willed, Rejuvenated, Healed Angel of Vengeance in The Charade

※※※※※※※※※※※※※※※※※※※※※※※※※※※※

Later that night, DeeDee came back into my room, "I forgot the second piece. Lorraine Holliday. Remember the fat slut and that fireman, the older guy in his early twenties, that Dale Bell. They 'screwed all the time which meant they were so in love' ... or is that vice-versa ... anyway, he was supposed to marry her this summer. She was gonna drop out and get a GED. Told her she had to lose weight first which I bet he thought she'd never be able to do or even try. But miraculously she started to ... real quick and a ton. **Then** ... she misses a couple periods, sure she's pregnant, tells this asshole Bell during one of their Bonk Nights. The Shit Hole goes nuts, tells her it's **her fault**, to get rid of '**it**'. Not going to marry her because **she's** knocked up. Says she won't get 'the big A' but what about their wonderful love. Says only thing he wonderfully loved was her huge tits ... now slightly less ... and screwing her. He dumps her! Really hurts her. Breaks her heart. You guys are such lying sacks of shit! He was never gunna marry her. Prick Bastard only wanted **ONE** thing! And getting it! On demand!"

"That's too bad. She's always a friendly, caring girl. Real chubby though. But incredibly amazing the amount of smoke that girl could suck in from one cigarette drag. And incredibly amazing how big-busted she is ... ... or was."

※※※※※※※※※※※※※※※※※※※※※※※※※※※※

Lorraine Lucille Holliday became deeply despondent when her 'one and only true love' broke his promise of marriage & abandoned her to deal with the stigma of being an unwed mother;

Reluctantly went to her Doctor for confirmation of the pregnancy;
To her surprising relief, he informed Lorraine she wasn't —
diagnosed the missed periods due to her intense, quick weight
loss combined with her heavy cigarette habit & the stress of her
marriage planning;

Greatly relieved she wasn't pregnant, but equally miserable
and in painabout being deserted, Lorraine debated what to tell
her mother; Walking home, she passed a Lutheran Church,
stopped in to pray for guidance and solace; While there, newly
ordained Assistant Pastor Phillip Jacobs asked if he could help;
Lorraine confessed everything to him, then continued to see him
on a regular basis;

During that three-year time period, she always took his
constructive advice; She quit smoking, went to Junior College
at night, kept the weight off, made new friends at Church and
practiced celibate activities in her spiritual growth;

The pastor was offered his own parish in Laramie, Wyoming;
During those first six weeks of separation, they both realized they
were truly in love; She immediately joined him and they married;
While she completed her degree in Social Work,
the couple had two boys;
Lorraine Lucille Jacobs is very happy and fulfilled,
she is a great help in her husband's ministry

****

Thank God for this Friday, it marked the end of exams, the end of school, and the end of Latin **forever**. DeForrest and I both were going to celebrate. We were going to pick up Autumn, then head to Blenders.

As we went into the study to say goodnight, our mother was standing over the leather couch, dangling a very fancy, lacy black bra. "Children, what is this? I found it stuffed under a cushion."

DeForrest and I quickly exchanged looks of total, utter shock.

Dee would have found it when she cleaned up where Caroline was 'displaying' herself. We assumed she was fully dressed when she left ... but maybe not? Left as an invitation/souvenir for me? Whatever! We're DEAD! Shit! ... SHIT!

However, DeeDee recovered to banter, "Mother, **that bra** is a quite elegant one. Beautiful floral embroidery atop sheer tulle. Expensive."

Not exactly knowing what she said, I added the male touch, "Yep, sexy too."

"Don't you two patronize me! You co-conspirators know all about this!" She shook the bra vigorously. "**A 32B**! Not close to your size, DeForrest Danièle! This is a 'smoking gun' from a very wild party last week, Forrest!"

Even though Linda was a good three inches taller, both Caroline and she have similar body frames. A quick mental comparison confirmed Caroline was easily bigger. Certainly not a 32B. And it looked more expensive than the plain one Caroline was wearing — at least during the outset when she had it on.

"Nope, just a 'smoking hot bra' from today." I regretted it as soon as I said it. That put me in the crosshairs, and judging by my mother's eyes, she was narrowing in on me for the kill. She was pissed off about her decree of 'absolutely no parties' being defied. An expensive errant bra left behind implied money for booze, hence drunkenness and carousing with at least one topless girl, followed by God knows what. I would spill everything in about ten seconds, then I would grovel for mercy for my sister and me.

Hearing all the commotion, Aunt Danae came in just in time to witness our executions. However she startlingly exclaimed, "Well, THERE it is. Now I remember. I grabbed it after it had dried in the laundry room then came in here to read the evening paper. Sure does look so much sexier on me than my others. Probably because it's Simone Pérèle, that French brand Mama told me to try when I was in Naples. This black lace one I wanted *finally* came in my size, so she sent it to me last month. I was going take it with me to Savoir-Faire or Farrar's on the Plaza to try to buy one in another color or something with a very similar design because it fit so well. Then Gi Gi, you brought Scott in here unexpectedly last night, so I jammed it into the couch to hide it. Great, now I can go shopping. Why all the strange looks?"

As DeForrest and I started to head for the door, my sister grinned, "Bye Aunt Danae. Bye Mother. Goin' to pick up Autumn. Celebrate! See ya both later.

"Case solved and closed. Bye Mother. Bye Aunt Danae." Then I teased, "Oh, hey Little Auntie, expensive bra ... seductively sexy. No wonder you didn't want Scott to see it. Saving it for a **private modeling**? Eh?"

DeeDee chimed in, "Him or maybe a showing for **some other** lucky guy? Byeee." This made our aunt turn a deep shade of red, which DeeDee and I had never seen.

We walked very slowly into the kitchen, barely containing our laughter from our aunt's complete embarrassment. We did hear our mother say, "Those two have always been thick as thieves. And they're getting worse! If I didn't give birth to them separately, **I** would think they **were** twins. I know something went on here last week. You should have seen their guilty looks, when I held up your bra. They **both** mistakenly recognized it as belonging to some girl they **both** know."

****

The three of us were sitting in a booth at Blender's, still snickering about the errant bra when suddenly DeeDee announced, "Gotta go tinkle." She got up quickly, striding to the toilets.

Autumn was quiet, so while we continued drinking our shakes, I teased, "Thought you girls could hold it longer. It's only been a half hour or so."

Autumn just smiled, "It happens."

"Are you feeling okay? You haven't been your normal self since ... well ... since last Friday night." As I leaned towards her, I whispered, "I swear to you, **nothing** has changed between us."

"Oh I know, Rich. Finally, all the exams are over and there is no more school. I'm just a little tired." She smiled, but weakly, "And starting my part-time job at the Hardy Design Studio Wednesday will make things better." Then Autumn just stared out the window.

Damn it, I KNOW something is wrong with her …… just won't tell me.

Suddenly, there was a muffled smack and a loud howl of pain. Almost immediately, a wailing Sheila Rhodes stumbled out of the girl's toilet, holding a noticeably inflamed left side of her face. She slightly staggered as she crossed behind a couple booths, then turned up the aisle we were sitting in. Sheila glanced at our table, her face registering shock upon seeing Autumn and me. She instantly lost her balance, fell against the table across from us, knocking it and everything on it to the floor. Her dive was punctuated with a loud ripping sound as the seam of her tightly constricted slacks had completely split up the backside from her crotch to her waist. As she started to get up, she slipped on some water, landing her sizable butt in the middle of some large puddles of dark chocolate malt. When she finally was able to stand and quit sliding around, there was loud laughter. Her voluminous white panties were easily displaying several wet, dark brownish splotches from the malt residue. She desperately tried to cover her exposed, stained undies, but too late — too large an opening and too much malt coloring. Her lower lip began to tremble.

The jeers, insults and mocking enjoyment began loudly and rapidly near a table close to us — classmates from Autumn's year. Ray O'Brien, the school's shot putter yelled, "Hey Rhody, nice pratfall but it looks like you crapped your panties and slacks doing it. Better go check."

His buddy crowed, "Didn't Mommy tell you to always wear clean undies in case of an accident! Oh yeah, the accident was *you shitting your drawers*."

His date piped up, "Wow! Who needs a sail for their boat? Just use a pair of your billowy Lane Bryant's."

Ray's steady, Sally Adams, a target of Rhodes' rumors some months ago, crudely scoffed, "The Coloss**ASS** of Rhodes tarnished itself nicely. But you really need a diaper more for that mouth. For all the vile shit that you spew out of it like this diarrhea you just farted out of your **whopping ass**."

During this ridicule, Sheila broke down, crying uncontrollably and painfully. Her girlfriends and a waitress had come over quickly and gathered around her. They all helped to try to clean her up and comfort her as Shelia leaned over the top of a booth, kneeling on the seat. While the waitress was retrieving another towel to finish wiping off her shoes, the toadies were scrounging for safety pins to hold her slacks together.

When Sheila looked up, it was almost into Autumn's face who had moved into the adjoining booth. Autumn brutally spat out in a low, ice-cold voice, "Your venomous, malicious plan was more coordinated than you, Bitch. **You ... vile ... hateful ... fat-assed ... repulsive cunt of a poxed whore!**"

Sheila broke away, bawling loudly, not waiting to be fixed up further. She hastily scrambled out the front door with the 'Rhodey's toadies' in her wake.

When I told Autumn she really nailed her, she frowned, "I was deeply upset by that nasty bitch's ruthless plan. She went out of her way to completely avoid Jacqui and me this past week. During *her* Greek tragedy, I decided to give the fat-assed piece of vermin shit those choice words."

✲✲✲✲✲✲✲✲✲✲✲✲✲✲✲✲✲✲✲✲✲✲✲✲✲✲✲✲✲✲

Sheila Faye Rhodes never went back to Blender's, became the 'butt' of Prescott jokes for a few years when someone slipped or lost their balance;

She graduated from UCLA's College of Fine Arts, majoring in Drama; During that time, she took Dexamyl or Purple Hearts and Menocil, exercised strenuously to successfully lose weight, significantly from her overly 'generous' derrière and thighs, yet unfortunately dropped some from her proudly prized bust;

She fancied herself a top notch, highly attractive actress, but failed miserably to realize her dream; Shelia had only a few lines in her sole movie role as a skimpy-dressed saloon floozy in a 'B' Western;

During her 'movie career', she supplied voices for Hanna-Barbera cartoons, then was offered a position for Walt Disney Pictures where she excelled remarkably well in some very challenging positions during her 18 years;

She dated a variety of guys and a few girls, became engaged three times, yet never married, had numerous affairs — all male but two, none lasting very long; Shelia always somewhat joked she 'would just simply die alone'

During a Friday morning, a decade younger co-worker Nicole,
whom Shelia had been seriously eyeing for weeks, asked her
to go out for drinks and an early dinner; They ended up at
Shelia's apartment, snorting her date's cocaine stash and
downing various pills from Shelia's amphetamine collection,
spending the entire night engaged in extensive sexual adventures;
Sheila christened her 'My New Love' as her fresh conquest
left near daybreak;

Sheila decided to continue celebrating more on their bed of
passion, downing more uppers and opening a new bottle of
Stolichnaya Vodka;

At two on Saturday, 'Almost a Fiancé' Alan came for
shopping, dinner and sex; He knocked several times
on the door, unlocked it and went in, calling for her;
Alan found her in a risqué, red negligée, face down on the bed;

The Coroner's verdict: 'Female, age 43; Death from extensive
cocaine and amphetamine use, highly exacerbated by intake of
near elevated level of alcohol';

Sheila was right — she died alone

❋❋❋❋❋❋❋❋❋❋❋❋❋❋❋❋❋❋❋❋❋❋❋❋❋❋❋❋❋❋❋❋

Autumn hesitated, "Oh damn ... I have used **that** four letter word **again** in **that** vulgar expression ... Jacqui's favorite. But I can't ... can't say that ... **never** going to say it again."

She looked pensive for a moment or two, then continued, "Oh Rich, I cannot get rid of these troubling feelings about what I did last Friday night ... they still bother me ... greatly. But you **needed** me to trip the guy. I truly **wanted** to stomp on that scheming mouth of the other piece of vermin shit. He hurt me! Terribly! **And** you! Poor DeeDee was still severely disturbed by **his ugly depravity**! He was going to ... to ... **to rap**—" She started tearing up, "I hate all this vicious meanness, but ... but—"

When she spoke again, her voice was resolute, adamant, "Richelieu, I am never going to swear again. Or be involved in physical violence. I detest what I am becoming. *I loathe it*. Nanna would not like what I am changing into."

In a prayer, she vowed, "Oh Nanna and God, I promise you ... I will return to be your kind-hearted, caring, virtuous girl ... whom you love so completely. I will keep my language blessed with no cursing."

****

No one ever found out or was told about Autumn's part as The Shrouded Angel of Vengeance in The Charade

****

That's what's bothering her ... the gentlest, kindest person I have ever known. Probably never had a vengeful thought before. Now can't understand or deal with those kinds of feelings.

DeForrest finally rejoined us, grinning, "Ooo, that still smarts," and showed us her vivid pink palm. "There *was* the strangest girl in the toilet ... thought her name was DeForrest. Can't be two of us. Hehheheh. I saw her come in the side door and go into there with one of her buddies while her other two little toadies grabbed a table. Gave her a few minutes or two, went in, waited until she came out of the stall and recognized me. She just ignored me like I was invisible. The other girl walked out the door, yelling at her she would order for her. Why didn't she just apologize when no one was in there? But she didn't! Meaning she wasn't sorry at all. So as she was walking to the door, I touched her arm. When she turned to look at me, I introduced myself with a friendly 'Never impersonate me, Bitch!', slapping that whore as hard as I could. Was that your nice footwork again, Autumn? Heh, heh. She was so comical, sliding around with that fat whale's ass of hers hanging out of those completely split slacks, looking like she had just soiled herself badly."

"I'm very glad you smacked her. But ultra-cool girls—"

DeForrest interrupted me in a serious tone, "Richie, I promise I will never do something like that ever again. Just this once. For *her* part in what she did to you two. She deserved much more."

"And she got much more, **so** much more. Your private slap quickly led to her complete public humiliation." I laughed sarcastically, "In her stained extra-large knickers she 'took her bows' in front of her 'adoring and loving' audience." We all laughed.

Autumn took DeForrest's palm and kissed it. "Thank you, Dee, for doing that for me. I couldn't have stomped or tripped anybody again. I just couldn't have done it. I could only tell her how truly despicable she most assuredly is. And that will be the last time for profane words like that." Autumn then smiled, "She was rather clumsy, wasn't she? Falling and knocking over that table on her way out? Such an ugly exit for the 'wonderfully great' actress!"

DeeDee emphatically stated, "Rich, this graphically illustrates one reason why ultra-cool girls always color coordinate everything. Always buy the best quality clothing, even if it means fewer outfits. And wear a thick, old lady's control girdle if your butt's huge. Like hers." She snickered, "Size ... EEEW! ... Means Extremely Extra Extra Wide."

I smirked, "That chubber's ass looked bigger since my 'outing' with her! Probably had her old lady's thick, control girdle on that night. Sure didn't tonight." We all laughed as I took the ice out of my coke, wrapped the cubes in my handkerchief. Autumn took it, bound up DeeDee's hand, patting it gently.

"Thanks Autumn. Got to get my palm ready for some serious handholding during the showing of the new James Bond movie, *From Russia With Love*. First weekend! Bartlett asked me where I wanted to go tomorrow night. Really surprised him with my choice. I'll go see it again with Karen. Oohh whee ... Sean Connery!" She mimicked deeply, "Bond. James Bond ... ... What an absolute *stud*!"

Later, DeForrest told the manager she hadn't seen anything — she thought a stall door swung open too quickly, accidentally clipping her face. We heard Rhodes' account a few weeks later, surprisingly very similar — the latch on the door wasn't fastened properly and it swung open, hitting her very hard at the same time she was getting off the toilet seat, pulling up her undies and slacks. She never saw it. Although similar, neither version was really believed, but then, there was no reason to ever dispute it.

The only link between them was remote — Bush. I was convinced that no "Charade activities" would ever surface, especially after the only tenuous possibility was from Maureen Modica about a year later. MoMo was a tall, full-figured, big boned, plain girl, seemingly nice and highly intelligent yet always looking unkempt. She would usually be drinking yet rarely drunk — but she was that night — consequently rather talkative and vulgar. And definitely on the prowl.

When asked what ever happened with Bush and Rhodes, she loudly declared, "All any of us girls ever knew was he sometimes would meet up with her when the girls were out together, then they would leave quickly. To fornicate. Only thing I ever heard was one night he came into Blender's, and they sat and talked for a while in the next booth. I overheard Shelia say to him that they had to figure out a way somehow to 'royally, completely screw **that** haughty bitch and her arrogant asshole boyfriend before we graduate'. Dunno know who they were. But if they would have succeeded, Shelia, the *real bitch* that she could be, would have talked and bragged about it. However, she left for California shortly after Bush was beaten to a pulp."

A new record, *You've Lost That Lovin' Feelin'* began playing. "But Sheila never lost **that lovin' feelin'** about **their fornicating** ... she would brag and brag to the Roadies! Oh, she loved him to 'F' her!

Said her first time ever was with him. She always claimed it was like kinda getting raped, "because she just didn't know how he got her pleated A-line skirt and slip over her waist so quickly, his pants already unzipped, then like lightening yanked her panties sideways more than enough to..." as her narrative was truncated by her throaty laugh.

Soon she continued, "Haha, 'kinda getting raped'? Yeah, sure! A consensual rape? Is that an oxymoron? That was just her usual rationalizing bullshit," and she whined for emphasis, "Acting like she **wanted** to keep her precious virginity intact. But she just was so overpowered and he simply **took** it from her. Oh alas, what could she do? Hahahaha."

"Weeks later she admitted she let him keep her apricot panties. When there was 'evidence' it was her first time, she proudly admitted it was her 'inauguration'. He happily tugged them off her 'to remember her and this night'. She told him he could keep them only if he 'F-ed' her another time. He heartily agreed. She said there was a third time, but none of us believed her. Regardless, when they left each other, she told him she knew they 'hugely satisfied' each other. He certainly agreed, saying this was just the beginning. And it was. Oh, many, many more times followed.

Since that night, she couldn't get enough of his ... haha ... can't remember her name for his ... his ... oh yeah ... 'Phallus Maximus'. She loved getting nailed by ole PM! Just loved it!"

A Kansas University junior named Crabtree came over and asked her to dance.

She happily accepted yet still finished her story, "She got her own memento too ... gave her a Path's Entry tied on some roses. Gloated as she showed 'em to us. But both got mosquito bites **EV-REE-WHERE**! Showed us some of those too!" MoMo started onto the dance floor to join her partner, mimicked scratching her genitals, yelling loudly, "**Calamine lotion for 'F-ing' MOTION**".

Later, our horny storyteller left the hall dance with Crabtree. She married him four months later inside his parents' Dunkin' Donuts store which became quite successful. The couple opened two stores of their own. Also successful.

✢✢✢✢✢✢✢✢✢✢✢✢✢✢✢✢✢✢✢✢✢✢

When we were making out at St. Victoria's the next night, I already had my hand a little under her full skirt, rubbing her lower left thigh. We started to French kiss as I began softly feeling her breast on the outside of her blouse. However, my recurring daydream of desire began to torment me.

The Elysian Fields exist magnificently inside her. Between her beautiful legs. Soft ... Warm ... Moist like dew. Be like touching Paradise.

I decided tonight was the night, so I would begin by caressing her on the outside of her panties — like I had done the first time with her breast — waiting for her invitation to gently proceed inside. My hand glided up her magnificent thigh and its garter strap, quickly sliding over to the portal of my dreams. However, something like a cushion was already there, blocking me.

Autumn grabbed my forearm, instantly pulling my arm out from underneath her dress.

Oh Shit, SHIT! She's having her period. ... ... "Sorry. I didn't know."

She began to cry softly, fixedly staring out the windshield. As a few minutes past, I silently waited, awkwardly.

She sniffed, "Probably tomorrow, maybe tonight. I'm the one who should be sorry. I should have told you. Most times I don't ... but you seem to know." Autumn continued to cry a little more, "Richie, you know I love you more than anything. I want you to stay with me." She tried to wipe her tears away and when I handed her my handkerchief, she continued distressingly, painfully, "I will ... go all the way ... with you. But **please, please** don't get me pregnant," the tears streamed down her cheeks, "I have my dreams ... you have your dreams ... all of them ... **ruined**."

What the hell is happening? I only wanted to touch inside Paradise, nestled between her magnificent thighs.

Then she almost screamed, "NOOooooo! Can't! Oh God! Can't let you! I'm **SO SCARED! I'm terrified**! You ... you ..." She broke down completely, becoming even more upset and her fists struck my chest four or five times but without any real force, then sobbing uncontrollably into my shoulder.

Oh God, this is crushing her. She's a mess. A complete mess! What the Hell is going on?

I wrapped my arms around her. "Victoria, listen to me. No, no! Everything's okay. Not all the way. I only wanted to **touch ... inside** you. Softly. Tenderly."

She continued to cry, moaning pitifully, "Oooh nooo Richie, not ... okay! Not." Through her tears and sobbing came, "Last Friday ... cruel deceitful trick ... an hour ... completely miserable ... vomited." She took a deep breath, but still brokenly continued, "Dee ... ex ... plained all ... to me. Made up ... my mind. Give you my ... virgin ... ginity." She blew her nose loudly with my handkerchief and resumed somewhat steadier yet still falteringly, "So you wouldn't ... find someone like that ... little tramp. I get sick ... think of you ... you touching **that thing** or another **piece of manure like it**." She hiccuped deeply, "But I can't ... go all the way! **I CAN'T** do it! You'll break my heart with **anyone** else ... into a thousand pieces." Autumn continued to weep fitfully, "Oh Richie, I'm sorry ... so sorry ... I'm just so scared! Oh God, I can't! **Can't** do it. So scared ... **just so scared**."

I could only hold her tightly as I was bombarded with all this shit to sort out.

All started when the whoring Caroline, coldheartedly taunted and challenged Autumn by obscenely describing the fanciful actions of our nonexistent 'Nookie'. Autumn, time to choose ... Start spreading your legs for me and take your chances on a pregnancy OR I use Caroline or someone like her for my 'silent slut'. Possibly lose each other as our relationship will be strained with my lies and deceit. When I tried to get into her panties, it forced her to try to choose. This is tearing her soul apart.

Time to end this SHIT! This has got to work!

As I continued to hold her, I reassured her, "Everything will be fine. You'll see. I know."

She began to calm down a little, and whimpered, "Richie, but how can it?"

"I can promise you something which is far better than just saying, 'It's all right if we don't go all the way, I won't break up with you'. I know you all too well. You're extremely sensitive, so easily hurt. You would worry, having all the doubts and anxieties in the back of your mind. Then they would fester into serious suspicions, especially given Friday's wild escapade at my house. You would lose your trust, your faith in me. Wondering if I was involved with Caroline, finally taking her up on her offer 'to be my silent slut' or someone worse, like one of her bragging buddy-whores ... that Phyllis. Or somebody you don't know. I'll bet a lot of unwanted thoughts about Caroline and me have already entered your mind this week."

"**Richelieu**! **NEVER** mention that name again! Please!" She sniffed heavily and again made her blaring sound with her nose into my handkerchief, "And yes, they have. They bother me. A whole bunch! Terribly! Keep seeing **HER** ... almost *completely* naked ... twirling her bra with those bare breasts ... **your** name on those garish panties ... her grin, telling you to come and ... oh darn it ... to ... **to have her**! Hurts me ... so much. Can't get rid of the mental pictures. I just can't. Oh, but Richie, but what can you do? How?"

I tried to explain, "I have thought about this before, but I never have mentioned because we are way, way too young. My idea kills your plans, kills my plans, *our future plans. And* anyway certainly none of those desired plans could happen now, but **I need you** with me **now**. Whenever I think about my future, you are always deeply imbedded in my thoughts. **I need you** with me in the **future**. I don't want somebody like Ginny or Judy, even Antoinette or Joanie or **anyone** else, now or ever. Oh God, *I want only* **you**! *Oh so much, Victoria*! So I will wait for you and you alone, my Victoria. You are immensely and incredibly worth it. Autumn Victoria Knight, will you **marry me** at some future date?"

She was completely stunned for a moment, not believing what I had just asked. As my proposal sunk in, she looked back at me thru her wet eyes. Then she said happily, "Yes, Forrest Étienne Richelieu Marlowe, I will most definitely **marry you**." She sputtered and laughed, "But I don't know when."

She grabbed my head with both hands and began kissing me all over my face — my cheeks, my nose, my eyelids, my forehead, even my mouth. "Oh, my sweet, sweet Richie! I am going to be Mrs. Forrest Étienne Richelieu Marlowe! Autumn Victoria Knight Marlowe or just wonderful Autumn Marlowe! Or even Victoria Marlowe!" And she snuggled up to me as close as possible. I kissed her salty cheeks and wiped them.

"I am such a huge mess. It seems like all I have been doing is worrying or studying for the past week. I didn't know **how** to tell you or even **what** to tell you. You know I can barely talk about intimate sex stuff, even with you, unless I am forced to, like when I had to tell you last February about my extremely painful period and needing my big bra or when we were first intimate." She giggled nervously, then continued, "All that stuff is so easy to talk to you about now and wonderful **to do** with you. But I don't think even Summer would be able to help me on this one. Guess it's a good thing you tried to get into my ... uh ... uh ... my panties tonight, otherwise I would have continued to worry until you somehow forced me to tell you. You knew all this week I have not been acting normal, especially with you. I'm so sorry. You deserved so much better." She started crying again but kissed me on my cheek. "The whole long week I worried needlessly but now I'm the happiest that I have ever been," she laughed through her tears. "The magician fixed it as he always does and I need to fix something … my makeup."

"Later, Victoria Marlowe. You will be my grandmother's namesake."

"Yes, Richie, and I will love having her name." She then began to fully explain her fears. "Regarding going any further than we have, I always become so scared … deathly afraid of becoming pregnant before marriage. You see, a couple of years ago, I had this vivid premonition … I don't think I was dreaming as it was so incredibly real, so vivid. Like when Nanna came to me. Regardless of whatever preventive measures would be taken, I would still get pregnant. Please, Richie please, nothing more, I can't do more than what we have been doing. I just *can't*. But I love what we do now."

"I understand, Victoria." Then I remembered the night we talked about teenage pregnancy. The more we spoke about it, the more she became visibly nervous and shaken.

"But hey, look, no blushing! Well, maybe a little. You have completely ruined me. I sure don't blush or get embarrassed like I used to, regardless who is around."

"For your complete, total ruination, you'll have to wait until our wedding night. Then …" And I made a very leering sound.

She laughed loudly, then kissed me very happily, "You know, I always sort of made fun of Summer with her engaged to be engaged status, but now she's really engaged. So I've replaced her as the lady-in-waiting. Just like what I was at the Dance. This is so amazing, so incredible. Richie, you always know how to make me feel wonderful, especially when I feel completely in the dumps. You always make everything right again. You are a true Magician. Like now. Like when you gave me this." She held out the locket.

I began faking like there might be a problem, "Yeah, about that locket—"

She interrupted, "Forrest Étienne Richelieu Marlowe, you are never getting **MY LOCKET** back! **I mean it! I do! I really mean it! It's MINE!"**

"Is your birthday soon? Sometime in June, around the 10th, I believe?"

"**You** know it is. Quit teasing me. I know you. You have something wonderful up your sleeve. I can't wait! Tell me! Tell me! Please! Oh Please! Pleasssse?"

I laughed, "It is unbelievable how you instantly turn into *such* a little girl! Okay, I've been carrying this with me for some weeks and when I touch it, it reminds me the way we are and the way I want us to be, why I need you. Ours is not like Summer's previous 'engaged to be engaged' status. We are really and truly engaged. Because ..." I pulled out the wad of Kleenex from my pocket and unfolded the crumpled tissues, "This is my promise to you!" and kissed her.

My talisman was the matching gold ring of the locket and chain. Autumn was completely speechless. I took the ring and placed it on the ring finger of her left hand which was a fairly good fit, only a little loose. The ring had the identical design with four smaller diamonds of the engraved pattern of the locket. Even with only the faint light of the distant light pole, she moved her hand all around to look at it from various angles. She still had not said a word. A few moments passed. Then some more.

"Oh Richelieu," she finally gasped.

I have never seen my little girl happier ... makes me feel incredibly happy too. Thank You Holy Ghost for showing me the way through this.

"Oh Richie ... ... Richie ... ... Richie."

She grabbed me and began to kiss me all over again. Even one of my ears got in on the action. "You are my Magician, a Wizard of the first class!"

"Victoria, you can keep the ring **ONLY** on the sole condition that **you have to promise to tell me** when something is wrong or bothering you. I can't take another intense breakdown like fifteen minutes ago or the silent, quiet suffering of this past week. I can't deal with it. **And I won't.**"

"Oh, I promise. I promise. I do. I really *will*. I *will* find a way. And I will always, always, always love you. You are unbelievable.

This is incredibly wonderful. You are incredibly wonderful. I'm sooooo happy!" She kissed me deeply, longingly. "You are the best boyfriend, no ... NO! ... fiancé there ever was and ever will be. I wish we could tell everybody. Uh ... should we tell *anybody*?"

"Sure, just a few! The Three Graces when we figure out how. Summer and Jake sometime after they come home. Jacqueline before she leaves. No one else!"

She began to French kiss me passionately while I gently pushed her puffed sleeved pullover over her bra which I quickly unhooked. The scent of the Chanel perfume and the powder on her breasts was extra intoxicating tonight.

Later, as I held her, I became serious and sighed, "Victoria, it's going to be a long, long time. Senior year plus all of college. Six long years!"

"I know. Richie, we will make it. We'll make those darn six years incredibly wonderful! And then the next fifty plus after them! Plus some kids! And dogs. Old English sheepdogs."

I laughed, then said, "Sure, whatever you want."

There is that determination, that resoluteness. It's back. O Thank You Holy Ghost. Damn it, six years is an eternity. Victoria's ring is reunited with her locket and chain. Wonder what she and my father are talking about now?

JUNE

Jacqueline had already said her good byes to her American family that first morning in June. She wanted just the four of us for her flight departure from Kansas City Municipal Airport. We were all talking, just waiting for the gate attendant to announce boarding. A few days before, Autumn had confirmed that Jacqueline's and Hal's relationship was deeply serious. Both looked distraught. Finally the gate attendant announced the departure of TWA Flight 113 to New York. DeForrest and Jacqueline first said their good byes, hugging and kissing each other on both cheeks, then on the lips. Autumn and Jacqueline did likewise but I could tell their farewell was painful for both, especially Autumn. DeeDee had already quickly walked past us to the high fenced area outside the gate. I was sure she was crying.

I said, "*Au revoir, mon* Jacqui," and we kissed on the lips.

She had tears in her eyes and we continued in French, "My handsome guy, **my** Richelieu, I will miss you most extraordinarily. You were there when I *desperately* needed someone. Take care of my sisters. Continue to watch over my 'little' DeForrest. Cherish your love and especially your engagement with our Autumn."

"Good times became the best times because of you. Without you, the ugly, nasty one couldn't have been remedied so thoroughly, so completely. I will take care of my two girls. I will greatly miss my third girl. Return, my beautiful French femme fatale. Goodbye **my** Jacqui." We kissed only slightly longer in good-bye and hugged again.

Autumn and I moved away as Jacqueline slowly went to Hal to say their good-byes in private. DeeDee was still standing outside at the gate exit, turning away when we walked out — not wanting to talk to anyone.

I translated for Autumn who also had tears in her eyes. She put her arms around me and hugged me tightly. She sniffed and a tear fell, "I am going to miss her terribly. She became my best friend. I told her that in French. Jacqui said I was hers. O this is terrible ... terrible! I hurt Rich. I hurt. Make my hurt go away. Please do something! Pleeasse!"

There is always the little girl ... my innocent little girl. I feel like I've been hit in the stomach. My 'outrageous girl' ... our Jacqui.

About five minutes later, she and Hal came out the door. The three of us joined DeeDee at the ten foot fence to watch her plane taxi and take-off. As she was walking on the tarmac to the movable boarding ramp, Jacqueline turned, forced a grin and waved a final goodbye. But I could see she was crying. That hurt *me*. Jacqueline was the toughest of all of us.

After the plane took off, we slowly made our way to the cars. As we started to say our good-byes, Hal said in a halting voice, "It hasn't even been a half hour. Oh God, I miss her terribly. God, what am I going to do?" Then he wailed, "She has to return! She has to!"

I said very seriously, "Hal, I guarantee you she will return. You will see her soon."

"Really, Rich?"

"**Really**, Hal!" He dejectedly got into his car and drove away. It was going to be a hard and lonely time for him.

"Richie, how do you know Jacqueline will come back to the States?"

"The Magician sometimes knows things." Truthfully, I didn't know *shit*, and for the next couple of months, I just continued nightly to pray an extra third decade to the Holy Ghost in the hope He would enlighten Le Ministère for Education to let Jacqueline return quickly. I missed her deeply.

※※※※※※※※※※※※※※※※※※※※※※※※※※※

No one ever found out or was told about Jacqueline's part as The Duplicitous and Seductive Angel of Vengeance in The Charade

※※※※※※※※※※※※※※※※※※※※※※※※※※※

Autumn sat as close as she could to me and put her hand on my leg and squeezed it periodically. DeeDee sat by the window and looked out of it the entire time until we dropped her off at The Hangout where she was meeting Karen and some other girls.

No one had said a word until DeeDee got out and simply said, "Bye."

The drive from The Hangout to Autumn's was fairly short, and I didn't want to talk about Jacqueline at all. So I brought up Mick and Pamela's break up. "There's a lot of guessing, but no one really knows why they broke up. When I went for a walk in the neighborhood yesterday afternoon, I saw Mick. He's been really, really down in the dumps for the last two weeks and desperately wanted to talk to someone he could totally trust ... like me. But couldn't make himself call me. Since I moved here, he and I have become more than just buddies ... we're close friends. Best friends."

"Well, I just assumed one of the usual reasons or maybe they just grew tired of each other. But after nine months?"

"No, it's much different."

"How so?"

"Here is what he told me. Pamela missed her period in mid-April which had happened once before. But this time, at the beginning of May, she started having morning sickness, some cramping, and having to urinate all the time."

Autumn inhaled deeply, "Oh, no, noo! Please Richelieu, tell me she's not!"

"Mick said she was too scared to go to the doctor as her mother would insist upon going with her. He just couldn't figure out how she could get pregnant so quickly, their first time was on that first Friday in April when his parents left for a weekend getaway and business meeting at The Lake of the Ozarks to meet with their biggest client. After their long, glorious 'special' night, he took Pamela home, but they resumed again when he picked her up late Saturday morning and they spent most of the day in bed until he had to take her home again. After that weekend, they had to use the back seat. I asked him if he double bagged* and he said yeah,

---

*Another myth of the '60s — the protection reality of "**Double Bagging**" *was worse,* not better since two condoms caused more friction, hence a greater likelihood of a split or break

he did, but a few times he didn't even single bag. It felt so great without one, so he would simply try to pull out. A couple times he couldn't make it."

"He didn't know what to do. It would mess up everything he had planned and what Pamela wanted to do. She would have to drop out of high school, get her GED. Over that weekend, after we beat the injured Mick and your Bears, he asked her a few times if she was absolutely positive that she was pregnant. He kept putting off talking to her about how it should be handled. Finally on Monday, he told her he was concerned about getting parental consent. He would approach them in a few days, when the time seemed right. You know, Pamela just turned seventeen in March."

As I pulled up in front of Autumn's house, I explained, "Victoria, his parents have never been too keen on Pamela. Thought he should date someone smarter, definitely on a college prep path and from a well-to-do family."

"Pamela said she knew hers would consent if only for the baby's sake. He told her this whole situation was affecting his life ... like his ball playing. He had distractedly clipped a corner edge of a wall on that game day Friday, injuring his wrist and hand. He knew there were things affecting her life too. She became really pissed off, saying, 'No shit ... I'm the one that's pregnant, what about *our* baby? To hell with *your* baseball!' He didn't mean it that way."

"Mick goes over to her house on Monday afternoon two weeks ago and tells her he got back too late from his cousin's wedding in St. Louis that Sunday night to call and she wasn't in school that day. He was worried. They slowly go out to his car, so she can tell him everything that has happened. She had begun to bleed like it was a light period on Friday night but it progressed quickly to very heavy bleeding ... worse than an extremely severe period ... even discharging some tissue with it and accompanying terrible, painful cramps. It finally had subsided early that morning.

So Mick, the idiot, says, 'that's great news, then it was just a period you missed. Sounds like this one doubled up its intensity for the one you didn't have.' She yelled at him, calling him an insensitive Bastard, threw her Path's Entry charm at him, told him to shove it up his worthless, uncaring ass, then screamed she just had a miscarriage, had been scared shitless the whole time, couldn't even tell her mother, called him a bunch of names I won't repeat to you, told him to go to Hell, and she never wanted to talk to him again. Got out of the car and tried to slam the door. She began crying as she walked slowly and painfully back to her house."

"I know she was in love with him ... maybe still is. He's sure she's gone to Chicago again. Probably for the entire summer this time. I don't think he really thought, even then or now, she was ever pregnant. But he is seriously messed up since their ugly break-up on that Monday. I think he probably was or still is in love with her too. Whatever his level of feelings, he *really* misses her. He only could glimpse her back twice at school. She avoided him like the plague ... like she said she would. So he didn't push it to see or talk to her, hoping she would come back ... like she did before. She didn't. Mick said he just has been straight lying to everyone, saying they grew tired of each other to protect her reputation. He then swore me to secrecy, so please, please don't tell anyone!"

"Oh, Richie, this is terrible. Poor Pamela! Oh God, that is horrifying. To miscarry and *no one there to comfort or help you.* She's right, Mick's a selfish, idiot shi— jerk. But at least she's not pregnant anymore. I would never tell anyone. I feel so terribly sorry for her. I wish I could have talked to her somehow, to help her through her pain. I ..." There was silence for a few moments. "I know I can't ... besides she's left town. This is dreadful. Exactly why I am so terribly scared, like when we talked two nights ago. Look what happened to them."

"Now I know exactly what you mean. Completely. She gives him her virginity and they had the ensuing four or five weeks of wonderful, secret pleasure. Then during the subsequent three weeks, things become tumultuously rough and they end up losing the baby. Worse ... each other. That's tragic, Victoria."

❋❋❋❋❋❋❋❋❋❋❋❋❋❋❋❋❋❋❋❋❋❋❋❋❋❋❋❋❋❋❋

Possibly because of her solitary ordeal with the miscarriage, Pamela Sue Parker decided to become a nurse, obtaining her BSN from Kansas University

Pamela began as an Emergency Room trainee nurse at Bethany Hospital, with increasing responsibilities and numerous successes throughout the years she became the Hospital's Director of Nursing;

Pamela and an office equipment salesman married after dating only a short time; Both ignored their marital mistake; he had a few short term 'flings' while she carried on an on-again-off-again affair with a married ER doctor; After only 2½ years of marriage, they decided to divorce, there were no children;

Three years later, she married an Executive of Quantum Medical Laboratories only days after his divorce was finalized — he had a year-old girl; A few months later, the ex-wife committed suicide & the baby came to live with them; Pamela already was four months pregnant; Unfortunately, both focused on their careers and the girls; causing their relationship to become more distant, then virtually nonexistent;

They waited to divorce when the girls were in college;

Only a handful of people ever knew about the miscarriage

❋❋❋❋❋❋❋❋❋❋❋❋❋❋❋❋❋❋❋❋❋❋❋❋❋❋❋❋❋❋❋

Michael Lee — Mick — Hayden signed after his senior year with the Cincinnati Reds, assigned to their AA team in Macon Georgia — had only mixed results; After two years he quit baseball, graduated from Kansas State College of Pittsburg;

He started his own successful construction company; Married a girl who was 7 years younger, only a high school graduate, his parents totally disapproved of her, but she loved Mick and baseball deeply;

Their marriage is very enthusiastic, warm and caring; They have two boys & a girl, all extremely good ball players, Mick always said Cat (Catherine) was the best of the bunch — another pitcher, playing four years on a scholarship at Florida State University;

When Mick was severely hurt on a job site, he was rushed to Bethany Hospital for his injuries where ER Head Nurse Pamela Matlock's quick and decisive actions ensured he didn't lose the use of his right arm;

Mick and Richelieu still remain close friends

✸✸✸✸✸✸✸✸✸✸✸✸✸✸✸✸✸✸✸✸✸✸✸✸✸✸✸✸✸✸✸✸

"What would **you** do if I got pregnant?"

"I would marry you in a heartbeat. But, of course, it would be my very last one I would have as my mother would kill me."

"O my God! Oh God! Oh Noooo! Gi Gi wouldn't have anything to do with me anymore! I never thought of that Hell. Richie, I couldn't take that. I can't be cut-off from your mother. That would completely devastate me. I truly need your mother. She's always there for me. I really love her so much! She's my earthly Nanna."

"Well, you're very wrong there. My mother feels like you are another daughter to her. But I know her and she would blame me completely ... *never* ... *ever* ... you. We have our agreement and you have defined those areas completely which exclude your amazing legs, specifically here." I placed my hand on her jeans, casually squeezing her left upper thigh within inches to the "portal of my dreams".

"Richie, *as usual*, you are so, so wicked. Is this all you think about?" She gave me my usual playful slug after she moved my hand much further down her jeans.

I kept massaging her thigh but only just above the knee. "Oh, there're other things, but right now it's on the top of my list."

"Oh, just darn you. I've got to admit I like you rubbing my leg. I know your mother likes me more than a lot. Does she really love me, like another daughter? Really?"

"I know she does. Give you an example. She was always, *always*, just *constantly* after me to date and marry a Catholic, *date and marry a Catholic*. Since the **day** we started dating and going steady, she has never mentioned it again or even suggested I date any other girls, Catholic or not. Oh yeah, my mother calls only **you**, 'Honey,' like she calls DeeDee, 'Angel'. Ya noticed? No one else. Ever! I could give you more ... like having you call her Gi

Gi, but I know she feels so strongly about you. She loves you very much. Deeply!"

"Wow, I feel so ecstatic, knowing that. And who knows, she might get *her* wish. Ooohh, but I still have the pain of Jacqueline leaving."

Her 'wish' comment went right by me. I was so focused on *not* wanting to talk about Jacqueline, I changed the subject quickly. "How do you think you will like your part-time summer job at Hardy's Studio?"

"It will be wonderful. Start tomorrow. Oh, I almost forgot to tell you, Summer is going to major in Pre-Law. And Miss Shea from Macy's called her to work as a salesgirl and sometimes teen model. Jake is going to work again for Templeton Construction, building duplexes. And will play baseball for Milgram's again in the Ban Johnson League. Maybe after this last year for you in the 3 & 2 League, you can go be teammates with him next summer."

"But you ... never thought I would see you going to school at Prescott. Seriously, I'm sure you'll like your Drafting class." She giggled, saying, "Are you going to conjure something up for the Gestapo?"

I laughed, "If the situation presents itself, you bet, sure enough. It's just a nine week summer class ... the only drawback of a college prep school. No Industrial Arts."

"My future husband, the big architect in training."

"Maybe, but I'm starting to get interested in what Mother does in the stock market and how finance works. Well, my future wife, the big interior designer, what do you want to do tonight? Do you want to eat dinner with us? I could pick you up at 5:30."

"Sure, but make it 4:30 so I can help your mother. Then I can just hang out with the Three Graces."

"Probably only two. I'm sure Dee has a date with Bart. Although, it might only be one. You *never* know about My Little Auntie. Since she put on some weight, she looks soooo much better, even a little younger too. Oddly, almost all of the Dating Queen's guys are younger than she. Hey, not hanging with me?"

"That's because she is so energetic, so full of life. Thank you, Richie, but nope. You can go buy some Eskimo pies. You do know what aisle they are in, don't you?"

"Would you show me?"

"Of course. Don't I always?" We both laughed heartily.

****

However, I dropped the class after only a week and a half. I had started reading my mother's introductory book on the stock market and after discussing some of its concepts and premises with her, my interest shifted rapidly and completely. Since she had only the one beginning textbook, I went to the Main Library where the wonderfully nice librarian, now MRS. Rosalind J. JACKSON, helped me numerous times to find books on my mother's topics list which I spent most of my summer reading and studying. As my knowledge level increased, my mother began to tutor me on the market, especially on my "puts and culls".

I wished I could go somehow play for the Cardinals again. My summer team, Basey's Market, was only going to be a .500, maybe a .600 team. We had won two and lost two but I was hitting .444. It wouldn't last. I was hoping around .375 for the season.

On my second library visit, I asked Mrs. Jackson about Mrs. Scott. Numerous times I relived that night when I first saw the dark-haired librarian, so truly stacked, so truly gorgeous, summoning me to follow her fabulously curved derrière and splendidly shaped legs that glided so effortlessly. She told me Mrs. Scott had twins the previous week, and she was not scheduled to return. Damn it! I remembered the very last time I saw her was during Christmas vacation. She was sitting at her desk, glanced up and smiled charmingly at me. I returned my very best smile. Oh God, she looked beautiful and appeared just magnificent in her tightly clinging black sweater with sequin beading. I'm sure **Mr.** Scott greatly appreciates the beauty of the Goddess of the Tomes. I know both Jake and I did. So much! She was one topic we *completely* agreed on. We could only marvel and compare our memories.

Strangely, Mrs. Jackson and Jake were always real chummy. When I asked Jake about her, he merely said she was a first-year librarian at Whittier when he was a freshman. She was always helpful, very nice then as she is now. Certainly became a valued friend over the years. Sounded like a tad too much bullshit. There was like a sort of bond between them. However, it wasn't any of my business.

****

Autumn called me before 10:30 on that third morning of June to say she had waited on her front steps for the mailman to get her grades. Her final numbers were: English 1, U. S. History 1-, Accounting 1-, and very happy that Advanced Algebra was a 2-, but ecstatic about Interior Design, the best for last ... it was a 1+.

She exclaimed, "Of course, I never made a 1+ in any subject, in fact, I've heard they're almost nonexistent. Even Summer never got one and she is *so smart*. So a **1.2** average. Richie, I owe it all to your mother. Could I speak to her, please?"

"Sure, I'll pick you up at 6 o'clock," and I called my mother to the phone.

After greeting each other, Mother began listening, then smiled broadly. "That's terrific, Honey! As DeeDee would say, 'Outta sight!' ... ... No, no. You were the one that did everything. You certainly deserved it. What did your mother say? ... ... Oooh, I see. You're coming over tonight to celebrate, I hope? ... ... Wonderful! ... ... Okay, I'll tell Richie 5:15, not six. Autumn, congratulations on those excellent grades and an extra, extra, so amazing, so special salute to you on the 1+ in Interior Design. ... ... Oh, I have had a nice compliment on the master suite already, but we can talk all about it tonight. Give you every detail then. ... ... Bye, Honey."

My mother hung up the phone, then began to pour herself a glass of orange juice. I asked, "So what's the deal with her mother?"

"Hasn't shown them to her yet. She wanted me to be the first to know. And a 5:15 pick-up to help me with dinner."

The postman brought mine around noon and I opened them:

Religion	86	English	93
Français III	91	Algebra & Trig	93
Ancient Civilizations	95	Latin III	82

"Congratulations to you too, Richie. First Honors. I'm very proud."

"Thank you. I know your trick. Father Hoyle showed us a couple weeks ago. If you expect an average to be around a certain value, then calculate the differences from that value and add. Easy, so we have -4, +1, +5, +3, +3, and -8, and adding on the fly nets to zero quickly. A 90.0 and First Honors by the skin of my teeth."

"Very good, Richelieu. I'll show you some more tricks this summer."

✻✻✻✻✻✻✻✻✻✻✻✻✻✻✻✻✻✻✻✻✻✻✻✻✻✻✻✻✻✻✻

That afternoon, I drove over to The Nu-Way to meet Bart and Jack to shoot the bull. Bart finished with a 92.2 average, making the top ten in the class at ninth. Jack had an 88.1. The three of us were happy about our final grades.

Bart exclaimed, "I just remembered. Jack won't be playing summer ball against Guy Frost. My father had to do some troubleshooting in New York last night and said he sat next to a guy who is a scout for the Yankees. This scout said that they were trying to sign him, but the A's beat them to it. So now the 'Guy' is a pro. Be in the papers."

"Shit, the guy was a pro two weeks ago when he beat us."

"We still hit him. Next year, Lou. The only starters we're losing are Thomas, Harris, and Todd LaFleur. We're going to kick that League's ass next year."

Then we talked about the teams we were playing summer ball for and what we were going to do this summer, talked some about school next year, and of course the girls — Autumn, Camille, and DeForrest as Bart preferred to call her, having said, 'I think that is such a cool name.'

As we broke up, Bartlett, as she calls him, said, "Lou, I'll see you later tonight, but much more importantly, your terrific looking sister. I just keep thanking God that she looks nothing like you. That would be a curse. And that He helps you find those missing bulbs for your marquee."

✻✻✻✻✻✻✻✻✻✻✻✻✻✻✻✻✻✻✻✻✻✻✻✻✻✻✻✻✻✻✻

After Mass and Sunday dinner, DeForrest already had gone over to Karen's, probably to go find some guys. She was already frothing at the mouth, counting down the days as she hardly could wait until her birthday next month when she could get her license. They were still threatening to go to Allen's to get picked up by some bikers. Both had even done some research, saying they wanted to be clever enough to talk with them about their bikes. Knowing those two, someday, they will do just that. I just hope they don't bring them back to the house. She keeps saying she wants to know what freedom feels like with the wind blowing in your hair, looking so bad-ass cool, zooming around town at 30 or 40 mph with only a panhead Harley engine between your legs, tightly holding onto a guy or the queen's seat. Autumn just cringes.

Danae had a picnic date at Wyandotte Lake. She often dates, looking for 'her great guy' to marry. She was going to begin law school at KU this week, hoping she would meet someone around her age — maybe even a professor — and they would fall in love.

※※※※※※※※※※※※※※※※※※※※※※

Danièle Madeleine Richelieu graduated in the top 10% of her class from Kansas University's Law School; became Ellis & Mullins first female lawyer; She regularly dated but never fell in love during those years at KU

※※※※※※※※※※※※※※※※※※※※※※

As I was walking out of the kitchen with a Coke, finalizing my plan for Autumn's birthday on Wednesday, my mother called to me, "Forrest, we need to talk about a few things. Very important things."

Awww Shit, it's Forrest.

I sat down and my mother came from out behind the desk and sat in the adjoining chair. She looked serious. *Does she know about Autumn and me?*

"Of course, having Father Fitzgerald for Autumn's birthday dinner will be highly enjoyable ... and entertaining. Wonderful to see him again so soon. So please confirm with him for 5:30. I know Autumn will love her surprise to see him. Those two love to talk about the soul and heaven, like last Sunday after his Mass. That girl is so wonderfully spiritual at times."

"But there are some matters we need to seriously discuss. There is a substantial amount of money from the investments I made over the years combined with your father's life insurance. I took some of that money and bought this house and the car. Most of it has stayed in the stock and bond markets. Over the years, I have virtually tripled the money. There is just under a half million dollars."

What? How much? God, I guess we're rich or something.

"**No one else** is to know this. I will tell DeForrest when the time is right for her. Danièle knows, since it was the only way I could persuade her to quit and go to law school full-time. There will always be enough money to live very comfortably but we are not going to spend it on unneeded things. We could buy a much larger house like the Reynolds' or drive a couple of expensive cars like a Mercedes, but I am very comfortable here and I *did* like my car. Since DeForrest is getting her license next month, I am going to buy another car and the Galaxie will be yours," she smiled happily.

"Wow, thank you, Mother."

"Now, we need to talk about Autumn—"

Maybe it was our secret engagement and agreement of a week ago which caused me to flared up, "No, we don't! Nothing …"

My mother put her hand up to stop me, "Forrest, just settle down and listen to *me!*" she said very adamantly, yet coolly. "Autumn Knight is the very best thing that has ever happened to you. Although it's been only seven months, I know the two of you are deeply in love. I can see it … I can feel it. I love her too. So does Danae, and well, DeeDee has worshiped her since the night she met her."

I calmed down quickly, "I know she loves 'My Three Graces' too. Why do you think she wants to be over here all the time?"

"I'm very glad to hear that … she is an incredible, truly magnificent daughter to have. Unfortunately, she definitely has a very unhappy home life, except for her dear sister. But Forrest, you both won't even start college until after next year. She could get pregnant. Then what?"

"She won't, at least for a long while. We have an agreement."

"*Listen to me,* maybe in two or three years, or whenever your so-called 'agreement' ends or changes, *don't you get her pregnant. Don't ruin both your dreams.* Please, please marry her before you start having intercourse. The money can make sure you both keep your dreams ... but a pregnancy, even before a possible marriage, could cause serious problems, even damage your relationship permanently. I've seen it. **I know.**"

"Father Fitz has warned me of the same thing ... ... repeatedly."

"You listen to **HIM**! And you listen to **ME**!"

Mick and Pamela's break up ... a miscarriage, not a baby ... HE was NOT ready. Dan Driscoll started cheating when Frances Parke was so pregnant. What a Bastard!

"I know you both are too young now to even think of marriage, but who knows in three years or so? Don't, **DON'T** you ever let the world get between you and her. Find a good university this year where you **both** can go next year together. Get to know her thoroughly and intensely. Don't you *ever* let go of that girl!"

This is her blessing! I've always known she's WANTED ME to marry Autumn.

"I don't know what to say, I knew there was some money. After all, you never talk about it. You don't seem to worry about it. You always make sure DeeDee and I have enough. There had to be a decent amount since that Jerk went after it. I had no idea it was *that* much."

She laughed, "See what happens when you study hard in school." Then returned to being serious, "When do you plan on getting engaged?"

I looked away and quietly said, "We already are, in secret. A week ago last night, I gave her the matching ring to the locket. It's really complicated, but it was very necessary for her. No ... honestly for both of us. We made our agreement then. She was so scared, so tormented. Oh Mother, I never saw her like that before. I can't take seeing her like that again. It was terrible!"

Again my mother held up her hand, "Forrest, I don't need to know anything more. I know how this can be for a girl who isn't ready. I have seen all of **its** ugly consequences, its terrible fallout.

When you are formally engaged, you will buy her an extremely nice ring, one that *she* picks out." Then my mother became strongly adamant again, "But so help me God, if you get that *sensitive, gentle girl* **pregnant**, **I promise you** will experience Hell on Earth! Just **promise me**, you two will marry before you start having intercourse. As I said, I'll take care of the dreams. That's what the money's for. Yours and Autumn's. DeeDee's and the one guy out of a thousand she finally falls for. Danae's and the Law and hopefully the right guy too."

"I promise you with all my heart, we will marry before the agreement runs out. Before we start having sex." If anyone could deliver Hell on Earth for me, it would definitely be my mother. The Jesuits and military drill sergeants are rank amateurs compared to her.

I changed the subject quickly. "So, are you batting .750, maybe .800 in the stock market?"

She laughed loudly, "Oh, heavens, no. You just need to know when to cash in your chips or double up."

"You make it sound like gambling."

"In a way, it is. You really have to work at it. I will continue to have my fun while you, DeeDee and Autumn, now Danae," and she laughed some more, "are toiling away in school. You can tell Autumn what you need to tell her about this, but it is for her ears *only*. I do truly love that girl an awful lot. She's another daughter to me. I am so ecstatic you are engaged to her."

"O don't worry about Valentina. They do talk somewhat more now, but still not much. That 1+ shocked her completely. She even thought, at first, it was a mistake. Autumn ... Summer too, think she's a self-centered fool who only worries about what people think. Summer even thinks their father always sexually plays around with whoever his current secretary is ... why he has late nights or gone some overnights for out of town 'Sales Meetings'. Autumn confides in you or Summer exclusively. I will tell her only some of this. About the money, I don't know how to tell her about it or more importantly, why? Is she going to love me more because there is a ton of money? No, that's not my Victoria. The important fact to know we don't have to wait forever. We may use it in a few years. Things will be much easier to deal with now. I love you for that and everything else you have ever done for me. You have been and are the very best mother always to DeeDee and me ... *and father* these past two years. And to my Victoria for some time."

"I will always unceasingly love my three children as your father and I deeply loved you two. Hmmm, all three pieces ... the chain and locket, now the ring of Victoria Marlowe are with a totally different, yet quite deserving ... Victoria Marlowe ... to be. Your father would be quite proud and happy that his mother's cherished jewelry is with Autumn and she is with you."

I went over, kissed her and hugged her tightly for a long moment. We continued to talk for the next couple of hours about different universities and colleges, the stock market, its financial aspects, what a financial analyst does, the investment class for next fall, and much more about Autumn. Then I told her about Mick and Pamela. How devastating it was. What Autumn is deathly scared of. We had our agreement. She told me I'd better keep it or welcome to her Hell. One of many things I truly loved about my mother — we could always talk about anything and I would always get unvarnished, straight answers. Sometimes I didn't like her answers, sometimes I hated her answers, but they were always honest, always from the heart and almost always right. DeForrest agrees with me 100%.

The front door opened with a loud, very cheerful, "Hello! It's just me!" She ducked her head in the study, sure that Mother was in here. The future Victoria Marlowe looked terrific with some light blue eyeshadow and very red lipstick. She was dressed in the Crepe de Chine silk blouse and that wonderful pair of form-fitting jeans with short heeled shoes. As she entered the room, my mother went over to hug her tightly and kissed her cheek. Autumn was quizzical, but of course, kissed her back. She didn't know why she got the hug and kiss. I knew it was my mother's way to welcome her newly confirmed daughter.

"Oh Autumn Honey, it is so really good to see you. Please take this male out of my sight and make him promise to do something extra special for your birthday. You deserve it so very much."

Autumn and I went to my room and I told her only the pieces of the talk concerning us. About the car, of course — but about the money, I was completely vague. Mother, especially, my aunt and sister loved her like she was already part of the family. They knew that we were in love and I had told her we were secretly engaged. When it was to be made public, I was to buy her a very nice ring of *her* choice. Autumn said she had already planned to have a diamond engagement ring designed to match both *her* locket and *her* ring. The latter would then become *The Victorias'* wedding band. We were both to finish college at the same school. If our feelings overran the agreement and we *both* were ready to have intercourse, we were to get married first. Autumn didn't blush, but smiled, then started to say something like 'How?' I told her any and all money problems would be taken care of. She was stunned but very happy. I was not, under any circumstances, to get her pregnant. If I did, I would be disowned, but Autumn and the child would never be. Judging from the look in my mother's eyes, I was quite sure she would borrow Dr. Nelson's scalpel.

Autumn said she had come to love my mother, heart and soul. She was a real, true mother, not a mother-in-law that jokes were made about and bad songs written for. She would be the best daughter to her that she could be. Ci Ci understood her so totally well. Autumn knew she deeply cared about her and even loved her more than her own mother ever wanted to or could.

"Rich, I will never know how you always manage to take care of any insurmountable problem that shows up, but you always do. Wow! We can be married much sooner! Maybe in three years or so? Oh Richie! My Magician! Oh! It's wonderful! Goody great! **Unbelievably** goody great!" We kissed and went downstairs to leave.

But this time I had a ton of help, an absolute ton from the Lady Master Magician.

"Rich, please wait here a minute. I need to take care of something extremely important." Autumn went over to my mother, and simply declared, "You are the most incredible person I have ever known, well, except our Richie and I will never, ever let go of him. I promise you we will be married when we first have sexual intercourse. I also promise you will get your fervent wish. **Richelieu will marry a Catholic**. I love you so much. My incredible, wonderful Mother. Thank you, **Mother**." They kissed and hugged each other tightly for a very long moment, kissed and hugged more, then kissed again and hugged for a third time. As we walked out the front door, a single tear fell down the cheek of a very happy and smiling Autumn. I looked back through the window to see my mother, dabbing her handkerchief at her eyes, glancing upwards, her lips moving. She was ecstatic, talking to my father — maybe God — more than likely, both.

❈❈❈❈❈❈❈❈❈❈❈❈❈❈❈❈❈❈❈❈❈❈❈

**Geneviève Georgette Richelieu Marlowe never remarried;
Richelieu, Autumn and DeForrest knew she wouldn't,
although she did continue to date often throughout the years;
She once said she unconsciously compared each
one to her late husband; None ever measured up;
She was still in love with him and missed her Forrest dearly**

❈❈❈❈❈❈❈❈❈❈❈❈❈❈❈❈❈❈❈❈❈❈❈

MARCH 1972

    One very cold spring night, a pregnant DeForrest showed an equally pregnant Autumn and me a small, slightly torn, folded piece of paper with semi-coded writing in our Father's hand. It had been originally contained in a blank envelope which she had found many years ago wedged and ripped in the mail slot. She had kept only the note, completely forgetting about it until she cleaned out some high school memorabilia the previous day. I accidentally remarked, "Ah, so that's where number 34 was." With that slip of the tongue, DeForrest and Autumn compelled me to tell the full truth about the missing number 34 and how its like companion folded notes were pieces of evidence for all the twists and tangles of deceit, blackmail, murders, and illegal drugs.

    I reluctantly related the full, unedited facts of the chain of events that occurred in Viet Nam, Wyandotte, The Lake combined with Fr. Fitz's inquiries. The expectant sister-in-laws were astounded and shocked even before I got a quarter of the way into the story. The three of us agreed these secrets of "The Investigation" would join "The Charade". Number 34 went into the crackling fire of the hearth. Neither my mother nor my aunt was ever told anything regarding these events. The evidence has remained untouched to this day since its deposit on March 12, 1964 in the St. Ignatius Jesuit Vault.

****

    That afternoon a package was delivered to my sister who happily and unbelievably surprised both Autumn and me. Earlier that morning, she had successfully bid on a silent movie at the memorabilia auction of the closed Jayhawk Theatre located next to Ball's. Five films from the twenties had been stored for decades in a forgotten corner of Ball's refrigeration room next to the huge freezer.

The 1922 movie was *The Desert Queen*, and our grandmother was in it! She played a supporting role as the favored harem girl, Désirée. The movie itself was OK, like a cheap copy of Valentino's *The Sheik*, but seeing our grandmother, Victoria Marlowe — alive, so young and so full of life — made it truly miraculous. Even in black and white, she was stunningly beautiful with deep dark eyes — like my father's and mine. A great "vamp" in her flimsy, risqué harem costume. I bet our grandfather certainly thought so — probably all the guys on the set too.

After the credits of the movie, there were two title cards proclaiming "Extra" then "Our Gorgeous and Wonderful Players' Cast Party". Although only a fifty-six second clip, the camera panned across the actors and their guests, all drinking, eating hors d'oeuvres, laughing, having a great time. Autumn yelled for DeForrest to freeze the frame. She rewound the film and there was Grandmother in the middle of the room, looking devilishly sultry in a backless black dress. Its highly suggestive V-shaped drape ended slightly below the small of her back, close to the beginning of her derrière's groove. About six inches above that area was strategically positioned a five-inch, thick gold chain with matching flat gold studs at each end for securing and keeping the dress in place.

I blurted out, "So that's what the chain is for! It's in my antique box." The girls began laughing, happily surprised. "And worth more than a few bucks. It's 18K."

Grandmother Victoria was now talking to a tall, seemly good-looking man whose appearance was greatly obscured. As she smilingly turned to wave at the camera, Autumn squealed happily, "Ooooh! **Our locket**!" She clasped it, crying out, "Back it up! Please!" As the picture rolled again, she whooped more, "That **IS** your Grandfather!"

Still my little girl and right as always. I kissed her cheek, then her tummy where my new little girl was growing. I kissed "My Little Dee," thanked her for the wonderful "family" movie, and softly patted my niece in her tummy. Lastly, I went to check on another little girl of mine. Her black hair fanned out on the champagne silk pillow, green eyes closed, fast asleep on her

Grand-mère's bed. Although they didn't need it, I still rearranged her covers then kissed her cheek. I stood and looked at "My Little Georgie" for a few moments, thanking the Holy Ghost for her, then rejoined the giggling sister-in-laws to watch the movie again. And again. Then two more times.

Autumn could hardly wait to see Victoria's 'V dress chain' tonight after we got home. She seductively invited me to watch her model it and I, of course, readily agreed. How she would, I wasn't sure. But I knew it would involve a garter belt in an alluring shade of blue with matching bra and panties, hose and heels. But probably less than that.

❋❋❋❋❋❋❋❋❋❋❋❋❋❋❋❋❋❋❋❋❋❋❋❋

JULY 1984

Hanging on my office wall is a large, beautiful, hand-colored professional photograph, entitled

CONVERGENT COINCIDENCES

It was taken at a black tie optional Christmas Gala party eight years after that first Christmas in Wyandotte. The four of us, Jacqueline, DeForrest, myself and Autumn, are standing in the front hallway of my Mother's house. People often comment, "How stunningly attractive and very tall all three girls are." I am, of course, rarely mentioned. Most people believe the title is based on their similar statuesque heights, styled dresses, even upswept hairdos or all three. Everyone is always very surprised when I explain to them the title was "conceived" as the result of each girl having just become pregnant, all being in their first trimester. Three baby girls were born within a three week period the following July. Growing up, they have become very close, worse than "thick as thieves," like their mothers still are. Worse than my sister and me.

Sometimes when I look at the picture, I smile without thinking about the chance timing of the pregnancies. My thoughts focus on a different set of convergent coincidences: How the three girls forged a powerful, lifelong bond, becoming exceptionally best friends, firmly rooted in a mutually distressing, painful experience one night in May a long time ago. How surprisingly extraordinary each one of those three Angels of Vengeance were during that fateful night. How wonderfully extraordinary each one of the Angels of Love and Friendship continues to still be. My smile always broadens, sometimes to a quiet laugh. Occasionally a moderate laugh. One partner prays it isn't a genetic trait. My other partner has often warned our associates that there are more than a few bulbs missing from my marquee then tells me I should go see the Doctor the three of us are patients of — the one who could play third base so well. I just laugh more. And louder. Much, much louder.

****

THE END OF RICHELIEU'S STORY
BOOK II —— THE LEAP YEAR SERIES

CPSIA information can be obtained
at www.ICGtesting.com
Printed in the USA
BVHW062255231121
622347BV00014B/644